Valley
of
The Purple Hearts

By

Rick DeStefanis

ISBN: 0996534237
ISBN 13: 9780996534239

...*Valley of the Purple Hearts* is a good addition to the professional reading library for the doctors and nurses working at a VA medical facility. Rick DeStefanis is a fabulous story teller and the author's descriptions of combat are vivid, and his writing is so descriptive that the reader can taste the muck at the bottom of the rice paddies, and smell the nuoc mam fish sauce of the Vietnamese patrols.

Robert W. Enzenauer, MD, BG, US Army Retired
Battalion Surgeon, 5/19th SFG(A) 1998-2010

Rick DeStefanis's new novel is one of the most powerful depictions of daily life for American soldiers in the Viet Nam War I've ever read. Reminiscent of Tim O'Brien and Joseph Heller, DeStefanis paints a devastating portrait of the chaos, boredom, violence and ironies that fill the lives of the combat units struggling for the single goal of surviving yet another day...Engaged as we are in current wars and trying to help our returning soldiers, this book should be required reading for everyone in this country.

Jonis Agee, author of *The Bones of Paradise*

A Note to My Readers

Realistic depictions of military events through the eyes of characters require the use of military terms and jargon. There is a glossary of military terms at the back of this book. Look it over before you begin the story. It will make your read easier.

I wish to express thanks to all those who helped me bring this story to print, my friends Carol Carlson, Chris Davis, Ellen Prewitt and Margaret Yates. Special thanks also goes to Robert W. Enzenauer, MD, BG, US Army Retired, Author William F. Brown, a former US Army Captain and Vietnam Veteran, as well as cover designer Todd Hebertson and Editor Elisabeth Hallett. If you enjoy this story, please post your written review on Amazon.com, Goodreads.com or on the vendor site of your choice. Your support is always appreciated. Learn more about The Word Hunter, at www.rickdestefanis.com.

This book is dedicated to all military veterans who have given themselves in some way to the service of our nation, and to those who have stood with them.

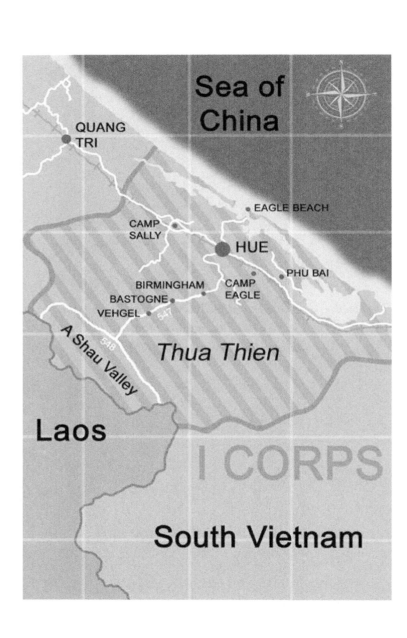

And if you gaze long enough into an abyss, the abyss will gaze back into you.

--Friedrich Nietzsche

1

DOWN THE RABBIT HOLE

Travis Air Force Base, California, February 1968

Buck Marino had once looked forward to this day. He thought it was going to be an adventure, but that was before he joined the military. It was a time when he imagined he would fly to Vietnam aboard a camouflaged aircraft, make a combat parachute jump into the jungle and heroically fight his way to a firebase. Instead he was sitting here on a lemon-yellow Braniff International charter jet staring out at the tarmac at Travis Air Force Base. Life was outrunning his ability to assimilate everything that was happening. Men like him, some wearing dress khakis, some jungle fatigues, were boarding, their eyes betraying the swagger they attempted walking down the aisle. Buck's sublime imaginations about fighting in Vietnam had taken a turn toward the bizarre.

Most of the soldiers looked as if they had leapt from the pages of their high school yearbooks, donned army uniforms and begun playing soldier, but not the sergeant with "Zwyrkowski" on his name tag. He was different. Stopping, he shoved something into the overhead bin before sitting down beside him. It was his eyes Buck first noticed. They were old man eyes, tired, not in a physical manner, but like he'd been to the ends of the earth and seen things he didn't care to talk about. There were three gold stripes on his shoulder, along with silver jump wings and a blue and silver combat infantry badge pinned above his pocket.

He grinned and stuck out his hand. "Rolley Zwyrkowski."

"Buck Marino."

The sergeant motioned toward Buck's silver jump wings.

"You're Airborne, too, huh?"

"Yeah," Buck said.

"I'm with the Hundred and First," the sergeant said. "Where are you headed?"

"My orders say I'm supposed to report to the 90th Replacement Battalion at Long Binh, but I'm going to the Hundred and First, too."

"Yeah, most replacements go through Long Binh. Where're you from?"

"A place called Bois de Arc, Mississippi. It's so small it doesn't even have a traffic light." Buck said. "You?"

The sergeant laughed. "My family lives south of Chicago, but we're originally from a small town up in Wisconsin."

A stewardess in a yellow uniform came down the aisle, closing the overhead bins and telling everyone to buckle up.

"I can't believe we're flying to Vietnam on a damned yellow jet," Buck said.

The sergeant raised his eyebrows. "Maybe they're sending us a subliminal message."

"Huh?"

"Well, take for instance that little hat the stewardess is wearing."

Buck glanced back at the stewardess, a knock-dead gorgeous woman too young to be showing the stress creases she had around her eyes—probably the price for delivering guys like him to war on a regular basis.

"Yeah?"

"Do you know what it's called?"

Buck shrugged.

"It's called a 'pill box' hat," the sergeant said.

Buck sighed and rolled his eyes. "Well, Sarge, at least they don't call it a 'fox hole' hat."

"Call me Rolley," he said. "My jokes are so bad, most cherries don't even get them."

Rolley was not like the hard-assed drill instructors that had put him through training. Facing twenty-something hours in the air, Buck figured he might ask him a few questions. And while most men read magazines or slept, Rolley explained how he had finished college with a degree in English lit and enlisted for NCO school when he was about to be drafted. He had already served seven months in Nam and was returning from an emergency leave. They talked quietly while the jet engines droned, and Rolley patiently answered Buck's endless questions about the war.

"You can't believe everything you read in the newspapers. The enemy in Vietnam is not some sort of peace-loving farmer. The VC are truculent bastards who work with the NVA. They kill and torture their own people, and they will do the same thing to you if they capture you."

"What's 'truculent' mean?"

Rolley smiled. "Sorry. I became a lexophile of sorts in college. When you spend four years with a bunch of English-lit professors you begin talking like them. Truculent means they're cruel and vicious, and I honestly believe the VC sometime kill for the fun of it."

"Good, I won't worry so much about killing *them*."

Rolley stared down at nothing in particular.

"Buck, you seem like a smart guy, but you're a tabula rasa."

Buck wrinkled his brow.

"Hang on. I'll explain. It's like this. By your own admission you've never paid attention to much of anything except hunting, fishing, and girls. 'Tabula rasa' is Latin for 'blank slate.' That means you have no preconceived notions about the mess we're in over there—but have no doubts, it *is* a mess, a big one.

"The biggest problem is you don't know what you don't know until you experience it. I don't have the answers. I wish I did, but where we're going there is no simple right and wrong. It's a crazy war and there are only you, me, and several thousand other GIs like us caught in the middle."

Rolley was right. Buck had seen the protests and other things about the war on television, but who had time for TV? It was all just so much noise to a teenager. He hadn't taken time to really learn what it was all about. If it was a war, he wanted to get a taste of it before it was over. Besides, who wanted to work all his life on a farm and end up dead like his parents in a car wreck? The problem now was he had grown into the realization that a taste of war could be just as fatal as their wreck.

Rolley glanced over at him and shrugged. "Look, I'm not trying to be a know-it-all. Just keep your eyes open. You're going to see some crazy shit in the next twelve months. Keep your head, keep your morals, and don't do anything you wouldn't want to think about for the rest of your life. And don't be a hero, either. We have a job to do over there. Do yours and come home."

Time seemed to creep and race all within the same thoughts on their long flight to the first stop-over at Hickam Air Force Base in Hawaii. Buck tried to make sense of the things Rolley had said. It was as if Vietnam was speeding toward him, but he was seeing it coming in slow motion. After the brief stop-over in Hawaii, he found Rolley and followed him on board for the next leg of the trip. Rolley gave him a sideways grin.

"What?" Buck said.

"I think I'm going to institute the 'adopt-a-cherry' program."

"Sorry, Sarge. Didn't mean to ask so many questions."

"Call me Rolley, and don't be sorry. I'll try to answer your questions, but keep in mind what I said about being ignorant. There's only one thing that can remedy it, and that's experience."

The hours dragged by while they talked, and Buck again drifted into a restless sleep. He dreamt that he was alone in a strange place, surrounded by strangers who looked past him as if he weren't there. Bright colors and lights surrounded him, and the people seemed intent upon one another, but not on him. He searched for someone he might know, but found no one. Growing desperate, he tried to greet them, but the people simply passed by seeming not to notice him. He wanted to ask what they were doing, where they were going, and if he could go with them, but it was as if he didn't exist. He jerked awake realizing the jetliner's wheels had thumped down on another runway. This time it was Guam—another step closer to destiny.

Rolley had been patient with his endless question, but they now both dozed, as the flight seemed it would never end. Another refueling stop in the Philippines, and more restless sleep was interrupted again by another landing. This time, though, it was different, and Buck somehow felt he'd reached a landmark in the journey of life. Sitting upright, he rubbed his eyes and peered out the window. A huge sign atop a building said:

TAN SON NHUT AIR BASE
WELCOME.

He took a deep breath. They had arrived. He was in Vietnam.

Turning, he found Rolley staring stoically at the back of the seat in front of him. Buck wanted to ask more questions, but it was too late. He was beginning to feel like a character in a low-budget B-grade movie, and just as Rolley said, he was blind-running drunk with ignorance. Low-budget movies were always better when you slept through them, but he had awakened right in the middle of this one—grainy film, sorry-ass acting and all.

Outside the window, sandbags and rolls of concertina barbed wire surrounded everything. Green helicopters with rotors churning lined the tarmac for a hundred yards. Trucks raced past, streaming clouds of black diesel exhaust, and beyond the fences in the distance was the hazy green countryside of Vietnam.

Rolley stood and retrieved his bag from the overhead bin. "Time to go down the rabbit hole," he said.

Up front the stewardess opened the aircraft door, flooding the cabin with a hot humid air that reeked of mildew and diesel fumes. Buck broke an instant sweat.

Smiling, Rolley shook his hand. "It was a pleasure traveling with you. Keep your head down, and maybe we'll cross paths again sometime. Good luck."

A young lieutenant standing on the tarmac below was shouting for anyone with orders for the Hundred and First to fall in there. That included Rolley, who didn't seem happy about it. The lieutenant began a welcoming speech, explaining how the entire division had just completed a month of in-country training when the '68 Tet Offensive began. Problem was an overabundance of job opportunities created by the killed and wounded meant replacements were getting the privilege of an abbreviated in-country orientation followed by OJT.

"On The Job Training," Rolley explained. "The military loves acronyms. Here in Nam it helps us identify cherries, because you guys don't know what they mean. Don't worry. The Hundred and First now gives you three days of SERTS training before sending you to your unit. You'll get courses like Booby-trap-101, Intro to Crotch Rot, and survey of Insect-Snake-and-Rat-Bite, as well as a broad range of other wonderful educational opportunities. Just make sure you pay attention."

Buck wanted to laugh. This guy was either crazy, or—

"Sergeant," the lieutenant called out, motioning Rolley out of the formation.

After a brief discussion, the lieutenant gave him a sheet of paper and turned back to the formation. Rolley stood beside him with his lips squinched at the corners and looking pissed.

"Okay, you men are going with Sergeant Zwyrkowski. Recover your duffel bags and climb aboard that deuce and a half over there."

"Where are we going?" someone asked.

""We're convoying twenty-five kilometers up to Long Binh, to the replacement battalion," Rolley said. "Looks like the whole of Nam has gone to shit, and I'm stuck with you guys for a while longer."

A thundering roar came from out on the runway where two jets streaked skyward. Splotched with dark green and tan camouflage, they sprouted rockets and bombs under their wings. Their flaming afterburners left smoky trails streaming behind.

"F-4 Phantoms," Rolley shouted.

The roar faded as the jets disappeared in the distance.

"Is it always this hot?" someone asked.

Rolley smiled. "Oh, no. It's normally much hotter."

Everyone was already drenched with sweat.

"Where's Long Binh?" Buck asked.

"Northeast of here. The lieutenant is staying here to meet another flight. So, I'm going with you guys. He said Saigon is off limits."

Rolley explained that parts of Saigon were still under siege by the Viet Cong, and the city was closed to all non-essential personnel. He was opting for the base

NCO club at Bien Hoa, and saluted Buck and the others a quick good-bye when they arrived. Two days later Buck spotted Rolley once again as he joined the new replacements walking across the ramp toward a Chinook. The big chopper was bound for a base near the city of Phu Bai, up in I-Corps.

According to the training officer, Phu Bai was just south of Hue. The 101st, the 82nd, 1st Cav, Marines, and the ARVN were all there and locked in close combat with several NVA regiments and main force Viet Cong battalions. Loaded down with gear that included an M-16, twenty magazines, six canteens, a poncho, a poncho liner, and a rucksack crammed with sixty more pounds of gear, Buck and the others leaned forward as they filed up the back ramp of the chopper. The rotors on the big helicopter were spinning rapidly as the crew chief impatiently motioned them forward.

"Let's go, men," Rolley shouted. He glanced at his wrist watch. "Hurry, or we'll be late."

"Late for what?" someone shouted over the drumming rotors.

"It'll be getting dark when we arrive, and there's heavy weather coming in off the South China Sea."

After shoving his rucksack under the nylon webbing, Buck sat down while the crew chief raised the back ramp and gave the pilot a thumbs-up. A few moments later the engine RPMs increased and the chopper lurched skyward. Everyone sat in silence, and after a while Buck looked over his shoulder through a porthole at the country below—miles of emerald green jungle, mountains, serpentine rivers, and a checker-board of glittering rice paddies. Villages and thatch-roofed huts lined the roads stretching all the way to the horizon.

"It looks like a garden paradise from up here," Rolley said.

Buck nodded.

Rolley grinned. "Yeah, but it's not."

He looked at the guy sitting across the aisle, another PFC like Buck who had been on the charter flight out of California. The young soldier stared off into space, his green eyes seemingly lost in a world of inconsolable despair.

"Hey dude," Rolley said. The guy looked at him. "What's your name?"

"TJ Arceneaux," the soldier replied.

"So, why are you looking so glum, TJ?"

The soldier pursed his lips. "Why do you think, Sarge? We're flying into a war, and I might just get ma ass killed, you know?"

He spoke with a heavy Cajun accent.

"Oh, hell," Rolley said. "Is that all you're worried about? Lighten up. Getting killed isn't the worst thing that can happen."

TJ stared back at him in silence, but Rolley's statement begged for an explanation.

"So, what's the worst thing?" Buck asked.

"Worrying about it till you go insane," Rolley said with a smile. "The enemy can't kill you but once. Insanity, on the other hand, can last a lifetime."

Rolley grinned, and Buck looked over at TJ, who remained somber.

After riding for several hours, Buck noticed the sun had dropped behind the mountains in the west. He gazed out the porthole window. Although it was still daylight up where they were, the ground below was enveloped in darkness. Despite the vibrations and occasional turbulence, the ride had been peaceful, but without warning Buck's stomach came up into his throat as the chopper dove earthward.

"Hold on to your nuts, troops," Rolley said. "We're going in."

The chopper was in a spiraling descent, and through the window Buck watched as they dropped into a darkened tunnel, falling, it seemed, forever. They went from a dusky evening daylight into total darkness, and when he thought they would never land, the chopper finally slowed its descent and touched down. Back to the east, flashes of lightning lit up the horizon, revealing a roiling bank of black clouds.

"Where are we, LA or San Francisco?" Rolley asked the crew chief.

"Sorry, Sarge. You're still in Nam."

Rolley turned to the rest of the men on the chopper.

"Listen up, men. We didn't fall far enough down the rabbit hole, so we're still in Nam. Sorry."

Buck studied the sergeant. He was either crazy as a loon or smart like a fox. The crew chief lowered the ramp, and Rolley motioned for the others to follow. "Stay with me and don't lag behind. There's a storm coming in."

A choking red dust swirled in the wind as they trotted down a dirt road. After running several hundred yards, Rolley dove through a sandbagged opening down into a large bunker. Buck and the others stumbled down the steps behind him. Inside, a gas lantern burned, and on a table were several radios along with several cardboard boxes marked "C-rations" although they were full of rolled maps and binders. A large collage of acetate-covered topo maps lined the wall above the table. A lieutenant stood holding one of the radio handsets as he turned around. Rolley saluted and handed him the sheaf of orders.

"Sergeant Zwyrkowski reporting, sir. I'm returning from emergency leave, and they told me to deliver these replacements here."

"Okay, Sergeant. Thanks."

With that Rolley turned and disappeared up the steps.

After a while a company clerk showed up with cases of C-rations and warm beer for supper, but no one complained. They hadn't eaten since early that morning. Buck and the others lounged around the bunker until later in the night when the clerk returned. He led them out into the pouring rain and down a muddy road to another bunker. Soaked, muddy, and exhausted, Buck and the other replacements wrapped themselves in their poncho liners and slept until shortly after daylight, when someone came in yelling.

"You fucking cherries, get your shit and fall-in outside. Move! Now! Let's go. You sorry sonofabitches are on my time, and I don't have much left in this sorry-ass place."

Bleary-eyed, Buck stumbled out into the morning light, expecting the soldier doing all the yelling to be some hardened NCO. He wasn't. He was a Spec-4, a grunt like him, probably another clerk. Basic and AIT had been the same way—always some cadre member with no real authority acting like a badass. Wet and tired from a sleepless night, Buck dropped his rucksack, and started toward him.

"Don't do it," TJ said.

It was too late. The Spec-4 stopped yelling and stared wide-eyed as Buck stepped in front of him. Feeling a hand on his shoulder, Buck turned expecting TJ, but there stood a squinty-eyed soldier in tiger-striped jungle fatigues. He wore a camouflaged bandanna and had a Car-15 slung across his back. His face was burnt brown, and his jungle boots were scuffed to raw leather. He ignored Buck while grinning at the clerk, except he wasn't really grinning, at least not with his eyes. The clerk stared back at him, bug-eyed.

"Uh huh," the soldier said. His voice was low and raspy, almost a whisper. "Almost got your REMF ass stomped by a cherry, didn't ju?"

The clerk stepped back, and the other soldier turned to Buck. "Be cool, cherry. You don't want to get stuck on shit-burning detail your first day."

"Here comes an officer," TJ said.

Coming up the road toward them was a lieutenant.

The clerk cut his eyes that way. "That's Lieutenant Liggons," he said, his voice now pitched more like that of a frightened rabbit. "He'll be taking over for me."

Buck glanced toward the lieutenant then back at the red-faced clerk and the now departing soldier. The soldier was right, and Buck heard his father's voice from long ago when he said, "A man who can't control his emotions is destined to be ruled by them." The adrenaline over-load had him on edge, but it wasn't something new. He'd been pissed off since the day they told him Joe and Margaret Marino had been killed in the automobile accident. He was pissed-off at the speeding truck driver, pissed-off at the highway patrol for not stopping the speeding trucks— he was pissed-off at himself for ending up here in Nam.

Overhead, a string of choppers drowned out the conversation while the young officer dismissed the clerk.

"Sir," Buck said.

The lieutenant looked his way.

"Who was that guy?" He motioned toward the soldier in the tiger-striped fatigues who was now well down the road.

"That's one of those crazy-ass lurps from the 75th Rangers. Why? Did he say something to you?"

"Uh, just said to be cool. I mean he seemed okay."

The lieutenant shrugged and began explaining that all replacements received three days of SERTS training before joining their units.

"That stands for Screaming Eagle Replacement Training School, and the Hundred and First is one of the only units over here that does that for our men." he explained. "Pay attention to your instructors and you will fare much better in the next twelve months."

After answering several questions, he led them up the road to a supply bunker where they were issued ammo, frags, smoke, trip flares, star burst flares, Claymores, C-rations, and more crap than Buck could imagine carrying.

Three rainy days later, loaded like pack-mules, Buck and the other replacements marched over to the base LZ. They sat along the edge of the acid pad leaning against their rucksacks while a staff sergeant and a medic walked down the line distributing malaria pills, bottles of Halazone purification tablets, and more last-minute instructions. The rain began again, and while several men examined their frags and flares, others began donning ponchos.

"Put those damned things away," the sergeant yelled. "You can't do an air assault in a poncho, and you'll have plenty of time to play with that other shit later. Now, listen up. The unit you're going to is in the hills west of FSB

Bastogne. The AO is covered with elephant grass and lots of jungle. It's mountainous, and there ain't nothin' good out there. You'll be met at the LZ by your platoon leaders. Listen to them. Do exactly what they say, and you might have a chance to come back here for R&R in six months. Go ahead and put a magazine in your rifle, but *do not* lock and load until you're coming into the LZ, and when you do, make sure your weapon is pointing outside the chopper."

With that he turned and trotted back down the road to a tent. The rain grew heavier, and the choppers stopped flying. Buck, TJ, and the other replacements sat out in the pouring rain for an hour until it decreased to a hazy mist. Soaked and shivering, the men were relieved when the sun reappeared and the tarmac began steaming. Morning passed into afternoon, and Buck had just dozed off when there came distant shouts from down the road. Buck cracked open his eyes. Men were sprinting from the sandbagged tents.

"What the fuck they yelling about?" TJ asked.

"I don't—" Buck suddenly heard it, "Incoming!"

Jumping up, he snatched TJ to his feet. "Let's go."

The men on the LZ scattered as the first incoming rounds exploded across the base. Buck and TJ sprinted down the road and dove through the door of a large bunker. Inside, it was dank and dark. Stacks of wooden crates lined the walls. So far, so good. Panting, Buck strained to hear what was happening outside. A jarring explosion filled the bunker with smoke and dust.

The impact of the rocket was incredible as Buck's ears popped and his chest felt as if it would cave in.

"Goddamn!" he shouted.

"Don't tempt him," TJ yelled back.

The two men huddled in a corner for several minutes, until they realized it was over—a dozen rockets and that was it. Cautiously peeking around the corner of the sandbagged doorway, Buck peered through the eerie haze of smoke hanging over the base. Somewhere nearby men were shouting. Tentatively he eased out into the open, slapping the dirt from his fatigues. TJ came out behind him. A lieutenant trotted by, but stopped and looked back.

"Hey. Aren't you the cherries who were up there on the LZ?"

"Yes, sir," they replied in unison.

"That's what I thought. Look—just a little advice— the next time we get incoming, try to find a better place to take cover."

"That was a first for us, sir," Buck said. "We just wanted some cover."

TJ gave a nervous laugh and nodded in agreement.

"Well, suit yourselves, but I'd go an extra step or two next time. An ammo bunker is a really bad place to be if it takes a direct hit from a 122 millimeter rocket."

The lieutenant pointed to the door of the bunker where they had been. Turning, he trotted up the road, laughing as he went.

TJ's face paled. "Shiiuutt."

"Sonofabitch," Buck whispered.

Looking back at the bunker, Buck noticed the crater just outside the door where the rocket had exploded. Streams of sand were still pouring from the tattered sandbags. An involuntary shiver ran down his back as he walked with TJ to the LZ.

The clouds returned once again and another misty rain began falling. The men huddled together until dusk when a clerk showed up. Weather up the valley had it socked-in. He told them to stand down for the night. All the adrenaline, the anticipation, was for naught. They trudged down the road for another restless night's sleep.

The next morning the sun rose and the sounds of the choppers came from overhead. The battalion clerk showed up again and quietly told them to gather their gear. Buck and the others ate a quick breakfast of cold C-rations before following him up the hill. Several Hueys had just arrived and their rotors were still churning as the six replacements trotted to the edge of the LZ.

"That's your chopper there," a sergeant shouted. "Take a knee, and stand by until the door gunner signals you to board. Good luck, men."

The co-pilot was removing a fueling hose from the side of the chopper while the door gunner crawled about on his knees inside with a towel wiping the floor. When he was done, he ran to a nearby drum, tossed the towel inside and returned.

"Load up," he shouted.

The co-pilot was buckling into his harness as Buck and the others climbed on board. Buck's hand slipped on something wet. That's when he realized what the door gunner had been wiping from the floor—smeared pink blood. TJ looked his way, and Buck turned toward the door gunner. He ignored them and began putting a new belt of ammo into his M-60.

The high-pitched whine of the turbine engines increased and the chopper lurched skyward. The pilot tilted the nose down and the rotors clacked loudly as the chopper climbed out of the LZ. Buck swallowed hard. This was it. He was going to war.

Time became a blur, and it seemed only a few minutes had passed before the pilot dove to treetop level. The trees streaked past as the chopper approached a smoky hilltop up ahead. Buck's heart was already pounding, but it jumped into his throat when the door gunner swung his sixty around and fired a burst into the jungle below. He looked back at them and nodded. He was only test-firing the machine gun.

Bending over toward Buck and the others, he shouted, "We've got a hot LZ." Buck could hardly hear him, and tried to read his lips. "We won't actually touch down. Just get the hell out when I tell you. Don't hesitate."

The chopper hovered into an open area where red smoke rose in arches. The rotors again clacked loudly. Buck clenched his teeth and breathed through his nostrils.

"GO!" the door gunner yelled.

Buck jumped, but with the eighty-pound rucksack and the M-16 in his arms, his leap turned into a belly flop as he plummeted face-down four or five feet. He struck the ground with a thump, knocking the breath from his lungs. Writhing in the grass, he fought to regain his breath. Someone grabbed his rucksack and jerked him to his feet. His head was spinning with stars, and the air refused to return to his lungs.

"Run," the soldier screamed. "Get to that ravine and stay down."

Buck stumbled into the trees and dove head-first into a steep ravine. Rolling downhill nearly twenty feet, he crashed into a tree. Every bone in his body had to be broken—he was certain. Several loud *KAROOMPHS* thundered and shook the ground beneath him. Smoke and a brimstone odor filled the air as shrapnel rained down through the trees. Buck raised his head to see where the others had gone.

Further down the ravine, TJ was stuck upside down between two trees, squirming like a turtle on its back. His rucksack held him hostage.

"Get your damned head down, cherry!" someone shouted.

Another explosion shattered the jungle canopy, sending more shrapnel and tree limbs flying across the ravine.

"Jesus!" someone yelled.

After a minute or two it grew quiet, and there came a shuffling through the leaves. Buck raised his head to see a pair of muddy jungle boots standing beside him.

"Buck?"

He looked up. It was Rolley. Reaching down, the sergeant pulled him to his feet.

"You okay?"

With his heart still wedged in his throat, Buck could only nod.

Rolley grinned. "Man, we can't go on meeting this way."

Shaking from an overdose of adrenaline, Buck again nodded. From somewhere not far away came the crackling pops of a firefight. Rolley cut his eyes that way then bobbing his brows, he turned back to Buck.

"That's the jabberwocky out there, my friend, and he's where we're going. So, you might want to lock and load."

Buck looked down at his M-16. He hadn't even chambered a round.

"You fellows better get a whole lot smarter real quick," Rolley said. He pointed at TJ, still stuck between the two trees. "Go down there and help John Wayne get his shit together."

Walking down the side of the ravine, Buck retrieved TJ's rifle and steel pot along the way. After pulling him from between the trees, he gave the little Cajun the rifle and helmet.

Rolley was talking in a low voice to the other replacements. "Okay, we're moving out. Don't let the man in front of you get out of sight. We're going to hook up with the rest of the platoon. They're over there about two hundred meters. Just do what I say without hesitation and you'll be okay. Let's go."

A few minutes later they met up with a lieutenant named Hensley. He had a first lieutenant's black bar on his collar.

"Did all the replacements make it off the LZ?" he asked.

Rolley looked around at them. "Yes, sir, all six, except this one here is a little addled. He collided with a tree down in the ravine."

"You okay?" the lieutenant asked.

Buck nodded. "Yes, sir. I think so."

"Go around the trees from now on."

Rolley motioned with his head. "Sir, I'd like to have this one and that one there, Arceneaux, for my squad, if that's okay."

"No problem. Take 'em. Get your guys together and take point while I get these other four squared away. Move out quick as you can, and I'll bring the rest of the platoon up, as soon as we get organized. Get across the river fast and try to flank those little bastards."

Buck thought it strange that Rolley wanted him and TJ in his squad, because so far they had been the biggest screw-ups. He fought to keep up with his new squad leader as they threaded their way through the under-growth. A few moments later they stopped behind a line of men lying along a small knoll.

"Okay, men. Third Platoon is in a world of shit over there. They're pinned down on the other side of the river below that ridge. We've got some gunships coming this way. Meanwhile, we're going to flank Charlie if we can. Crowfoot, you and Nguyen take point. Blondie, you walk slack for them. Head down that way toward the river. Try to make time, but don't walk us into an ambush."

The men began pulling one another to their feet. Rolley turned to TJ and Buck. "You two cherries stay right on my ass, and be quiet."

Crowfoot began heading toward the river, but he was angling away from the firefight.

"I thought we were going toward the firefight," Buck whispered to Rolley.

"Yeah, that's the direction Charlie expects us to come, and he'll likely have an ambush waiting for us if we go that way."

They arrived at the river a few minutes later. It appeared no more than waist deep, but it was roiling with a muddy froth of sticks and leaves. Blondie glanced back and shrugged. Rolley motioned for him to continue down the bank and followed as Blondie, Crowfoot, and the other guy slipped into the water.

The current was treacherous as the men fought to stay afoot. Crowfoot and the other man had nearly made it to the far bank. Blondie was over halfway and Buck was behind Rolley about a third of the way across the river. Crowfoot started up the steep bank but slipped and fell backward, knocking the man behind him off his feet. The two men thrashed wildly as they were swept away by the current. Blondie and Rolley lunged downstream toward them. Buck followed, and before long they reached quiet water where the men struggled to regain their footing and reach the far shore. They had drifted nearly seventy meters downstream.

Buck was beside Rolley as they made their way toward the bank, but when he looked up a Vietnamese was standing there holding an M-16.

"Look out," Buck shouted.

He brought his M-16 down from above his head, but before he could aim, Rolley pushed the barrel downward.

"That's Nguyen, our Kit Carson," he hissed, "and don't shout like that again."

Nguyen was the other man who had been with Crowfoot on point, and Buck hadn't realized he was Vietnamese. The scout had lost his helmet in the river, and looked like a VC waiting on the far bank to take them prisoner. Buck's head spun. If he got through this first day without getting killed or killing one of his own, it was going to be a miracle.

When the squad finally reached the opposite bank, Rolley didn't allow them a break. Rapidly circling behind the ridge, they drew ever closer to the firefight still raging on the other side. They were now only a few hundred meters from the battle. In the distance there came the thump-thump-thump of the approaching helicopter gunships. Buck's heart pounded in his chest, not from the physical exertion, but because he was about to be in his first firefight.

2

EYES OF FLAME

Thua Thien Province, February 1968

The squad was nearly at a trot as they approached the backside of the ridge. The incessant popping and cracking of the firefight continued on the opposite side. Buck felt the hair rising on his neck, and he could only imagine that Third Platoon had been ripped to shreds by now. Feeling lightheaded, his every nerve tingled as he followed Rolley through the thick undergrowth. They were still moving rapidly when the squad leader came to a sudden stop. Buck nearly ran into him as TJ bumped him from behind. Up at the point, Blondie stood directly behind Crowfoot and the Kit Carson, Nguyen. Crowfoot was frozen in place, holding his hand in the air while staring into the jungle.

Nguyen crouched and pointed at something. Crowfoot quickly threw up his sixteen, fired a burst and crouched.

"Get down," Rolley said, dropping to a knee.

Blondie had gone down on one knee as well, but he turned back to Rolley. "Bunker complex," he said. "I think it's abandoned, but Crowfoot just greased a scout."

Rolley crawled forward, and Buck followed. A quick assessment revealed several bunkers along the base of the ridge. Inside were fresh stores, arms, ammo, and other supplies.

"Where's the guy you shot?" Rolley asked.

Crowfoot motioned up the ridge. "Uniformed NVA," he said.

"You sure he's down?"

Crowfoot nodded, but before he could say more, the whooshing sounds of multiple rockets and the buzz of mini-guns came from the ridge above as the helicopter gunships lit up the enemy.

"Crowfoot," Rolley called out. "You and Blondie move over and cover the left flank from behind that last bunker." He turned, looking past Buck and TJ. "Lizard, you take Mo and Romeo. Go over behind that other bunker and cover the right flank. I'll take the cherries and cover the center. The gooks will be coming back down to these bunkers pretty quick, so hurry."

Rolley turned to Buck. "Move over there on the left about twenty meters. Find some cover. Wait for me to shoot first. TJ, you go over there on the right. If we get in a drawn-out firefight, move. Don't stay in one position too long."

Buck knelt behind the adjacent bunker and peered up the slope. Exploding rockets crashed through the jungle canopy at the top of the ridge, and though he couldn't see the helicopters, he heard the clacking of the rotors as they made their runs. It couldn't have been more than a minute when he spotted the first movement up the ridge to his front. It was the enemy. They were coming.

He glanced over at Rolley. With a grim nod, the squad leader gave Buck a thumbs-up and looked back up the ridge. Immediately, Buck spotted two NVA soldiers wearing pith helmets. They carried AK-47s, and with their free hands they were pulling a wounded comrade down the hill behind them. Disappearing and reappearing in the dense undergrowth, they were now less than forty meters away and coming straight at him. Buck flicked the selector switch on his sixteen to full auto and glanced over at Rolley. The squad leader apparently couldn't see the approaching enemy soldiers, but he had said not to fire until he did.

The soldiers popped out of the undergrowth less than twenty meters away, and for whatever reason Buck was totally calm as he raised his sixteen. Aiming carefully, he squeezed the trigger and swept back and forth until all three NVA soldiers lay dead on the opposite side of the bunker.

Quickly ejecting the empty magazine, he shoved in another as more gunfire erupted on the left, then the right. Rolley came up on a knee and fired several quick shots. Another enemy soldier fell between them. Spotting more movement to his front, Buck realized they were about to be overrun and began scattering suppressing fire across the ridge. A streak of sparks shot down the ridge and a loud thump shook the ground as a rocket-propelled grenade exploded inside the bunker near where Rolley was kneeling. The enemy apparently thought the squad was inside their bunkers.

Explosions mushroomed across the ridge as Lizard began firing round after round from his M-79 grenade launcher. As quickly as it began, the fight ended and a total silence fell over the ridge. A fog of dust and smoke hung in the surrounding jungle. After a moment there came the distant sound of the helicopter gunships departing. The acrid odor of burnt cordite filled Buck's nostrils, and the sound of the choppers faded as the eerie silence continued. No one moved. A moment later he heard a slight metallic sound and glanced over at Rolley. The sergeant was changing out the magazine in his M-16.

From the south, where they crossed the river, came a burst of gunfire that quickly echoed into more silence. A few moments later the same thing occurred to the north where Second Platoon had set up a blocking guard. Apparently the enemy had scattered in a panicked effort to escape.

Rolley crawled over to where Buck knelt, and raised his eyebrows. *"The vorpal blade went snicker-snack,"* he whispered.

"What?"

"We definitely need to get you some education, troop. For now, though, I want you to ease over there and tell Blondie to pass the word to Crowfoot to stay in position until I say otherwise." With that he turned and crawled over to TJ, apparently telling him the same.

Second Squad held their position for a half-hour before there came the sound of someone approaching from the rear. Buck rolled over, readied his M-16 and glanced at Rolley. The sergeant held up his hand, signaling him to wait, but he too held his weapon at the ready. The bushes below shook and swayed. Buck lowered his cheek to the stock of the rifle, taking aim as sweat ran in rivulets down his face. A moment later the palm leaves parted and a soldier pushed his way out of the jungle less than fifteen meters away. Buck centered his peep-site on his chest. Tom Jenkins, point man for the rest of the platoon, stepped out of the undergrowth and smiled. Buck exhaled, but his insides trembled uncontrollably.

Second Squad and the rest of First Platoon won the day, but half of Third Platoon's men were medevac'd that afternoon. Six men were KIA, several others were seriously wounded, and at least a dozen more received lesser injuries. A half-click to the east the terrain was flatter and more open, and after policing the ridge, the company was ordered to form an NDP on a couple of knolls out that way. They were to act as a blocking force in case the enemy retreating from Hue tried to re-occupy the ridge. The company had accounted for twenty-eight enemy dead that morning, eleven of which were credited to Buck's squad alone. Because of that, they were given inside perimeter security around the company CP that night.

Rolley gathered the squad in a shallow ravine where they heated C-rations and reloaded their magazines. Conscious of his still relatively clean and new fatigues and jungle boots, Buck glanced around at the other men. The sweat-streaked dirt on their faces intermingled with a three-day growth of beard. Their flak jackets and fatigues were faded and ripped, but it was their eyes, blood-shot and sunken, that revealed the most. While holding a can of ham and lima beans over a heat tab, Rolley introduced TJ and Buck.

"I'm putting both of you guys on Crowfoot's team."

He said Crowfoot was a Dakota Sioux from Montana. Skinny as a snake, he had piercing dark brown eyes, a hawkish nose, and a permanent scowl on his face. Drawing deeply on an unfiltered Camel, he didn't speak, but Rolley said he was the best point man in the battalion. Crowfoot gazed away from the group toward the distant horizon. Buck didn't know why, but he liked him.

The Lizard was a short, baby-faced guy from North Carolina, but he was all business. He carried the M-79 and a forty-five automatic. His claim to fame, Rolley explained, was that he was the platoon tunnel rat, and a damned good one at that. Lizard nodded without looking up. "Fuckin' A," he said.

Blondie was the other team leader. From Minnesota, he was tall and muscular, and toted the M-60. Rolley said he could throw a frag farther than anyone in the company. Buck eyed him. Blondie probably best represented them all with his easygoing demeanor.

Romeo Lopez was also on Blondie's team. He was from LA, and sported an Errol Flynn mustache. He was also stuck with his real name. "We couldn't come up with a better one than that," Rolley said, "especially since he was the first one to get the clap from a Vietnamese whore in Phu Bai."

"Aww Sarge," Romeo said, "you know that's some shit."

Rolley grinned. "Just keeping it real, my man. Too much boom-boom for *Romeo*."

Mo rounded out Crowfoot's team. He was from Detroit, and the only one in the group who smiled, but like his eyes, the smile seemed tired and strained. Rolley said he wanted to be called Mo-Town, but they'd tagged him with Motor-Mouth instead, because he never shut up.

"At least when I talk, Sarge, everybody be knowin' what I'm sayin', you know?"

"Take off your helmet and show them your fro-hawk," Rolley said.

Mo obediently removed his helmet. Although the webbing had deformed it, his Mohawk haircut gave him a sinister appearance.

"We call it a fro-hawk," Blondie explained, "because he had an afro before he cut it."

Mo ran his hand over his head. "I just wanted to look like them badass D-Day muthafuckas you see in them pictures."

Buck felt something strange inside his shirt and opened his flak jacket. "Oh, shit!"

"Muthafucka!" Mo said. "Dude's ate up with the leeches."

Buck unbuttoned his fatigue shirt to find his neck and armpits infested with them.

"Damned," Lizard said. "He's covered with the little blood-suckers."

TJ jumped to his feet and stripped off his flak jacket and shirt. "They on me, too," he said.

For the first time several of the men began laughing.

"Crowfoot," Rolley said, "Bring your cigarette, and let's get these cherries de-leeched. Romeo, you fire one up, too, and get started on TJ while I help Crowfoot. You cherries go ahead and strip off your britches, so we can check your legs."

After a couple minutes, they had singed at least a dozen leeches from Buck and that many more from TJ.

"Didn't you guys check yourselves after you got out of the river?" Rolley asked.

TJ shrugged.

"Reckon not," Buck said.

"Well, I was going to stop calling you 'cherries' after what you did this morning, but I think we're going to wait a little longer."

"Yeah. Don't rush it, Sarge," Mo said. He looked at Buck. "Hey, how come they call you Buck? I mean is that buck like a deer, or buck like a dollar or what?"

"It's buck like the car."

"Huh?"

Mo looked pissed, like he thought Buck was messing with him.

"My mama had a Buick Skylark she let me drive to school, but the 'I' was missing from the logo on the hood. The guys at school saw it and started calling me Buck."

Mo glanced around. "Maybe we should call him 'Buick.'"

"I think 'Buck' works. Let's stick with that," Rolley said.

Mo turned to TJ. "Hey, how about you? How come you talk so funny? Where you from anyway?"

"I'm from Louisiana, but you don't worry none 'bout my talkin', boy, 'cause you sound funny, too."

"Hey, cracker, who you callin' boy?"

Buck threw up his hand. "Chill, dude. Everybody is called 'boy' in Louisiana. Now, if *I* call you boy, you might have a reason to get hot, because I'm from Mississippi."

Mo's eyes widened. "You from Mississippi?"

Buck nodded.

"Oh, shit. I done heard about you muthafuckas. You gotch your hood in your ruck?"

"Not everybody from Mississippi is in the Klan."

Mo looked off to one side and cut his eyes back at Buck.

"Yeah, right."

"Why don't you give it a rest and eat your C's," Rolley said.

Rolley was not only the squad leader, but the resident sage as well, or so it seemed. He was able to talk about most anything, except Nam. Mention of Vietnam, or at least the war, left him unresponsive. He tried to explain their mission to Buck and TJ, but to hear him tell it, there was an inherent irrationality about the war and everything they were doing. "It's kind of like Alice in Wonderland," he said.

"He's always saying what we're doing is like that crazy shit he learned in college," Mo said.

Buck looked around at Rolley, but the squad leader simply shrugged.

"Why don't we talk about pussy or something good?" Romeo said.

"And *that* is why we call you Romeo," Blondie said.

"Let's get dug in," Rolley said.

"Beaucoup Charlie in these hills," Lizard said. "We'll probably get a visit from them tonight."

Buck had found the jungle wasn't much different from the Mississippi Delta where he grew up. The heat and humidity, along with the insects, snakes, and near-impenetrable vegetation were nothing new. It was the fighting that first day that had left him wondering if he could make it an entire year without getting hurt.

He and TJ were waist-deep and still digging their NDP when the lieutenant showed up near dusk. A tall sergeant first-class walked with him. Rolley saw them approaching, and turned to Buck and TJ. "We don't salute officers in the field."

No explanation was necessary.

Rolley stood and introduced them. First Lieutenant Hensley was the platoon leader, and the platoon sergeant was Dixie Greenbaugh. Hensley had an Errol Flynn mustache like Romeo's, but seemed laid back. Dixie, who was at least six-foot-three, probably weighed close to two-fifty.

"How did your cherries do today?" he asked Rolley. Dixie spoke with an Appalachian drawl—northern Georgia, or perhaps east Tennessee. He eyed Buck and TJ carefully.

"They did well, real we—"

"Good. Send them down to the platoon CP. I need some help." He turned to Buck and TJ. "You two, bring your entrenching tools and a canteen of water."

"They need to finish their own hole first," Rolley said.

"They can do that after they help dig one for me and the lieutenant."

"These guys were put through the wringer today, Sarge. Marino here killed three NVA at point-blank range this morning. Why don't you give them a break?"

"You killed three NVA this morning?" Hensley asked. The platoon leader seemed impressed.

Buck nodded.

Hensley turned to Rolley. "Write that up for me. I'll put it in my AAR with some recommendations. I believe this young man has already earned himself a Bronze Star."

"*All* my men did," Rolley said. "Those eleven gooks in front of our position didn't kill themselves."

"Write it up," Hensley said. "We'll put it in the report and see if we can get all you guys some hardware. Hell, you deserve it."

"You boys hurry up and di di mau your butts down to the CP," Dixie said. "It'll be gettin' dark soon, and we need to dig in."

Rolley glanced at the lieutenant, but Hensley turned away. It was obvious he didn't agree, but he didn't want to cross the old platoon sergeant. "You guys go help Sergeant Greenbaugh," he said. "We'll all pitch in here and finish digging your night position."

TJ and Buck walked down the hill and dug a hole for Hensley and Greenbaugh. Returning later, they found their hole finished in the squad perimeter surrounding the company CP. They thanked Rolley, who was the only one still awake.

"You guys get some sleep. We'll wake you when it's your turn for watch."

Wrapping themselves in their poncho liners, Buck and TJ squatted shoulder to shoulder in the hole. It was their first night in the Nam, and Buck figured he wouldn't sleep much, but the next thing he felt was someone pulling the poncho liner from over his head. It was Lizard.

A gray light revealed a milky fog that had settled across the hillside. TJ stood up, but Buck was locked in place. Every muscle in his body ached, and the slightest movement was met with shooting pain. It was the collision with the tree in the ravine near the LZ.

"Help me up," he said.

TJ locked arms with Buck and pulled him up. Lightning bolts of pain shot through his body. "Damned!"

"What's wrong with you?" Lizard asked.

"I fell down in a ravine yesterday and crashed into a tree. I'm sore."

"Okay, well, Rolley said for y'all to eat you some Cs, 'cause we'll be moving out soon."

Only then did Buck realize Rolley had skipped him and TJ for watch that night.

The company humped a couple clicks to a nearby LZ where the choppers were coming to pick them up again. Rolley said they were going to CA into the mountains to the west and run some RIF patrols. TJ glanced at Buck with a blank stare and shrugged.

Buck turned to Rolley. "What the hell are a CA and a riff patrol?"

"There you go," Rolley said, shaking his head in resignation.

"There he go what?" TJ said. He was obviously pissed.

Rolley grinned. "There *he* go looking like a damned cherry, again."

"So, tell us what the fuck you a'sayin', Sarge."

"Damned," Rolley said. "You Cajuns have a high threshold for humor, don't you?"

Buck put his hand on TJ's shoulder, but the little Cajun pushed it away.

"No, I'm tired of all this CA, OBQ, riff gonna run, bullshit. Just talk to me some English, you know?"

Rolley smiled. TJ took off his helmet and ran his hand over his head. In the distance there came the sound of the approaching slicks.

"Okay," Rolley said. "Be cool. CA means Combat Assault. That means we're going to land on an LZ and kill any of the little bastards we find around there."

"If they don't kill us first," Romeo added.

"Yeah," Mo said.

Rolley continued, "RIF stands for Reconnaissance In Force. That means we go out and poke around—bring the war to Charlie. You know?"

Buck put his arm around TJ's neck. "See, there ain't nothing to it. We're gonna go stir up some more shit, swat some hornet nests and get shot at some more. Now, what part of that don't you understand?"

TJ finally grinned. "Hey, I can't say it to the sarge, here, but you can kiss my ass, ma friend."

The company's combat assault back into the hills was going to be accompanied by a variety of TAC, which Rolley was kind enough to explain was Tactical Air Cover. It included Cobra gunships and jet attack aircraft. Apparently a LRRP team had found a treasure trove of enemy sign, and the company was going to search the area. Divided into six-man groups, Second Platoon was first to board the choppers and get airborne. No rain and a night's rest had been a reprieve of sorts. Buck felt a momentary relief as he realized that his fatigues had dried and the wind rushing through the chopper actually felt good.

He glanced down at the floor, half expecting to see more smeared blood, but there was something else. It wasn't quite the lump-in-your-throat bad as the blood, but it was ominous. Little holes were everywhere—bullet holes. They were in the floor, the side panels, and up front in the Plexiglas. The noise from the wind and rotors prevented much conversation, but he nudged TJ and pointed them out.

TJ looked down at them then looked up at the door gunner. Already watching them, the door gunner shrugged and dropped his head to point at a gash across the top of his flight helmet. It was apparently where an enemy round had grazed it. His eyes were sunken and tired as he slowly grinned and shook his head side to side.

After a while Buck noticed the chopper was dropping rapidly. Looking out at the hills up ahead, he saw they were approaching a hilltop where puffs of dark gray smoke mushroomed through the treetops. The area around the LZ was being prepped with artillery. A moment later two Cobra gunships shot past. Again, that lightheaded feeling came over him, and Buck's heart pounded as he clenched his teeth and breathed through his nose. Twice in as many days, he was again part of an air assault.

Rolley bent across TJ and shouted in Buck's ear. "There's a LRRP team already down there. Don't get trigger happy till you know what you're shooting at." Rolley pushed his mouth close to TJ's ear, probably saying the same thing. Afterward he turned to Blondie, Crowfoot, and Lizard on the other side. Several green tracers floated up out of the jungle as the chopper passed over an adjacent ridge. The rounds zipped past, and the door gunner swung around and began chugging away at the ridge. His red tracers disappeared into the jungle canopy below.

The main rotor clacked loudly when the chopper flared and set down on the LZ. Arches of green smoke swirled upward, and this time Buck and the others were able to step off the skids onto hard ground. They ran forward to cover. Rolley motioned for them to spread out along the edge of the undergrowth. More choppers approached, and within a few minutes the entire platoon was deployed around the LZ. Sergeant Greenbaugh walked over to Rolley.

"Did you see that trail on the way in?" he asked in a low voice.

Rolley nodded.

"Take your squad down there and set up where you can watch it. We don't want the little bastards moving in on us while the rest of the company is coming in."

What Dixie had called a "trail" looked more like a red ball road. It was little more than a hundred meters down a ridge from the LZ, and four men could easily walk abreast on it. When they reached it, Rolley pointed to the jumble of tracks in the red mud. "It's a well-used trail," he whispered. "So, be quiet and be ready." After setting out their Claymores, the squad spread in the undergrowth along the trail and waited.

Buck fingered the selector switch on his M-16 and glanced over at TJ. The little Cajun was bug-eyed. They were sweating as much from the tension as from the heat and humidity. The rhythmic thumping of more helicopters came from the hills to the east as the next flight of choppers approached.

3

BILLY THE LIZARD

Across the Song Bo

The squad continued watching the red ball trail below the LZ, while the choppers ferried in the rest of the company. Flight after flight of choppers came and went, until it grew quiet again. There came a sound from up the hill behind the squad. It wasn't much, the scuff of a boot perhaps, but it was definitely something. Buck turned, as did Rolley and TJ. It was easy to assume that someone was coming down from the LZ, but making assumptions often put men in body bags. The enemy was everywhere, and they could easily have slipped between the squad and the LZ.

There was movement in the trees a few meters above, then nothing. The jungle was ghostly quiet. Buck eased around with his M-16 and thumbed the selector switch to auto. Rolley held up a hand signaling for him to wait.

No one moved. After several long seconds there came a soft voice, "Roman."

Buck exhaled. It was the challenge.

"Candle," Rolley answered.

A guy from second platoon stepped into the open. He was walking point and locked hands with Rolley as he explained that the CO had sent them down to find First Platoon's Second Squad. The Second Platoon lieutenant and RTO came down the hill behind him and squatted with Rolley in the undergrowth.

"Lieutenant Hensley said your chopper took some incoming from a ridge over this way. Captain Crenshaw told us to get with you to see if you could show it to us."

Rolley pointed to a rise in the terrain, probably four hundred meters away. "Right out there, sir."

The lieutenant nodded. "Okay. My platoon is going to do a RIF down that way. Lieutenant Hensley said you're to pull back to the LZ."

The squad trudged back up to the LZ, while Second and Third Platoons recon'ed the area. Another heavy rain had begun falling by the time the squad arrived back at the LZ. The men huddled beneath their ponchos, eating cold C-rations and waiting for their turn in the shadows of the jungle below. Rolley and Lieutenant Hensley were talking with the Kit Carson scout, Nguyen, while Buck sat off to one side with TJ listening. Rolley had called Nguyen "Mouse" and Hensley wasn't happy.

"Call the man by his name, Sergeant," the lieutenant said. With that he turned to the Vietnamese scout. "You think beaucoup NVA here?" Hensley asked. His words were metered and pronounced carefully as he pointed to the ground at his feet.

Nguyen nodded rapidly and also pointed at the ground. "NVA here, yes."

"Yes," Hensley said, "but do you—"

"Sir!" Rolley said. "With all due respect, may I?" He motioned toward Nguyen.

Hensley looked at Nguyen then back at Rolley. "Go ahead, if you think you can do any better."

Rolley turned to the scout. "Okay. Enough fun and games, Nguyen. What's our situation here? I take it you're familiar with this area, right?"

The lieutenant started to say something, but Rolley held up his hand as he stared steadily at the Kit Carson.

"Sergeant, we are in a bad position here," Nguyen said. "I was here a year ago, and we had several base camps and beaucoup men. I am very much afraid that they are still here, and that we will all be killed because we are too few."

The joke was on the lieutenant. Their Kit Carson scout spoke almost perfect English, something only Rolley had realized.

"Why did you come over to our side if you had so many base camps and men?" Lieutenant Hensley asked.

"I was forced to join the NLF, but my family always hated the communists."

"Okay, Mouse," Rolley said, "here comes the tough question: What would you do if you were in our position?"

"Get more men," Nguyen said.

Buck choked back a laugh at the scout's laconic reply.

"Best damned advice we've heard all day," Rolley said.

"Why did the lieutenant object to the name 'Mouse' you are calling me?"

"Because he doesn't realize I mean no disrespect," Rolley said. "I do it to relieve the tension amongst us. Do you remember how I told you a couple months back how you reminded me of a character named Mouse in a story I once read?"

Nguyen nodded. "Yes, you said he slept at every opportunity, much as I do."

"What story is that?" Hensley asked.

"Alice in Wonderland."

Hensley slowly shook his head side to side. "Sometimes, you really scare me, Sergeant."

The radio broke squelch, and the lieutenant's RTO, Blanchard, stuck his head out from under his poncho. He gave Hensley the handset. "It's the CO, sir. He's calling for you."

After the lieutenant talked with Captain Crenshaw, he gave the handset back to the RTO and turned to Rolley. "Captain says Second Platoon found a large bunker complex down the mountain to the west. Pass the word to the other squad leaders to form up. Put Crowfoot on point and let's move out. Second Platoon is going to move past the complex and secure the area. We're going to search the bunkers."

Dixie, the platoon sergeant, stood in the rain without a poncho as he organized the column. He motioned to Crowfoot. "Okay, Chief, take your time, and let's see if we can find that bunker complex."

The stoic Crowfoot seemed to take no offense at Dixie calling him "chief." He nodded and walked off down the hill. Romeo followed as his slack-man, and the rest of the platoon fell in behind them. Once again, the men were swallowed in the shadows beneath the jungle canopy as the platoon made its way down the mountainside. The rain stopped, and up ahead, there came the occasional ping of Crowfoot's machete as he was forced to hack away a vine or some other obstacle in the wet undergrowth. Other than that, it was quiet. No one spoke. No one coughed. No one made a sound. Thirty minutes later Crowfoot brought the platoon to a halt. There came the hiss of excited whispers from the jungle on the hillside below. Crenshaw and his RTO walked past, down the hill.

Rolley turned and motioned with his head toward something on the slope a few meters away. Buck did a double-take. It was an enemy bunker hidden in the growth of vines and trees, all but invisible. Rolley turned and pointed the opposite direction. It took a moment to see it, but there was another bunker twenty meters to the left. The squad had walked right into the middle of the complex, and Buck had seen nothing until Rolley pointed them out. After a few minutes the odor of a cook fire became evident, along with the foul odor of rotting fish.

Lieutenant Hensley knelt beside Rolley. Buck listened. "These boys haven't been gone long. Take your time. I'm sure there are booby-traps, but we need to search for weapons and documents. We'll blow the rest in place. Take your men around the hill to the right. I'll send Third Squad to the left. This will be our assembly point once we've completed the search."

Rolley nodded and motioned for the others to follow him toward the first bunker. From there he sent Crowfoot, Lizard, Romeo and Mo around the hill toward the other bunkers. They disappeared into the undergrowth.

"Don't touch anything unless I tell you to," Rolley said. "Watch for trip wires and anything that looks like a booby-trap." His voice was little more than a whisper.

Removing his rucksack, he took a coil of rope with what appeared to be a small grappling hook and crawled into the bunker with his flashlight. A few moments later he emerged and motioned for Buck and TJ to back up. He had tied it to something down in the bunker, uncoiling the rope as he returned.

"Get down," Rolley said. He pulled the rope. The line stretched and grew taut. He yanked it. Nothing happened. He began pulling until he had taken up several more feet of rope.

"Good," he said. He stood and walked back to the bunker where he yanked a wooden crate up through the opening. "That's how you move shit and check for booby-traps," he said. "There's not much in there except this crate and a couple haversacks. These guys must have been in a hell of a hurry when they left."

Romeo appeared from out of the undergrowth. "Blondie says you need to come around to the next bunker. They found a tunnel."

Rolley sent Romeo back to find Lieutenant Hensley, while he led Buck, TJ, and Blondie to find Lizard and the others. When they arrived, Lizard was already stripped to his waist and held his forty-five and flashlight as he stared down into a hole. There was a hidden tunnel entrance inside the bunker.

"Lizard...Billy," Rolley said, "don't take any unnecessary chances."

"Don't worry, Sarge." Pulling a guide rope behind him, he dove head-first into the hole.

"Why did you call him Billy?" Buck asked.

Rolley didn't answer.

"That's his name," Mo said. "Sometimes Sarge gets uptight and he calls us by our real names."

Within minutes Hensley arrived with Dixie just as Lizard crawled back out of the tunnel.

"Big tunnel," Lizard said. His eyes were startled and wide. "Big, big tunnel, and a shitload of arms and ammo. There's a room down there that's bigger than—hell, I don't know. It looks like a warehouse. It's probably got enough RPGs, AKs, mortar rounds, and other shit in it to arm a battalion. It's huge."

Hensley got on the radio with the CO. A few moments later he called out. "The captain said to bring it all up."

"No way, LT," Lizard said. "Ain't gonna happen. It'd take us a week. Like I said, there's beaucoup shit in this hole, besides, I think I heard dinks down there, too. They were further down the tunnel."

The LT got back on the radio with Captain Crenshaw. The men watched and waited.

The lieutenant gave the handset back to Blanch, his RTO. "Okay. The captain wants a solid count of everything down there. Then he wants us to blow it in place."

"I'll count it best I can, sir, but it's going to take a while. I'm tellin' you, there's *beaucoup* shit in this fucking tunnel—more than I've ever seen, anywhere."

Lizard's voice was becoming louder with each exchange.

"Take it easy, troop," Dixie said.

"Do you want someone to go back down with you?" Rolley asked.

Lizard nodded. "Yeah, they can carry the C-4 and the fuses, and give me a piece of paper and a pencil."

Rolley tore a sheet of paper from his notepad and looked around at the other men. Other than Crowfoot, TJ was the next smallest man.

"TJ, strip down," Rolley said.

"Let's put enough C-4 down there to close that tunnel where they can't dig it out," the lieutenant said.

Rolley gathered several blocks of the explosive from the men and gave it to TJ along with a timed fuse and detonator. The two men disappeared down into the hole.

He turned to the LT. "Sir, I'd get the rest of the platoon and move away from here. They took enough C-4 down there to blow a really big hole in the side of this mountain. I'm staying here till they come up, and then we'll all haul ass together."

Rolley told Blondie to take the squad with Lieutenant Hensley and move out with the rest of the platoon, but Buck didn't go. Mo stayed behind as well. Rolley looked over his shoulder at them, but said nothing. Several minutes elapsed, and Buck stood at the bunker entrance, glancing skyward. The clouds broke and shafts of sunlight found their way through the treetops. Birds began squawking and singing. He looked at his watch. Lizard and TJ were somewhere down there in the tunnel with enough explosives to blow the side off the mountain, but it seemed they had been gone way too long.

There came a faint scuffling sound, and TJ popped up out of the tunnel. Rolley reached down and pulled him up.

"Where's Lizard?"

"He told me to di di. He's setting the charges."

TJ cleared the hole, and Rolley grabbed the guide rope. It was wrapped around TJ's boot. He had dragged it with him as he crawled from the tunnel.

"Did Lizard tell you to bring up the rope?"

Realizing what had happened, TJ dove toward the hole, but Rolley caught him by the boot and pulled him back.

"No way he's gonna find his way out of there, mon," TJ said. "There's too many ladders and tunnels."

He pushed Rolley aside and lunged into the hole, but the sergeant again caught his boot. TJ scratched futilely at the dirt.

"Sit tight," Rolley said. "Lizard knows his shit."

They waited.

A minute that seemed like an hour passed, then another. After several more minutes the men began making nervous eye-contact until there came a tremendous rumble from deep in the ground below. The earth quivered beneath their boots. It was an instantaneous reaction in Buck's mind as he assumed Lizard was dead, but there came a whoosh of smoke and dust from the hole along with Lizard veritably clawing at the air as he flew out of the tunnel. He tumbled head over heels, ending up on his back, cross-eyed and panting.

"And there comes Lizard," Rolley said.

Mo winked at Buck. "He's happy, now."

The bunker filled with smoke and dust, while it rained trees, dirt, and rocks outside. When the debris stopped falling, they dragged Lizard out into the open. On the slope above there were several plumes of smoke and dust rising from the undergrowth—additional outlets to the tunnels. The entire hillside below had collapsed into a smoky crater of trees and vegetation. Lizard coughed and sat up. He stared hard at TJ. The freckle-faced North Carolinian looked pissed.

"You took the damned guide rope, dude. What the fuck?"

"I'm sorry," TJ said. "I didn't know it was loose. It must have tangled around my boot when I was crawling out." Lizard lay on his back staring up into the tattered jungle canopy, but said nothing more.

Up to then, Buck had not noticed any insecurity in Rolley. His squad leader always seemed confident, but the seams in his façade were exposed when he thought Lizard had bought it down in the tunnel. Buck now realized Rolley joked, not for the humor, but as a means of coping with his responsibilities as squad leader. It was pretty obvious that he cared for his men, but his role as a non-commissioned officer carried with it the responsibility of sending them in harm's way.

Lieutenant Hensley showed up a few minutes later and pulled First Platoon's squad leaders together for a briefing. The CO had ordered the company to do a RIF over to the next ridge. Alpha Company was to the west, and Charlie Company was down the mountain to their east. The plan was to converge on the ridge. They moved out in platoon columns, along the crest and on either side of another long ridge that ran into a small valley. The company had to move through nearly fifteen hundred meters of dripping double- and triple-canopied jungle to reach the next objective. A spooky twilight world, it seemed almost subterranean.

Crowfoot was on point again, leading the platoon down the first ridge. After humping several hundred meters, they climbed another ridge and broke out of the jungle into an open area of scrub and elephant grass. Buck was awed as he stopped and gazed out toward the horizon. Miles upon square miles of nothing but green surrounded them—a huge panorama of jungle, rivers, and mountains. Under the clouds scattered below, he caught occasional glimpses of a broad valley. And it came to him: clearing the enemy from the vastness of this remote country might be an impossible task.

Blondie came up behind him. "Let's go. Move out," he said.

Buck snapped out of his daydream and hurried to catch up with Rolley, who was already entering another darkened tunnel of canopied jungle. The squad's progress slowed in the heavier cover. The sun broke through the clouds somewhere above, and the jungle went from hot and steamy to nearly unbearable. It was stop-and-go, and without the hint of a breeze, the men were red-faced and soaked with sweat.

Buck sipped warm, iodine-flavored water from his canteen as he waited for the column to move. The platoon struggled as they pushed through the undergrowth along the side of the steep ridge. Crowfoot was in no hurry as he hacked and pushed through the vines and vegetation. Behind him, Romeo walked slack, never taking his eyes off the wall of green in front. They worked as a team, leading the platoon toward the next ridge.

Occasionally Lieutenant Hensley and his RTO worked their way to the front and consulted with Rolley. Hensley seemed patient and smart. He told Rolley the platoon wasn't keeping up with the others and if possible to move a little faster, but he didn't push—he led by walking near the front of the column.

There came a sudden commotion along with Crowfoot's subdued voice from the point. Romeo threw up his M-16, but didn't fire. Everyone hit the ground.

Hensley and Rolley crawled up between Buck and TJ. "What is it?" Rolley whispered.

Romeo was still standing frozen in place staring straight ahead. After a moment or two, he turned to the others. "NVA scout," he said. "Got out of sight before we could get a shot."

Rolley came up on his knees, and looked toward Lieutenant Hensley. "What are your orders, sir?"

"I'll call the CO, but I'm fairly certain he's going to tell us to pursue. We'll follow, but double-slow for now. That guy wouldn't have been seen unless he wanted us to see him. He's probably leading us into an ambush."

They moved out again, but after only a hundred meters the column again came to a halt. Rolley and the LT moved forward. Up ahead Romeo was kneeling, but Crowfoot wasn't visible. They had reached the base of the next ridge, and it was only another four hundred meters to the top, but no one was moving.

The weird thing about hours of grueling work interspersed with adrenaline rushes was that Buck found the damnedest thoughts overtaking him at the worst possible times. He was suddenly looking out over a panoramic nighttime view of Grenada Lake back home in Mississippi. Lying on a blanket beside him was Debra Sue Lindsey, and he was looking down at the most fabulous tits in all of Sunflower County. Borrowing his mother's Buick Skylark, Buck had driven Debra Sue to the huge reservoir that evening, and the moonlight warmed her breasts as he buried his face between them. Debra moaned, seeming to enjoy herself almost as much as he did—if that was possible.

"Buck!"

It was Rolley. "Come on, man. Get your head in the game."

Rolley was almost clairvoyant that way. He knew when someone wasn't engaged.

"Move up there with Romeo."

Buck eased up to where Romeo was kneeling. Romeo jerked him down, but said nothing.

"What is it?" Buck whispered.

"More bunkers."

"Where? I don't see anything."

"I don't know, but Nguyen says they're here. He's somewhere up ahead with Crowfoot."

Having a turn-coat VC for a Kit Carson scout at first seemed like a bad idea, but Buck was rapidly falling in love with Nguyen. They would have likely blundered into the bunkers had he not warned them. Romeo shed his rucksack and began crawling on his belly through the undergrowth. Buck followed, but they stopped when a pair of jungle boots appeared in the bushes up ahead. It was Crowfoot, and he was slowly backing toward Buck and Romeo.

"What is it?" Romeo asked.

"Bunkers. They're occupied."

"Where's Nguyen?"

Crowfoot motioned with his head to the jungle where he had come from. "He's coming."

A moment later Nguyen appeared, scooting backward on his belly. His eyes were wide and hard with tension.

"Number ten," he whispered. "Beaucoup NVA. We too close. We di di mau len now or we die."

"Let's move back quietly," Crowfoot said. "We'll get with Rolley and the LT to see what's next."

They found Rolley and Lieutenant Hensley kneeling a few meters behind them. Crowfoot began relating what they had found when a firefight erupted on the left. Second Platoon had blundered into the bunker complex. After moving the squad back down the mountain, Hensley and Blanch began plotting the coordinates for a fire mission. Everyone hugged the ground as occasional stray rounds zipped and cracked past.

The LT brought the rest of First Platoon up and deployed them on line, telling everyone to stay down and wait. After a couple minutes the first artillery round impacted on the hill above.

Hensley yelled at Blanch, his RTO. "Tell them to fire for effect."

Moments later the hill above erupted with thundering explosions. The ground trembled with each impact and shrapnel whirred overhead as Buck buried his head beneath his arms. The artillery barrage continued for several minutes sending shrapnel, rocks, sticks, leaves, and debris raining down through the jungle canopy.

When the shelling finally ceased, an eerie silence ensued before there came shouts from Second Platoon as they fell back. Hensley ordered First Platoon ahead. Buck came to his feet, and began pushing through the vegetation. He had gone barely fifty meters when a .51 caliber opened up from somewhere above. He dove to the ground as the huge rounds shattered the trees sending more debris fluttering down from above.

Buck had heard them say a .51 caliber round anywhere in the body, instantly turned a man into multiple pieces of body bag material. He looked over at TJ on his right. He was bug-eyed, white and sweating. To the left Mo was curled up behind a tiny sapling, holding his helmet with both hands. Rolley crawled up from the rear and grabbed Buck's boot. Buck looked under his arm back at the squad leader.

"Pass the word," he said. "Pull back. Stay down, but pull back."

Buck motioned for TJ to go back down the hill. He began a backward crawl.

"Mo," Buck hissed. He didn't move. Buck crawled over to him and grabbed his arm. Mo jerked in panic and rolled over, looking up. "Pull back," Buck said.

Further to the left, he spotted Blondie. He was already looking his way. Buck motioned him back down the hill. By the time they were assembled a couple hundred meters back, the lieutenant was on the radio again.

"What now?" Buck asked.

"Sit tight," Rolley said. "The lieutenant is calling in some fast movers."

He must have seen the puzzled look on Buck's face. "TAC, Tactical Air Cover."

A moment later Hensley tossed the handset back to the RTO and turned to Sergeant Greenbaugh. "Pass the word for everyone to get small. The fast movers are already on station, and they're inbound with nape."

From somewhere overhead came the buzz of a small aircraft, followed by the whoosh of rockets. A moment later they impacted up the mountain near the bunker complex. Trails of white phosphorus sprouted from the trees above. The Bird Dog was marking the target for the jets. After that, it again grew deathly silent. Buck strained to hear the jets, but there was nothing—not a bird calling, nothing but a void of total silence. The men lay sweating, swatting mosquitos and waiting.

Wiping the sweat from his eyes, Buck lay prone, still trembling from an overdose of adrenaline. It was twilight under the trees, and the extended silence was spooky. He continued listening for the inbound jets, but there was only the eerie silence. A distant shout came from one of the other platoons, then more silence. After a while Buck could hear the breathing of the men in the surrounding bushes and an occasional staccato of rifle shots somewhere in the distance, nothing more.

Perhaps silence was good. Maybe the enemy had retreated. He sucked down a trembling breath. His heart was finally withdrawing back into his chest, and he tried to relax. A bird actually began singing somewhere in the jungle canopy above. He lit a cigarette, drawing in the warmth of the smoke and holding it, before slowly exhaling. The tension that had held his body captive was finally receding.

4

THE SACRED WU FUC SOCIETY

The Hills Above the A Shau Valley

IIIEEEEOOOOHHHHFFFFOOOMMMPPHHH—a screaming roar filled the air around him, and Buck clawed into the dirt, certain he was about to pee in his pants. He balled up, burying his head beneath his hands. The silence had been wrecked by the thundering roar of afterburners mere feet above his head. Burnt Jet-A fumes, smoky white, filtered down through the jungle canopy. The F-4 Phantoms were already rocketing skyward when the hill above exploded into a monstrous fireball and roiling black smoke. Sucking the oxygen from the air, the mass of flames and smoke rolled down the hill, stopping only forty or fifty meters away. The heat was nearly unbearable as the men shielded their faces against the blistering flames. After a few moments Buck looked over at TJ, red-faced and sweating, as he stared up the hillside.

"Whooo, Fuck!" TJ said in wide-eyed amazement.

Buck nodded and looked over at Rolley who was lying beside Blondie. They were both grinning.

"Welcome to the fraternal order of the Wu Fuc Society, gentlemen. You have responded with the secret password for those who witness their first napalm strike."

A few minutes later Lieutenant Hensley crawled up and began motioning for the platoon to move back up the hill.

"This is crazy," TJ muttered. "Sooner or later, we all are gonna die."

"Shut up," Rolley hissed. "And spread out."

Buck agreed with TJ. Two days in the field and they'd been in almost constant contact with the enemy.

The company advanced up the hill, finding a couple dozen crispy corpses along with more weapons and ammo, but the NVA who survived the napalm strike had apparently di di'd to points unknown, probably across the A Shau Valley into Laos a few clicks to the west. Buck looked about at the enemy dead. The odor of their burnt bodies was nauseating. Rolley was right. Only experience could teach you about this shit.

After blowing the bunkers, the company cleared an LZ atop the hill to take out the wounded and KIA. It was hard physical labor after a day of combat, and by the time the last chopper departed that evening Buck was exhausted, but it mattered little. There was always more to do. The company formed a night perimeter and dug in around the LZ. It was dark by the time he had dug his hole. Everyone would take his turn on watch for what Rolley said would be the inevitable probes by the enemy during the night.

The first trip flares went off sometime after midnight and the nighttime jungle became a beehive of clashing red and green tracers, punctuated by rocket-propelled grenades and Claymores. Captain Crenshaw had formed the company into a relatively tight perimeter, and the enemy was unable to penetrate despite several attempts. They gave up shortly before daylight, but it was a night with no sleep and with more casualties. One of the KIAs was from Third Squad in Buck's platoon—one of the new replacements. They had flown in together that first day on the chopper, but Buck could not recall hearing the soldier's name or seeing his face. He began wondering if after only two days the war was already affecting his mind.

Buck knew little about his dad, except that he'd come to Bois de Arc after World War II, made a cash purchase of nearly four hundred acres of land and developed it into one of the largest vegetable-growing operations in Mississippi. Joe Marino had fought in Sicily, landed at Anzio, and fought his way up the Italian peninsula, but that was about the extent of Buck's knowledge. His father seldom spoke of the war, except to mention losing both of his brothers at Normandy, and when Buck mentioned the possibility of someday joining the army, his father had simply said, "Patrick, that would be a very bad mistake." After his first two days in the field, Buck now saw the wisdom in those words.

A high school senior not yet eighteen years old, Buck was left in a world of confusion and anger after his parents were killed. His maternal grandfather, now his closest adult relative, had sworn never to step inside a Catholic church and didn't attend his own daughter's wedding, yet stood proudly on the front row at the funeral mass. He had stepped in immediately with his lawyer, telling Buck he would hold his inheritance in a trust and run the day-to-day farm operations until he was old enough to do it himself. It was the first time Grandfather McKinney had ever put his arm across Buck's shoulders and the first time he had spoken more than two or three words to him. The problem was he didn't know about the Last Will and Testament Joe Marino had the foresight to leave behind.

A young lawyer out of Batesville, Jerry Baker, had written the document covering almost every possibility, including a trust in the event Buck wasn't of age—a trust that Joe Marino had made certain didn't include anyone remotely related to the McKinney clan. Buck understood little of the legal machinations after his grandfather retained a lawyer and challenged the will, but he understood well his own anger at his grandfather's greed.

Buck was determined to get away. He wanted to escape the Mississippi Delta, the McKinneys, and the nightmarish memories of his mother and father dying. And for good measure, after enlisting in the army, he left the daily farming operations in the hands of a family friend, a young black preacher named Son Freeman. It was a message Buck was certain his grandfather would understand. Buck's only problem now was the 356 days remaining on his tour of duty. If he didn't survive, his mother's and father's land would certainly be divvied-up amongst his greedy cousins.

For the next three weeks the company continued humping from one hill to the next searching for the NVA, all the while knowing the enemy would be found only when they wanted to be. Day after day, valley after valley, ridge after ridge, hill after hill, they walked, they climbed, and they sweated. The rain fell and despite their ponchos they were soaked to the bone, their skin becoming white, wrinkled, and swollen. Their feet rotted, and their fatigues became ripped and muddy and stank of mildew and body odor.

When the sun came out, their exposed skin blistered and their crotches became raw from the salty sweat and constant friction. The water in their canteens was hot and tasted of iodine purification tablets. Sleep, real sleep, was impossible. The medic began distributing "green bombers," big green amphetamine pills, so the men could keep their eyes open. It was nearing the end of another hot day when the company gathered around another nameless hill in another perimeter and dug in.

Buck decided TJ was right. It wasn't a matter of *if* he'd get wounded or killed, but *when*. The odds seemed stacked against them. If it wasn't a sudden firefight, it was snipers taking out an occasional point man or RTO, or a sudden barrage of incoming mortar fire from a nearby ridge. And there were the ever-present booby-traps. The best thing that had happened in the three weeks they had been in the field was the last two days. There hadn't been a single contact of any kind by any-one in the battalion. It was as if the enemy had disap-peared altogether.

After their first night in the field Rolley had put Buck and TJ in night defensive positions with one of the experienced squad members, but this night he put them together again. It suited Buck just fine, because after nearly a month, TJ had become a pretty good grunt. They began digging their hole, and filling their sand-bags, when Buck paused. He gazed down at the wall of vegetation only a few yards from their position. He wasn't certain, but he thought he had heard something in the jungle somewhere below. It was a sound so subtle that it seemed almost subliminal, something he had learned to recognize back home in the Mississippi Delta.

TJ hadn't noticed as he continued hacking with his entrenching tool down inside the hole, but Buck stopped and listened. It *was* something, even if it was so vague that it didn't fully register for a moment or two. After a while, TJ noticed Buck was still looking down the steep mountainside and listening. He stopped working and looked up. TJ had taken off his helmet and flak jacket. Stripped to the waist, he was covered with a sheen of sweat and coated with dirt and leaves.

"What'ju lookin' at, ma friend?" He drove his entrenching tool into the dirt beside the hole and stood up beside Buck.

Buck held up a hand to silence the little Cajun as he continued listening and searching the jungle below. The sun had dropped into the trees and the undergrowth was a solid wall of green in the gathering shadows before dusk. He continued straining to hear whatever it was that had first gotten his attention. TJ, sensing his alarm, quickly picked up his M-16 and took a knee beside him.

Buck bent over and whispered in his ear. "Go over to Rolley's hole, and tell him I think I heard something."

TJ nodded, grabbed his helmet and trotted in a crouch toward where Rolley was supposed to be. Buck pulled a frag from his web gear, knelt and continued listening. The jungle was still. The only birds calling were somewhere in the distance. The hillside immediately below was unusually quiet—no birds, no frogs, nothing. He watched. He waited. He listened, and it reminded him of when his mean-spirited cousins would try to sneak up on him when he was hunting back home in the forests along the Mississippi River. After a while, his instincts and senses grew to be like those of the deer. He sensed things others seldom noticed until it was too late.

A minute later a stick broke behind him and he heard the scuff of boots. Buck glanced over his shoulder. It was TJ and Rolley. Following them were Lieutenant Hensley and Dixie Greenbaugh, the platoon sergeant. Hensley and Rolley knelt beside Buck.

"Whatcha got?" Hensley asked.

Buck glanced at Rolley. The squad leader nodded his approval.

"I heard something, sir."

Dixie was still standing behind them with his hand on his hip, looking down into the jungle.

"What did it sound like?" Hensley asked.

"I'm not sure, sir, but it was something—footsteps, maybe or…I really don't know."

"Come on, troop," Dixie said. "Was it footsteps, voices—what was it?"

Buck looked over his shoulder at the platoon sergeant. "I'm not sure, Sarge. It was…I don't know, maybe a sound that didn't belong, but there's something or somebody down there not too far."

Rolley put his hand on Buck's shoulder. TJ went to a knee, while the Lieutenant looked back at Sergeant Greenbaugh and shrugged.

Dixie laughed. "It was probably just the men out there on the LP. I shit you not, Sergeant Zwyrkowski. You need to split these cherries up and put them with experienced men." The platoon sergeant had seen more of the Nam than anyone in the platoon, but he was standing and talking with no effort to keep his voice down.

"You don't think we need to check it out?" Hensley asked.

Dixie pointed to an adjacent hill. "Sir, Alpha Company is right over there on that hill, and Charlie Company is down there on that ridge below us. We have three men on an LP back over that way, a hundred meters or so. If the dinks are gonna probe us tonight, it's gonna come from the other side of the perimeter. There ain't nothin' down there but some figments of these boys' overworked imagination."

"You're wrong, Sarge," Buck said.

Rolley squeezed his shoulder, and Buck realized he wanted him to shut up.

Dixie spit a stream of tobacco juice from the wad in his jaw, and grew red-faced. "Cherry, you don't need to be telling me I'm wrong. You need to listen—" A stream of green tracers cracked and zipped past, followed instantaneously by the clatter of an AK-47 from only a few meters down the hillside. A Chi-Com grenade thudded in the dirt beside the hole. Buck grabbed it and threw it back down the hill. An NVA soldier with a pith helmet and an AK-47 with fixed bayonet popped from the undergrowth, charging their way.

Rolley fired a string of rounds, until the enemy soldier tumbled dead at Buck's feet. Three more NVA burst from the jungle only yards away. The first one sank his bayonet into Lieutenant Hensley's thigh. Buck shot him in the side of the head. Rolley emptied his sixteen in the second, grabbed TJ's entrenching tool and swung it like a baseball bat at the third. TJ was firing indiscriminately into the jungle below. Dixie, who dove for cover during the first burst of gunfire, regained his composure and pulled a frag from his web gear. He threw it into the undergrowth on the hillside below.

Two more NVA charged from the jungle. TJ and Buck took them out, but another grenade landed only a few meters down the hill. TJ dove into the foxhole, but the explosion knocked Lieutenant Hensley off his feet. The concussion was so powerful, Buck barely noticed the sting of shrapnel as he, TJ, and Dixie continued pouring fire into the jungle below. A moment later Lizard showed up and began pumping rounds from his M-79. The explosions from the grenades were deafening, and the shrapnel zipped lethally through the trees all around. Within minutes it grew quiet again.

Buck grew dizzy and sat down. TJ pushed him onto his back, while Lizard tore open a bandage and pressed it to his neck. What Buck had thought was sweat soaking his fatigue shirt was blood. Rolley held a pressure bandage on Hensley's thigh wound, while Dixie held pressure on several shrapnel wounds on the lieutenant's torso. The lieutenant was going into shock when Doc Gilbert, the company medic, showed up. He hooked up Buck and Hensley to plasma bags and hit them with syrettes of morphine.

Buck was getting woozy as he looked up at Dixie. "Like I was saying, Sarge."

"Shut the fuck up, Marino. You made your point."

Red-faced, Dixie lit a cigarette and pressed it to Buck's lips. "Just take it easy," he said. "We've got a dust-off coming. If they can make it in before dark, we'll get you guys back to Phu Bai."

It was probably the loss of blood, but Buck remembered little of that night—only the medevac coming in at last light, the thundering rotors, the wind buffeting through the open cabin of the helicopter, and Lieutenant Hensley moaning. It all seemed like a bad dream—probably for the better—a nightmare forgotten.

5

JANIE

22nd Surgical Hospital, Phu Bai, March 1968

When he awoke, Buck had the distinct feeling he had been asleep for a long time, perhaps days. He was on his side, and when his eyes opened he was looking at someone in fatigues standing beside the bed. The fatigues weren't bleached of color and ragged like his, but fresh and green. He stared at them, and after a while he realized the soldier wearing them had—well—breasts—a woman's breasts. Buck cut his eyes upward. She was staring down at him.

If there is one thing that quickly connects two people, it is usually their eyes. At least that was Buck's thought as he gazed up into a woman's brown eyes. They were tired, but young, clean brown eyes—sympathetic and honest. He didn't move, and she said nothing, but he felt her fingers gently pushing through his hair. His senses returned, and he remembered the dust-off, the wind, and a distant nightmare.

"Lieutenant Hensley," he said.

"He's going to be okay," she said. "They evacuated him to another hospital. I'm not sure where, but he's going to make it."

"Good."

Afraid he would find instantaneous pain, Buck didn't want to move.

"Were any of our other guys hurt?"

"You and the lieutenant were the only ones that came in on the chopper."

"Good."

She continued running her fingers through his hair. Buck slowly rolled onto his back, finding to his relief almost no pain. After a minute or so he began to realize there was no body odor either. He had been in the bush for three weeks with no bath, but he no longer stank. Pulling the sheet away, he discovered several gauze bandages on his neck and chest. He drew a deep breath through his nostrils. Other than the iodine and alcohol, there was nothing particularly foul smelling. He looked down at his arms. They were clean, as were his hands and fingernails.

"Where am I?"

"22nd Surgical, Phu Bai," she said.

"Am I…?" he paused, unsure how to ask.

"You're fine," she said. "Maybe, too fine. You'll be going back to your unit before long."

"How did I get a bath?"

"I gave you a little sponge bath," she said. "Who are Rolley and TJ?"

"How do you know their names?"

"You talk a lot when you're on pain meds," she said.

"Are they okay?"

"As far as I know. Sounds like you guys were having a really bad time."

Buck stared up at the ceiling where a naked light bulb burned.

"Okay," she said. "I know you are Specialist 4th Class Patrick Marino—"

"No, I'm a PFC."

"Sorry, dude. Whether you like it or not, this says you are a Specialist 4th Class."

She held her clipboard where he could see it.

Buck thought about it a moment and nodded. "Hell, a few more holes in me and I'll probably make general."

She laughed. "Well, let's hope that doesn't happen."

Buck thought of the odds if he went back. It could happen.

"Do you need more pain meds?"

He really wasn't hurting—not physically, anyway.

"I don't reckon."

She removed her army baseball cap and pulled a shirtsleeve across her forehead. Her hair was blond, her cheekbones high, and she had a natural beauty that normally got women better jobs before they became army nurses. Another nurse walked up behind her. She didn't have the drop-dead good looks of the first woman, but she was nonetheless a hell of a lot better looking than any other woman he had seen since leaving the States.

"I see your boyfriend is awake," she said.

"Shut up," the first nurse said.

"Did you ask him who those other guys were that he was talking about?"

"I think they're his buddies."

The second nurse rolled her eyes. "Well, duh."

"Get out of here," she said, giving her a playful shove.

"Specialist, this is Spec-Five Janie Jorgensen," the second nurse said, "and she's madly in love with you, so you better act right and toe the line."

"Will you please…?"

"I'm going to make the rounds," the second nurse said.

"Good. Go!"

She walked away, looking over her shoulder, smiling and nodding as she went.

"So, your name is Jane," Buck said.

"Yes."

She was a thin, almost gangly-looking woman.

"Is that like Tarzan's Jane?"

"I'm from Montana, mister smart ass, and we don't have a lot of vines to swing on there."

He looked up into her eyes. "Thanks for cleaning me up."

She ran her fingers through his hair again.

"My friends call me Janie."

Buck had three small shrapnel wounds, the worst one in his neck. A week later he was released for light duty. Janie told him to return at the end of the week so a doctor could give him a last checkup before he returned to his unit. The battalion was now working the line of hills east of the Laotian border, doing air assault vertical envelopments, landing high in the mountains and working their way down into the adjacent A Shau Valley. The company was setting up another NDP when Buck arrived that afternoon. Lizard and Mo met him at the LZ and led the way across the hill to where the platoon was digging in.

"You should'a tried to stay longer," Mo said. "Things done gone to shit 'round here."

"It's not like I had a choice. What's going on?"

"New platoon leader's a real dick," Lizard said.

"Somebody gonna frag his ass if he don't start actin' right," Mo said.

"He did six months behind a desk down at MAC-V and thought he was gonna walk into the XO's job, but they dumped him on us instead. He's pissed off at the whole damned world."

"Great," Buck said. "Just what we need, a gung-ho asshole with an attitude."

They walked past a foxhole with a poncho stretched above it. Dixie was sitting there eating a can of C-rations and talking with Tom Blanchard, the RTO. The platoon sergeant looked over his shoulder and promptly did a double-take. "Hey, Buck," he said. "You're looking good, my boy. Welcome home."

It was a totally different tone of voice from the one Buck heard the last time they had spoken. And the sudden realization struck him that he had been promoted from "cherry" to Buck.

"Hey, Dixie. Hey, Blanch."

He continued down the hill with Mo.

"They both hate that new muthafucka," Mo said.

Rolley popped up out of a hole, smiling. Crawling to his feet he wrapped his arm across Buck's shoulders. "Good to see you, baby brother. How are you feeling?"

"Neck and shoulder are still sore, but I was feeling halfway decent till these guys started telling me about our new platoon leader."

Rolley looked up the hill behind Buck. "Yeah, he's quite a bit different from Lieutenant Hensley."

"Different?" Mo said. "Muthafucka's crazy."

TJ came up the hill trailing the wires from the Claymores. He dropped the ends beside the hole, walked up to Buck, pressed his face close and began examining the wound on his neck. The entire side of his neck and lower jaw were still purple and swollen. TJ touched it lightly with a finger. Buck drew back.

"Easy," he said.

"You should still be on light duty," Rolley said.

"Yeah, I know. I was, but that chicken-shit battalion clerk put me on shit-burning detail the very first day, so I told the Sergeant Major I wanted to go back into the field."

"Well, keep that bandage dry till you heal," he said.

"Word is we might stand-down back at one of the firebases in a few days," TJ said. "Did you get any decent food while you was back there?"

"Well, they didn't serve crawfish etouffée or filé gumbo, if that's what you mean, but the hospital food wasn't bad."

"Yeah, mon, what I wouldn't give for a bowl of filé gumbo," TJ said, "I'd even settle for a good hamburger and some french fries, right now."

Buck looked down at the ground and grinned.

"Oh, no, mon. Please, tell me you didn't get no hamburger and french fries while you was back there," TJ said.

"There was this really great nurse I met, and she went out and got me a burger and fries one day."

"Oh, shit, you done met a nurse, too?" Mo said.

"Okay, guys, let's knock off the bullshit and finish digging in," Rolley said. "I'm going down and check on Blondie and Romeo. They're going out on LP tonight. Mo, go on back down there with Lizard and finish up your hole."

The men were about finished with their NPDs when the clouds blotted out the evening sun. There came the rumble of thunder and the storm clouds rolled in over the mountains. By nightfall, Buck was soaked as the rain continued unabated, but it was better than burning 55-gallon drums of shit back at Phu Bai.

For once it remained quiet that night, but the rain was relentless, still falling straight down when the gray light of another dawn came. With no choppers able to fly, and several NVA regiments known to be in the vicinity, Captain Crenshaw held the company fast in their secure perimeter. The men huddled beneath their ponchos, watched and waited while their foxholes filled and overflowed with muddy rainwater.

Life in the Nam came in schizophrenic jolts of agony and pleasure, and Buck was never certain which was coming next. He could never make sense of the madness, and Rolley had given him a little book called *Alice in Wonderland*. He told Buck to read it. It would explain everything. And it did.

The comparisons seemed uncanny. One moment he was up to his armpits in a foxhole full of muddy water and the next he was sitting high and dry in a chopper with the wind blowing in his face. One day he was receiving a medal from some colonel, and the next afternoon he was on latrine duty, burning shit in 55-gallon drums.

This time it was one of the better days. Buck had been snatched from hell and delivered, maybe not to heaven, but perhaps to a higher level of purgatory. The company had been ferried back to the base at Phu Bai for a few days of R&R—not rest and recuperation, the way Buck had it figured, but what was certain to be ranting and raving from the new platoon leader, Frank Mallon. The men called him Molly, because he reminded them of Shirley Temple in *The Little Colonel*, except Molly wasn't cute. He was an asshole.

Buck, TJ, Mo, Blondie, Crowfoot, Romeo, and Lizard were sitting inside their hooch with Rolley that night, smoking cigarettes, drinking beer, and singing along with Jackie Wilson on Mo's transistor radio. It was Wilson's hit *Higher and Higher*. Everyone in the squad, even Crowfoot, was singing at the top of his lungs.

That's why your love (your love keeps lifting me)
Keep on lifting (love keeps lifting me)
Higher (lifting me)
Higher and higher (higher)
I said your love (your love keeps lifting me)
Keep on (love keeps lifting me)
Lifting me (lifting me)
Higher and higher (higher)

This was heaven. They'd had their first hot meal since late February, a hot shower, and downed at least four or five beers apiece. After washing their gear and cleaning their weapons, there was nothing left to do but look forward to a few days of rest and relaxation. Life was good.

The new platoon leader ducked inside the hooch. The men continued singing. Rolley glanced up. "Oh, hey LT," he shouted. "Come on in."

Mallon eyed Rolley with a cold stare and silence. He was wearing his web-gear and packing his forty-five, but he had on newly cleaned fatigues and his jungle boots were polished. The men's voices faded into silence and they gazed up at him while the lieutenant stared back at them with something resembling disgust. Mo turned off the radio.

"Something wrong, LT?" Rolley asked.

Lieutenant Mallon jerked his head around and looked down at him. "Outside!"

Rolley had a puzzled look on his face. "Sir?"

"Outside, Sergeant, now!"

Mallon strutted back to the door and stepped outside. Rolley turned and made eye-contact with Buck. He smiled and winked. "Look up the Queen of Hearts in that book I gave you."

After they'd gone, TJ looked bewildered. Buck slapped him on the back. The little Cajun didn't seem to understand what was happening. Buck wasn't sure himself. He looked over at Lizard. The platoon tunnel rat pressed his lips together, shook his head but said nothing.

"Muthafucka's crazy," Mo murmured.

Romeo stared at the wall, but Blondie smiled. "Don't worry," he said. "Rolley will play his game—all the way to checkmate."

Crowfoot, always the silent one, simply nodded.

Buck began turning the pages, looking for the Queen of Hearts.

Mo turned on the radio, again. *You are listening to the Armed Forces Radio Network – Vietnam.…* The music began. It was The Platters singing *The Great Pretender.*

Buck listened as Rolley told the men that despite his best efforts to explain the deference of protocol in combat areas, their failure to at least acknowledge Molly's presence had pissed him off and the squad was getting extra duty. That night they walked together down to the base perimeter where they were assigned guard duty in the bunkers. It was a magnificently beautiful starlit night and their rucksacks were stuffed with beer. When the squad arrived, the men on duty there were sitting atop the bunkers, talking and listening to a radio. There was the distinct odor of reefer in the air.

"Wassup?" one asked. "You the relief?"

"I suppose so," Rolley said. "Anything happening out there?"

The soldier looked as if he didn't understand. "Out where?"

"Out there," Rolley said motioning with his head. "Outside the wire."

The soldier looked around as if he had only that moment remembered his guard duty responsibility. "Oh, man. You're like totally paranoid. The gooks haven't been around here since Tet."

They were obviously REMFs who had never been off the base. Rolley sent them on their way and turned to his men. "We have to cover this bunker and that one over there. Buck, you stay here with me, Romeo, and Crowfoot. Blondie, you take TJ, Lizard, and Mo, and set up the sixty in that next bunker. Take one of the rucksacks of beer, but don't get so shit-faced you can't stay awake. And don't chamber a round in your weapons unless you need to. We don't need an accidental discharge. It'll give the lieutenant another reason to fuck with us."

The men passed the early evening hours sitting atop the bunker, talking, smoking, and drinking cans of lukewarm beer. A little before midnight Romeo and Crowfoot went inside and bedded down. It was amazingly quiet, no outgoing artillery—and only an occasional illumination flare. A pleasant breeze made the evening almost enjoyable. Overhead, a bright sliver of the new moon cast shadows amongst the surrounding bunkers. Both Buck and Rolley sat in silence for over an hour before Rolley lit a cigarette.

"Want one?" he asked.

"Sure."

Rolley flipped the cap on his Zippo and lit Buck's cigarette.

"Cup your hands around it, so it can't be seen. So, tell me some more about Buck Marino," Rolley said.

"Not much to tell."

And in Buck's mind there really wasn't.

"What are you going to do when you get back to the world?"

"I don't know. I'd like to find a girl, look after my parents' farm, whatever."

"You know you can go to school on the GI Bill," Rolley said.

"Yeah, I know, but I haven't given it much thought. I figure I'll be lucky if I don't die over here. I have to deal with that first, and I don't want to die for no good reason or by some stupid stroke of fate. You know?"

"You're looking at it all wrong," Rolley said. "It's not about how you die, but how you live—what you did while you were here. Stop focusing on dying. Hell, everybody dies eventually, but only some really live. And if it happens over here, you don't have a lot of choice in the matter. Live while you can, drive on, and keep looking forward."

"I reckon you're right. Maybe, I do need to go to college when I get out."

"You should. You might find something you really like doing."

"What are you going to do?" Buck asked.

"I'm going to keep re-upping till this war's over, then I'm going to buy a Harley and ride across the country."

"You're crazy, Sarge."

"You noticed, huh?"

"I didn't mean you were *really* crazy."

"Don't worry about it," Rolley said.

"Do you have a girl back home?" Buck asked.

Rolley dropped his head, paused, then flipped his cigarette in the dirt. He snuffed it out with the toe of his boot.

"Are you getting sleepy?" he asked.

"I slept all night and half the day today," Buck said. "I couldn't sleep if I wanted to."

"Okay, I'm going down and take a nap. Wake up Romeo or Crowfoot when you're ready."

Sometime later Buck heard someone coming up out of the bunker. It was Romeo. He sat down atop the bunker beside Buck, lit a cigarette, stretched and yawned.

"Reminds me of nighttime in the hills outside LA," Romeo said.

Buck slapped at a mosquito. "Yeah, I feel almost human again. I'm dry, got a full night's sleep, and I'm wearing clean fatigues."

"I know what you mean, dude."

"So, what's the deal with Rolley?" Buck asked.

"What do you mean?"

"I don't know. I mean, he always seems like he's got something hanging over him."

"Oh, yeah," Romeo said. "He's really been sort of zoned-out since he got back from his fiancée's funeral."

"Is that why he was on emergency leave?"

"Yeah. You didn't know?"

"What happened to her?"

"She was at nursing school in Chicago and some drunk fraternity asshole ran over her in a crosswalk one night. The sarge is really tore up about it. Hasn't been the same since it happened."

Buck looked up. Something moved in the shadows behind the adjacent bunker where Blondie and the others were on guard. He put a hand on Romeo's arm and motioned with his head.

"Put out your cigarette. We've got company," he whispered.

Romeo started to turn. "Don't look," Buck whispered. "There's someone sneaking around over there behind the other bunker. Go down and wake up Rolley and the others. I'm going to walk back down the road like I'm heading back. I'll circle around and try to see who it is."

"Be careful," Romeo said. "It might be a sapper."

After nonchalantly strolling up the road, Buck ducked behind a hooch and quickly circled to where he had seen the movement in the shadows. The person was still there, hiding behind a pole and peering steadily at the bunker. It appeared to be another GI, but Buck wasn't certain.

Treading softly, he eased up behind the unsuspecting intruder. Only then did he realize he hadn't chambered a round in his M-16. Snatching the charging handle on his weapon he let it go. The 5.56 mm round chambered with a metallic *CACHINK*. The soldier dropped to his knees, spun and thrust his hands in the air.

"Don't shoot!" he screamed. "First Lieutenant Mallon, Bravo Company, 2nd of the—"

"What the fuck are you doing sneaking around back here?" Buck couldn't restrain his rage. "I almost shot your ass."

Mallon jumped to his feet and dusted the dirt from his fatigues.

"At ease, troop! You're addressing an officer."

The entire squad ran up with their weapons at the ready.

"I thought you were a sapper. I damned near blew your dumb ass away, *Sir*."

Buck couldn't believe what he had just said, but his anger was uncontrollable.

"Identify yourself, troop," Mallon said.

"It doesn't matter who he is, sir," Rolley said. He motioned to the rest of the squad. "You guys get back to the bunkers. I'll deal with this. You too, Buck. Go, now."

"I didn't dismiss these men," the lieutenant said.

"I did, sir. Now, let's go to the company CP and wake up Captain Crenshaw so you can make a full report on this incident."

"I can handle this matter myself," Mallon said. "I don't need to involve the CO."

The squad had stopped to listen. Rolley turned their way. "I told you men to go back into the bunkers. Now, go!"

The men began filing back into the bunkers, all except Buck. He stopped long enough to hear the discussion between Mallon and Rolley.

"That's fine, sir. You handle this matter, but I want you to think about how you're going to explain to the CO why one of his officers was sneaking around out here in the shadows behind the bunkers, and were it not for a damned good soldier challenging him, he might have got his ass shot off."

"Go get your men squared away, Sergeant Zwyrkowski. I'm going to think on this awhile. I'll let you know tomorrow what action I will take."

Buck quickly ducked into the bunker as Rolley turned his way. Inside, Romeo and Crowfoot were still mumbling and cursing.

"You should'a shot his dumb ass," Romeo said.

"I almost did."

"Bummer, man—a real bummer. Maybe next time."

Buck glanced at him. Romeo's eyes were set hard. He was dead serious. Still trembling, Buck wondered if he would be court marshalled. Rolley made his way down into the bunker.

"The next time you see someone sneaking around like that, wake me up before you go after them."

"Sorry, Sarge. I was just—"

"Don't worry about it."

"Are you going to report his dumb ass to the Captain?" Romeo asked.

"We'll wait and see what comes of it first. If he's smart, he'll keep his mouth shut and move on."

6

MOLLY TAKES CHARGE

Round Trip Back to Phu Bai, April 1968

Lieutenant Mallon seemed satisfied with restricting the men to the battalion area after the incident at the bunkers. Nothing more had been said for several days, and Buck did his best to avoid the lieutenant, who seemed to have actually learned something. Their next mission would probably tell for certain. A few days later, with Mallon still absent, Dixie brought the news to the platoon.

The battalion was headed back into the A Shau Valley, to an area where the 4th and 5th NVA Regiments owned the real estate. The Long Range Reconnaissance Patrols were reporting the enemy not only had numerous motorized vehicles, but some armor as well. The Hundred and First Airborne "traveled light" and facing an enemy tank was something Buck had never considered. For the first time, they were issued the new LAWS rocket, something Rolley said using against Russian-made tanks would be like hunting elephants with a pistol.

This was the Light Anti-Armor Weapons System, with "light" being the keyword, as Rolley explained it. The NVA were said to have the T-34 Russian-made tank. A direct hit with a LAWS in the right spot would take one out, but you had to be within a couple hundred meters. Buck stared at TJ with the realization that the ante had just been upped. Worrying about surviving was no longer worth the effort. They had been in-country a little over three months, and Buck had already resigned himself to the inevitable. It was the only way to maintain his sanity. With his usual intuitive nature, Rolley must have realized what he was thinking. He gave Buck a friendly slap on the back. "Let thee embrace me, sour adversity, for wise men say it is the wisest course."

"What the hell does that mean?" Buck asked.

"It's a quote from Shakespeare. Accept what may happen, and stop worrying about it. Take charge. Embrace it. Own it. Like I said a long time ago, it's the worrying that drives you crazy."

Buck realized that his platoon had been relatively lucky, because Third Platoon had been all but decimated in the last few months, and even with a flood of replacements they had only two full squads in service. Being in the wrong places at the wrong times, they'd taken heavy casualties in two different NVA ambushes. Buck figured First Platoon was merely lucky, and it wasn't a matter of "if" but "when" their luck too would run out. He could worry about it, but as usual, what Rolley said was right. If he wanted to stay sane, he needed to stop worrying and simply go out and fight.

They were aboard the choppers, making another combat assault, and Buck looked down at hundreds of water-filled bomb craters stretching as far as he could see. The battalion was flying into the A Shau Valley up Highway 548. Rolley described it as the dead-end road to Purple Heart Valley. The combat assault became a routine insertion as the platoon began assembling along the road. It was quiet. The enemy was apparently giving them a pass. Rising on both sides of the valley, the mountains were huge dark shadows, laced with misty fog.

"Which way are we going?" Buck asked.

"That depends a great deal on where you want to go," Rolley said.

Buck eyed him carefully as he tried to figure what he was saying.

"Okay, I really don't give a shit which way we go, as long as you tell me. Why don't we just go somewhere and dig in?"

Rolley grinned and threw his arm around Buck's neck. "Sorry, little brother. I'm just messing with you."

"Was that more of your Alice in Wonderland shit?" Buck asked.

"You're kidding, right?"

"Why?"

"Because I thought you knew it was. Your answer was nearly like it's written in the book."

"Damned! I must be going nuts," Buck said.

"We're all crazy here," Rolley said. "You are. I am."

"Yeah, you're probably right. At least, I'm beginning to feel that way."

"You must be," Rolley said, "or you wouldn't be here."

"Wait a minute. Is that more of your…"

Rolley nodded. "Where's the book I gave you?"

Buck motioned with his thumb over his shoulder. "In my ruck."

"Good. Read it. If you don't agree it's about this fucking war, I'll kiss your ass."

Buck motioned with his head. "Better get ready. Here comes your Queen of Hearts."

It was Lieutenant Mallon, strutting up the middle of the road. He had the hardened stare of a man on a mission. Dixie came up the road behind him looking down and wagging his head side to side. Behind Dixie was Blanch, the platoon RTO. He too appeared pissed.

"When he gets up here," Rolley said, "come to attention and salute him."

"I thought we weren't supposed to salute officers in the field."

"Why are you standing around talking, Sergeant Zwyrkowski?"

Rolley glanced at Buck, raised his eyebrows then turned and snapped to attention. He gave Mallon a snappy salute. Buck did the same. The lieutenant gave a half-hearted return salute.

"Awaiting orders to move out, sir," Rolley said.

Mallon turned back to Dixie. "Sergeant Greenbaugh, why haven't these men been told to move out?"

"Because you haven't given the order, sir."

Blanch stepped around Dixie and held the radio handset out to Lieutenant Mallon. "Sir, it's the CO. He wants to know what the delay is."

Mallon batted Blanch's hand away. "Tell him we are moving now, and I'll give him a sit-rep as soon as I can."

"Somebody gonna frag that muthafucka," Mo muttered.

Rolley turned to Crowfoot. "Take Buck and walk slack for him, but don't let him screw up."

"Be careful, chief," Dixie said.

Crowfoot nodded and motioned for Buck to follow him. The squad was spread out up the road, and they walked to the head of the column. It was a surprise for Buck, but a hell of a vote of confidence from Rolley. Up to then, Crowfoot and Romeo had been the only two who had walked point. Granted, it was by far the most dangerous place to be anywhere in Vietnam, but you put only two types of men on point—those you trusted with the lives of your men, and those you wanted to get rid of. Buck took it as the former.

"Do you see that little valley up there to the west?" Crowfoot asked.

Buck nodded.

"White Knight says we are going up there."

A couple clicks away a fog-filled fold in the mountains extended out into the main valley.

"Who is White Knight?"

Crowfoot motioned toward a Kiowa observation chopper that had been circling several thousand feet overhead. "That's what Sarge calls the battalion commander."

"More of Rolley's 'wonderland' crap?"

Crowfoot shrugged. "Head out through that elephant grass. Try to keep that big mountain on the left in sight. Watch out for punji-pits, there are hundreds of them out here. And if you see anything in front that looks like a trail, or a place where people have been, stop. I'll move up and take a look at it."

Buck felt something sting his neck and reached up to slap it, but hesitated. Carefully, he pulled his fingers over the spot on his neck. It was one of his shrapnel wounds. The skin was hot and swollen, but there was nothing he could do about it now. He was leading the platoon through the elephant grass and into a thick growth of cane and palms along the edge of the valley. By midday they had reached the canopied jungle at the mouth of the little valley. Buck stopped to catch his breath. He was feeling unusually exhausted and slightly nauseated.

After sipping water from one of his canteens, he poured some on his chin and neck. The water felt good on the wounds. A moment later the lieutenant appeared from back in the column.

"Why are we stopped, Marino?"

"Just getting a quick drink of water, sir."

"You need to learn to walk and drink at the same time. Stop wasting time and move out."

"Uh, sir."

Buck showed Mallon his neck, now swollen under his jaw and burning hot. Rolley eased up behind the lieutenant and listened.

"Looks like a bug bite," Mallon said. "Get the medic to look at it this afternoon when we form-up for our NDP."

Rolley stepped around the lieutenant and peered closely at Buck's neck. "Sir, this isn't a bug bite. It's an infected wound."

"Like I said, he can get the medic to look at it later. Right now, we need to move out."

"Sir, before we get up there under that jungle canopy, I recommend we call for a dust-off and get this man to the rear for some medical attention."

"We need every man, and I'm not going to medevac him for a little infection. Move out, Sergeant, *now*."

With the corners of his mouth turned down, Rolley grew red-faced. He turned to Buck. "Go back to headquarters group and find Doc Gilbert. Let him take a look at that wound."

He turned and motioned to Romeo. "Come up and walk slack for Crowfoot. Move up the side of the ridge and take a heading parallel to the valley. We need to reach that hilltop before dark."

"It looks like there's a good trail down here," Mallon said, "and the walking will be a lot easier if we stay in the valley. We can reach the hilltop a lot faster."

"Yes, sir, we can, but it will also leave us exposed to higher ground on both flanks, not to mention the possibility of booby-traps and bunkers. I don't think Captain Crenshaw will be very happy with us if we lead the company up through there."

The lieutenant cut his eyes back down the trail as if he might see the CO coming. "Okay, then, take us up the ridge, but no more slacking."

Rolley winked at Buck. "Report back to me after you see Doc. Let me know what he says."

The medic was Doc Gilbert. Texas born and bred, he had an easy western drawl, and it wasn't difficult to imagine him wearing a Stetson and Santa Fe cowboy boots with saddle bags thrown over his shoulder. Instead he wore a steel pot, green canvas jungle boots, and carried a medic's bag. He was walking with the company headquarters group when Buck found him. The CO noticed when Buck came back down the column.

"Where are you going, son?"

"Sergeant Zwyrkowski told me to see Doc about my neck."

Buck paused as Captain Crenshaw looked at his neck. He turned to Doc Gilbert. "Come take a look at this."

The doc walked over and carefully touched Buck's neck. Buck drew back.

"Hold still, partner."

He pushed with his finger against Buck's neck. Buck flinched as a flashing pain shot through his jaw.

"Oh, hell!" Gilbert turned to the CO. "It's bad. Pus is running out."

He put his hand on Buck's forehead. "You feelin' feverish?"

"Yeah."

"He's burning up. We need to medevac him, if we can, sir."

Captain Crenshaw turned to his RTO. "Tell First Platoon to hold up and put out flank security, then get the Six on the command net."

Buck had let his buddies down. The entire company was delayed for nearly an hour, and now he was on a Huey headed back to Phu Bai. His neck and jaw were swollen and tender, and he really *did* feel like crap, but leaving his buddies behind in the A Shau was the last thing he wanted to do. Some might even think he was ghosting. Hopefully, he could get some antibiotics and be back within a few days. He lay against the wall of the chopper and closed his eyes.

When they landed at Phu Bai, a stretcher crew ran out on the LZ, but Buck waved them off as he stepped onto the acid pad. He could walk to the ambulance on his own, but he took only three steps before the ground spun beneath him. He dropped to his knees and promptly puked his guts out. The next thing he remembered was a nurse inserting an IV. Feeling as if he had awakened with the flu, Buck was too exhausted to move. He looked up at her. It was the nurse who had introduced him to Janie.

"Where's Janie?" he muttered.

Even talking took a lot of effort.

"Oh, don't worry," the nurse said. "She went off duty a little while ago, but I sent word that you were here. She'll probably show up as soon as she showers and smears on some lipstick. But don't plan on a big date, pretty boy. You're in bad shape."

Buck worked up a weak smile.

A while later he felt a warm hand resting on his forehead and opened his eyes. He was shivering with feverish chills, as he gazed up into Janie's light brown eyes.

"You were supposed to report back here before returning to duty, Mr. Knucklehead."

Buck stared into her eyes. How was it that this nurse had suddenly decided he was the man for her? She had to be at least a couple years older than he was.

"They missed a tiny piece of that shrapnel in your neck. It was all festered up. The doctor got it out a little while ago, but you've got a bad infection. He put you on some antibiotics. I think you'll feel a lot better by morning."

Buck realized he had fallen asleep again only when he awakened to more voices.

"Go get some sleep, Janie. I'll check with the captain to see if we can get you a couple days off. Besides, I don't think your boy is going to be released for a day or two, anyway."

Buck tried to force his eyes open, but they wouldn't cooperate. The pain killers had him zonked. He drifted back to sleep.

He wasn't sure how long he had slept when he awakened again, but he felt a thousand percent better. The fever was gone, and his head was clear. The other nurse was standing over him, looking at a thermometer. She glanced down, noticing he had opened his eyes.

"How are you feeling?"

"Where's Janie?"

"Better, I take it," the nurse said with a smile.

"Sorry," Buck said. "Yeah, a lot better."

"What happened between you two?" the nurse asked.

"What do you mean?"

"I mean, did you two have sex or something when we weren't looking? We've had scores of men come through here, and I've never seen her act this way."

"All we did was talk, but I don't remember much of what I said."

"That's what she told me. I mean, she said you two had a day-long conversation, but she said you were mostly delirious the whole time. I sure wish I knew what you said to her."

"Why?"

"Because I've never seen such a dedicated, no-bullshit nurse change like she did when you came along. For months now, she's had Army, Air Force and Navy officers trying to date her, but you're the first man she's shown more than a passing interest in getting to know."

"Who are you?" Buck asked.

"I'm the senior NCOIC here, Miriam Anderson."

"Nice to meet you, Sergeant Anderson."

She smiled. "And according to your dog tags, you're Patrick Marino."

"I'm usually called Buck."

"Well, hey Buck."

"Hey, Miriam."

"So, when's Janie coming by?"

"I'll be damned if you don't have it as bad as she does. I made her go get some rest. She was in here sleeping beside your bed."

The nurse hung the clipboard on the end of his bunk.

"She comes on duty in a couple hours. I'm sure you'll be her first stop as long as we don't have any new incoming."

"Is he awake?"

It was her voice. Buck tried to look past Miriam.

"I thought I told you to get some sleep?"

Janie walked up beside the bed and grasped his hand. She talked to Miriam, while looking down at him. "I did, but I woke up and couldn't go back to sleep."

Buck heard the loud slap of boots on the floor as someone came running up the center of the ward.

"We've got incoming wounded," he said. With that the orderly turned and ran back the way he had come.

Miriam put her hand on Janie's shoulder. "I made some notes in the log. When you come on duty, check them and follow up. I'll catch up with you later. I'm heading over to triage to see if I can help out."

Two days passed, and Buck had hoped to spend some time with Janie, but more wounded arrived, and the best she could afford were short visits and snippets of conversation. Miriam said the doctor was likely releasing him in a day or two, but she arranged for Buck and Janie to spend an afternoon over at Eagle Beach east of Hue. Bending over the bed, she smiled and pinched his cheek on the side that wasn't sore. "You can thank me later."

The weather cooperated that day as he walked with Janie out to the water's edge. They stood hand in hand, gazing out at the South China Sea. The sun was shining through a light haze, and the salty air filled Buck's nostrils. Off shore, patrol boats cut foamy wakes, and a Huey came up the coast, thundering overhead before disappearing to the north. He couldn't believe he was standing here, holding hands with this beautiful woman, and she seemed as attracted to him as he was to her. It was a dream in the middle of a nightmare.

All around them were GIs with flak jacket tans trying to imagine that they were having fun and not destined to return to the war in a day or two. Several eyed Janie with the lonesome eyes of men too long and too far from home. Buck was pretty sure the sight of a round-eyed woman in a two-piece swimsuit was no less than a mirage from heaven for most of them. He could hardly begrudge them for staring.

"This is the first beach I've ever been to," Janie said.

"Really?"

"My dad has a cattle ranch and runs a guide service up in Montana. I suppose that has always taken up most of his time. We never traveled much."

"You should visit the Gulf Coast when you get back home. It's even nicer than this. The sand is white as sugar."

"The Gulf of Mexico?"

"Yeah, there's a place in Florida called Saint George Island. That's where my grandparents had a beach house, and my mother always took us there for summer vacation."

"Maybe we can go there sometime," Janie said.

Buck could think of nothing better than spending a week in a beach house with Janie, yet there was this huge obstacle between them—the nearly eight months remaining on his tour of duty.

"If things work out, maybe we can."

She noticed.

"Keep your chin up. You'll be okay."

"What did we talk about when I came into the hospital last month?"

"You don't remember?"

"Well, yes, some of it. I mean, I know the first place I'm going to visit when I leave Nam is the Bitterroot Valley. Then I'm going up to Glacier National Park and all those other places you talked about. I remember you describing the Rocky Mountains until I began dreaming about them."

"You don't remember telling me that your mother had brown eyes and blond hair, too, or the story about saving the baby flying squirrels?"

"Oh, no. The squirrels, really? I must have been totally out of it."

"Yes, you said the Mississippi River had flooded everywhere and you found them on a log floating along. You kept them until they began chewing the wires on your stereo, then turned them loose in the woods behind your house."

"Did I tell you their names?"

"Lester, Clyde, and Billy Bob, except you figured out later one of them was incorrectly named because a whole new family of them raised out there."

Buck led her by the hand as they walked along in the shallow surf. Simply being here beside a beautiful woman on a beach, in the sun, seemed too perfect to be real.

"What else did I talk about?"

"Just about everything."

"Oh, shit."

She gave him a flat smile and nodded.

"Anything personal?"

Janie blushed. "Some of it. You're definitely all man, but you have a way of expressing things that sound… well, honest."

"What didn't I tell you?"

Janie motioned to a corner of the beach where no one was around. "Let's go up that way and spread our towels. I need to put some suntan oil on before I get burned."

"I told you some things about me, as well. You don't remember?"

Buck felt as if he'd known Janie for a very long time. There was almost none of the caution that came with new relationships, and he found himself saying things he would never say to a new acquaintance.

"In all honesty, I feel like I know you well, but I can't remember much of anything we talked about. How long did we talk?"

"I had a rest day, and sat on that chair beside your bed the entire time. Miriam, that's Sergeant Anderson the head nurse, made me go back to the quarters to sleep, but I spent several hours with you the next afternoon after I got off duty."

Janie uncapped a brown plastic bottle of Coppertone suntan oil with cocoa butter. After she rubbed it on her arms and legs, she rubbed some on Buck's back.

"Do you mind returning the favor?" she asked, handing him the bottle. She rolled over on her stomach.

"I'm not sure who is doing who a favor," Buck said.

"Just don't let your hands wander where they don't belong, tiger."

Buck poured the oil onto her back and carefully worked it in, tenderly massaging her shoulders and lower torso. He pushed the oil beneath the shoulder straps of her swim suit and softly worked her muscles with the tips of his fingers. Simply touching a woman this way was heaven, and after several minutes, Janie moaned and turned over. She took the bottle from him and capped it.

"Sorry, I can't stand any more of that."

She sat up and wrapped her arms around him, pulling him close. Their lips met and her mouth was soft, wet, and warm. His body burned, and Buck became worried that he might lose himself right there on the beach. When they parted he was nearly panting, but so was she.

"I've got to go in the water and cool off," he said.

Janie grinned. "Me too."

They ran splashing into the surf.

The next morning Buck was released. He stood with Janie out on the road awaiting the ride back to his unit. A tear slipped from her eye and rolled down her cheek.

"Buck, there's something I didn't tell you yesterday about how you said you would do anything for your buddies. Please take care of yourself. Come back to see me. I'll save my R&R, and we can go somewhere together."

It was as if God were dangling this vision of heaven before him, but sending him back to hell. What could he say? What could he tell her that wouldn't give her false hope? Surely, she could see the number of wounded coming in every day. The odds weren't good.

"It may be too soon for us to use words like love," Buck said, "but we—"

"No, it's not." Janie grasped his fatigues and pulled him close. "It's not too soon. It may sound crazy, but I already know I love you. I mean it. I love you. I've never felt this way. Please, come back."

Buck looked into her eyes. They were firm, not desperate, but truly passionate. Janie had to be at least two years older than he was, maybe more, and even with his eighteen years, he still saw her as having a wisdom predicated on experience that was beyond his. Surely she didn't believe in fairytale things like love at first sight.

Yet she was here, baring her soul before him as if he had earned it. And Buck knew at that moment that he probably loved her as well. Perhaps it was the war that drove people together so quickly. After all, he had similar strong feelings for the men in his unit—grungy dudes he had known barely three months, and he would give his life for any of them. A deuce and a half rolled to a stop beside them—his ride. He pulled her chin up and softly kissed her lips. Her brown eyes were pooled with tears.

"I love you, too, Janie. I'll do my best."

7

FIXED BAYONETS

Highway 547, May 1968

Buck caught a chopper back to the bush that afternoon. On board with him were several replacements. They had on new jungle fatigues and shiny new black and green jungle boots. Beads of sweat formed on the upper lip of the one sitting beside him, and Buck felt sorry for him, but there was little other than silent sympathy he could offer. It was a while coming, but only recently had he realized the agony he had put Rolley through with all his questions during the flight out of California.

There was no way to describe this mess. There was no way to tell a man how to survive it. Probably, nothing he could say would make a difference. Each man had to figure it out for himself. And sometimes, no matter what a man did, the beast chose him.

As soon as he stepped off the chopper at FSB Bastogne, Buck knew something wasn't right. Rolley was waiting on the LZ when the choppers landed. He wore a grim countenance and said nothing as Buck ran from beneath the churning rotors with the new replacements. The stone-faced squad leader looked past him and the others as if he were staring into eternity.

"What happened?" Buck shouted.

They made eye-contact, but Rolley only shook his head and turned away. The unit had returned to the firebase after only a week up in the A Shau.

"Follow the sergeant, men," Buck said to the newbies. He hurried to catch up with Rolley.

"What happened?" he asked again.

Rolley stared straight ahead and swallowed hard. "Romeo is dead. Dixie and Blondie both got hit. They were medevac'd. Word is they're going to be okay and back in a week or two. First Squad lost Ramirez and Jackson. Third Squad lost Willis and a new guy, don't know his name. There were seven other casualties, a couple who might not make it."

"What the fuck happened?"

"Some bad decisions were made."

"Mallon?"

Rolley pressed his lips together hard, and kept walking without answering.

"What the fuck happened, Rolley?"

"Doesn't matter, now. Let's get these newbies squared away, and we'll talk later."

"When did Romeo get it?"

"Yesterday afternoon."

Buck felt the blood pressure swell in his chest until he was sure his heart would burst wide open. Yesterday afternoon, he was at the beach with Janie. He was getting suntan oil rubbed on his back and looking out at the sparkling waters of the South China Sea—all because of a damned little infection.

Yesterday, he should have been back with his unit, but he was pretty sure Janie and Miriam had pulled some strings to allow them that afternoon at the beach. When he arrived with Rolley at their hooch, Mo and Lizard were sitting outside on the sandbags smoking cigarettes. TJ was sitting on the ground cradling his head in his hands.

"Where's Crowfoot?" Buck asked.

"I am in here." Crowfoot's voice came from inside.

"Anyone else in there?" Buck asked.

"Only Blanch, our new machine gunner," Crowfoot said.

"Blanch?"

Rolley turned and walked up the road—no doubt a calculated move where he wouldn't witness the discussion.

"We tried to warn him, but that dumb ass Molly pushed us into an ambush. We got pinned down," Lizard said.

"Dumb muthafucka thinks he's John fuckin' Wayne, yellin' at us and tellin' us to keep moving," Mo said.

Crowfoot stepped outside the tent and hunched over his Zippo, shielding it and lighting an unfiltered Camel. He inhaled deeply and blew the smoke out into the dank afternoon air. Only then did Buck notice Rolley had left two of the new cherries there with the squad. They stood shifting foot to foot still wearing their rucksacks and holding their M-16s.

"You guys go on in there and find a spot to bunk," Buck said. "Take it easy."

"It might not have ended up so bad, if he'd a let Blanch call in some artillery," Lizard said.

Blanch stepped through the opening between the sandbags, and swayed side to side as he came out of the hooch. "Yes, shir, meet your new official pig totin' machine-gunner, Pa-private First Class Thomas Blanchard," he said.

His eyes were bloodshot, and he was obviously feeling minimal pain.

"PFC?" Buck said.

"Yeah," Mo said. "The chicken-shit lieutenant busted him back a stripe."

"What the fuck for?"

Blanch put his hand on Buck's shoulder. "Fret not, my friend. It's an—" He let out a beer belch. "—an absolute fucking blessing."

"Getting busted?"

"No—not being that stupid fucker's RTO."

"What did you do?"

"Blanch was callin' in a fire mission after we got hit," TJ said. "I was there with him, and we was taking some serious fire from up the road and a ridge on our right. The LT come out of a ditch while Blanch was calling for a fire mission, and grabbed the handset. Blanch told him he had already called in the fire mission, but Molly got all crazy and started yellin' at him. Said only an officer was authorized to call in artillery. Dumb fuck called in a check-fire over the command net and grabbed Blanch's map—told him he wasn't authorized to have a map, neither."

"He busted you for that?"

"No," Blanch said. "He busted me for telling him he could take the radio and map and shove them up his little Pollyanna ass. He is also ma-making me tote the sixty from now on, because I'm too lazy and wanted to get out of carrying his radio."

"So, how did Romeo get it?"

"After Mallon check-fired," Lizard said, "the stupid fucker called in the wrong coordinates. Blanch tried to tell him, but it was too late. The first round landed on the road up near where Romeo was laying. Killed him dead right there, and Sergeant Greenbaugh caught some shrapnel, too."

Buck swiped at a tear of anger before the others saw it. Rolley had been right about the book he had given him. Having finished reading the two stories, it became more obvious every day what he meant. *Alice in Wonderland* and

Through the Looking Glass and What Alice Found There were stories exactly like the things his buddies were telling him. Vietnam, like the book, was an experience on the bizarre fringes of reality.

"How did Blondie get hit?" he asked.

"He was the first one hit when the gooks popped their Claymores," Crowfoot said. "He's gonna be okay. He got a little piece in his chin, and some in his shoulder."

"We gotta frag that muthafucka," Mo said.

"No!"

Buck wasn't sure why he said it, but there had to be a better way.

"Whatta you mean, 'no'?" TJ said.

Buck thought about what Rolley had said to him when they first met on the flight from Oakland. He looked around at Crowfoot and Lizard. Crowfoot took another deep drag on his cigarette, turned and stared up the road. Lizard briefly made self-conscious eye-contact but shrugged.

"Okay, guys. I know this fucker has cost us all some serious grief, but think about what you're saying. Do you want to go to Leavenworth for the rest of your life?"

"Better Leavenworth than a body bag," Lizard said.

"Ain't nobody gonna know no difference, anyhow, ma friend," TJ said.

"What do you say, Crowfoot?"

"Something needs to change. Otherwise, he is going to get us all killed."

"Why don't we go to Captain Crenshaw? He's pretty cool, and I'm sure—"

"Rolley already tried," Blanch said.

"What did Crenshaw say?"

"There wasn't much he could say," Crowfoot said. "He told the sarge he'd look into it, but for now he had to follow orders or turn in his stripes."

"That's it?"

"Somebody said they heard the captain yellin' and cussin' at the lieutenant later," Lizard said, "but the dumb fucker is still struttin' around here like a peacock."

"I just wish we had Lieutenant Hensley back," Blanch said. "He was a *real* officer."

"Okay, guys. Let's not do anything stupid. We've got to think. I promise I'll come up with something. Just don't do something that will bring CID down on our ass."

Buck had no idea what to do, but he wanted no part of killing an officer, no matter how much the prick deserved it. He could go to Rolley, but the squad leader didn't deserve having something like this put on his shoulders. It was a conundrum with no simple answer.

The company's reprieve lasted a few more days, while more replacements came in and the men rested and recuperated. It was early June when word came down that the battalion was going to begin working with the ARVN forces and the 1st Cav in an area up southwest of Hue.

Blondie and Dixie had returned to the platoon, and Lieutenant Mallon seemed to have calmed down after his ass chewing from Captain Crenshaw. Dixie explained to the men that their mission was interdiction and pacification in the villages and hills in Thua Thien Province along Highway 547 between Hue and the A Shau Valley. There were still main-force Viet Cong units as well as some NVA units in the area. He also said there would probably be some messy village fighting, something he hated more than operating back in the hills.

With their canteens topped off, magazines cleaned and reloaded, and a fresh supply of C-rations, the men trudged up the road that morning to the base LZ. The choppers were there, rotors churning, fueled and ready. The only thing Buck could do now was turn his back on thoughts of Janie and get his head in the game. It was that or risk losing it.

The weather had gone from months of rain, drizzle, and fog to miserably hot, dry, and dusty. The company was part of a joint task force encircling a series of villages and hamlets near the highway. A day earlier, the lead elements of Delta Company had come under heavy fire while approaching this area, and careful reconnaissance revealed a winding trench in the tree-line along the southern edge of the main village. Further north between the village and a couple of secondary hamlets were bunkers and on the higher ground beyond, there were several enemy machine gun and mortar positions dug into the side of the slope. At least two companies, one NVA regulars and the other main force VC, occupied the positions. Bravo had moved up on line with Alpha and Charlie Companies and the men watched while the Air Force blanketed the tree-line and far ridge with napalm and two-hundred-and-fifty pounders.

Buck, TJ, and the others marveled as the jets streaked in dropping their ordnance. And afterward, with afterburners roaring, they rocketed skyward while the entire ridge was engulfed in a mass of orange flames and black smoke. They were taking great care not to strike the village or hamlets, but the ground to the north and south was getting pummeled. After a half-hour of nonstop airstrikes, the jets disappeared, and an artillery barrage began. The loud *Karrooomphs* of the impacting artillery shook the ground as Mallon came down the line crouching low behind the men.

"Leave your rucksacks, men. Carry your ammo and canteens. Squad leaders, form your men on line, and let's move out."

They walked out into a dried rice paddy, overgrown with waist-high grass and scrub. Bravo Company was making a direct assault on the village while Alpha and Charlie provided flank security to the east and west.

Buck could think only of Janie and the pleasant odor of the cocoa butter suntan oil as he rubbed it gently on her back and shoulders. He could still smell the sweet scent of her hair and taste the sweetness of her lips. Across the dried rice paddy he walked on line with the rest of the platoon. TJ was on his left acting as ammo bearer and assistant gunner for Blanch toting the M-60. Mo was on the far left beyond them, and Rolley was to Buck's right with Crowfoot and Blondie. Lizard was behind Rolley with his M-79.

"Spread out," Dixie shouted. "Squad leaders, dress your ranks."

Mallon followed behind Dixie with his new RTO—a cherry. It was four hundred meters to the tree-line near the village and there was little more than grass and scrub brush for cover.

"Buck!"

He couldn't understand why this beautiful nurse had fallen so totally in love with him. What else had he said to her while he was unconscious? It must have been something that touched her deepest feelings.

"Buck!"

He glanced to his right, and only then did he realize Rolley was shouting at him.

"You okay, dude?" Rolley asked.

They were walking, almost trotting, forward, now less than three hundred meters from the trees. Mortars and artillery were still impacting on the enemy positions behind the village and along the ridge beyond.

"I'm good," Buck said.

A stream of green tracers spewed from the ridge, cracking and zipping past. Buck looked to his right as plumes of dust shot up several meters away. Third Platoon had stopped their advance, and there came shouts for a medic.

"First Platoon, keep moving!" Mallon shouted.

"Run," Rolley said.

Buck looked his way.

"Forward. Run forward. We've got to get clear of this open ground."

Rolley took off at a dead run straight for the trees. Blondie and Crowfoot followed. Buck went after them. More enemy machine gun rounds cracked past, plowing the ground behind them. The air was alive with the zipping and cracking of enemy bullets. Second Squad was ahead of the entire company line, sprinting toward the trees and the enemy trenches. From the rear Mallon shouted at them to slow down, silenced only when the first enemy mortar rounds began exploding around him, shattering the advancing skirmish line.

Second Squad reached the trees and dove into the enemy trenches. They were empty. Rolley signaled for the men to spread out and stay down. Three hundred meters to their rear the rest of the company had stalled and hunkered down in the open. They were getting raked and blasted by machine gun and mortar fire from the ridge beyond the village. After the napalm and artillery strikes, Buck figured the trenches would be full of enemy dead, but they weren't. He glanced over at Rolley. The squad leader pointed into the village. "Get ready."

Through the smoke and dust, Buck spotted villagers, mostly women and children, walking toward the trench. He glanced over his shoulder. The company was falling back toward the highway. He turned back to the village. The villagers were now less than seventy-five meters away, and behind them came a line of men carrying Ak-47s and RPGs. The Viet Cong were using the villagers as a human shield.

"Fix bayonets," Rolley shouted.

Buck snatched his bayonet from the scabbard and pulled it down on the barrel of the M-16. He never thought he would actually use it in combat. It also seemed he was about to break his first and only promise to Janie—to come back alive.

"Come get you some of this, muthafuckas," Mo muttered, caressing the trigger on his M-16. Sweat ran from beneath his steel pot and down his neck.

"Okay," Rolley shouted. "Try not to hit the women and children, but we've got to take some of those bastards out. Pick your shots."

With that he rose up and squeezed off a round. One of the VC dropped in a heap sending up a cloud of dust. The villagers scattered, screaming in panic, and it was on. The VC rushed the trench. Buck shot the first one at point-blank range, but the second enemy soldier dove into the trench on top of him. He caught the soldier on the end of his bayonet. A third and a fourth VC dove into the trench behind the others. Buck wrenched his bayonet free and fired point-blank into the chest of the next attacker. The enemy soldier's blood and bits of his clothing spattered into Buck's face.

The fourth enemy soldier shoved his rifle at Buck. It was a fraction of a second, but time froze to eternity as Buck stared into the bore of the rifle only inches from his nose. It was a mere flash in time, but Buck saw his mother and his father, the Bayou Bois de Arc and home. There came a loud *Whhaap,* as Rolley crushed the enemy soldier's head with his rifle. The guerrilla's weapon either misfired or was still on safe. A moment later Blanch opened up with the sixty. Villagers and Viet Cong alike were low-crawling back into the village.

"Who's hit?" Rolley shouted. "Anybody hit?"

Buck gathered his wits and looked up and down the trench. Seven or eight dead VC lay amongst them. Another half-dozen lay dead a few meters in front of the trenches, along with several of the villagers.

A pop and a thud sounded a few feet away as Mo put another round in a still squirming enemy soldier. Further up the trench to the right, Blondie and Crowfoot were pushing an enemy soldier's body up over the edge.

"Swap magazines and stay down," Rolley said.

The dirt around the trench squirmed and spattered from the impact of bullets. An RPG streaked overhead, exploding in the trees behind them. A second RPG came in and exploded at the edge of the trench. Mo yelped and threw his hand over his jaw. Rolley held his M-16 over his head, above the edge of the trench, firing blindly into the village. Buck crawled past TJ to Mo, who was curled in the bottom of the trench still holding his jaw. Another RPG exploded just outside the trench, raining dirt down inside.

Buck grabbed Mo's hand. "Come on, buddy. Move it. Let me see your jaw." Mo was wild-eyed as blood seeped from between his fingers.

"Iii ma mouuuu," Mo tried to talk.

"Open it," Buck said. "Come on. Open your mouth." The blood was running from a hole in Mo's cheek, but when he opened his mouth, he spit out two bloody teeth, and a chunk of shrapnel. Buck picked up the teeth and the piece of shrapnel and shoved them into Mo's breast pocket.

"There's you some souvenirs, if we make it out of this shit."

Ripping open the first aid packet, he shoved the gauze bandage against Mo's jaw and wrapped the ties around to the other side of his head, tying them tight. He took the bayonet off his rifle, cut the loose end of one of the ties and rolled it into a ball.

"Open your mouth." He shoved the ball of gauze in the gap where the two teeth had been. "Bite down on it, and don't spit it out. It'll stop the bleeding."

Rolley crawled up beside them. "How bad is he hit?"

"It's pretty bad, but I don't think it's life threatening."

"Good job," Rolley said. "Lock your bayonet back on your rifle." He grabbed Mo's M-16, inserted a fresh magazine and handed it to him. "Sorry, buddy, but we're cut off, and there aren't any medics around. You'll have to keep fighting till they send up some relief."

With his eyes crossed and his mouth clenched shut, Mo nodded.

"Why did the rest of the platoon stop?" Buck asked.

"Because the lieutenant ordered them to," Rolley said.

"Where's Lizard?"

"I don't know. He must have fallen back with the rest of the company."

Buck looked back across the dried rice paddy. There were several bodies visible out in the grass. Lizard would never leave the rest of his squad while they were still moving forward.

"Listen up," Rolley said. "I'm not sure why the gooks haven't come at us again, but it can't mean anything good. We need to secure our flanks. Buck, I want you and Mo to go to that bend in the trench on our left. They might rush us by coming down the trench from that direction. I already have Crowfoot and Blondie watching the other end."

There came a sudden lull in the enemy fire. Buck jumped up and peeked over the top of the trench. A half-dozen VC had run out from behind the huts in the village and were flinging grenades toward the trench. He opened fire, spraying them as they ran back to cover. The grenades rained down. *Whap, whap* they struck the tree trunks, ricocheting to the ground, but one didn't.

It landed directly in the trench. Buck grabbed it and tossed it back. The grenades went off in a near simultaneous roar, showering them with debris.

"Get ready," Rolley shouted as he ran back up the trench. "They're coming."

Buck looked to his left—movement. Only the tops of their helmets were visible as a line of NVA regulars came running down the trench seventy-five meters to his left. He grabbed a frag, snatched the pin and threw it their way. Snatching another from his web gear, he threw it as well. He had one grenade left, a white phosphorus. Several of the enemy soldiers crawled from the trench and began running parallel to it, straight at him and Mo.

"Shoot!" he yelled at Mo, but his partner was already in the act, knocking down two of the advancing enemy soldiers. Mo's muzzle was only inches from Buck's ear as he continued laying down suppressing fire. Buck pulled the pin on the willy peter, let the handle fly, and waited a couple seconds before throwing it in a high arc. It worked as the grenade exploded several feet above the ground. More enemy soldiers scrambled from the trench. Some squirmed and rolled in the leaves, while the others ran back the way they had come. Buck began shooting, first at the ones running, then the ones still crawling about and clawing at the phosphorus burning through their clothes.

After emptying his magazine, he squatted and turned to see two VC locked in a hand-to-hand fight with

Mo. They had attacked from the village. With his helmet gone, the Detroit boy looked like a mad Mohawk as he held one VC by the throat and wrenched the other's AK from his hands. Buck lunged, burying his bayonet in the chest of the one Mo held by the throat. Down the trench Blanch had dropped the sixty and pulled his forty-five. He shot the other VC with the pistol. Buck spotted TJ. He was face-down in the trench squirming and holding his chest.

He glanced toward the village. Another line of VC was sprinting toward the trench. Blood, bright crimson, was pooling in the dirt around TJ. Buck had no choice as he turned away. Despite the shower of AK-47 bullets shredding the ground around him, he began picking targets and firing rapidly. He dropped one, then two, but the line of enemy soldiers didn't slow as they ran toward him. It looked hopeless.

The line of Viet Cong attackers was only meters away as Buck slammed another magazine into his M-16 and thumbed the selector to full automatic. Blanch retrieved his M-60 and began firing. The attackers were nearly upon them when an explosion sent them tumbling like puppets. A second explosion ripped the earth apart only meters from the trench. Buck crouched, covering his head. A third and a fourth explosion bracketed the first two with incredible accuracy.

After a moment or two, Buck peeked over the top of the trench. The line of attackers had been totally annihilated. And only then did he realize there was but one weapon that could have delivered such accuracy. He looked back toward the dried rice paddy. Crouching in the grass nearly a hundred meters behind him was a familiar figure. It was Lizard, reloading his M-79. He'd used his grenade launcher like a mortar, dropping the rounds amongst the advancing enemy.

Buck motioned him forward. The little tunnel rat came to his feet, but he was hobbling as he made his way to the trench.

"You hit?" Buck asked.

"Took some shrapnel in my ass from that first mortar barrage."

Lizard's fatigue pants were a muddy, bloody mess.

"Drop your trousers, and let's have a look," Rolley said. He turned to Blanch, who was working on TJ. "How bad is he hit?"

Blanch shook his head. "It's not good. He's lost a lot of blood."

They bandaged Lizard and TJ while Blondie and Crowfoot maintained a lookout. When they were done, Rolley glanced at his watch.

"It's 17:30. We're going to move out as soon as it gets dark. Be ready. I want everyone to leave their steel pots behind. We'll line them along the edge of the trench when we go. It'll give the gooks something to shoot at when they start trying to sneak up on us."

Dusk came and Rolley began planning the with-drawal. "Blanch, you and Crowfoot will cover us from the rear. Blondie, you and I will carry TJ. Buck, you help Lizard. Mo, you take the lead. Can you handle it?"

Mo, still unable to talk, nodded.

"When I give the word we'll move out slow and quiet, until we get out into the rice paddy. When we get close to the other side, we'll stop, and I'll call out. We don't want our own people to shoot us."

Rolley began unscrewing the handle and fuse mechanism from a fragmentation grenade. "Buck, open a C-ration can. You can eat it or dump it out. I don't care, but open the can on both ends."

After shortening the fuse, he screwed it back into the frag and tied the end of a wire to the handle. It was nearly dark when he crawled forward with the frag, C-ration can and wire. Tying off the wire on a small tree, Rolley stretched it across in front of the trench, drew it taut, pulled the pin on the grenade and carefully slid it into the C-ration can. He set the can atop a dead enemy soldier and laid an Ak-47 over it to hold it in place.

Scooting backwards on his belly, he slid feet-first back into the trench. "That should slow them down when they come. Let's move out. Stay low and be quiet."

The men crawled out of the trench, crouching and moving slowly at first. When they had gone nearly a hundred meters, Rolley paused and stood upright. "Okay, let's make some time," he whispered.

The squad had put nearly three hundred meters between themselves and the trench line when there came the cracks of AK-47s behind them. Buck and Lizard looked back. A moment later, the grenade Rolley had left behind flashed in the night as it exploded, silhouetting several attackers.

"Keep moving," Rolley hissed. "They'll start shooting out this way when they realize we're gone."

Up ahead the shadow of the highway berm became visible. They had come to within a hundred meters of it. Rolley signaled for everyone to stop.

"Second Squad, First Platoon, we're coming in," he shouted.

"Council," someone shouted from up near the road. It sounded like Lieutenant Mallon calling the challenge for a password.

"Lieutenant, sir, I don't know the fucking password," Rolley shouted, "but I have wounded and we need help."

"Hold up, Rolley." It was Dixie's voice. "We've got trip flares and Claymores out there. I'm coming your way."

8

PURPLE HEARTS, SILVER STARS, AND R&R

I Corps, 1968

When they finally stumbled up on the road that night, Buck and the rest of the squad were beyond exhaustion, and their only hope was to get help for TJ, Mo, and Lizard, but it was too dangerous to call for a dust-off after dark. Doc Gilbert gave them all morphine and hooked them to plasma bags. After cleaning and re-bandaging all the wounds, Buck and the others helped wrap the three wounded men in poncho liners. Buck sat cradling TJ's head in his lap. The little Cajun had not regained consciousness, and his breathing was low and shallow. He lay deathly still. Buck held him while dozing and jerking awake continually through the night.

Mo began moaning. The forceful extraction of two teeth and the hole in his jaw had to be one of the most painful wounds Buck could imagine. Doc Gilbert talked to him in his soothing Texas drawl. "I'll hit you with another shot of morphine in about an hour, Mo. You just hang in there. We're gonna get you fellas outta here at first light, you hear?"

Thankfully, it remained quiet, and sometime in the night Buck must have dozed, because he could hear choppers coming in his dreams—coming to get TJ, Mo, and Lizard. The steady thumping of their rotors seemed so real that he wanted to jump up and guide them in. Although utterly exhausted, he cracked his eyes open. The eastern sky was glowing orange. It *was* choppers, and they were inbound. He looked down at TJ still resting in his arms. Buck's heart all but stopped.

TJ's face was gray, and he was very still. Buck pressed two fingers against his neck. He breathed a sigh of relief. There remained a weak pulse. Doc Gilbert pulled Lizard upright. Rolley and Blondie helped Mo. Dixie and Crowfoot made a makeshift litter with a poncho, and Buck helped them as they carried TJ and the others up the road to the LZ.

After the choppers departed with the wounded, Dixie told Rolley to get the remainder of his squad squared away, reload magazines, refill canteens, and be ready to move out in thirty minutes. The company was going to make another assault on the village.

"You're fucking kidding, right?" Rolley said.

Buck couldn't believe what he was hearing. He looked over at Rolley, but the squad leader looked away. While Second Squad had fought for their lives in close-quarter combat the entire afternoon before, everyone else in the company had been resting. Buck's body ached, and he could hardly move.

"My men don't have helmets, Sarge, and we're all out of ammo," Rolley said. "We don't have any grenades, either."

"I'll get your boys resupplied," Dixie said. He glanced over his shoulder then turned back to Rolley. "I tried to get you some slack," he said, lowering his voice, "but the lieutenant said he wants every available man on the line."

Rolley stared back at the platoon sergeant.

"So, what the hell happened out there?" Dixie asked. "I thought you were all dead."

"They were all over us," Rolley said. "We were using our bayonets and clubbing them with whatever we had in our hands. There are probably twenty of them dead in front of that trench and a dozen more down inside. I don't know how any of us made it back here."

Dixie's eyes got big as several of the other platoon members stopped and listened.

"You see that dried blood on Marino's face?"

Only then did Buck reach up to feel the crusted layer on his face.

"That's blood from a VC he shot. That's how close they were. You see this?" Rolley held up his M-16. The stock was gone. "I broke it bashing a gook's brains out.

"You want to know what happened over there?" Rolley's voice grew louder. "My men fought like *hell*, and had the rest of the platoon done the same, we might be in that 'ville right now, instead of getting ready to assault it again."

Lieutenant Mallon came strutting up the road. "Is there a problem, Sergeant Greenbaugh?"

Dixie turned to face the lieutenant. "Sir, Sergeant Zwyrkowski and his men are exhausted. We need to—"

"Good! Maybe they'll stay with the rest of the platoon today and stop trying to be a bunch of John Waynes."

Rolley lunged, but Dixie caught him and wrapped him in a bear hug. Buck jumped up and grabbed the squad leader from behind. Rolley started to say something, but Dixie clamped a huge hand across his mouth. Crowfoot, Blondie, and Blanch all stood up and walked up beside Rolley, staring hard at the lieutenant.

Mallon stared, wide-eyed. "What's this man's problem, Sergeant?"

"Let me handle this, sir. Please. He's just upset about his wounded men. Go see if you can gather some ammo and frags for us. I mean, sir, if you don't mind. And get Sergeant Zwyrkowski a weapon. His is busted."

The lieutenant paused, eyeing them.

"Sir," Dixie said, "you need to listen to your NCOs. We know this war. You don't."

The lieutenant's lip curled. "Sergeant Greenbaugh, I know a hell of a lot more than you seem to think I do."

With that he turned and stalked away. Dixie slowly lifted his hand from Rolley's mouth. "I'm not lettin' you go, till you calm down, Rolley. You hear? Relax, now. I mean it."

"If we had stayed out there in the middle of that paddy, we'd have been chopped to pieces. I did the only reasonable thing besides turning tail and running."

"I know," Dixie said. "I tried to get the rest of the platoon to move forward with you, but the lieutenant was yelling for everyone to get down. It was a cluster-fuck, and we still have several men missing somewhere out there because of it."

The company got on line once again, and began the second assault on the village. There was no artillery or air support this time, because a battalion of ARVN Rangers had circled behind the village. They had come over the ridge, and pushed down through the outlying hamlets without resistance. The enemy had retreated during the night, disappearing back into the hills. As the company crossed the dried paddy that morning, they found their missing members. The bodies were still lying in the grass where they had fallen the previous day. The CO radioed for choppers to pick them up, and the company continued moving toward the village.

When they reached the trench line, Buck and the rest of the squad retrieved their helmets, while their fellow platoon members and the rest of Bravo Company stared wide-eyed at the bodies piled around the trench. Captain Crenshaw walked up with his RTO. Dixie began explaining to him what Rolley had told him earlier. Crenshaw looked over at Rolley and motioned for him.

He turned to Mallon. "Lieutenant, while I talk with Sergeant Zwyrkowski, I want you to get me a body count and a weapons tally."

The captain turned back to Rolley. "What the hell happened here, son?"

Rolley gazed across the trench at the piles of bodies, then to the right and left. "The enemy came from the village using the villagers as a human shield. We couldn't use our grenades, and I told the men to pick their shots. Actually, sir, all of the villagers' bodies are gone and some of the enemy bodies are, too." He pointed up the trench to the left. "Specialists Marino and Joyner killed seven or eight NVA regulars right over there. Those bodies are all gone now."

The captain made eye-contact with Buck.

"How many villagers do you think were killed?"

"At least four or five, sir. Maybe more. The VC were shooting them when they turned to run. Like Rolley... ah... Sergeant Zwyrkowski said, he told us to pick our shots, and try not to hit the women and children."

The captain nodded and turned back to Rolley. "Who is Joyner? Is that Mo?"

"Yes, sir."

"Damn," the captain said. "I hadn't made the connection with his real name before now. He was one of the men we medevac'd this morning, wasn't he?"

"That's right, sir. He took a chunk of shrapnel in the jaw from an RPG. It knocked out a couple of his teeth."

The captain grimaced and looked over at Crowfoot and Blondie. He nodded as if to give his approval before turning back to Rolley. "I want a detailed after-action report on this fight, Rolley. I'm going to see that you and your boys get the medals you deserve. And let me know if there is anything else I can do for you."

Lieutenant Mallon returned and stood with a pencil and paper, checking his numbers.

"Sir," Rolley said to the captain. "I need one thing."

"What's that?"

"My guys are hurting pretty bad right now, and we're exhausted. I want to take them back to Phu Bai to check on our wounded, TJ, Lizard, and Mo. Twenty-four hours, that's all I'm asking, sir."

Mallon raised his head. "Uh, sir, with all due respect: I've already addressed that issue with Sergeant Zwyrkowski. I told him we can't spare a single man."

Buck noticed a vein swell on the captain's neck as he turned to the lieutenant.

"With all due respect, Lieutenant, get me my goddamn numbers, and I'll handle this matter myself."

The captain turned to Rolley. "There are some choppers coming in to recover our dead back there. Take your men back to the paddy. Tell the XO I said that you and your men are to ride those choppers back to Phu Bai for a three-day R&R."

Rolley looked drained. "Thank you, sir."

"I'll need you to keep me updated on our wounded, and I want that report when you return. Understood?"

"Yes, sir."

Captain Crenshaw called out to Dixie. "Sergeant Greenbaugh, deploy your men and put out flank security. I'll be back in a few minutes."

The captain turned to Lieutenant Mallon. "Frank, come, let's go for a walk."

As soon as the choppers landed back at Phu Bai Rolley flagged a ride for the squad over to the 22nd Surgical. Still covered with dirt, mud, and blood, and carrying their weapons and rucksacks, the men didn't stop until they found Mo and Lizard in beds adjacent to TJ. They were hooked up to a variety of IVs and monitors. TJ and Mo were in deep drug-induced sleep, but Lizard was awake. He was on his belly with an iodine soaked bandage taped to his butt.

Buck and the other men stacked their weapons and filthy gear on the floor and gathered around. "How about it, dude?" Rolley asked. "Are they going to send you guys home?"

Lizard shook his head slowly side to side. "Hell, no. Leastwise, not me and Mo. They ain't said nothing about TJ, yet, except that he's gonna make it."

Rolley let out a whoop. Buck felt it, too. They thought TJ wouldn't make it more than a few hours when he was first wounded. The elation Buck felt was like nothing he had ever experienced.

"You men quiet down, and get those rucksacks and weapons…"

It was Miriam, and she was struck silent when she saw Buck. He was pretty sure he looked like crap, scratched, bruised, and coated with dried blood and dirt.

"This is Sergeant Anderson," Lizard said. "She and a nurse named Janie have been asking about our boy Buck, here. I think that other nurse has a crush on him."

Rolley extended his hand to Miriam. "Rolley Zwyrkowski," he said. "It's good to meet you."

Miriam shook his hand and glanced at the pile of weapons and muddy rucksacks on the floor.

"My apologies, Sergeant," Rolley said. "We'll get that cleaned up and out of here ASAP."

Miriam took Buck's hand and gazed into his eyes. "You okay?"

Buck nodded.

"You look pretty beat up. You sure?" She gently scratched at something on his cheek. "This is dried blood."

"It's not mine."

"Okay. Why don't you and your buddies go get cleaned up and come back later. You really don't want Janie to see you looking like this. She worries enough as it is."

It was late afternoon when Buck, Rolley, Crowfoot, Blondie, and Blanch returned to the hospital. After hot showers, a clean change of fatigues and more than a few cans of beer, they were still exhausted but in better spirits. Mo was awake when they arrived. Miriam was still there as well.

Mo's face was swollen and his lips didn't move, but his eyes were smiling as the men gathered around his bunk. His Mohawk haircut had been trimmed and shaped.

"Mo, my man," Buck said. He bent over the bed and pressed his head against Mo's chest. Mo patted him on the back. Buck felt self-conscious as he straightened and stepped back.

"He won't be able to talk for a while," Miriam said. "He's got a lot of trauma to his face, and he lost some teeth, but believe it or not, his jaw isn't broken."

"I can't believe they aren't sending him home," Rolley said.

Miriam pursed her lips as if she were fighting the urge to say something she shouldn't. She shrugged instead.

"Well," Blondie said, "At least we finally have him where we want him."

Miriam furrowed her brows.

"His nickname is Mo," Rolley said, "which is short for motor-mouth."

Mo reached toward Miriam and tapped her clipboard. She gave it to him, and he motioned to the pen in her breast pocket. Miriam handed him the pen.

"Wait," she said. "Don't write on my report." She pulled a blank form from the clipboard and flipped it over. "Write on that."

Mo scratched a note on the clipboard and handed it to Rolley. It said, "Fuck You."

Rolley smiled. "You are a poet, Mo, an absolute master."

Mo grabbed the clipboard and began writing again. "I..." He paused a moment then continued writing. "... love you guys."

Crowfoot, who seldom spoke, stepped up and ran his hand over Mo's Mohawk. "Someone has been trimming your hair, my friend."

"I did that," Miriam said, "just a little while ago."

"It *was* getting a little nappy," Rolley said.

"Okay," Crowfoot said, looking down at Mo, "just don't let them take it all. I've been thinking how such a scalp would look so fine hanging from my rucksack."

Everyone broke into laughter. This was the first time Buck had heard Crowfoot say much of anything. Mo began scribbling on the clipboard.

"Indian boy, I make..." He stopped writing and the clipboard fell on his chest. His eyes slowly closed.

"He's falling asleep," Miriam said. "I gave him a pretty good dose of morphine just before you guys got here."

Rolley turned to TJ's bed. "How about this man?"

TJ slept soundly. Miriam paused and looked off to one side, still seeming reluctant to speak. "He's going to recover, but it's up to the doctors to decide if he'll return to duty. I think they'll send him off-shore and eventually back to the States, but there's no guarantee."

"What do you mean?"

"He's young. We've seen men come in here with some pretty serious wounds, and they go back to their units within a couple weeks. His is T&T with no broken bones or organ damage. They'll watch him for a few days, before they decide."

"Don't worry, Sarge," Lizard said, still face-down in the next bed. "They put about a thousand stitches in my ass, and they already told me I'm coming back."

"So," Blondie said, "how do you shit with that bandage on your ass?"

Lizard smiled. "Don't know. Haven't tried yet. You better ask that foxy nurse."

Miriam stepped up to his bed. "Don't worry, soldier. I will personally make sure you get through that chore with no problem."

Buck made eye-contact with Miriam. She may not have been out in the boonies fighting to stay alive, but she was every much as brave as the ones who were.

"Where's Janie?" he asked.

"She's sleeping. She's exhausted from dealing with the incoming wounded we received yesterday and last night. The First Cav has been in a serious fight for two days, and several more arrived this morning. She was up for over twenty-four hours."

"Let her sleep," Buck said. "Tell her I love her."

The entire squad turned at once and stared at him. He looked around and shrugged. Rolley slapped him on the back. "Apparently our boy had the savoir faire to hook this sweet nurse named Janie by the heart."

"He had the what?" Blondie said.

"Savoir faire."

"What the fuck is that?" Lizard asked.

"Means he said all the right things to make her fall in love with him."

Blondie turned to Buck. "Okay, man. You gotta come clean. What did you say to that chick to make her want a country bumpkin like you? I gotta know those magic words."

Buck shrugged. "I don't remember."

"Awww, man, don't give me that—"

"Seriously, I swear. I was out of it. They had me on premium blend, you know? It was straight morphine or something. She called it truth serum, but I don't remember anything I said."

Buck sat with Rolley that night admiring the stars above the South China Sea. He was exhausted and Rolley no doubt was as well. The only thing that kept them awake was knowing their R&R would be gone in a flash. With their feet buried in the sand, they drank cans of beer until the pain receded ever so slightly—enough that they could maintain some modicum of sanity for a while longer.

"So, you're pretty serious about this nurse, huh?" Rolley said.

"Yeah, I reckon so. I've never met a woman with looks like hers who didn't think she was the center of the universe. Janie is different."

"You know most of them hook up with officers?"

"I suppose, why?"

"I just don't want to see you get down if she sends you a Dear John letter someday."

Buck shrugged. Rolley was right. People change, and things happen.

"Do you have a family back in the world?"

"My folks were killed in a car wreck the year before last. I was starting my senior year of high school, and..." Buck paused. "I don't have any brothers or sisters."

Rolley's face flushed such that it was visible even in the night shadows.

"The guys told me about your fiancée," Buck said.

Rolley said nothing as he opened another beer and handed it to him.

"I mean, I said that because I wanted you to know... well..."

"It's okay," Rolley said. "I appreciate it. Right now, we need to focus on what we'll be doing when we head back into the boonies. I think we're going to end up in some more nasty fights."

"Do you think it's worth it?"

"What do you mean?" Rolley asked.

"Every time we go up in the choppers I look out, and there are miles of jungles and mountains as far as I can see. And those LRRPs we talk with say there are thousands of NVA soldiers out there. I just don't see how..." Buck paused.

"...how we can win?" Rolley said.

Buck nodded.

Rolley stared steadily out at the nighttime sky blanketed with a million stars.

"And that wasn't the first time it ever occurred to me that this world ain't run like it ought to be run a heap of more times than what it is."

"Huh?"

"That's a quote from a story written by another man from Mississippi, William Faulkner. Do you know who he was?"

"Give me a break, Rolley. I'm not that damned stupid."

"Sorry."

"So, what are you saying?"

"Look. You aren't the average dumb grunt, Buck, so I don't think this is going to be any great revelation for you, but I don't think we're fighting to win. I don't know who is really calling the shots, but it's not our officers. What the politicians are telling the American public denies the reality of our situation, and we're caught in the middle. The men running this war tell us what to do, and we're like pawns on the chessboard, but they're applying a kind of logic where there is none. We're stuck in this Sisyphean Hell where we go out every week and do the same thing with the same results."

"What's a Sisyphean Hell?"

"Sisyphus was a Greek mythological figure who was doomed to endlessly roll a boulder up a hill in Hades only to have it roll down again. You see, we walk up and down the same godforsaken mountains till the enemy thinks he wants a piece of our ass. He ambushes us, kills two, three, a dozen, hell, sometimes entire platoons. We call in air and artillery and kill a bunch of them. The higher-ups inflate the body count and call it a victory. Then we do the same thing the next day, the next week, again and again. They feed us their specious bullshit about body count, God, and country, and we're supposed to lap it up like Mom's pot-roast gravy."

"What's 'specious' mean?"

Rolley grinned. "Sorry. I was being a little redundant. Think of 'specious' and 'bullshit' as being somewhat the same. It means everything they tell us sounds good and plausible, but it's just bullshit."

Buck turned up his beer, emptied the can and set it aside. "So, what are we fighting for?"

"I think the original intent was to stop the spread of Communism, but that doesn't seem to be working, so I really don't know what the hell they're trying to accomplish."

After a few moments Rolley turned up his beer, finishing it.

"Grab your weapon, and let's head back. These damned mosquitoes are eating me up. Besides, we aren't supposed to be out here after dark."

The next morning Buck awakened from a deep sleep. He glanced at his wrist watch. "Oh, shit!" Throwing back the mosquito netting, he jumped from the cot. The rest of the squad was still sleeping.

Blanch rolled over. "Where the hell are you going in such a big hurry?"

"It's after ten. I'm heading back over to the hospital to see the guys."

"Hold on. I'll go with you."

Buck didn't look up while lacing his boots. "I'm not waiting. You can catch up when you get dressed."

Rolley was lying in his bunk with his back toward them. "He's going to see his girlfriend, the nurse."

"How in the hell did you land a good-looking nurse in Vietnam, anyway?" Blanch asked.

Rolley rolled over and pushed back his mosquito netting. "We're all going to meet after lunch, Buck. I need you to be back here so we can write up that after-action report for the CO."

Buck stopped at the door of the hooch, and his shoulders slumped. "Don't worry," Rolley said. "It shouldn't take more than a couple hours, and you'll have the rest of the day and all day tomorrow to spend with your girl."

Buck realized he must have looked like a love-struck fool as he nodded rapidly, but he didn't care. He took off at a trot down the road. When he arrived at the 22nd Surgical, he went straight to Mo, TJ, and Lizard. TJ was awake and looking around. He spotted Buck.

"Hey Lizard, wake up, mon. It's Buck. Whatchu doing back here, ma friend?"

His voice was soft and labored.

"I came to see you, dumbass. What do you think?"

TJ grinned. "Mon, you lookin' good—real good."

"Well, you look like shit."

"I know, but the doctor, he said I'm a doing real good. T&T—and not much damage."

"Just don't let them send you back out there with us. Go back to the world. Get out of this place. Go home to Louisiana, and have a real life."

"Oh, no, that ain't gonna happen. I already told him I was going back to ma unit to be with you boys."

Buck bent over the bed and looked down at him. "Don't be a dumbass, TJ. Tell the doctor you feel like shit and you can't go back. Tell him anything. Just go home and—"

"Ain't gonna happen, ma friend. I ain't leavin' you and Rolley. We all go home together or we won't, but I ain't leavin'."

Buck sat with TJ, and later Rolley showed up with the rest of the squad. Only then did he leave to find Janie.

A woman came walking up the road nearly a quarter-mile away, but Buck knew it was Janie as soon as he spotted her. He had never felt this way about anyone. Not even his first teenage crushes had left him quite so unable to control his emotions. When she realized it was him approaching, she began running his way. They met as a truck sped past blowing its horn. Oblivious to the world around them, they were enveloped in a cloud of red dust as they embraced. She pushed away too soon and pulled his collar down to examine his neck.

"It's okay," Buck said. "You did a magnificent job."

Tears spilled from her eyes.

"What the hell are you crying for, baby? It's not like we weren't together a week ago, you know?"

She said nothing, and he gazed down into her eyes. She knew about the fight out on Highway 547. It was the only explanation.

"Did those guys feed you a bunch of their bullshit war stories?"

"Your friend, Lizard, told me what happened, and TJ, the little guy from Louisiana, told me more."

"It wasn't that bad."

And he hoped she didn't see the lie in his eyes, because it *was* bad—*real* bad. It was a fight where he had killed men face-to-face with whatever he had in his hands. It was a fight where he truly believed he was about to die at any moment. And it was a fight where he thought at least one of his buddies, TJ, had been killed. It came to him at that moment what he needed to do.

"Look. I need a favor."

"Anything," Janie said. "What is it?"

"Get TJ sent home."

"Oh, Patrick."

She buried her face against his shoulder.

"What?"

She looked up at him with tired eyes. "I can make recommendations, but it's up to the doctors. They make the final determination."

"What do you think they'll do with TJ?"

"They already said last night that he was going to remain in-country on limited duty before being re-evaluated in two weeks."

They walked back up the road to the hospital.

"How long will you be here?" she asked.

"The rest of today and tomorrow. We fly out with the supply choppers the next afternoon."

"The Vietnamese woman who does my laundry has a little room above her shop in Phu Bai. I have to work until noon tomorrow, but I thought maybe, we might…" Janie paused.

"I thought the city has been off-limits since Tet," Buck said.

"It's safe there," Janie said.

"Are you sure—"

"She does my laundry. I go there—"

"No," Buck said. "I mean, are you sure this is what you want to do?"

Janie looked up into his eyes as she spoke. "I've never been so sure about anything in my life."

His high school crushes had always seemed predicated more on curiosity and the potential for sex, but this was different. If it happened, it would validate something already developing much deeper in his heart. Anything sexual between him and Janie would be a commitment.

"How do you know I'm not going along just so I can get into your pants?"

"Patrick Marino, I know you. I bathed you head to toe. I changed your bandages. Heck, I even inserted your catheter. I know your body as well as I know my own, but more importantly, I know your heart and mind. So, don't even try to bullshit me. You said you loved your mom and dad, and you told me how since they died you could no longer focus on life till we met. I'll see you here at the hospital tomorrow afternoon. Bring an overnight bag."

9

A NIGHT AT THE LAUNDRY

Phu Bai, June 1968

Evidence of the Tet offensive was everywhere in Phu Bai: burned-out homes, walls pock-marked with shell holes, and the sad but nervous faces of a people facing an ominous black cloud of uncertainty. Janie's friend, a young male orderly, drove the jeep and delivered them to the laundry shop that day. An aged Vietnamese woman with stained teeth eyed them as they stepped inside. Buck nervously glanced about. The shop smelled of incense, hot steam, and laundry soap. The old woman said nothing as she smiled, nodded, and motioned with her hand toward a small beaded curtain in a doorway.

"Come on," Janie said, taking Buck by the hand.

"You call," the old woman said. "I bring you hot water for tub and fresh tea."

The stairway was little more than shoulder-wide and steep. Buck followed Janie up to the room above the shop. It was relatively spacious with a bed and a black lacquered table with a lamp. On the opposite wall sat a large bathtub with clean towels and a chair. A flowered porcelain tea pot with cups sat on another table near the window.

Buck eyed her every move, the curve of her hip, her soft jutting breasts beneath her fatigue shirt. This woman was about to be his, but he suddenly felt clumsy as he looked into Janie's eyes—honest eyes that left him feeling like a thief. This wasn't a simple romantic affair—not for her and not for him. For whatever reason, this girl had chosen him, and he wondered if he could provide what it was she wanted beyond this room and today.

She smiled up at him—her eyes and lips glistening with moisture. His boiling passions were already out of control, but he faced another sudden realization—romantic encounters weren't exactly his forte. Lightheaded, he walked to a ladder-back chair, where he sat and began unlacing his jungle boots. Janie fell across the bed and stared up at an ancient ceiling fan turning slowly above.

"It feels so good, just knowing I don't have to be anywhere for the next twenty-four hours," she said.

After removing his boots, Buck moved the chair over beside the bed and began unlacing Janie's.

"I don't reckon I've ever taken boots off a woman before," he said.

She laughed. "And I didn't think the first time a man undressed me I'd be wearing boots."

"The first time?"

"Yup. I grew up in Montana. My mother passed away when I was a baby, and I'm a daddy's girl. I've busted the chops of more than one over-aggressive cowboy."

Buck felt a weight on his conscience like he'd never felt before as he held up Janie's boot and gazed at it in a beam of sunlight coming through the window. It was small. And for whatever reason, her petite boot made him all the more aware that this was so much more than a sexual encounter. In a way it was almost frightening.

"Janie dear, the way I feel right now, I don't think I would even notice, unless you had spurs on these boots."

She laughed.

It was true. He couldn't have been more aroused than he was at that moment. There was no turning back. She began unbuttoning her fatigue shirt exposing a lacy white bra. Buck gently pulled her upright and pushed the fatigue shirt from her shoulders as their lips met and he pushed his tongue deep into her mouth. She worked desperately with the buttons on his shirt, making her way down to his trousers. She didn't stop, and within a few moments they were both naked, and staring at one another as if each wanted the other to make the next move.

Buck brushed the back of his hand gently over her erect nipple, and carefully bent over to kiss her breasts. Janie clutched the back of his head and pulled him close. Working his way up the side of her neck he kissed her behind the ear and once again found himself gazing into her wet brown eyes. He gently brought the palm of his hand up flat against her. She was soft and warm between her legs. He massaged her gently before softly probing with his fingers. Janie groaned with passion. Buck pushed her legs apart, rolled over and slowly sank inside her. The silky warmth inside her body enveloped him, and he drew back slowly and pushed again gently, this time deeper. Her body came up to meet him, and they began sharing a slow and gentle rhythm, pausing each time to savor the mutual pressure of their joined bodies.

And when Buck thought he could no longer restrain himself, Janie suddenly bit down on his shoulder, not so hard that it was painful, but just on the verge. Grasping his buttocks, she arched her back and let out a sudden gasp as she stifled a near scream. With her legs wrapped around him, she shuddered uncontrollably and Buck burst inside her.

Two more times that afternoon before it grew dark outside they made love, and Janie was sleeping, clutched in his arms, when Buck heard someone coming up the stairs. He pulled the sheet to cover their naked bodies, and the Vietnamese woman came in followed by two younger women carrying large pails of steaming water. They made two more trips until the tub was sufficiently filled. Janie still slept soundly, as the old woman stopped in the doorway.

"I bring you tea," she whispered. "Then you take bath. I bring you food later."

A few minutes later the old woman returned, filled the teapot on the table and left again. Janie was still sleeping. Buck blew softly into her ear, and she stopped breathing so heavily. He blew again. Her eyes remained closed, but she smiled.

"Again?"

"No, not now. Our bath water is ready."

Her eyes opened and she grasped the sheet, pulling it under her chin as she looked around the room.

"Oh, my. I don't think I've slept that soundly since I left home."

Later, after a meal of rice, shrimp, and sweet peppers, they slept again, waking one more time after midnight. This time they made love for nearly an hour until again drifting off to sleep.

When the morning light crept through the window, Buck lay on the bed while Janie cleaned herself and dressed. He watched her every move with a fascination bred not by curiosity alone, but by a growing love the likes of which he had never before felt. She buttoned her shirt, then brushed her blond hair and pushed it beneath her cap.

"Well," he said. "I suppose it's time to go back to the OD Green world."

She turned and smiled. "It may take me a week to recover from this little R&R."

"At least I can now die a happy man."

Janie's smile disappeared and she paled. "Don't ever say that. You are *not* going to die."

Buck sat up and took her hand. "It's okay. It's okay. It was just a lame joke."

Janie lay on the bed beside him, and wrapped her arms around his neck.

"I just want to go home with you when this war is over."

"I'm not sure you will like it where I'm from," Buck said.

"I've never been to Mississippi," she said.

"And I've never been to Montana."

Their lips met softly. Buck was still amazed at the uncontrollable desire he had to be with this girl, to hold her, to love her and now, to spend his life with her.

"Montana winters can be pretty rough," Janie said.

Buck grinned and pulled her closer. "Summers in Mississippi can be hotter than a bitch." They kissed again, passionately this time.

After a moment she pushed away. "Boy, we've got to save some for our R&R in August. Get up. Get cleaned up and let's go out and look around town."

"I can't. I have to get back to the unit."

"Why?" Janie asked.

"We're supposed to catch a resupply chopper out to the field today. Rolley told me to be back by oh-nine-hundred this morning."

Janie pulled her watch from her pocket and glanced at it. Her shoulders slumped and she looked up at Buck with a flat smile. "Next time, call me sooner."

10

A ROUTINE PATROL

Fire Support Base Vehgel

Clean dry socks and new fatigues did wonders for a man's spirits, and despite being on board a Huey heading west into the mountains, Buck felt pretty good that day. Word was the battalion had worked its way further west and was now on a two-day stand down at FSB Vehgel. Buck and Second Squad found the company area that afternoon and joined the rest of the platoon. As usual the last to arrive got the leftovers, and the squad was assigned the only remaining empty bunker, one just below the artillery battalion.

Rolley met with Dixie, and moved away from the men to talk in private. Because both NCOs were shaking their heads in resignation, Buck was pretty sure Lieutenant Mallon was the subject of their conversation. After a while, Rolley returned, and the squad sat around outside the bunker smoking cigarettes and talking. He explained that the company was going to deploy the next morning in platoon-size units and run a series of cloverleaf patrols at the base of the mountain below the firebase.

"It shouldn't be a big deal," Rolley said. "We'll just work our way to the bottom of the mountain, circle part way around and hopefully be back here by dark."

"Yeah, *right*," Buck said.

"Perimeter patrols are usually pretty routine," Blondie said. "We don't go that far out, and the other two platoons will be doing the same thing on the other sides of the firebase."

"Sorry, but the only *routine* I've seen the last five months has been us getting our asses kicked—"

"Lighten up," Rolley said. "The terrain is going to be rough, and the climb back up here will be a killer, but the dinks usually don't mess with us close to a firebase. Get some rest. We're moving out at first light."

The first barrage from the outgoing 105s erupted just after dark. Jolted awake, Buck sat upright. He felt for his flashlight and switched it on. Sand was trickling down from the roof of the bunker. Again and again the howitzers thundered and shook the bunker. The guns were so close he could hear the conversations of the artillerymen and the metallic clank of the breech closing. And when it grew quiet for a few minutes, sleep began soothing his frazzled nerves, only to be jarred awake again by another outgoing barrage.

By dawn Buck and the rest of the squad were bleary-eyed and exhausted as they stumbled about, preparing for the patrol down the mountain. Mallon said that since Second Squad had just finished a three-day R&R, they would walk point for the platoon. Buck stared at the young lieutenant who refused to meet his gaze and for a moment, from the exhaustion of a sleepless night, he saw how some soldiers justified fragging idiots like Mallon.

Fragmentation and smoke grenades were distributed while they heated C-rations for breakfast. Two belts of ammo for the M-60 were issued for each man to carry, and everyone grabbed an extra box of C-rations for later. Afterward they topped off their canteens with fresh water and iodine tablets. PJ Goodson, Mallon's new RTO, was busy copying the list of radio frequencies on his note pad, while Dixie and the lieutenant marked their maps with points of origin and issued last-minute instructions. As the first rays of the morning sun lit the sky, the men locked and loaded, then eased out through the wire. Buck was walking point. Crowfoot walked slack behind him. The morning sun had crept higher above the hills back to the east. It seemed quiet for now.

From his vantage point atop the mountain, Buck gazed out at the sweeping landscape of hills and valleys stretching away to the horizon. The treetops below shimmered and sparkled in the morning sunlight. It was a stunning view, but it was a magnificent deception—something he had learned after only a week or two in-country. The terrain beneath the trees was rugged and dark—a reality-check for any would-be admirer. The jungle with its insects, vines, snakes, hills, ravines and streams, was merely a prerequisite that qualified a grunt for the privilege of searching for an enemy that always seemed ready and waiting.

The dry season held, and the temperatures climbed rapidly as the platoon zigzagged across the face of the mountain. They worked their way down the steep slope bathed in a shadowy steam-bath of itchy sweat, flies and mosquitoes. The thick jungle prevented even the hint of a breeze as Buck and Crowfoot silently led the platoon down the mountain from the firebase. Buck refused to relax or to let down his guard. There were enough opportunities to get killed without creating more. He remained alert and moved with deliberation.

After a couple hours, Rolley passed word for them to come to a halt. It had been an uneventful descent, but the platoon was now strung out in an area of steep ravines, covered with vines and thick vegetation. With their field of view limited to only a few feet in any direction, Dixie conferred with Lieutenant Mallon. Buck shoved a cigarette between his lips and shook one out for Crowfoot. Striking a flame with his Zippo, he lit both cigarettes.

Crowfoot inhaled deeply. "Good cigarette," he said.

Buck nodded. It was true. Even something as simple as a cigarette was a unique pleasure when you realized your next step might be your last. Rolley and Dixie quietly eased up to the front of the column and gave them a new azimuth. It would take the platoon across the base of the mountain before they turned back uphill to the firebase. Buck led off carefully, pushing his way through the undergrowth. He had gone less than a hundred meters when he came to a gorge. Its steep walls, overgrown with trees and vines, made it a formidable obstacle.

He signaled for Rolley to come up and take a look. The walls of the gorge were nearly vertical, and it was several hundred feet to the bottom. After looking things over, Rolley went back to discuss the situation with Dixie and Lieutenant Mallon. He returned a few minutes later.

"We need to go ahead and cross here," Rolley said.

"Huh?"

Buck couldn't believe what he was hearing.

"Right here?"

"Yeah," Rolley said. "The lieutenant thinks it will take less time than going further down the mountain."

Buck gazed down at the treetops rising nearly to the top of the rim. A fall, if not fatal, certainly had the potential for severe injury and a lot of pain. Carefully, he began making his way down, grasping trees and vines, sometimes sliding on his backside, but never letting go of one hand-hold till he had another. After reaching the bottom, he paused and looked back up the wall of the ravine. Dirt and loose rock tumbled down from above. Crowfoot was only halfway down.

Buck turned and started across the ravine. It was only a couple of hundred feet across, but the lieutenant had put them in a bad position. Split up in rough terrain, there was no way they could cover one another. After only a few steps, Buck froze in his tracks. There was something odd—bare dirt shining beneath the undergrowth. Something or someone had been digging.

A jolt of adrenaline sent him into hyper-awareness as he discovered a well-worn trail coming up the center of the ravine. The path disappeared into an opening on the opposite wall. Almost clumsily, Buck fell to the ground and looked back at Crowfoot who by now was squatted several meters behind him. Above, Rolley and Blanch were halfway down the wall of the ravine, still clinging to saplings.

Buck signaled to Crowfoot, pointing toward the trail, but the more experienced point man had already spotted it. Pointing two fingers toward his eyes, he gave Buck the fingers down signal for booby-trap. Buck nodded while Crowfoot signaled for Rolley and Blanch to wait. They clung to trees and stopped their descent into the gorge.

Buck pushed through the undergrowth. Carefully, he crept the last few feet, reaching the wall of the ravine where he found the trail disappeared into a tunnel. His fatigues were soaked with sweat, but his mouth was dry. *Breathe,* he told himself. Dropping to his knees, he crawled ahead, searching every leaf, every blade of grass, and every clump of dirt for trip wires or signs of a booby-trap. He reached the tunnel entrance. The fresh tracks of those using the tunnel were everywhere.

The entrance was large enough for a man to stoop down and walk through, but he dare not expose his head to the darkened abyss. Instead, he switched on his flashlight and held it above his head. He waited, half expecting a burst of automatic weapons fire from inside. Nothing happened. Buck raised his head and looked into the opening. The beam of the flashlight faded into the depths of the tunnel. It was quiet—deathly quiet. He moved the light around, searching the entrance. He froze. The flashlight's beam had found a shiny black wire.

Tracing the path of the wire with the light, Buck's eyes fell on a two-hundred-pound bomb, less than ten feet away. A jolt of adrenaline made him lightheaded. The bomb was an apparent dud, one of the thousands dropped on the enemy. It was now rewired and ready to explode with a command detonator. Large enough to vaporize anyone in the ravine, the bomb wouldn't leave enough of him to scrape up and put in a body bag. Buck gave Crowfoot the booby-trap sign, and backed away from the tunnel entrance.

"What is it?" Crowfoot asked.

"Two-hundred-pounder on a wire. It's huge."

The usually emotionless Crowfoot raised his brows slightly.

"You sure? That's a hell of a big booby-trap."

Buck nodded rapidly, "I know."

"Let's go back and see what the LT wants to do," Crowfoot said.

They began scaling the wall, as the others retreated ahead of them. When they reached the top, a red-faced Lieutenant Mallon was waiting for them. "What the fuck is the problem?" he asked.

"I would move the men back away from this ravine, sir," Crowfoot said. "There's a pretty big booby-trap down there."

"Why didn't you blow it in place?"

"Because, sir, it's a two-hundred-pound bomb."

The lieutenant's eyes grew big, and he turned to Dixie. "Okay, let's move the men back. I'll get on the horn with the CO and see what he wants us to do."

A few minutes later, Rolley came over to where Crowfoot and Buck were lying. "Lieutenant wants a volunteer to go back down and set a charge on that bomb," he said.

Crowfoot nodded. "I'll do it."

"No," Buck said. "You didn't see exactly where it is. It'll be better if I do it."

He could hear his voice, as if someone else were talking. It was a violation of the enlisted man's cardinal rule, "Never volunteer for anything."

"He's right," Rolley said. He turned to Buck. "Reckon you can handle it?"

"No problem."

Someone had taken control of his voice. It certainly wasn't him. *I'm a fool,* he thought. Rolley dug in his rucksack and tossed Buck a block of C-4 explosive along with a time delayed detonator.

"All you do is set this beside the bomb. You don't have to touch it. Remove the cap, and push the detonator into the C-4. Pull out this cotter pin and pull the detonator ring. You'll have plenty of time, ten minutes or more. You got it?"

"Yeah," Buck answered.

He pushed the packet of plastic explosive into one pocket and the detonator into another. Leaving everything behind except his sixteen, ammo pouches, and hand grenades, Buck eased back down the wall of the ravine. When he reached the bottom, he paused to listen. It was quiet, but it seemed even darker than before, and he suddenly felt terribly alone. Taking a deep breath, he started forward.

Easing back to the mouth of the tunnel, he paused and toweled the sweat from his face. Less than a foot away was enough explosive to send him into eternity as a fine mist. Removing his helmet, he set his sixteen aside and pulled the C-4 from his pocket, but the craziest thing kept running through his mind—a memory from high school.

It was the fall day in October when they came and got him out of class. He asked what was happening, but no one said anything. "Where are we going?" he asked. Again, he was met with silence as a school secretary and the principal walked him to a waiting sheriff deputy's cruiser. "Am I in trouble for something?" he asked.

"No, Patrick," the secretary said. "It's your parents. They've been in a car wreck."

He remembered the principal eyeing the secretary with a hard stare.

"Everything will be okay," the secretary added.

But it wasn't. His parents were both dead. An eighteen-wheeler had run over them from behind when they stopped at a traffic light on Highway 61. The county coroner gave him their wedding rings.

After his parents were killed, Buck lost focus and his grades went south. He wasn't even sure he would graduate, but he no longer cared. His English teacher, Ms. Jackson, a thirty-six-year-old spinster who always wore a string of pearls, said to him, "Patrick, I know of no good purpose which can be achieved by failing you in your senior year. It would be a waste of everyone's time to hold you back. Therefore, I am granting you a grade of 'D' in English, and sending you on your way. I doubt seriously you will ever make much of yourself, therefore I strongly suggest that you find some type of manual work with your hands."

Bitch was right, and she would certainly be proud of him now. Holding his breath, he carefully removed the cap and pushed the detonator into the soft cottony-white explosive. Tucking it at the base of the bomb, he removed the cotter pin and pulled the ring on the detonator. If everything went according to plan, he had enough time to climb out of the gorge and run like hell. Backing away, he grabbed his helmet and M-16, and started back toward the opposite wall of the gorge.

He froze. There were voices, cracking, nasal voices, coming from further down the ravine. An NVA soldier walked around the bend in the trail stopping less than five meters away. His AK-47 was slung over his shoulder. Like Buck, he was young, very young. Buck could smell the odor of smoke and fish on his uniform. The men stood staring at one another in a moment of mutual stunned paralysis. A fine sheen of sweat coated the man's face, and his dark brown eyes widened as he stared back at Buck.

Both went for their weapons, except Buck's M-16 was already in his hands. Their eyes never parted, and Buck knew he had him as he flicked the selector switch and mashed the trigger. The enemy soldier's body shook from the impacts of the bullets, and his eyes lost focus as he stumbled backward into the brush. Buck continued spraying the trail behind him as more shadowy figures scattered into the underbrush. With his first magazine emptied, he sprinted toward the wall of the gorge, less than a hundred feet away.

An explosion ripped the undergrowth behind him, probably a grenade. From the rim above, the rest of the platoon opened fire, quickly suppressing the enemy attack as sounds of breaking brush indicated their panicked retreat. Buck began scrambling up the wall of the ravine. From further down the gorge the enemy opened fire. Several rounds thudded into the ground beside him, spraying his face with dirt and sand. He stopped and slid back down into the shelter of the brush below.

With less than nine minutes remaining before the bomb detonated, he had a decision to make. An overdose of adrenaline pumped through his body as more enemy soldiers appeared. They were little more than a hundred meters away. His only hope was that the men above would provide cover while he began crawling up the ravine wall. He lunged upward, clawing at the dirt. More bullets cracked near his head.

There came a commotion from above, and Crowfoot came tumbling wildly down the steep incline. The enemy fire became more intense, and Buck turned, cutting loose on full automatic. Rolley and several others had crawled to the edge of the ravine and were firing from above.

"Did you already set the charge?" Crowfoot asked.

Buck nodded. Crowfoot's face was contorted with pain.

"What happened?"

"I thought you were hit, and my ankle gave way coming down," Crowfoot said. "I think it's only twisted, but—"

A sharp metallic sound sent Crowfoot's helmet spinning crazily into the air. A hole was clearly visible as it spun past. His body jerked spasmodically and his eyes rolled back in his head. Buck grabbed for him but missed. Crowfoot's body tumbled into the ravine below.

An RPG streaked in and exploded. When the smoke and debris cleared Buck heard only the ringing in his ears. His helmet was gone, and he clung desperately to a sapling.

Looking up, he saw Rolley on the rim above as he raised a LAWS rocket to his shoulder. The rocket whooshed down the gorge, and the enemy attack abruptly ceased. A moment later Dixie appeared, sliding down the wall of the ravine. He grabbed Buck by the collar of his flak jacket.

"No," Buck shouted.

"Get Crowfoot, first."

He lay in a crumpled heap below, unmoving.

"I think he's gone," Dixie said. "Come on."

"Not without Crowfoot."

A moment later Rolley appeared. "Is the charge set?"

Buck nodded, and Rolley made eye contact with Dixie. "I'll go down after him."

"No," Dixie shouted. "You take Buck. Get back to the top and give me some cover fire. I'll get Crowfoot."

Rolley began climbing with Buck in tow. When they reached the top, they looked down. Dixie had Crowfoot's limp body on his shoulder, carrying him up the side of the ravine. He was sweating, red-faced and gasping for air. Buck and Rolley reached down and pulled Crowfoot's body over the edge while Dixie crawled the last few feet up the slope. They all scrambled for cover away from the ravine.

Buck was beginning to think the detonator was a dud when the ground shook violently, erupting as if the earth itself were coming apart. An incredible shock wave sent debris skyward, and moments later trees, dirt, and shrapnel rained down everywhere around. Several secondary explosions followed as the entire side of the gorge collapsed in an avalanche of trees, rocks, and dirt. Smoke and flames shot from out of the ground from several tunnels. A nightmarish pall of smoke and dust hung in the air.

After a moment or two, Buck realized it had grown ghostly quiet. With his head beginning to clear, he glanced around. The ravine below was denuded of vegetation. Crowfoot's body was still lying beside him, brown eyes glazed and staring straight up. He had fought his last battle. His hair was matted with blood and his mouth gaped open. Buck's mind raced, and he wanted to scream. Crowfoot's eyelids quivered, no doubt a reflex signal from his dying brain.

"Crowfoot?" he shouted. "Crowfoot! Dammit! Crowfoot! He's alive."

He knew it wasn't true, but he couldn't help himself. He was losing it.

Rolley grasped his shoulder. "No, Buck."

"No. I swear. His eyelids, they—"

"Buck—no," Rolley said. "It was just nerves."

Buck knelt over the body.

"Let him go, Buck," Dixie whispered, putting his hand on Buck's shoulder.

Then, slowly, Crowfoot's hand elevated as if it were defying gravity. It moved toward his head. Dixie scrambled over and looked down at him. Crowfoot's eyes were now shut tight, but he spoke.

"Where am I hit?"

Buck ran his hand around behind his head. Warm blood dripped between his fingers as he parted Crowfoot's matted hair.

"All I can see back here is a big knot and a cut," Buck said.

"Chief, I think you just spent another one of your nine lives," Dixie whispered.

Crowfoot opened his eyes, but they were crossed.

"My uugghhead," he groaned.

A round had apparently struck his helmet a glancing blow putting a hole in it and knocking him unconscious, but it left only a cut and a knot in his scalp. Doc Gilbert bandaged Crowfoot's head, while Dixie radioed for a dust-off.

11

WHAT HAPPENED TO ALICE?

August 1968

The company was still on stand-down at FSB Vehgel when Buck first heard the news. The 101st was changing from Airborne to Airmobile, which meant replacements no longer had to be paratroopers. As always, things were changing, and he wasn't quite sure what to think. He had good friends who weren't Airborne—legs they called them, and most were damned good soldiers, but someone returning from Camp Eagle had already warned Rolley he was getting three troublemakers.

Albert Gruenstein, Doyle Henderson, and Maurice Boggs had all been in-country for several months and blown rear echelon jobs at a motor pool near Bien Hoa. They had been reassigned to a line-company after getting busted for dropping acid, going AWOL in Saigon, and fighting with the MPs. Lieutenant Mallon had apparently also heard, and informed Rolley that they would be assigned to Second Squad. Buck figured it was Mallon's way of screwing with them. It was pretty much a consensus amongst the men—Mallon wanted Rolley and Second Squad taken down a notch, because they had inadvertently exposed him for the hapless idiot that he was.

Mo and TJ had been reassigned to Camp Eagle where they were put on indefinite light duty, while Crowfoot and Lizard returned on a chopper with the three new replacements. Walking back toward their hooch, the squad gathered around their returning members, slapping backs and trading news. The last six months had been the longest of Buck's life, but this was one of the brighter moments. His fire team leader, Crowfoot, was standing upright and looking healthy again, and in some way this validated Buck's hope that he too could make it through this war.

"So, all you motherfuckers is gung-ho paratrooper types, right?"

Everyone went silent and turned toward the replacements. Gruenstein, Henderson, and Boggs all stood staring at the rest of the squad who were gathered around Crowfoot and Lizard. Boggs's upper lip was curled in a surly smile, belied only by his hate-filled eyes. Rolley stepped forward facing the much taller Boggs who had just spoken.

"Why don't you men follow us inside. We'll get out of the sun, and get to know one another."

"Why don't you just get outta my muthafuckin' face, whitey." The soldier shoved him. Caught off-guard, Rolley stumbled backward, landing on his butt in the dust.

Buck didn't think. He reacted. Lunging, he plowed into Boggs, knocking him to the ground. And with his shoulders behind every punch, Buck pounded him with his fists. Only when Rolley and Blondie pulled him away did he realize what he had done. Boggs lay addled, groping his bloodied face. Blanch, Crowfoot, and Lizard had backed the other two replacements against the wall of a bunker. Both held their hands high in surrender.

"Okay," Rolley said. He pointed at the two replacements. "You two help your buddy up and follow me into the hooch."

He glanced around the compound then turned to the other squad members. "Don't any of you talk about this with anyone, and Buck, you hang around. We need to talk."

The sun shone bright above the firebase, and a light breeze filtered up the hillside from the jungle below. Buck rubbed his bruised knuckles. In a way it had felt good, pounding the loud-mouthed asshole, but it also frightened him. He had again lost control, and had the others not pulled him away, there was no telling what he might have done. His emotions owned him.

"Holy crap!" Lizard said. "You waylaid that big fucker."

"Good job," Blanch said.

"Yeah, he deserved it," Blondie added.

Buck glanced at Crowfoot. Crowfoot nodded and said, "Wicasa Igmuwatogla."

Buck raised his chin and maintained eye-lock with Crowfoot.

"Actually my native language is more secondary to me than English. I did not live on reservation land and went to a Catholic school in Montana. I don't know it as well as I should, but it is your new name. You are Wicasa Igmuwatogla, the man cougar."

Buck pulled a cigarette from his pocket, fired it with his Zippo, inhaled deeply, then gave it to Crowfoot. Crowfoot took it and also drew deeply on the cigarette. As he exhaled, the breeze carried the smoke away, and he smiled. "Good cigarette."

A while later Rolley came up out of the hooch. He motioned for Buck to follow and walked across the side of the hill to another bunker where he leaned his M-16 against the sandbags and sat in a sliver of shade.

"What did you tell them?" Buck asked.

"I told them their life expectancy in the boonies would be about a day or two if they alienated you guys."

"Reckon they listened?"

"I don't know. Boggs, the one you jumped, seems dumb as a brick, but he's been hanging out with a bunch of Black Panther wannabes and thinks he wants to start a revolution. They all have lousy attitudes. Al Gruenstein, the guy with the big nose, said he was going to the CO. I think he's their ringleader."

"What'd you tell him?"

"I told him to go ahead, and the next time we went on patrol, he was going to be on point, and I was going to have Boggs walking slack for him."

"He doesn't sound too bright, either."

"Yeah, they screwed up some pretty good jobs by going AWOL. The Judge Advocate gave them the option of either going to the Long Binh Stockade or coming up here to join us."

"No shit? And they chose us over the LBJ?"

Rolley grinned. "No. They all chose Long Binh, but the Judge Advocate sent them up here, anyway."

"Karma can be a real bitch."

Rolley laughed.

"Speaking of karma, Captain Crenshaw is putting you, me, and Crowfoot in for Silver Stars, and he's putting Dixie up for the Congressional Medal of Honor."

"No shit?"

"Yes, you and Crowfoot are good men. You deserve it. And old Dixie does too. By the way, I noticed you and Crowfoot have this thing."

Buck knew what he meant, but he wasn't sure how to respond.

"Yeah. I like him. He's a no-bullshit kind of guy."

"You know his people went through this same kind of thing?" Rolley said.

"I know. He gave me a book, *Disinherited*. I read it, too."

Rolley smiled. "You're going to be a scholar by the time this war is over."

"The Indians got fucked by our ancestors."

Rolley nodded. "I know. All we can do now, though, is look ahead. I think that's what Crowfoot is trying to do."

"So, me and him and Dixie and you, too—we're getting these medals for trying save each other's asses?"

"All of you guys showed unselfish bravery, and I told Captain Crenshaw as much. He's the one that threw my name in the pot as well, but don't get too excited just yet. Politics come into play when they start talking about Silver Stars and Medals of Honor. And frankly speaking, for all I care, they can keep their damned medals."

Buck glanced over at him. Rolley was changing, or maybe it was he who had changed, and only now was he becoming aware.

"What happened to Alice in Wonderland?" Buck asked.

Rolley grinned—something he hadn't been doing much, lately.

"Did you read both stories in the book I gave you?"

"Yeah. It took me a while, but I understand now what you were talking about. Lewis Carroll had to be writing a parody of Nam, and I'm pretty sure he was smoking pot, too."

Rolley gave a half-assed grin. "Damned, Buck! You impress me. Yeah, a parody that was a hundred years before the fact."

"So, the question still stands."

"What question?"

"What happened to Alice?"

Rolley furrowed his brows, and his grin shriveled. "What do you mean?"

"I mean you don't joke much anymore. I kind of liked your corny jokes."

Rolley looked down at his dust-covered jungle boots and slowly shook his head.

"I made fun of this mess to keep my sanity, but the jokes got old. This war is exactly like the two Alice stories, chaotic and strange, a surreal world of absurd logic, but the more I see men like Romeo getting killed, and guys like Mo and TJ getting fucked-up, the less I can hide it. I'm tired."

Buck didn't like what he was hearing. Rolley was his only lifeline to sanity, and now *he* was slipping.

"We're wasting our time over here, aren't we?"

"I think so. It is a kind of alternate reality, and this body count thing is pretty much the pinnacle of stupidity."

"What do you mean?"

"You know, Mark Twain said there are three kinds of lies: lies, damn lies, and statistics. Statistics—they're what this whole damned war is based on. The higher-ups give everyone these numbers of enemy killed to prove we're winning, but if you statistically analyzed buffalo dung, you'd come closer to the truth. It's called bullshit, and it's now the strategy for this entire war."

Buck nodded. "Yeah, it's like we're killing fire ants one or two at a time."

"Have you heard about the US Public Affairs Office in Saigon?"

Buck shrugged. "Don't reckon."

"They hold a press conference every day at oh-five-hundred. It's where they paint the roses for Mr. McNamara and the President, who by the way I think are the real provocateurs behind this war."

"The Queen's croquet ground," Buck said.

Rolley looked around and smiled. "Dammit, boy! You *have* been reading. There's hope for you yet."

Buck simply smiled.

"The press calls it The Five O'clock Follies. It's all a bullshit charade where the spokesmen for the military use body count as proof we're winning. And I suppose if you're the lucky bastard who isn't part of the body count, you might call it a victory, but they aren't fooling anyone. We're in a mess over here, and there's no easy way out."

"At least you're getting short," Buck said. "When's your DEROS?"

"Doesn't matter. I already extended. I'm not leaving you guys."

"We can take care of ourselves," Buck said. "I can't believe you signed up for more of this shit."

"That's a discussion for another day. Right now, I want you to keep your head in the game. You can't let those new guys cause you to do something stupid. I appreciate what you did back there, but we need to function as a unit."

"No problem, but I'm dreading going back out in the bush with those idiots."

"Me too," Rolley said, "but I think if we work on Recalcitrant Al, the others will fall in line behind him."

"What's that mean?"

"It's my new name for Gruenstein—Recalcitrant Al. It means someone who refuses to obey authority."

Buck laughed, and Rolley stood up.

"I'm going to help Recalcitrant Al and his buddies get their rucksacks squared away. Pass the word to the men. We'll be moving back into the field in the next day or two, so the 508th can come in for some rest."

"Back to the A Shau?"

"Not sure yet. By the way, TJ is coming back."

Buck nodded. He didn't know if he should be happy the little Cajun had recovered or angered that they were sending him back into combat.

Late that afternoon a hell of a thunderstorm blew up and turned the red dust back to mud. The black clouds drifted away across the mountains, and Buck spread his poncho on top of the bunker. He began reading a letter from Janie for the tenth time. When he looked up, the evening sun had appeared in the clouds on the horizon. The sky and mountains were aflame with another spectacular Vietnam sunset. Foggy mists were rising from the surrounding valleys, and almost as if on cue, a radio somewhere back in the compound began playing an old Platters song.

...Deepening shadows gather splendor as day is done
Fingers of night will soon surrender the setting sun
I count the moments darling till you're here with me
Together at last at twilight time....

Buck sucked down a breath, exhaled, and folded Janie's letter. She had stolen his heart, and moments like this one left him an emotional wreck. Rolley was right. He had to get his head back in the game.

12

VALLEY OF THE PURPLE HEARTS

The A Shau Valley, August 1968

Choppers, choppers, choppers. Buck gazed skyward. They were everywhere in Nam, and the rhythmic thump of their rotors was the cadence of life. Kneeling at the edge of the LZ with the rest of the platoon, he was listening to someone's radio playing Steppenwolf's "Born to be Wild," but it was quickly drowned out by the incoming Hueys. Swarming onto the LZ, they touched down as Buck and the others ran forward ducking beneath the churning main rotors. They were headed back to the A Shau Valley for another date with the beast.

Gruenstein was doing a pretty bad imitation of a limp, claiming he had twisted his ankle in a volleyball game. Since no one had seen him playing volleyball and Rolley found no swelling after a forced personal inspection of

Gruenstein's foot, he denied him sick-call and told him to saddle up. Henderson, too, had tried by puking up his C-rations in front of Rolley and the squad. Claiming a bellyache, he asked to go on sick-call. Rolley laughed and told him to load up. Boggs simply gave everyone the evil eye and swore he and Stokely Carmichael were gonna kill them all when the great revolution began.

Gruenstein and Henderson both climbed onboard the first chopper with Rolley, while Buck, Boggs and Crowfoot jumped in on the opposite side. As was becoming the norm, Lieutenant Mallon, had put Rolley and most of First Squad in the lead chopper. Crowfoot broke into one of his rare grins. "Dumbass LT doesn't know the second chopper is the one the dinks always go after," he said.

Within seconds the turbines grew to a high-pitched whine as the RPMs increased and the choppers lifted away from the firebase. The checkerboard of sandbags and bunkers below quickly grew distant and was replaced by an ocean of rolling green mountains. Buck glanced at Boggs and Crowfoot. Both stared out at the mountains, their eyes sunken and lost in thought.

The sky was filled with Hueys, thundering and vibrating over the mountains as the battalion ferried down into the valley. They were headed to the base of the high ridges along the Laotian border. Once there, the plan was to form a perimeter for an NDP, and patrol in company-size units the following day. The chopper began dropping closer to the trees, and Buck again glanced at Boggs sitting beside him. His eyes had become big as saucers, and he was licking his lips. The selector switch on his M-16 was in the "Fire" position, and he had his finger wrapped around the trigger. Buck reached over and flicked the selector to "Safe." Boggs didn't seem to notice.

The choppers came in fast on an LZ near the western edge of the valley. Green smoke streamed from the grass. It was a cold LZ. Buck ran forward and took up a defensive position. When he looked back, Boggs was still kneeling on the LZ looking up in wonderment at the departing choppers. Buck motioned to Crowfoot and pointed at Boggs. The second wave of choppers was approaching.

"Hey, dumbass!" Crowfoot shouted. "Over here."

Crowfoot motioned him his way. Boggs didn't move, seemingly frozen in fear.

Crowfoot screamed louder. "Get out of there, dumbass!"

Boggs finally seemed to hear him. He looked their way and began running. The next chopper nearly hit him as he ran from the LZ. Dixie jumped from the skid of the chopper along with Molly and his RTO. They followed Boggs.

Dixie shoved Boggs to the ground. "Get down, dumbass."

The platoon sergeant dropped to the ground beside Buck and turned toward Crowfoot. "Dammit, Chief, you gotta take care of these dumbasses. What was that idiot still doing out there on the LZ?"

Crowfoot shrugged. "I tried, Sarge."

Rolley trotted up with Gruenstein and Henderson close behind. He was red-faced as he shouted at the three replacements. "I told you dumbasses before we left the firebase to stay close behind us and to do what we did. If you don't want your first trip out here to be your last, you better start listening."

Dixie described it as a "cluster fuck," but the platoon finally gathered its collective wits and started up the side of the valley. Buck volunteered for point and Crowfoot took up the slack position. Behind them Gruenstein, Henderson, and Boggs clomped along like a herd of water buffalo, bitching and whining. The platoon led the rest of the company as they humped up the valley toward a secondary ridge to rendezvous with the other companies. After pushing through thick elephant grass, Buck climbed the ridge and hacked through walls of vines and brush. Near exhaustion, he reached a clearing at the top late that afternoon.

Cotton-mouthed, Buck turned up one of his canteens, sucking down the warm water. Crowfoot took a knee beside him, hanging his head in exhaustion, while Blondie and Rolley walked away from the group. TJ came up and knelt between Buck and Crowfoot and watched while Blondie and Rolley engaged in an animated argument of hissing and whispering. Buck looked over at Crowfoot and motioned with his head toward the two men.

"What's up?"

Crowfoot, his fatigues soaked with sweat, didn't bother to raise his head. "Blondie is pissed off."

"Well, no shit, Chief!"

Crowfoot smiled, but still didn't look up.

"It's about the noise the legs been making all day," TJ said. "Blondie's pissed 'cause they givin' away our position to every gook in the valley."

Buck had heard enough. Pushing the straps from his shoulders, he dropped his rucksack. He walked down the hill to where the three troublemakers lay on their backs pouring water from their canteens over their faces.

"You turd-heads better listen up, 'cause I'm only going to say this once."

"What the fuck, now?" Henderson said.

Red-faced and panting, his mouth hung open as he sat up, hanging his head between his knees. He cut his bloodshot eyes upward at Buck.

Gruenstein glanced around. "Can't you gung-ho cocksuckers give it a rest?"

"Sure," Buck said, "but if you dumb fucks want to get out of this place alive, you better listen."

Boggs turned and looked up. "Fuck you. Take yo Chuck ass on back up that hill 'fo I light yo ass up."

Standing over them, Buck forced himself to remain calm. "I've had enough. You stupid fucks have been talking loud, banging your gear and making noise all day.

Every gook scout in the valley knows exactly where we are by now. Sooner or later they're going to ambush us and kill some of us, and you better hope they kill me, because if they don't, I'm coming for your sorry asses when it's over."

Buck felt a hand on his shoulder. It was Rolley.

"Be cool, little brother. I'll take it from here. Go on back up the hill. Dixie is assigning sectors and fields of fire."

Buck looked Rolley in the eyes but remained silent.

"Go on. I'll handle it. I promise," Rolley said.

Buck started back up the hill, but stopped and looked back. "And tomorrow when you dumb fucks are out of water, don't come begging me for mine. I hope you—"

"Go! Go on, Buck," Rolley said.

The company dug in that afternoon, filling sandbags, cutting trees for overhead and setting out Claymores and trip flares. It rained, and Rolley showed up and sat in the mud beside Buck. A cold rivulet of water ran through the neck of Buck's poncho, down his back and into the crack of his butt. It wasn't dark yet, and Rolley lit a cigarette, handing it to him. After he lit one for himself, he gazed out at the jungle and misting rain.

"You need to lighten up some, little brother. Those replacements will either figure it out on their own, or…" He paused for a long moment. "Or, well, they won't."

Buck sucked hard on the unfiltered cigarette. He was miserable, both physically and mentally. Rolley continued gazing into the darkening wall of rain and vegetation.

"We're all chasing our own white rabbits. We've been called for whatever reason, and we've all fallen down this hole called Vietnam. But each one of us has to figure it out on our own. Just don't let what they do make you lose focus on doing what's right."

Buck finished his cigarette, and after a while Rolley patted him on the back, stood and walked away. The jungle sounds maintained a steady rhythm throughout the night—a good indication there wasn't a lot of enemy movement in the area. Dawn came, and after a breakfast of cold C-rations chased with iodine-flavored water, Dixie explained that the company was going to work its way down the ridge to the west and up another trackless ravine further into the mountains.

Buck glanced down the hill in the direction they were going. A half-klick below, a sluggish pool of dense fog filled the crease at the bottom of the small mountain valley. Tinged by the first hints of sunlight, the fog had an almost luminescent quality—beautiful, surreal, but ominous. He wasn't one for premonitions, but gazing into the valley made the hair on his neck tingle. He prayed the fog would burn away before they reached it.

Buck was again on point with Crowfoot walking slack as they led the company down the hillside. It was slow going as he was forced to hack through tangles of vines and dripping wet vegetation with his machete. He did so as quietly as he could. By mid-morning they had reached the bottom of the little valley, and began working their way up a rocky stream. Wading and climbing over boulders, the men slowly made their way up the steep incline. Buck's wish finally came true as the fog dissipated and the mountain air went from cold to miserably hot.

Lieutenant Mallon sent word up for them to leave the stream and turn up the mountainside to the north. Shrouded by the thick jungle canopy, the air was heavy with humidity and permeated with the odor of rotted vegetation. Buck paused to wipe the sweat from his face. He was glad to get away from the open ground in the middle of the stream, but he couldn't shake the feeling that something wasn't quite right. The never-ending twilight and occasional animal sounds made the jungle spooky as hell. He began climbing again, pushing through more overhanging vines, when without warning Crowfoot knocked him to the ground.

The jungle became an instant hornets' nest of cracking and zipping bullets. Several explosions sent rocks, tree limbs, and shrapnel flying. Buck's heart pounded as he fought to regain his wits. Someone in the column below was screaming in agony. Looking under his arm, he tried to see who it might be. The man's screams echoed from the far hillside as automatic weapon fire poured in, not only from the attackers on the ridge above, but from his own men still in the stream below. Crowfoot, who was lying beside him, yelled for them to cease fire.

The person screaming suddenly stopped, but the enemy fire continued intense and unabated as Buck flattened his body against the ground. The thudding *karoomph* of mortar rounds sent showers of rocks and vegetation raining down. Bullets were striking everywhere, and Buck expected any moment to feel one shred his insides.

"They're above us and some are on our left," Crowfoot said. His voice was eerily calm.

Buck shed his rucksack. It already had two bullet holes in it. Pinned down, he and Crowfoot pushed their rucksacks in front for cover. Two men dashed across the stream below and up the mountainside into the jungle. It was Blondie and Rolley. The intense gunfire quickly shifted as the enemy focused on these new targets.

Leaves and branches fell as the bullets made salad of the undergrowth. Down below no one else was moving. The enemy began flinging grenades down the mountain while a machine gun somewhere upstream fired steadily, tearing up the mountainside and occasionally spraying a burst down the stream. Jets of water, rock shards, and ricochets scattered everywhere.

Only a few covering shots came at irregular intervals from below. It was Dixie, but every time he fired, he was met with a torrent of return fire from above. Buck rolled onto his back.

"Quit moving!" Crowfoot said. "They think we're dead. When Rolley and Blondie open up, we'll try to get close enough to throw a grenade at that machine gun."

Kaaroomph! Kaaroomph! The thudding explosions of grenades tossed by Rolley and Blondie came from above. Their sixteens rattled on full automatic. The enemy machine gun continued firing across the mountainside. With the enemy now concentrating their return fire on Blondie and Rolley, it was time to move. Crowfoot left his rucksack behind and began crawling up the mountainside.

Buck paused, momentarily paralyzed with fear, but the next minute he was crawling like a snake, under logs, over rocks and through the brush, steadily getting closer to the sounds of the machine gun. He spotted them. Their helmets camouflaged with leaves were all that was visible. The muzzle blast of the machine gun shook the bushes and the tinkle of spent brass followed every pause. He was close, almost too close, but they had no idea he was there.

Pulling a pin from a frag, Buck tossed it through an opening toward the machine gun nest. The firing stopped immediately, and one of the enemy soldiers tried to jump up and run, but the explosion of the grenade caught him before he took two steps. The concussion knocked Buck's helmet off. Momentarily stunned, his ears were ringing as he caught a glimpse of more movement. Two enemy soldiers darted across a small opening twenty meters to the left and disappeared up the mountainside. He had apparently crawled inside their ambush line.

After snapping off four or five shots at the fleeing NVA, Buck crawled forward. A burst of M-16 fire erupted only a few meters away in the brush to his right. Something or someone tumbled down the hill. There came a loud splash and the sounds of thrashing in the water below. Sweat saturated Buck's fatigues as he crawled up a little further. It grew quiet except for an occasional shout somewhere down the mountainside. The adrenaline flowed like electricity through his body. His heart raced, and he waited and watched the area around the machine gun nest. There was movement on the other side. Buck held his M-16 at the ready.

Drunk with adrenaline, he steadied himself as a black head rose slowly from behind the enemy bunker. Sweat ran into his eyes, but he was ready as he looked over the barrel of his rifle and waited for a clear shot. The man's eyes darted back and forth. Tightening his finger around the trigger, Buck prepared to fire, but the man raised his hand and gave the two-fingered peace sign. Hesitation in combat could mean instant death, but he did just that. Buck wiped the sweat from his eyes, and only then did he look into the other man's eyes. They were the eyes of a wolf. Without his helmet, he looked like an enemy soldier, but he wasn't.

"Damn, Crowfoot, I almost shot you."

Crowfoot put his finger to his lips as his eyes darted about.

"Did you do this?" He pointed to the two dead enemy soldiers.

Buck nodded. "Yeah. What now?"

"Let's link up with Rolley and Blondie and move back down to the stream."

By the time Buck and the others returned to the rest of the platoon, Captain Crenshaw had come forward. Three men had been hit, but the screaming had come from Lieutenant Mallon's new RTO, PJ Goodson. A machine-gun round had pierced his lower abdomen. He was dead. Doc Gilbert poured water from a canteen as he washed the blood from his hands. His fatigues were covered with blood. There was blood on his face and his arms, and it looked as if someone had splashed a bucket of red paint on the ground. Goodson's body had already been wrapped in a poncho. His jungle boots protruded from one end.

Lizard explained how Gruenstein, Henderson, and Boggs had hidden behind a large boulder and never moved. Dixie tried to get them to provide suppressing fire on the left for Rolley and Blondie, but the cowards refused to move. Lieutenant Mallon and Doc Gilbert were too busy trying to save Goodson.

The enemy apparently had planned their kill-zone for the mountain stream just ahead of where Buck and Crowfoot had turned up the mountain. It was a blind stroke of luck when they left the creek and turned uphill. Although the platoon had turned directly into the face of the enemy ambush, the cover was so thick the NVA were unable to bring the largest part of their weapons to bear. In the end, the final score was seven enemy KIA to one

American dead and two wounded. And like Rolley had said before: if you weren't PJ or his family, you might call it a victory.

Dixie made Gruenstein and Boggs carry PJ's body, while a newbie from Third Squad was temporarily assigned as the new platoon RTO. The company worked its way to the top of the hill and cleared an LZ. By early afternoon the two wounded along with PJ's body were put on a dust-off to Phu Bai. The company was ordered to dig in around the LZ and await further orders.

13

THE NIGHT ON THE MOUNTAIN

Late August, 1968

While Dixie assigned fields of fire and defensive positions, Buck glanced about at the jungle terrain. The landing zone had been hurriedly hacked and chain-sawed out that afternoon in order to get the two wounded medevac'd. The LZ was on a ridge, jutting from the side of the mountain. On the high side of the perimeter, the positions were exposed to higher ground, a lousy situation, but there was nothing the CO could do about it. He put an extra M-60 and a couple of extra M-79s there, but the men were still ducks in a shooting gallery if the enemy decided to attack. Everyone hurriedly put out Claymores and trip flares, and it was nearly dark when the first sniper fire began.

"Don't give your position away by shooting back at them," Rolley whispered to Boggs and Gruenstein, "at least not until you have to. If you think they're getting close, use your frags."

Buck was at least thankful that First Platoon had been placed on the downhill side, where the timber cut from the LZ was tossed in loose piles. He was on his knees digging in when there came a loud *SSSHHCRRACCCKK-WUMP.* A single enemy round had passed within inches of his head, striking the ground behind him. He dropped to the ground. Crowfoot pointed down the ridge into the darkness. "I have him," he whispered. "Stay down. I'm going to move back up the hill and try to get him the next time I see the muzzle flash."

Buck lay flat on his belly, knowing he had avoided an early visit to eternity by inches. With his cheek against the ground, he continued digging while Crowfoot crawled back up the hill to the pile of trees that had been cleared from the LZ. There came another crack as another round passed over Buck's head. Crowfoot opened up with his sixteen. The red tracers ricocheted and bounced crazily on the mountainside below. The jungle came alive as rounds hissed and cracked hitting the trees around Crowfoot. Someone on the backside of the perimeter fired several rounds from an M-79. The explosions flashed brilliant white in the growing darkness, and the enemy fire ceased.

"They'll move closer," Rolley said. "Just keep your heads down, and once they get in close, keep moving so they can't zero in on your position."

"Hey. You okay?" Crowfoot whispered in the darkness.

"I'm good," Buck called in a hoarse whisper.

A stick cracked down the hill. It was only a few meters from where the men lay. Buck rolled quietly on his side and pulled the pin on a grenade. Holding the spoon in place, he paused and listened intently. Night had fallen, and little was visible in the pitch-black darkness, only the massive outline of the mountain looming against the night sky behind him. He could feel it. This was going to be a bad night.

There came another sound from below, a mere scratch in the leaves. Buck tensed, then lobbed the grenade down the hillside. The blast showered him with debris as all hell broke loose. Rolling onto his belly he looked down the ridge and detonated his first Claymore.

There were at least eight or nine figures outlined by the flash of the mine. He detonated the second Claymore as the entire side of the perimeter opened up. Buck fired his sixteen into the darkness as screams of pain came from below. Behind him someone began shouting for a medic. A person landed with a thump beside him. Buck didn't have time to react, but thankfully, it was Blondie.

"Rolley said you guys need to move. Let's go."

Buck followed as they crawled up the hill and hid between two of the downed trees. Another explosion lit the night sky and the position they had just vacated was inundated with orange flame. Voices came from mere feet away. Two figures appeared silhouetted against the night sky. They moved cautiously toward the center of the perimeter. Buck and Blondie opened up simultaneously on full automatic with their M-16s.

The artillery support came, first with illumination rounds, followed by HE rounds slamming into the hillside below. Shrapnel whirred and thudded all around as the exploding artillery shells bracketed the perimeter, but it was too late. The enemy had already gotten inside the protective ring of fire and breached the perimeter. Several bursts of gunfire came from up the hill near the company CP.

Buck could hear Blondie breathing beside him. He poked him. "Where's Crowfoot?" he whispered.

"I saw him running toward the Platoon CP, when we were crawling up here."

All around the perimeter, sputtering small-arms fire swelled then quickly died away to one shot, then two, then silence. What seemed like hours slowly passed, while the artillery barrage continued, illumination rounds drifted eerily overhead and sharp clashes of automatic weapons continued inside the perimeter. No one was moving. Doing so made you an instant target for both sides.

Sometime after midnight Buck heard something to his left only a few feet away. Holding his M-16 at the ready, he watched and waited. The seconds passed, then minutes, but he refused to lower his guard. He waited until the faint glow of an illumination round revealed a solitary figure standing just the other side of the felled tree trunk. It didn't move. Buck's mouth was dry with the metallic taste of fear. Whether or not Blondie saw it, he wasn't sure, but he was afraid to blink, much less warn him.

The figure stood unmoving for a minute then two, until Buck began to doubt if it really was a man. Perhaps it was just his imagination. During training the drill instructors explained how something called "visual purple" aided a man's night vision. You simply rotate your eyes around the object you wish to see without looking directly at it. Perhaps so in theory, but they forgot to mention what to do when your eyes were filled with the floating white haze of multiple grenade and artillery explosions.

Buck's body ached with tension. Blondie must have sensed something was up. He wasn't moving. Buck's head spun with adrenaline as he prepared to snatch his M-16 into firing position. There would be no second chance. If he blew it, they might both be killed in a split second.

"Buck, don't shoot. It's me, Crowfoot."

He had been standing no more than seven or eight feet away for several minutes. Stepping carefully over the tree trunk, he squatted between Buck and Blondie.

"I almost blew you away," Buck whispered.

"I sensed you were about to do something," Crowfoot said. "Sorry, but I wasn't sure who you were."

"Where's Rolley?" Blondie asked.

"The last time I saw him was around ten o'clock," Crowfoot said. "He was over there with Boggs and Henderson. He and Dixie were moving up and down the line checking on the men, but now everyone's afraid to move. We've got dinks inside the perimeter."

"Yeah, I know," Buck answered. "There's a couple laying right there." He motioned toward the two NVA he and Blondie had killed a few hours before.

Crowfoot was holding something in his hand opposite his M-16, but it was too dark to see what it was.

'What's that?" Buck asked.

"My bayonet," Crowfoot whispered. "I'm hunting dinks." And as if he had never been there, he again disappeared into the darkness.

Crowfoot had shown Buck how to hone his bayonet until it could peel the skin from a grape, but only now did he realize just how fearless a warrior Crowfoot really was. He was a man he was proud to call a friend.

For the next several hours, Buck and Blondie lay silent, listening and watching for movement. Time moved slowly as each hour seemed unwilling to yield to the next, and each time when Buck thought perhaps it was over, there came more bursts of gunfire and grenade explosions from somewhere inside the perimeter.

After hours of being half blinded by the explosions, and his body buzzing with adrenaline, Buck noticed the stars overhead beginning to fade as the mountains slowly began to lighten. He wanted to jump to his feet and yell "Yes!" The artillery barrage abated, and other than the moans of the wounded and an occasional scratch of a radio breaking squelch, it remained silent. Buck lay on his back, his muscles rigid and sore.

Jet contrails shone high in the sky overhead, but they were too late. The enemy was gone. Other than the bodies of their dead and some wounded left behind, they had disappeared back into the mountains. The sun rose, and the American dead and wounded were loaded aboard choppers. Gray, lifeless forms wrapped in ponchos lay next to men wrapped in bloody white gauze. The wounded held plasma bottles for themselves with one hand and the bodies of their buddies with the other as the choppers lifted into the sky. The company had nine KIAs and fourteen wounded.

After being resupplied early that afternoon, Buck and the others heated their C-rations over wads of C-4, while nervously sucking on unfiltered Camels and Lucky Strikes. Later, the company formed up and began working its way back down the mountain toward the valley to rendezvous with the rest of the battalion.

For once, no one had to tell Boggs or Henderson to be quiet, and even Recalcitrant Al seemed willing to join the program. They moved like hollow-eyed cats—skittish and brandishing their weapons at the slightest sounds. Buck was beyond exhaustion, and his nerves were shot to hell, but he couldn't help but smile at the clowns. They now understood their places in this godforsaken war.

14

R&R

Bangkok, Thailand, September 1968

With over six months in-country, Buck was now eligible for R&R. Janie said she would go wherever he chose, but his choices were limited. Bumped from the lists for Hawaii and Australia, he had to settle for Thailand. The men who had been there said Bangkok was the Asian version of a Wild West boomtown. It sounded like fun, except he had seen enough of Southeast Asia. The week with Janie was what mattered most—that and delivery from the mundane hell of combat into the open arms of a loving woman. It seemed like a dream.

The resupply choppers were coming in with replacements that afternoon, when Dixie told him to report to the LZ. Late that evening, after arriving in Phu Bai, Buck hurried to the R&R center where he contacted Janie's

CO. After the officer's explanation of his reluctance to rearrange schedules, it seemed a miracle of sorts when Janie called back a few minutes later. She said she would meet him the next day to catch a Pan Am flight to Bangkok. He hung up the phone, and stared out at nothing in particular. His heart should have been soaring with anticipation, but he suddenly realized it wasn't, and he couldn't explain it.

Buck wanted more than anything to once again gaze into those radiant brown eyes, lose himself in her arms and forget about the war, but he was tired. He was a wasted human wreck. He was physically tired, mentally tired, and emotionally tired. If he spent the next several days in a hotel room, drinking himself into oblivion, it would be just the same—except for Janie. For her, he had to get his head right. He had to, because on the phone he heard a tremor in her voice, and an unmistakable excitement. It was as if his call had validated all her hopes. She needed him as much as he needed her—perhaps more.

When he first saw her, Buck gave in to a moment of euphoria as he smiled broadly. Janie was no longer an Army nurse in boots and OD green fatigues, but a beautiful young girl again. She wore a yellow dress and a ribbon in her hair. More gorgeous than he remembered, this beautiful woman pressed close against him and they embraced with a passionate kiss there on the tarmac before boarding the big jet. When their lips parted, she gazed breathlessly up into his eyes, her soft brown eyes smiling as she caressed his cheek, but the corners of her mouth suddenly turned down and her face clouded. Buck tried to smile again, but there was no hiding it. She saw it in his eyes. She had seen through his façade. Rings of moisture gathered in hers and she reached up to touch his face again, this time tracing her thumb carefully across his chin. The line boarding the aircraft began moving around them, but they stood gazing at one another.

"It'll be okay, Buck," she whispered. "You'll see. Let's just go spend this week together, and make the best of it."

If there was so much as a teardrop left in him, a hint of emotion or hope, Buck wanted to find it for Janie, but for now, he simply nodded. Taking her hand, he walked with her up the stairway into the aircraft, hoping things would change for the better.

Later that day, Janie held his hand in hers while they rode in the taxi from the Bangkok Airport, gazing out at a wondrous countryside of pagodas and Buddha statues. The people at the airport, the cab driver, everyone was smiling and helpful. And when they arrived at the Windsor Hotel the driver carried their bags and guided them to the US R&R Center. There Buck explained that he and Janie were together and needed a room voucher. After repeated assurances that only one room was needed, the staff finally understood, and he and Janie began receiving VIP treatment. Becoming instant royalty, the young soldiers were assigned their own private concierge and the best room in the hotel.

It seemed almost surreal. Less than forty-eight hours ago, Buck had been fighting desperately in the night, sweating, and fully expecting he might die at any moment. Now he stood at the door of a grand hotel suite, arm in arm with Janie. The concierge set the bags on a bench at the end of the bed, turned down the covers and quickly disappeared.

When the door closed behind them, there was no freshening up, no unpacking bags, only a mad scramble to pull one another's clothes away, punctuated with passionate kisses, quick embraces and a dash to fall into the huge bed. For the next twenty-four hours Buck and Janie did not leave the room. They ate nothing and drank only bottled sodas. They became lost in one another's body, at first making love, hard and fast. Later they made love soft and slow, and then they slept tangled as one. When they awakened, they again made passionate love, and only the following evening when the neon lights on the street below began flickering to life did they begin to realize there was another world awaiting them.

Janie stared up at him, dreamy-eyed and smiling, and Buck could only imagine that this had to be as close to heaven as a man could get in this world.

"Are you hungry?" he asked.

"Starving," she said.

After bathing one another, something that nearly resulted in starting over, Buck helped Janie into a new dress. She insisted upon wearing dresses, saying she was tired of boots and fatigues. He loved it. She would have stood out in a crowded city anywhere in the world, but here, on the backside of nowhere, she was an icon of what he and every other soldier in Nam dreamt of every night. After buttoning her up the back, he smoothed her soft blond hair with his hand. She was a dream in the middle of a nightmare.

There came the quietest of knocks at the door. Janie turned and looked up at him. "Room service?"

He grinned and turned toward the door. "Just a minute," he called out. He slipped on his new jeans and opened the door. It was the Thai concierge. The little man nodded respectfully.

"I bring you clean linen and towel. If you wish, I am to be your guide, only five hundred Baht for week."

Behind him stood two women with the towels, linens, and a basket of soaps and oils. Buck looked over his shoulder at Janie. She gave him a sideways grin and shrugged.

"Come in, come in," Buck said, motioning them into the room. He turned to Janie. "How much is five hundred Baht?"

She began thumbing through the literature they had received at the front desk.

"If I may, sir, it is twenty-five American Dollar—very good deal. Escort get twenty dollar *every* day."

"Of course that include something I cannot do for you…I mean—" The young man paused and seemed embarrassed.

Buck laughed. He had already learned that a twenty-four-hour female escort was the norm for most visiting GIs. They charged around 400 Baht a day, and provided guide service, companionship and unlimited sex.

"No problem. What is your name?" Buck asked the little man.

"I am Sarathoon."

The young Thai stood erect, his lips set firm. Buck met his stare and looked him in the eyes. At first it was a proud stare, but after a few moments Sarathoon looked downward.

"I want you to be our guide," Buck said. "Take care of me and Janie, and I'll take care of you."

Sarathoon raised his head and smiled. "You have no worry. You have great R and R. You see. I take care of you."

That first night they clutched one another and danced to a Platters song.

> *Only you can make all this world seem right*
> *Only you can make the darkness bright*
> *….you are my destiny*
> *You're my dream come true, my one and only you*

Buck was certain that was the way it would be. There was no doubt. Janie was his, but after a night barhopping on the American Strip down New Petchaburi Road, they agreed the people-watching was interesting, but they were ready to take a pass on the rowdy mix of drinking, sex and music. The next morning Sarathoon packed them a lunch basket and a bag with towels and a blanket. He also had a taxi waiting out front and took them down a coastal road where they found a quiet beach.

"This is more like it," Buck said, gazing out at the Gulf of Thailand.

Gentle waves of crystalline water lapped onto the beach while they spread a blanket beneath the palms.

"I take it you like this a lot more than the bar scene," Janie said.

"If I were single, the bar might not be so bad."

She removed her sunglasses and turned toward him. "What do you mean by 'if you were single'?"

Buck grinned. "My mother was always direct. I mean, she wasn't rude, but she didn't mince words. I'm kind of the same way. So, I suppose we need to determine just exactly where we want to go from here."

Buck pushed his aviators up on his head and met her stare.

"I like that," Janie said. "I'm the same way."

"What I mean about not being single is I feel I'm committed to you, and I was kind of hoping you felt the same."

She took his hand. "I'm ready to go as far as you want to take me. Like I said that day in Phu Bai, I love you."

"I love you, too, but what's next?"

"Are you proposing?"

"No. I have to get past this war, first. I suppose I want to know where you want our relationship to lead."

"You know…." Janie paused for several long seconds. "I've been wined and dined by several officers since I got to Vietnam. As their guest, I've visited Saigon, Hue, and a couple cities in between, and despite my insistence on separate rooms, every last one attempted to bed me. For a little girl from a not so rich family in Montana, it was pretty difficult to say 'no' to them, but I did—to all of them. Hopefully this tells you how much you mean to me."

"Do you think Sarathoon and that taxi driver are where they can see us?"

Janie glanced around. "He said they would be out at the road. Why?"

"Because you're fixin' to lose your pants, again."

Buck ran his hand down into the front of her shorts and gently cradled her as their lips met. She moaned and Buck again found himself lost in a place where all the tensions of the war drained away. The sun was low on the water that afternoon when they made their way back to the road. Buck was lightheaded from the wine Sarathoon had put in the basket, and Janie rested her head on his shoulder as they walked through the now cooling sand.

Not since losing his mother and father had he imagined he could again become so attached to another person. Janie seemed forthright and honest, and all too vulnerable. She had given herself totally to him. Best of all, she was fun to talk with, and he loved her company. They spent the next few days visiting places like the Mae Klong Market, Wat Phrakaew, Thermae, Khao Takiap, and so many other places he could no longer remember all the names. At night they dined on exotic foods and drinks and talked about their lives and families. And it all came and went in the blur of a few days' time.

15

THE BOTCHED FRAGGING

October 1968

Buck left Janie back at Phu Bai. The 101ˢᵗ was now at the new base called Camp Eagle, where the company was on a three day stand-down. They were bivouacked in large thirty-man tents. As he approached, he spotted a familiar face. It was TJ.

"Wassup, ma friend?" the little Cajun shouted.

He was coming up out of one of the sandbagged tents where the men were billeted. Buck wrapped his arm around his neck. TJ, who was wearing his normal camo fatigues and jungle boots, had what appeared to be a new suit, tie, and white shirt draped over his arm.

"What's that stuff?" Buck asked as he stepped back.

"A suit I had made in Hong Kong while I was on R&R."

"Where are you going with it?"

TJ said nothing as he turned and walked across the dusty red-ball road to a roadside trash bin. Opening the side door, he tossed the clothes inside, turned and shrugged. "Ain't gonna need that stuff no more."

"Aw, come on man. You can't think like that. Five more months of this shit and we're home free."

"You haven't heard, have you?" TJ asked.

"Heard what?"

"Dixie is dead. The platoon got ambushed by NVA regulars, and that dumbass Mallon was doing his usual, hunkered down but yelling at everybody else to move out while they were taking grazing fire from a .51 cal. Dixie ran forward to get Nguyen and one of the cherries who got hit. Yeah, Nguyen is dead, too. And word is that right in the middle of the fight somebody tried to frag the dumbass lieutenant, but it killed Boggs and the new RTO."

"Oh, shit. Who did it?"

"Blondie said he thinks it was Henderson. He was closest to them when it happened. A couple of RPGs came in, but Blondie said he's pretty sure it was one of our own frags that got Boggs and the RTO. It landed right between them."

"What about the lieutenant?"

"Not a scratch, and they said he ain't none the wiser. He thinks it was an enemy grenade."

"Holy shit. Does Rolley know all this?"

TJ shrugged. "I don't know, but maybe you can ask him." He pointed toward the steps coming out of the tent. Rolley was coming up through the sandbags.

"Hey, Buck. How was Bangkok?"

"Good, real good."

"Were you able to hook up with your nurse friend?"

"Yeah. We spent the week together."

TJ pursed his lips and shook his head. "I just don't get it. How does this country-ass get the best looking round-eyed woman in I-Corps?"

"What's this shit TJ is telling me about somebody trying to frag Mallon?" Buck asked.

Rolley's grin disappeared, and he glanced around. "It's nothing we can prove." He had lowered his voice to just above a whisper. "Go square away your gear. I'm running over to the company CP. I'll meet you up the road in ten minutes. We'll talk where no one can hear us."

A few minutes later, Buck walked with Rolley down the red ball in the middle of Camp Eagle. Kicking at nothing in particular, he watched a dust devil swirling through the tents below. Any day now, the dust would become mud again when the monsoons returned, but for now a jaundiced sky hung over the huge base and the distant hills.

Buck had to thread his way through the maze of Rolley's thoughts, because it was pretty obvious the squad leader wasn't telling him everything. Rolley was an Army NCO doing his best to maintain the discipline inherent to the chain of command, but he was also putting a trust in Buck that wasn't to be taken lightly.

"A lot happened while you were on R&R. With Dixie gone, I'm now Acting Platoon Sergeant. Blondie is taking my place as squad leader. Buck, I need you to talk with the men. Don't tell them I put you up to it, but tell them to stay cool. Tell them don't do anything they'll regret for the rest of their lives. I will do my best to cover for you guys. And I promise I won't let that… I won't let anyone make a bad decision that will get you guys hurt."

"What's his problem, Rolley?"

Rolley stopped, pulled a pack of Camels from his shirt pocket and shook two out. He put both in his mouth and scratched his Zippo. After lighting the two cigarettes he gave one to Buck. "He's less than a year out of OCS, and thinks he has something to prove. He made a comment about Lieutenant Vinton getting the XO job over him because Vinton is a West Pointer. I think Mallon is jealous and wants to prove he's some sort of super-trooper officer, but every time the shit hits the fan he gets scared shitless. He also overcompensates by acting cocky when he should be listening to his NCOs. The result is he makes mistakes."

"Why doesn't Captain Crenshaw do something?"

"Don't worry, when the CO has sufficient cause it will be game over. Crenshaw isn't going to let him get our people hurt."

"Dammit, Rolley, he already has! What about Romeo? What about Dixie, Nguyen, and the cherry?"

"Be cool, little brother. The friendly fire incident that got Romeo has already been investigated, but that's all the captain will say. Don't worry. I'll cover our butts."

It was pretty plain that Rolley had already said more than he wanted. Buck appreciated the trust, but Rolley was walking a fine line. As the new platoon sergeant, he could say only so much, and he wouldn't challenge a commissioned officer, no matter how incompetent, until it was absolutely necessary. Buck respected him for it, but he wasn't going to let Mallon get any more men killed—not while he was still standing.

"That sonofabitch keeps volunteering us for point platoon and puts our squad on point every time. What's with that?"

Rolley's face turned red, and he bit at his lower lip. Only then did Buck realize the position Rolley was in.

"Okay," Buck said, "I'm sorry. I know you're in a tough spot, but just so you know, I'll go to Leavenworth before that stupid bastard gets any more of us killed."

"Just listen to me, Buck. You don't have to do anything. I have your back."

Rolley wrapped his arm around Buck's neck. "How about some good news?"

"What's that?"

"Top said they're sending Mo back stateside to get reconstructive surgery on his jaw. He's out of here, home free."

"Does he know yet?"

"No. I'm going to tell him now, and then we're all getting gloriously drunk."

16

THE SHADOW OF DEATH

Thua Thien Province, October 1968

Rolley had again returned from the company CP that morning, and Henderson stood beside him in stunned silence. His face was milky white. Rolley had just told him he was going to be Lieutenant Mallon's new RTO, and it was suddenly obvious to everyone including Henderson that they knew who tossed the frag that killed Boggs and the RTO.

"Get your gear and report to the lieutenant."

"Ugh, Sarge, wait. Can't we—"

"No, we can't," Rolley all but shouted. "Get your shit and go, now."

"Paybacks can be a real bitch," TJ whispered.

"Sshhh," Buck said.

Rolley turned to the rest of the men in the huge tent. "Okay, men, listen up. Fall in outside, platoon formation.

We're going up the road, draw ammo and C-rations then head over to the LZ. The battalion is going up west of Camp Sally. We'll be working with the Marines and the ARVNs to recapture the hearts and minds of the local villagers in the northernmost part of Thua Thien Province."

Rolley's voice was dripping with sarcasm. "The problem is that several large NVA units have infiltrated into the hills in that area. We have to find and destroy them before we can convince the local populace it's okay to associate with us."

The ARVN troops and the Marines had secured several LZs, and the battalion air assault was relatively uneventful that day. The company deployed in platoon-size units, patrolling westward along the base of the mountains to the south. Second Platoon had reached the edge of the palm trees and faced an open area at least four hundred meters across. A light breeze swayed the palms and grasses, making it seem almost pastoral, except it was anything but that.

Blondie called Rolley up to the point where they knelt with Crowfoot and Buck. Across the open ground to the southwest, an ancient pagoda stood on a rise at the base of the hills, and a small canal came out of the hills, meandering across several hundred meters of open terrain. A well-worn path led from a small village to the north to an arched stone bridge that crossed the canal near the center of the open ground. The path eventually turned south and led to the pagoda.

Rolley put his hand on Crowfoot's shoulder and gazed out across the canal. "What do you think?" he asked.

"It's not good," Crowfoot said.

"Looks like a sucker hole to me," Blondie said.

"What do you say, Buck?" Crowfoot asked.

Buck said nothing, but simply nodded. And only at that moment he realized he had taken his place with the vets he most respected. They now respected him. He thought like them, saw what they saw and knew when things weren't right.

Crowfoot nodded in return. He was right, and it wasn't only the obvious signs that he had pointed out. Buck could feel it. Call it a sixth sense, intuition or whatever, he knew with a certainty that something wasn't right.

Rolley motioned to Buck. "Come with me. We'll go back and check with the LT to see if we can detour toward the 'ville over there."

They walked back only twenty meters before meeting Mallon and his new RTO, Henderson, coming their way. Henderson still had the look of a man on the way to the gallows—rightfully so, Buck figured.

"What's the holdup?" Mallon asked.

"We have an open area that's too risky to cross, sir. I'm going to suggest we turn north and cross in the trees along the backside of the village. That will give us more cover."

"Shit!" Mallon glanced at his watch. "Let's go have a look."

When they got back to where Crowfoot and Blondie were kneeling, the lieutenant stood with his hands on his hips studying the open ground.

"Seen anything?" Rolley asked.

"Nothing," Blondie said, "not a farmer, a water buffalo, nothing."

"Too damned quiet," Crowfoot said. "Should be some villagers around, or at least a water buffalo out there."

The lieutenant stepped out of the palms and into the open. Buck held his breath as the platoon leader squinted in the open sunlight, studying the hills to the south and the slight rise where the pagoda stood further west. After a few seconds he turned and stepped back inside the trees.

"I don't see the problem. It looks like the dozens of other clearings we've crossed."

"It's not the same, sir. The terrain is diff—"

"White Knight wants all the platoons at the assembly point on those next hills by oh-sixteen-hundred. I want our platoon to be the first one there, and there's no way we can detour all the way over to that village and beat the others. We'll go straight across. Tell the men to maintain good separation and put the point element well out front. We'll be fine."

Rolley shook his head.

"Sir, if we walk out across that canal on that open ground, this chess game could be over. That rise around that pagoda is an ideal place for the enemy to ambush us. I suggest that—"

"White Knight has given us our orders. We don't have time for—"

"Sir, at least let me run a quick recon out beyond that bridge. We may be able to see if there's anyone around that pagoda, and—"

"Oh, Jesus! Are you scared? I need a platoon sergeant who can—"

"No, sir. I just don't want to lead my men into—"

"Just fucking go, Sergeant Zwyrkowski, but make it fast. We're losing time."

Rolley was red-faced with anger as he trotted to the edge of the palms. Crowfoot and Blondie jumped to their feet and followed, but Rolley motioned them back. They ignored him. The three knelt at the edge of the clearing. Buck walked up behind them.

Rolley turned back to the lieutenant. "Sir, if you will, deploy the men along the edge of the trees here in case we need cover fire. Buck, you stay here and take care of your squad." With that he turned and trotted out across the open ground, followed by Crowfoot and Blondie.

The three men were nearly to the bridge, but the lieutenant was still kneeling and watching. "Sir," Buck said, "do you want me to go back and bring up the rest of the platoon?"

The lieutenant wagged his head. "No. If we deploy, it'll take too long to get everyone moving again. You can take some of your men out there where you can see if you want."

Buck started to object, but there was no time. Crowfoot was a silhouette crouching low as he followed Rolley and Blondie, trotting over the arched bridge at the canal.

"TJ, Lizard, you guys go over that way and be ready to give them cover fire if they need it. Gruenstein, you come with me." By the time he got into place, Buck could see all three men had crossed the bridge and were cautiously moving ahead, less than two hundred meters from the pagoda. Perhaps the LT was right. All remained quiet.

It was still silent when it seemed an invisible scythe took the legs out from under all three men. The sounds of weapons firing followed a second later.

"Cover fire!" Buck shouted. "Aim for the trees around the pagoda."

Gruenstein and TJ began firing their M-16s while Lizard unleashed round after round from his thump gun. The enemy began redirecting their fire. Rounds cracked all around and several rockets exploded in the palms nearby. Buck spotted movement as a helmetless figure crawled from the canal, running and stumbling back toward the tree line. It was Blondie. He fell, but rose again and continued running. Buck emptied his sixteen on full automatic, slapped in another magazine and emptied that one as well. Mortar and rocket rounds were now exploding all around. Lines of green and red tracers crisscrossed the open ground.

Blondie fell again, this time eighty meters from the trees. He didn't move. Buck jumped up and ran forward. He felt a hammer blow to his side, and a liquid mist struck his face as he was knocked off his feet. The jolt took his breath, but there was no immediate pain. It had to be the numbness of shock. The right side of his face was wet, and he carefully ran his hand across it as he looked down, expecting to see his leg mangled or gone. It was still there. He looked at his hand. It was coated with the liquid from his face, but it wasn't the bloody mess he expected. It was clear.

The enemy fire continued cracking over his head, and only then did Buck notice that one of his canteens was blown inside out. The spray had come from the water inside. Rattled and relieved in the same instant, he fought to gather his wits. Blondie was still lying out there sixty meters away.

Buck came back to his feet again, zig-zagging across the open ground, until he reached Blondie. His left arm was nearly severed above the hand and hemorrhaging badly. Quickly Buck wrapped it with a bandanna and cinched it tight. Enemy rounds continued zipping past as he came to his feet and began dragging Blondie by his collar.

"Medic!" Buck yelled as he reached the trees.

Doc Gilbert was there in seconds.

"Take him back where you guys have some cover," Buck said. "Where's the damned lieutenant?"

Doc motioned with his free hand. "He's over there in a ditch."

Buck pushed his way through the scrub palm until he found Lieutenant Mallon curled up in a ditch with Henderson and two others. He stood over them ignoring the enemy rounds cracking all around. Mallon and the men in the ditch looked up in wide-eyed fear.

"Get up, sir," Buck said.

He reached down and pulled Mallon to his feet. The lieutenant's face went white as more bullets cracked and hissed past them.

"Get the men organized, sir. Bring them up and start laying down some suppressing fire. I'm going forward to find Rolley and Crowfoot."

"You can't go forward," Mallon screamed. "I'm calling for artillery."

"You have two men out there, sir."

"They're probably dead," Mallon said. "I saw them go down as soon as the enemy opened fire."

"You don't know for sure they're dead. You do what you think is right, sir. I'm going to find our men and bring them back."

TJ crawled up. "Buck, you're crazy, mon. Get the fuck down."

An enemy round grazed Buck's helmet with a loud metallic ping. Mallon dove into the ditch and looked up at him. Buck straightened his helmet, reached down and grabbed the lieutenant by his fatigue shirt. He jerked him to his feet.

"Sir, you can't direct artillery fire from down there. Stay on your feet, and bring the men up to give me some cover fire."

With that he turned and trotted out of the palms toward the canal. Crossing the open ground, he fully expected to get hit at any moment. Grazing fire from an enemy machine gun was pulverizing the stone bridge. That route would be instant suicide. Instead, he ducked and crawled into the tall grass near the canal. After wading the chest-deep water, he crawled out on the other side, where he spotted them. Crowfoot and Rolley lay together where they had first fallen. He reached Crowfoot first.

He lay unmoving in a pool of blood. Pressing two fingers against his neck, Buck felt for a pulse. Crowfoot was dead—bled out. Buck crawled over to Rolley. He was face-down in the grass. Setting his rifle aside, he rolled Rolley over onto his back. There was a huge bloodstain on the front of his fatigue shirt. He groaned and opened his eyes.

"Buck, get out of here. Go back before you get hit. I'm finished."

"Let's get you bandaged."

He ripped open Rolley's fatigue shirt, but paused at what he saw. He looked up, and the young platoon sergeant grimaced. "Now, do you see? Go. Get the hell out of here."

There was no way he was leaving Rolley.

"No, you can't die. Come on, man. Don't give up."

Buck ripped open a first aid dressing.

"Please, Buck, leave me here. There's nothing you can do. I'm…"

Rolley closed his eyes, and the blood that had been flowing from his shredded abdomen with each heartbeat ceased. Buck pushed the bandage into the gaping wound, but it was useless. It was too late. He thought of the day in the sheriff's squad car when the deputy told him his parents had been killed in the car wreck. He had gone instantly numb. There were no tears—only a haze of shock. Pulling Rolley close, he began weeping. He wept for Rolley, and he finally wept for his parents. He wept uncontrollably.

Buck wasn't sure how long he had held Rolley in his arms before he suddenly realized the cover fire from the platoon had faded. He looked up as two NVA soldiers dashed from the trees near the pagoda, running in his direction. Carrying their weapons at the ready, they ran straight for him, obviously intent upon making him their prisoner. Buck reached over, picked up his M-16 and killed them both. He emptied the remainder of the magazine into the nearby trees.

Sporadic enemy fire continued as he pulled Rolley's body back to the canal and crossed to the opposite bank. Leaving him there, he returned and retrieved Crowfoot's body, dragging it too across the canal. By now he was exhausted.

When the first howitzer rounds exploded, Buck was well inside danger close range and felt the sting of shrapnel on his side. The cargo pocket on the right side of his fatigue shirt was ripped open. It was only a glancing blow, but his hip was gashed. Burying his face in the mud, he huddled between the bodies of his two buddies. Several more artillery rounds shattered the tile roof of the pagoda and splintered the nearby palm trees. The concussion of the explosions sucked the air from his lungs and his head began spinning with stars as he felt himself losing consciousness. After a moment it became silent.

Buck didn't realize he had passed out until he awoke to the sound of footsteps nearby. He raised his head. It was TJ walking down the side of the canal. Buck tried to call out, but managed only a weak moan.

"Hey," TJ yelled. "Over here. They're over here." He was motioning to the other men.

"Crowfoot and Rolley are dead," Buck muttered.

TJ, Lizard, and Doc Gilbert knelt beside him, and from the looks on their faces, he realized he too might be dying.

"I'm thirsty."

"Give him some water," TJ said.

"You just lost a little blood, podna, but I'm gettin' you bandaged and hooked up to some plasma," Doc said. "You're gonna be fine—real fine, 'cause you're a two-timer, now. Second heart means you might get a free pass for a job back at Eagle."

"Come on, man," TJ shouted. "Don't close your eyes. We gotta chopper comin'."

But he did as the voices around him faded and it again grew quiet.

17

TAKING ROLLEY HOME

22nd Surgical Hospital, Phu Bai

Buck smelled alcohol and iodine, and he heard a gruff voice talking over the others. It was the unmistakable voice of the Battalion Sergeant Major, but amongst the other voices was the one he wanted to hear most. It was Janie's. It took a while before he realized he had been sleeping, but he opened his eyes to a blur of faces standing over him.

"Janie?"

"Son, you are truly fucked up if you think that I am that good-looking nurse."

"No, Sergeant Major, you're way too ugly. Where is she?"

Buck was waiting for the ass chewing he deserved when Janie's face appeared only inches above him.

"Janie?"

He felt tears flowing from his eyes.

"It's okay, Buck. You made it. You're going home, and in a few weeks I'll be going home, too. We both made it."

"Son," the Sergeant Major said, "Your CO, Captain Crenshaw, has put you in for the Congressional Medal of Honor. The battalion commander has already pushed it up to brigade. I just wanted you to know. That was a damned brave thing you did out there."

"Top, where is Rolley's... I mean, where is Sergeant Zwyrkowski's body?"

"The Graves Registration Unit here in Phu Bai," the Sergeant Major said.

"Can I go home on the plane with him?"

There was a long pause.

"If there is any way possible, son, I will make it happen, but you need to get released from this hospital first."

Buck's hair was freshly cut, his jump boots spit-shined, and he wore his dress summer khakis that day as he walked up the ramp of the C-141 beside Rolley's casket. The soldiers loading the caskets wore clean green fatigues and baseball caps, but they maintained a stern solemnity as they strapped casket after casket to the floor of the aircraft. After a while an airman came down through the rows of flag-draped caskets and raised the rear ramp.

Although he did his best not to let it show, Buck walked with a slight limp. It was the stitches in his hip. Lost in a world of shock and grief, he was on auto-pilot, going through the motions and hoping to do the right things. The Army had given him orders for escort duty, and he was accompanying Rolley's body home to Illinois where he was to meet with a military honor guard and attend the funeral.

The big jet lifted off the runway and climbed into the sky while Buck peered through the window. Below, the distant paddies and jungles disappeared as the plane climbed into the clouds. He should have been elated, but he wasn't. Back there, still on the ground, were TJ, Lizard, Doc Gilbert, and Blanch. It was as if he were running away, abandoning the men who had stood beside him in the worst of circumstances. He was leaving them with the unfinished business of trying to survive in a paradoxical war with no possible good outcome. And if individual survival was the only achievable victory, his felt more like a loss. He felt an unexplainable anger.

Trying to make sense of all that had happened since February was to walk a maddening maze of dead-end thoughts. Crowfoot, Rolley, and Blondie had to have known they were taking a terrible gamble when they volunteered to recon toward the pagoda that day. It simply didn't make sense. They were seasoned veterans. And who was to blame? Was it Mallon, the colonel Rolley called "the white knight," or was it the politicians in Washington? And Buck knew he could have done more. He had the experience to know they were doing something risky. He could have stepped up and spoken out, but he didn't.

Blondie, by some miracle of God, had lived, but he lost part of his left hand and would be hospitalized for several months. Henderson, too, had been severely wounded, and likely wouldn't make it. He had been struck by the same machine gun round that killed Lieutenant Mallon. In all, the platoon lost four men that afternoon, along with six wounded. Buck could only wonder why he was going home, while Crowfoot, Rolley, and the others died and Blondie was permanently maimed.

His thoughts were a jumbled confusion of flashbacks. He remembered that day on the plane at Travis Air Force Base when he first met Rolley, and he thought of Crowfoot with the rangy body of a dark-eyed wolf, leading them through the jungles. And his thoughts of those final good-byes to Janie earlier that morning still worried him. It was a constrained and awkward few minutes where he promised to stay in touch. Even their final parting kiss was devoid of the passion that they had so eagerly shared in recent months. It was as if he had died inside. She saw his pain, and again said those words: "It'll be okay, Buck. You'll see."

18

THE FUNERAL DETAIL

Illinois, October 1968

After several days in transit, Buck reported to a National Guard Armory in a town south of Chicago. He was told to meet with the soldiers there who were performing Rolley's Military Funeral. The town bustled with workday activity and seemed unaware of the funeral taking place less than twenty miles away in the country. The air was cool, almost crisp, something Buck hadn't felt in almost a year, and the trees were emblazoned with their full autumn colors. The leaves of the silver maples along the sidewalk were turned inside out by the breeze, fluttering and sparkling in the new sun. Buck walked into the armory to find a sergeant with his feet propped on a desk.

"I'm here to meet with the detail for Sergeant Zwyrkowski's funeral."

The sergeant, an E-5, dropped his feet to the floor and sat up, obviously studying Buck's uniform for rank insignia. Buck had changed into his dress greens.

"Damned, you caught me off-guard. I thought you were a general or something."

Buck studied the young sergeant behind the desk. He, too, wore dress greens, but his shoes were scuffed, the brass insignia on his uniform was tarnished and his hair was long and unkempt.

"Uhh, yeah. They went up the street for coffee and donuts. Have a seat, Specialist. They'll be back in a little while."

The sergeant grabbed a paper from the desk and studied it as if it were something important. After a moment, Buck nodded. "I have a rental car. I believe I'll go get a cup of coffee, too."

"I'm not sure where they went, but the guys are in two green Ford LTDs. If you see them, tell them to get back here, because we need to be leaving soon."

Buck already knew this, and he drove up the highway into town where he spotted the two Army sedans parked in front of a restaurant. When he walked inside he found seven men in uniforms seated at two tables. They looked like their sergeant back at the armory: wrinkled uniforms, scuffed shoes, and long hair. Buck walked to the tables where they sat.

"Your sergeant said for you guys to go back to the armory, now."

The men eyed him carefully, their eyes scanning the Purple Heart, Bronze and Silver Stars and other ribbons pinned above his pocket. After a few moments one of them responded. "Don't worry about him. That's Eddie. He just made buck sergeant—thinks he's a fucking general, now. Pull up a chair and have some coffee."

"Where are the men for the flag detail and the bugler?" Buck asked.

"That's just some gung-ho lifers who come in from somewhere out of town. They'll meet us at the cemetery. We do the twenty-one-gun salute. They do everything else."

Buck nodded and glanced out the restaurant window. There was little traffic. It was still early, but the lights were already lit in a variety store across the street.

"I'm going to pass on the coffee. I need to run across the street and get some things. I'll meet you guys back at the armory."

Buck walked into the variety store, and the clerk behind the counter greeted him. "Can I help you, sir?"

"Yes, I need a couple cans of black shoe polish, some shoe brushes and a can of brass polish. And do you know where there's a barber shop and a sporting goods store?"

"Sure. The barber shop is up the street about a block or so on the left, and Enderson's Sporting Goods is a little further up on the same side. There's a sign out front shaped like a fish."

After purchasing polish and brushes, Buck thanked the clerk and drove to the sporting goods store. The man behind the counter greeted him as he walked inside. Buck eyed a long glass case containing pistols and rifle scopes.

"Looking for a handgun, today?" the man asked.

"What do you have that's affordable?"

The clerk slid the glass door open on the back of the case and took out a 1911 Model Colt .45 automatic. "I have this army surplus .45 for a hundred and fifty bucks. It's a little rough, but it shoots."

He handed the pistol across the counter to Buck, who pulled open the slide action and examined the weapon.

"Throw in a box of shells and you have a deal."

The old man shrugged. "You got it. You got some I.D.?"

When Buck got back to the armory, the seven men had returned from the restaurant and already drawn their M-14s. He motioned their young sergeant into an adjoining room.

"Where are your officers and senior NCOs?" he asked.

"The ones on duty went into Chicago to meet with some people. We're going to march in a Veteran's Day Parade up there. Why?"

"So, you're the ranking person in charge here?"

"Yeah, why?"

Buck gave him the bag containing the brushes and polish.

"What's this?"

"I want you to have your men polish their shoes and their brass with that stuff. When they're done, we're all going up the street to the barber shop and get haircuts."

"You're fucking kidding, right?"

Buck swallowed hard as he fought back his anger.

"Sergeant, for the last eight months, while you and your men have been living the good life, Sergeant Zwyrkowski and I have been in the Republic of Vietnam fighting a war. Our platoon has taken over sixty percent casualties, and the man you're burying today was my platoon sergeant. He was also my best friend, and he died in my arms."

Buck rested his hand on the forty-five in his waistband. The sergeant's eyes bulged as he looked down at the weapon.

"You and these bastards you call soldiers *will* give him and his family the proper respect they deserve by cleaning up your uniforms, cutting your hair, and polishing your brass, or we will all go to hell together. Do you understand?"

Buck felt tears pooling in his eyes, and the sergeant's face paled.

"Yeah, yeah. No problem, dude. It's okay. Just stay cool."

The sergeant walked into the room where the others were watching television. He tossed the bag on the table.

"Okay, guys, gather 'round. We're going to have a little shoeshine and brass polishing party before we go."

"What the fuck?" one of the men said.

"Just shut up and do it, Tony."

The sergeant opened a can of shoe polish and began brushing it on his shoes. The others joined him—all except the one he called Tony. He sat watching the TV. Buck walked toward him.

"Wait a minute," the sergeant said. Buck stopped and looked back at him. "Please, let me handle this."

The sergeant turned toward the man still watching the TV. "Tony, get your ass over here, now, and polish your shoes, or I'm putting you on report."

The soldier jumped to his feet. "You got to be fucking kidding me."

"Don't give me any shit, Tony. Just do it."

Buck stood by, and when the men finished polishing their shoes and the brass on their uniforms, they put their rifles into the trunks of the cars.

"I'll lead in my car," Buck said to the sergeant.

A few minutes later he pulled up to the front of the barbershop and got out. The other two cars pulled in and parked beside him. The doors opened and shut as the soldiers got out with quizzical looks.

"Let's go, men," Buck said. "Everyone inside. We're going to get a haircut and look sharp for this detail."

The men milled about on the sidewalk, gathering around their sergeant. One with longish blond hair glared at Buck while he spoke to his sergeant. "Damn it,

Eddie, you know I play in the band, and I'm not cutting my hair to please this fucking lifer."

"Then please yourself," Buck said. "Do as you are told, or I'll see you're put on active duty with immediate deployment to Vietnam."

"You can't do that," the soldier said.

The soldier was calling his bluff. Buck doubled-down.

"No, but I have friends in your chain of command who can. It's your choice."

"Come on, guys," the sergeant said. "It's not like we don't have to get trimmed once a month anyway."

Grumbling and muttering, the men filed into the barbershop where two barbers began trimming their hair. The last man to get into the barber chairs was Tony.

"What about your sideburns?" the barber asked.

"Leave 'em," Tony muttered.

He eyed Buck.

"Take them off," Buck said.

"Fuck you!" Ripping away his barber's cape, Tony lunged from the chair.

"No!" The young sergeant stepped forward, grabbing him around the shoulders. "No, man, Tony. Trust me. This guy is...well... Look, just get back in the chair. Please?"

Tony looked over the sergeant's shoulder with a burning glare.

"Come on," the sergeant said. "Just get back in the chair, and let's get through this. Okay?"

With his eyes fixed on Buck, Tony slowly backed to the chair and sat.

Buck looked at the barber. "Take off the sideburns."

The cemetery was in a hilly wooded area, quiet except for the subdued voices of the gathering mourners. Buck met Rolley's parents and his teenage sister. The girl was a beautiful young woman with eyes like Rolley's. Her parents clung to one another, red-eyed and seemingly lost in a grief only parents could feel. Buck surprised himself by maintaining a stoic demeanor while talking with them. Not once did his voice crack. Not once did he shed a tear. It was important, because it reflected the man Rolley had made him become.

He told them how he had first met him on the flight over to Vietnam, and how he had served under him the entire time. He told them about their friendship, Rolley's inspiring leadership and his unselfish bravery. He told them everything positive he could think of, anything that might somehow assuage their grief. And when he was done, he hoped the least he had accomplished was to leave them believing their son's life had not been wasted—that it had mattered.

"Would you introduce yourself and say something about our son to the people here?" the father asked. He motioned to the family members sitting under the tent and the large crowd standing all around. "I mean—it would mean a lot to his mother and I."

Buck didn't blink, nor did he let them see the slightest indication of his shock and surprise. These were smart people—people whose son was so much smarter than he could ever hope to be. He wasn't sure what to say. It was an enormous responsibility, but prepared or not, it was now his. He nodded, and when the priest motioned to him, he stepped forward and removed his cap.

> "My name is Patrick Marino. I served under Rolley. He was my squad leader and my platoon sergeant in Vietnam. Rolley, Roland Zwyrkowski, was a paratrooper and a warrior like none I've ever known. More importantly, he was a leader whose service to his nation and his men deserves more than what I can say here today. He was my friend, and he taught me a lot about the things that are most important in life."
>
> Buck paused, bowed his head and cleared his throat. He had to keep it together. Rolley would have expected that of him.
>
> "I was allowed to escort him back home from Vietnam."
>
> Buck again paused, and swallowed hard.

"So, here we are, and I sincerely believe I am here today and still with the living, because of Rolley. And there are others from our platoon still back in Vietnam who are also alive because of the leadership and guidance Rolley gave us. And more importantly, more so than just surviving, at least for me, is that Rolley taught me how to be a soldier and a man.

"Sergeant Roland Zwyrkowski, Rolley, was my closest friend. He was only a few years older than me, but a whole lot wiser. His memory will live with me and the other men who served under him for the rest of our lives.

"I hope someday, God willing, to pass down to my children the traits of kindness and fearless loyalty that Rolley taught me."

With that, Buck stepped back and replaced his cap. When the prayers were done, the National Guardsmen rose to the occasion—shiny shoes, shiny brass and all. Marching in step to a nearby hillside, they stood at rigid attention. And when the time came, the seven riflemen fired their M-14s three times in perfect unison. The total silence that followed the twenty-one-gun salute seemed a terrible void, until from somewhere back in the trees the lone bugler began blowing taps. Buck fought the lump in his throat as he stood at attention beside the color guard.

Later that afternoon, Buck checked into a local hotel. His flight out of Chicago didn't depart until the following morning. After carefully hanging his uniform and changing into civvies, he got directions from the desk clerk to a local place called The Oak Street Tavern. The sun had set and the street lights were flickering to life when he parked his rental car out front. He needed the quiet time and a stiff drink.

A few after-work patrons wandered in, and Buck had finished two bourbons over ice when he heard someone cursing in a low voice somewhere back at the tables. He turned on his barstool and looked back. It was Tony. Sitting back in the shadows with two other men, he was still wearing part of his dress green uniform, but his shirt was hanging untucked and he had changed into white tennis shoes. Buck turned back to the bar, but thankfully there was a mirror behind the liquor bottles stretching the length of the wall.

After a few minutes, Tony stood and walked to a pay phone hanging near the restroom door. Buck watched him carefully in the mirror as he inserted coins, dialed, talked and hung up. He did this three more times, before returning to the table. A few minutes later, as Buck figured, other members of the guard group began arriving. A hissing of argumentative whispers ensued, and Buck decided he needed to go.

Standing, he paid the bartender as the whispers grew to a low crescendo behind him. In the mirror he saw Tony stand and pull the hand of one of his buddies away from his sleeve. He walked around the table and toward the door. Buck turned.

"You still packing your piece, lifer?"

Tony was obviously bent on a fight. Buck was emotionally exhausted.

"No, and I don't feel like fighting right now."

Tony laughed and turned to the others. "What'd I tell ya? Fucka ain't so badass when he's not wearing his uniform."

A man at the table stood. "Come on Tony, let it go." It was the sergeant.

"No, Eddie. We ain't on duty now, and this asshole is mine."

"Why did you call them here?" Buck asked, motioning toward the other men at the table.

"I called them so they could watch me kick your ass."

Only after having several drinks and calling his buddies did Tony seem to have worked up his courage. Buck eyed him. He was a coward and not worth his time.

"Well, you wasted their time. I'm not fighting." With that he pushed past Tony to get to the door. The stinging slap on his jaw was more surprising than damaging as Buck spun to face him. Rolley's funeral had drained every last emotion from his body, and Buck's response surprised even himself. He paused, and although angered, he simply glared at the stocky guardsman in silence.

"You pussy. If you ain't fighting, you're going to apologize. Say it! Tell us all you're sorry."

Despite growing lightheaded with a pulse of adrenaline, Buck remained calm.

"Sorry, I had to..." He couldn't finish. Turning, he started for the door, but a jarring jolt to his butt sent him stumbling forward.

"See. I told yuss guys I was going to kick his ass."

The two shots of bourbon and a flood of adrenaline had eliminated the last of Buck's restraint. He lunged, catching his opponent flatfooted. The two men sprawled on the floor, and Buck grabbed for the man's throat. He realized Tony was pulling something from his pants pocket. A switchblade clicked open beside Buck's face. He grabbed the wrist with both hands and came hard with his knee into Tony's ribs. Raising the arm that held the switchblade, Buck rammed it into the edge of a table. It snapped with an audible crack as the knife skittered across the floor. The fight was over in seconds, and Tony curled on the floor holding his broken arm against his ribs. Buck sprang to his feet and faced the others. They stood in wide-eyed silence.

Tony regained his breath and groaned. No one moved. Buck exhaled and turned toward the door. Early the next morning he caught a flight out of Chicago that would eventually take him to Fayetteville, North Carolina, and the 82nd Airborne Division at Fort Bragg.

Buck was emotionally fried, and whatever stoicism he had displayed at the funeral was lost as tears filled his eyes and he continued hearing the bugler's taps. Even as he curled up and fell asleep on the plane, he saw the flag-draped casket that contained his friend, and he dreamt of the war that had taken Rolley's life—a war that was a hard-fought struggle of futility and death.

That afternoon when Buck reported to the replacement company, headquarters battalion of the 82nd Airborne at Bragg, he realized something was up. The captain told him to take a seat in an adjacent room and disappeared. Buck sat, first for thirty minutes, then more, before he dozed. He was dreaming of Janie and their R&R when something jolted him awake. Through the open door he saw the clerk in the next room standing at rigid attention and saluting someone who was obviously a high-ranking officer.

After a while the clerk, a sergeant, stepped into the room. "Ugh, Specialist Marino?" It was the tone of the sergeant's voice that caught his attention. It was one of respect. "The captain wants to see you in his office."

Buck examined his uniform, smoothed the wrinkles and walked into the captain's office. He stood at rigid attention but cut his eyes toward another soldier sitting in the room. He was in a chair on the opposite wall. Buck's eyes did a double-take when he saw his rank. The soldier wore the insignia of a full bird colonel.

"At ease, Marino. Take a seat," the captain said. "This is Colonel Allen, the division XO."

The colonel leaned forward. "Specialist Marino, anything you say to us, stays here in this room. What I want from you is the truth. I have nothing to do with the Judge Advocate's command. I'm not saying I won't hold you accountable, but I *do* have your best interest in mind. Now, tell me what the hell happened up there in Illinois. There are some pissed-off people up there wanting your head on a platter."

"Sir, Sergeant Zwyrkowski was my Acting Platoon Sergeant when he was killed in Vietnam. I carried him off the battlefield, and he was my closest friend in this world. I was wounded for a second time in the same action, and my CO let me escort his body back to the United States for burial."

"I understand, Specialist Marino. You have my deepest sympathies," the colonel said. "Right now, I want you to focus on what happened in Illinois."

"Sir, the soldiers at the National Guard armory looked like a bunch of ragamuffins. I made them polish their shoes and their brass, and I made them get haircuts."

"Did you assault anyone?"

"I roughed up one named Tony after the funeral, sir. He jumped me in a bar. I was only defending myself."

"I would say a double-compound fracture of his arm, two broken ribs and a collapsed lung exceed the definition of 'roughing up,'" the colonel said.

"He pulled a switchblade knife on me, sir."

The captain and the colonel eyed one another, and the colonel glanced down at a notepad in his lap.

"No mention of that here," he said.

"Sir, I was only trying to disable him enough to get the knife away from him. The fight couldn't have lasted more than ten or fifteen seconds."

"Did you have a .45 automatic with you at the time?"

"No, sir."

"Did you have one earlier in the day?"

"Yes, sir."

"Did you draw it or threaten anyone with it?"

"No, sir, but I suppose there was the implied threat."

The colonel nodded. "Did you verbally threaten anyone?"

"A few hours before the funeral I told their sergeant that if he and his men didn't give Rolley—Sergeant Zwyrkowski and his family—the respect they deserved by cleaning up their uniforms, we would all go to hell together."

"Did you have the .45 at that time?"

"It was in my waistband, sir."

The colonel eyed him carefully. "I understand you were wounded in the hip. How is that coming along?"

"It's a little sore, sir. The stitches haven't been taken out."

"Send Specialist Marino over to Womack for a physical exam, Captain," the colonel said.

He turned back to Buck. "You'll be billeted here at Headquarters Company until this issue is resolved. I can't make you any promises, but we'll do our best. You'll have no extra duty and are free to come and go as long as you make morning formations each day. Hopefully, I can let you know something in a few days."

Two days later the CO sent for Buck. He was not a mind-reader, but Buck sensed something was about to be tossed into his lap. Whether it was a grenade or an honorable discharge, he didn't have a clue. The captain would have been a good poker player. Buck sensed it wasn't altogether good, but there might also be some sort of reprieve forthcoming.

"Have a seat, Marino," the captain said. "What are your plans as far as the military?"

"I want to serve out my remaining time and go home."

The captain nodded and pressed his lips together.

"We're having a problem resolving the issue in Illinois. Look, I can't say I wouldn't have reacted the same way, but apparently that fellow from the armory you *roughed up* is well-connected. Even after we told them you were under consideration for the Medal of Honor, a district attorney and some civilian big shots are still pushing the Guard chain of command for a Courts Martial.

"What do you think will happen, sir?"

"What do you think about returning to Vietnam to serve your remaining time?"

"Will that prevent me getting court martialed?"

"No guarantees, but I believe it will."

"Do I have to go back to a line company?"

"What do you want to do?"

Buck shook his head. "Sir, anything is better than walking around tripping booby-traps and walking into ambushes. Are there any recon slots available?"

"I'll get with the colonel, and we'll see what we can do. Don't unpack your bags."

Buck was growing antsy. He had visited Special Forces friends at Smoke Bomb Hill, wandered through the PX, and driven out to the Sicily and Normandy Drop Zones to watch the 82nd make jumps. Three days had come and gone when a sergeant came to him and told him to report to the CO's office. It came almost as a relief, and he all but ran to get there. After returning Buck's salute, the captain told him to take a seat.

"I've got some bad news and some good news. The good news first. We were able to get you orders for the Ranger LRRP Company with the Hundred and First at

Camp Eagle back in Vietnam. We were also able to get you a slot that came open at the MAC-V Recondo School at Nha Trang. There's a hell of a waiting list, so we were pretty damned lucky. The school is run by 5th Special Forces. It's tough as hell, but you will get thorough training there and you'll be well ahead of anyone who hasn't. Problem is the class starts in four days. We have people jumping through hoops to get your travel arrangements in order. You may need to report directly to the school before going to your new unit. We'll see.

"Now, for the bad news. That incident in Illinois may be cause for your recommendation to receive the Medal of Honor to be—well, modified. This wasn't anything done by us here at the 82nd or by your previous chain of command in Vietnam. Let's just suffice to say we did our best, but the recommendation is that it be modified for you to receive the Army Distinguished Service Cross. That's still one hell of an award, and one you well deserve."

Buck gave the captain a one shoulder shrug. It no longer mattered. Nothing mattered, except that he was ready to get back to Nam. He couldn't explain it. It wasn't a simple compulsion. It was something that owned him. Not unlike the heroin addict who craves his next fix, all the while knowing it might be the one that kills him, Buck had to go back. There was no replacement for the adrenaline high of combat, but more importantly, there was unfinished business back in Nam. Rolley, Crowfoot, Romeo, and Dixie did not die for nothing. There somehow had to be a reckoning for someone. Despite everything that said otherwise, there had to be a way to put an ending on it, put it to rest and move on. Only then could he get on with the rest of his life.

"When will I leave?"

"I'm not sure yet. Make sure all your gear is packed and you're ready to travel. Check in at S-1 when you leave here, and make sure all your pay and shot records are squared away and up to date. Your orders are being typed up. We may be able to get you on a flight as early as this afternoon."

PART II

Combat drenches the soul in a river of adrenaline and blood, leaving a veteran forever afterward facing a random specter of mutilation and death. It returns in the night, stealing sanity and reinforcing the reality that tomorrow is never guaranteed. Nothing is ever again the same. Even while still young, the combat veteran feels old. It is as if his life has already been lived and he has nothing more to give. Combat changes a man until he doesn't recognize even himself. He wants to be normal, but he no longer knows what that is. His entire life is driven by some inescapable sense of desperation.

--*Rick DeStefanis*

19

THE CENTRAL HIGHLANDS

October 1968

When Buck's military charter landed in Vietnam he had two days remaining before he was scheduled to report to the MACV Recondo School at Nha Trang. Wasting no time, he caught a flight up to Phu Bai. Within hours he was hurrying down a road toward the 22nd Surgical Hospital. It took only a few minutes before he found her.

Janie was sitting at a table in the shade writing a letter. She glanced up at him, then turned back to writing her letter. A moment later she sat bolt upright and looked again. Screaming, Janie jumped to her feet and tripped over her chair as she lunged into his arms. Locking a leg around his, she clung to Buck's neck, kissing him passionately.

"What are you doing here?"

Tears streamed from her eyes, and she trembled in his arms. Gazing up at him, she searched his eyes. She was the most delicate creature he had ever held, but she also possessed an intuitive sixth sense that seemed almost supernatural. She already sensed it, and it wasn't going to be easy explaining what had happened.

Buck ran his fingers through her soft blond hair, and he couldn't imagine being any more attached to a person than he was to Janie. How an otherwise intelligent and beautiful young woman could become so totally infatuated with him was beyond reason. Now, he was left with a sense of responsibility that required he protect her heart, but he had to tell her the truth. With the greatest willpower he could muster, Buck freed himself from her embrace and held her hands in his.

"I'm going through some training down at Nha Trang for my next duty assignment."

She wrinkled her brows. "Nha Trang? What's down there?"

He thumbed a tear from her cheek. "The MAC-V Recondo School."

"Recondo? But that's…. You're not supposed to go back to combat duty. You said that."

Unable to look into her eyes, Buck glanced off to one side. "I got into some trouble back in the States."

"What do you mean? What kind of trouble?"

"It was something stupid I did the night after Rolley's funeral." Buck took a deep breath. "I met a funeral detail of National Guardsmen at their armory, and…." By the time he finished telling his story the color had drained from Janie's cheeks and tears streamed from her eyes.

"This war…it has you, doesn't it?"

It was transparent to her that no matter what had happened, it was his choice. And it was true. If it hadn't been for the incident in Illinois, he would have found another reason to return. Buck couldn't turn his back on Nam and walk away. Janie was right, this war *did* have him, and during his short time back in the States he had peered into the darkened abyss of the future and seen nothing. He was determined to return, to stare the beast in the eye, to meet it face to face once again and take some measure of reparations for Rolley, Crowfoot, Romeo, Dixie, and the others who had given everything.

He looked into Janie's eyes. "What do you mean?"

"Oh, Buck, you're just too honest of a person to even try that."

She was beyond intelligent. She was a woman he couldn't lie to no matter how much he tried. He again looked over her shoulder, and she rested her head on his chest. A long minute passed, before she looked up at him.

"I'm going to postpone my DEROS and stay, so I can—"

"No!"

"Why not!? I want to be here, where we can at least see one another once in a—"

"No, Janie. Please. Just go home. Find a job somewhere as a nurse. You need to get out of this godforsaken place."

Janie looked up at him, and Buck gazed into her eyes. There were things she could say that she mercifully didn't. It was true. In her own clairvoyant way she always seemed to know exactly what he was thinking.

"I already have a job offer from the hospital in Missoula, but I'd rather stay here to be near you."

"Just because I'm a fool doesn't mean we both have to be. Go home. I promise I will come home when I can."

He could say anything, but Janie's eyes were open windows to her soul, and she needed only to respond with a silent gaze for him to know what she was thinking. He saw in them the fear and doubt.

"I mean it," he said. "I will take care of myself and do everything I can to come home to you."

Getting through the MAC-V Recondo School was not automatic, but the patrolling techniques came almost as second nature for Buck, thanks to his cousins back in Mississippi. He remembered that first incident far back in the river bottoms when he was thirteen years old. This was before getting his nickname, and he still went by Patrick. Having taken three young gray squirrels with his .22 rifle, he was headed home where his mom had promised to fry them for supper with cheese grits, gravy, and biscuits.

He was walking along the edge of a "drain," which was what they called the huge dry ravines created by the powerful runoff in early summer when the flooded Mississippi dropped back out of the woods and into its banks miles away. Other than the cane thickets and piles of driftwood, Buck could see for several hundred yards down through the wooded bottoms. The first yellow leaves of October had begun drifting from the trees. He still had nearly a half-mile to go to reach the river levee, and was walking steadily when a loud crack snapped past his head.

Patrick had never heard a rifle round pass this close, but he instinctively knew what it was as he jumped into the drain. Running sixty yards down the drain, he spotted a cane thicket on the same side from where he had leapt. Climbing up the steep bank, he slipped into the thicket. There he studied the woods, spotting almost immediately two of his older cousins sneaking to the edge of the drain.

The boys stood glancing about and scratching their heads. It was Wade and Nick McKinney, and he could barely hear their voices. "Don't reckon you hit him, do ya?" the younger Nick asked.

"Nah. I just shot close enough to scare him. He's probably still running, little chicken-shit. He's probably halfway home by now."

The older Wade was a senior in high school and was carrying a deer rifle, but Patrick found his anger overwhelming. Near them was a huge cypress tree, and he circled to put the tree between him and his two cousins before creeping back toward them. When he stepped from behind the cypress the two teenagers' eyes widened. Obviously rattled, Nick threw up his hands, while Wade brandished his rifle and stumbled backwards nearly falling into the drain.

"How'd you get behind us, you little shit?" a red-faced Wade asked.

"Don't matter. How come you shot that round past me?" At thirteen years old, Patrick wasn't near as sure of himself as he hoped to make them think.

"You're huntin' on posted land, dago."

"I'm hunting on granddaddy's land."

"Yeah, and he don't want no dagos on his land. Just ask your mama."

"We'll see," Patrick said. "Just be careful where you're shooting that rifle."

With that he turned to walk away.

"Hey, dago."

Patrick stopped but didn't look back.

"Those are our squirrels you got there."

With his .22 snug under his arm and pointed at the ground, Patrick turned slowly.

"No, they're my mama's, but you can try to take them if you want."

"Come on, Wade," Nick said. "Let the little shit go."

Wade gave a nervous laugh, while Patrick only hoped his bluff had worked.

"Go ahead, dago," Wade said. "Get your ass out of here, and don't let us catch you killing any of our deer, either."

Patrick turned and walked away, and later his mother suggested that it would be better if he didn't return to her father's land. She offered no explanation, but he knew. It was one of his first and hardest lessons on life and humanity. His mother had been ostracized by her own father for marrying an Italian truck farmer.

For his next birthday, Patrick asked for a bow and a set of arrows with broad heads. Every fall for the next four years he took a couple of deer from his grandfather's land with the bow, and he did it right under his cousin's noses. In the process he learned what it took to move undetected through wooded terrain. The patrolling techniques he learned on Hon Tre Island near Nha Trang merely honed and solidified his abilities. There now remained one final test—an actual long range reconnaissance patrol in enemy territory with one of his instructors.

This was the final exam, the make-it-or-break-it test that determined if Buck and his classmates were fit to be LRRP team members. He'd been through immediate action drills so many times until his reactions became automatic. He had rappelled from choppers and ridden the strings out of the jungle in a Swiss seat. Now, he was ready. All his gear was taped and silenced, his CAR-15 meticulously cleaned, and his face was blackened.

The Special Forces instructor accompanying the five-man team was Sergeant First Class Garrity, but he went by "Irish." Having served two tours with Special Forces Strike and Hatchet teams, this was his third tour in Nam, and he was all business.

The previous day the entire team had done a flyover of the ops area. Their visual recon included scouting possible insertion points from the chopper. All went well, and after observing each man give a detailed mission briefing to the rest of the team, Irish inspected their equipment. When he finished, he simply nodded. He was satisfied. A single Huey was on the LZ, its rotors already churning as the pilots went through their checklist.

The team would rotate assignments during the five-day patrol, and Buck started as the assistant team leader. He also packed one of the PRC-25 radios in his rucksack. Buck, Jack Minders from the 173rd Airborne, and a young lieutenant named Percy from the 23rd Infantry all had combat experience. The other two men, Jack Lefler and Don Baker, had come straight out of Jump and NCO schools at Benning. Minders started off as the team leader, with Buck on point and the lieutenant as tail-gunner. The tail-gunner guarded the team's back trail and covered their tracks. Irish assigned himself to walk behind Buck and Minders.

The chopper lifted out of Nha Trang and climbed across the winding Song Tau River. They were headed approximately twenty clicks westward to the highlands just beyond the Highway One corridor. There they would recon several trails coming down out of the mountains into a broad area encompassing the Suoi Cat Valley. The cool air of the highlands blew through the chopper cabin bringing a brief respite from the thick, humid heat of the coastal plains. Buck was ready, and confident that he could handle anything they required of him, but there came that ever-present voice from his past. It was Rolley saying he didn't know what he didn't know. Only experience could teach him that.

Buck was again feeling young and stupid, knowing he had to keep his eyes open and his mind clear. He'd promised Janie to be careful, but for now, he had to put her out of his mind. He loved her, but he needed to focus on his job. There was no choice. If he hesitated, if he blinked, if he spent even one luxurious moment thinking about life in Montana with Janie, he could die, or worse, cause one of his buddies to die. He had to focus.

It seemed like a continuous diorama of roads, hamlets, and villages passing below. The area was more heavily populated than the mountains where he had fought in I-Corps. If the enemy seemed to know their every move west of Hue, here they no doubt knew even more. Below were more villages, many more people, and many more eyes. The vast array of roads, villages, and rice paddies stretched to the horizon. Buck gazed down in amazement. Hell, this place was so populated a soldier couldn't fart without it being reported to Hanoi.

The chopper crossed a mountainous area, then another dense area of villages and roads—the Highway One corridor. Up ahead was their destination, the foggy mountains of the Central Highlands. Buck couldn't help but think how many enemy eyes were in the villages below watching this lone helicopter and reporting it to enemy units in the mountains. The chopper dove earthward then climbed up a mountain valley.

A small clearing appeared at the top of the mountain. The chopper dipped and made a tight turn, flaring as it dropped into the opening. The pilot hovered a few feet above the ground before slowly lifting the chopper up over the trees. It was the first of two false insertions. The chopper climbed over the next ridge then turned down another small valley back toward Highway One. With an abrupt left turn, the pilot steered the helicopter over another small opening on the side of the next ridge. The team jumped from the skids, and the chopper shot skyward.

Buck glanced left and right, then at Minders. Minders silently motioned for him to take the point and move out. Soundlessly, they moved single file into the jungle. After moving a few hundred feet into dense cover, Buck stopped and listened. The sound of the chopper became more distant, before momentarily growing louder—the second false insertion. Buck glanced around at his fellow team members. A fine sheen of sweat covered their green and black camo faces. There wasn't a hint of a breeze or even the hint of a sound. This void of sound was his world. There was no mumbling, no canteen cups banging—nothing but silence. For the first time in Nam he felt more like a hunter than the hunted.

Buck clicked the mic button on the radio twice sending the "all clear" signal to the chopper still circling somewhere in the distance. Surrounded by a solid wall of visually impenetrable jungle, they were on their own now. Training dictated they needed to put some distance between themselves and the insertion point. After checking the prearranged azimuth with his compass, Buck motioned for the team to follow. They crossed over the ridge, waded a shallow stream and quickly climbed the opposite ridge. They had gone barely four hundred meters when there came a faint shuffling sound from somewhere on the slope above. Buck threw up his hand and went to a knee. Whatever sound there had been was brief, faint, and unrecognizable.

It was almost as if he had heard nothing—something easy to dismiss had it not been for the sixth sense he had developed hunting his grandfather's land. He glanced back at Minders. The team leader had also heard it, and it *was* something—nothing more than a faint rustling in the brush above, probably a monkey or some other wild animal, but it was something they couldn't ignore.

The team had become bunched up, and Irish motioned the others back, while Buck and Minders waited, listening. Ten minutes passed, and Buck came to his feet. He turned to signal the team ahead. *SSSH-HHRACKKK*! It felt as if his rucksack had been struck by a sledge hammer as he was spun sideways and fell backward.

"You hit?" Minders hissed.

Buck shook his head. "Check my ruck," he whispered.

"Can anyone tell where that sonofabitch is at?" Irish whispered.

No one answered.

SSSSHRRRRAACCKKK!! Another round cracked in their midst.

Buck raised his CAR-15 and fired a burst up the ridge. Minders examined his rucksack. There was a sniper somewhere up the ridge targeting them, and he was close, very close.

"The good news is he missed your Claymore, but the radio is shot to shit."

Minders was grinning. Buck could only shake his head at the team leader's nonchalant sense of humor. Had the sniper's round struck the Claymore the entire LRRP team would likely have been wiped out. Buck shed his rucksack and rolled to his right, crawling into the roots of a nearby tree. He motioned with a cupped hand to Minders his intention to flank the sniper.

SSSHHRRACCKK—ZZZZZZZIIIIIIIINNNGGG. The bullet ricocheted with a whine out across the little valley. There came a low moan from one of the team members. Someone was hit, but now Buck had the sniper's position pinpointed. He was almost on top of them—no more than sixty meters away, but there was too much under-growth between them. There was no time for hesitation.

Snaking out of the tree's roots, Buck crawled into a shallow depression. Rapidly but silently, he crawled uphill through clumps of scrub palms as he attempted to flank the sniper. The team was now sixty meters below and to his left. The sniper's hide had to be within a few meters of where Buck lay, but there was no sign of him.

He held his breath and listened. The hillside was a solid mass of vegetation. Nothing stood out. His only advantage was the sniper likely still had his attention focused on the team below. Slowly and carefully Buck stood and took a step. Again, he paused.

There came the slightest tick of a metallic sound—someone slowly chambering a round with a bolt action rifle. It was no more than four or five feet away, directly in front of him. It had to be the sniper, but Buck had gotten too close to toss a frag. Raising his CAR-15, he sprayed the underbrush to his front. As he fired, he stepped forward, one, two, then three steps before nearly falling over the wounded sniper. The enemy soldier was struggling to climb from a spider hole. Buck fired several more rounds, and the soldier slumped back into the hole.

Kneeling beside the body, he picked up the sniper's weapon. They had displayed one like it during his previous week's training at Nha Trang. It was a Soviet Dragunov sniper rifle with a scope. This wasn't one of the local boys. The clip-clop sound of sandals and someone running came from the ridge above. Buck dropped the sniper's weapon and swung his CAR-15 up the hill. He fired two rounds before the bolt on his CAR-15 locked back. It was a stupid rookie mistake. He'd forgotten to reload with a fresh magazine.

Quickly ejecting the empty magazine, he inserted another and waited. A moment later Minders and Irish crawled up beside him.

"Whatcha got?" Minders whispered.

Buck pointed to the spider hole. Both men did a double-take. They hadn't seen it until Buck pointed it out.

"I think there's another one up the ridge," Buck said. "I heard him running."

"Okay," Minders said. "We're obviously compromised. We need to un-ass this AO and get over into the next valley. Problem is we don't have a radio. Help me pull this sumbitch out of the hole, and let's check him for documents."

They grabbed the dead sniper by his clothes and pulled him from the spider hole.

"What happened to the other radio?" Buck asked.

Irish spoke quietly while Minders went through the dead man's pockets. "A bullet hit it, too."

"What about Lefler?"

Lefler had been packing the second radio.

"He took some shrapnel in his shoulder and neck, but I think he's okay for now. We'll see." Minders stuffed some papers he took off the body into his pocket. "Grab this bastard's weapon, and let's get the hell out of here."

With both radios destroyed and the enemy likely searching for them, the team had to move quickly. A thunderstorm erupted overhead, helping mask the sounds of their movement as Buck led them rapidly eastward along the ridge. Pushing through heavy cover, they put as much distance as possible between themselves and the insertion point. When the team finally came to a stop they had moved nearly three clicks. A light rain was still falling. Minders and Irish crouched beside Buck on a high knoll overlooking the next valley.

Buck pointed to a small village several hundred meters below. It was barely visible beneath the jungle canopy. They lay studying it for nearly twenty minutes while the morning sun broke through and a brisk breeze began blowing. The wind would also help mask the sound of their movements. An ocean of swirling elephant grass and a winding stream separated them from the village.

"What do you want to do, Team Leader?" Irish asked Minders as he examined Lefler's neck. It was wrapped with a blood-soaked bandanna.

"You good?" he whispered.

"Yeah. I don't think it's serious."

"Maybe, maybe not. We'll see," Irish whispered. He turned to Minders. "My suggestion would be we get this man some medical care. We can start over again tomorrow."

Minders nodded and motioned for the rest of the team to gather closer. "That village down there isn't on the map. I think we inserted right in the middle of an enemy staging area. We've got a whole bunch of these little fuckers around us. I want to circle back a couple hundred meters and set up watch on our back trail. We'll put the Claymores out. If they're following us, we'll put a hurt on them and E&E eastward from here. The TOC will send a chopper when we don't check in, but that'll probably be at least a couple hours. We're on our own till then."

Escape and Evasion training was a big part of AIT back at Fort Polk, and again during LRRP training, but Buck hadn't realized how soon it would come into play. Now, Minders was saying it, and Irish was nodding. It was a reality. The Tactical Operations Center would send a chopper out to look for them when they missed the scheduled sit-rep. Until then, they had no other choice. Escape and evasion was their only means of survival.

After circling back, the team set out the Claymores and waited. Watching their back trail, they hoped an ambush wouldn't be necessary. With both radios down, they were in a hairy situation, especially if they ran afoul of a large enemy unit. An hour passed, then another, but it remained quiet. Eventually, there came the distant buzz of a helicopter approaching. Irish moved the team back to the knoll, and when the chopper began circling the area, he fired a starburst, popped smoke and laid out a panel. After several passes and confirmation of the team's identity, the chopper hovered over the knoll while the men climbed aboard.

A shower of green tracers came from the village below, and the door gunner returned fire as the chopper scooted down the valley and out of range.

Back at the MAC-V training compound in Nha Trang, Buck rested. The mission debriefing by Irish affirmed his confidence in the team. Despite the aborted mission, they were going back into the same area the next morning, minus Lefler. This time Buck would act as the team leader. The plan was to get a better look at the village they had discovered and possibly call in some airstrikes if it was as they suspected, strictly an enemy compound.

Although the sky was heavy with clouds, the weather held that morning as they inserted once again a few clicks from the village. Lieutenant Percy was on point with Minders walking slack as they moved off the LZ. Other than a mild breeze it was again quiet in the twilight beneath the jungle canopy. After ten minutes laying dog Buck nodded to Percy and clicked the mic twice to send the "all clear" signal to the chopper. They began climbing the ridge northward toward the next valley where the village was hidden.

Percy was cautious as he moved slowly and silently up the steep hillside. The baby-faced lieutenant was sharp, and Buck was glad he had put him on point. If all went well, they would reach the vicinity of the village by midafternoon.

The team had nearly reached the top of the mountain ridge when there came two distant shots from across the valley behind them. They went to a knee and waited, listening. A moment later another shot came from down the valley to the east and one from higher up the mountain to the west. It was something they had learned about only the week before. The enemy trail watchers were signaling one another. They had seen the chopper and knew a LRRP team was in the area. At the rear of the column Irish was helping Baker sweep the back trail. Buck turned and nodded to Percy to move out.

Only a sparse mottling of sunlight penetrated the trees overhead, and the men moved silently in an eerie underworld of shadows. After a few minutes, Percy again halted the column and signaled for Buck to come to the front. Before him was a well-used trail paralleling the crest of the ridge. It came from up on the mountain to the west and led eastward out toward the Suoi Cat Valley. Four-wide and rutted with tracks, it was obviously a main thoroughfare.

"Looks like we found what we were looking for," Buck whispered. "Let's cross and set up a watch while I contact the TOC. I've got a feeling they'll want us to watch this one for a day or two."

After crossing, Buck sent Percy and Minders up the ridge to find an observation post and set up the long range radio antenna. He watched up and down the trail while Irish and the tail-gunner stirred the mud on the trail to obliterate their footprints. When they were done, the three men turned and started up the hill, but there came voices from further up the trail. Someone was coming, and they were close. Too late to get further away, all three squatted in the underbrush less than ten meters from the trail.

Buck eased a fragmentation grenade from his pocket and cut his eyes toward Irish. Their eyes met and they both looked toward Baker. Baker was the wild card with no combat experience. He was rock-steady and calm. All three had their weapons at the ready. Then they were there, two men at the front of a column. Their body language wasn't tense, but neither man was being careless. Studying the trail at their feet, obviously searching for signs of anyone crossing, they walked slowly while scanning the surrounding jungle.

Buck could hear his heart thumping in his chest, so loud he feared the men on the trail would hear it. The first two passed, followed by twelve more. Buck smelled the ammonia-like body odor of the guerrillas as they passed, glancing about and seeming to look right through him and the two lurps squatted beside the trail. He now fully understood why the instructors refused to allow lurps to use insect repellents, soap, or anything with an unnatural odor.

He counted the enemy's weapons: Besides a rifle, one wore a pistol on his belt, two carried RPGs, three SKS rifles, eight AK-47s and one a Soviet RPK light machine gun. Several carried extra rounds for the RPGs. Seven were in nondescript shorts or black pajamas. The rest were in unmarked NVA uniforms. All carried haversacks or backpacks. After the enemy patrol passed, Buck realized he had been holding his breath the entire time. He panted as he scrambled with the others up the hill to where Percy and Minders were burrowed in a thicket of grass and scrub palms.

"Did you see them?" Buck whispered to Minders.

The sergeant nodded rapidly.

"You guys looked like you were sitting right beside them," Percy said.

"We were," Irish answered. He turned and looked expectantly at Buck.

"Okay," Buck said. "Let's finish erecting the antenna and contact the relay team."

Within minutes they got their orders. Hold tight and watch the trail the rest of the day and night. They would follow up with additional orders in the morning. A pitch black night followed with a veritable parade of shadows passing on the trail only forty meters below. It lasted till near daylight. The birds and monkeys were awakening around them when the team radioed in for the sit-rep. The relay team answered immediately.

"Roger, Lima Tango-One-Zero, Tango Oscar requires response from Irish. Are you guys up for trying a Papa Sierra of one of the northern visitors up there?"

Irish took the radio handset, glanced around at the team then put it to his ear.

"What the fuck are they talking about?" Minders asked.

Buck and the others shrugged.

"They want us to do a prisoner-snatch," Irish whispered, "but they want an NVA." He keyed the mic. "Roger, X-ray Alpha, this is Irish. I think we're up for it, but we'll need to relo closer to Echo Papa Two, and request assets on standby. This place is crawling with opportunity. Over."

"Roger, Irish. Tango Oscar sends: you take One-Zero position for continuation of the mission."

Buck and the others had run several prisoner-snatch drills during training, but here it was his first LRRP mission, not even yet out of actual training and they were preparing to try one. Prisoner snatches could get hairy in an instant. Buck watched and waited with the others while Irish studied his map. Finally he turned to them.

"Alright. They want me to take over as team leader, but I want to use this as a learning opportunity. Percy, tell me how you would set this thing up."

"Well," the young lieutenant said, "with the largest concentrations of the enemy up the mountain to the west and around that village to the north, I like your idea of using the secondary extraction point to the east."

"Outstanding, Lieutenant." He turned to Minders. "What's your take on it, Sergeant?"

"I agree. Relocating closer to the extraction point is smart, and I say we parallel the trail along the ridge till we find a good ambush point closer to the LZ."

"Good, good," Irish whispered. He turned to Buck. "You got anything to add?"

"I suppose they covered the most important things, but there are a couple things," Buck said.

"Go ahead," Irish said.

"Well, yesterday when that patrol passed us, the NVA regulars were walking at the center of the column, and one of them wore a sidearm. I figure he was an officer. If we have that opportunity again, I say we set our Claymores to blow up and down the trail to take out the front and back of the column and grab somebody in the middle. We might get lucky and capture an officer."

Irish pressed his lips together and nodded. "I like the way you think, boy."

"One more thing," Buck said. "We know the coordinates on that village, and that's probably where a lot of their people will come from when the shit hits the fan. I say we call in prearranged airstrikes on it and this trail too, as soon as we blow the ambush."

Irish grinned. "Damn it, son. I believe you have a future in this business. Plot the coordinates, and we'll call them in with our next sit-rep."

Buck smiled. If nothing else, ten months in Nam and hunting posted land as a kid had taught him the value of attention to the details. The LRRPs began a slow and tedious movement along the ridge as they paralleled the trail. After several hours Irish called them to a halt. The terrain had become slightly more open, and they were nearing the extraction point. Taking Lieutenant Percy, Irish slipped down the hill to examine the trail. They returned a few minutes later.

"We lucked out," he said. "The trail actually splits just below here, but there's a place up this way where we can see fifty or sixty meters in both directions. We can strap the Claymores to some trees, and we'll have pretty good cover. Let's get moving."

The sun had dropped into the trees at the top of the mountain by the time they were in position. The wait began and ended almost immediately when Baker signaled from the right. Not daring to move his head, Buck cut his eyes up the trail where a single point man stood motionless nearly sixty meters away. The soldier was wearing an NVA uniform. No one moved.

Several long seconds passed, and Buck began wondering if they had been spotted. Finally, the soldier scooped his hand forward at waist level to signal the others ahead. More soldiers came around the bend in the trail, all wearing NVA uniforms. The problem was determining how many more there were. Blowing a five-man ambush on a platoon-size or larger unit would be suicide.

The point man passed through the kill zone. Buck again cut his eyes up the trail. NVA soldiers were steadily rounding the curve—way too many. Irish sat cross-legged with a clacker in each hand, ready to fire the Claymores if necessary. The team's primary goal now was to remain undetected. The Claymores were masked with palm fronds, and the team was well hidden, but one inadvertent movement or one sharp-eyed enemy soldier could bring down an instant world of shit. A bead of sweat trickled into Buck's right eye. He dared not blink as he kept a mental tally of the enemy numbers and weapons as they passed by only a few meters away.

It was probably no more than three minutes, but it seemed like an hour had passed when the last man in the column finally disappeared down the trail. The sun had set, and the already dim light of the jungle was quickly fading into the nighttime shadows. The sky opened suddenly in a gush of pouring rain as Irish moved the team up the hill. There they lay dog the remainder of the night, shivering, wet and again listening to the sloshing sounds of enemy troops moving down the trail toward the valley.

20

THE REUNION

The 101st Airborne LRRPs

Buck was curled up against his rucksack on board a C-130 headed up to Phu Bai. By the time the training mission ended he was feeling a hundred years old and a lot smarter than he had five days earlier. The team managed a successful prisoner snatch, but it wasn't the prized NVA officer they had hoped for. A lone VC trail watcher had wandered into their midst and all but pissed his pants when the team stepped from the shadows on either side and pressed their weapons against his head.

The training, the activity, the sense of accomplishing something, all helped Buck regain a grip on life, but he still found himself in an emotionally desolate place when he thought about Rolley, Crowfoot, and the others. His thoughts of Janie were his only islands of sanity. She was his best hope. Janie was probably home by now, back in

Montana, wearing dresses or jeans, and enjoying just being alive for once. He wished he could be with her, if only for a few minutes, but that wasn't possible—at least for now.

He sat up, pulled a sheet of paper from his rucksack, and despite the jostling of the aircraft, he began writing a letter:

November 24, 1968

Dear Janie,

I know you still don't understand why I felt a need to come back here. I'm not sure I know the answer myself. Rolley and Crowfoot didn't have to die, that's the one thing I know for sure and maybe that's the reason I'm here again. Maybe I can make a difference for some of the men who are still trying to make it through this war. Hell, I don't know. We all tried our best, but when I read the newspapers it makes me just want to stay here forever. The people at home call us criminals. I don't know where the center of life lies anymore. Sorry. I don't mean to be so morose. That's a word Rolley taught me. He was the best friend I

ever had, besides you. Maybe when
I get back home you can help me
figure all this out and we can
make a better life for our kids.
Love,
Buck

When he finished, he reread the letter. It wasn't what Janie needed to get from him, especially now. He tore it up and stuffed the paper in his pocket. With the assassinations, riots, and all the other crap going on back home—not to mention her worries about him—she needed some good news. He pulled another piece of paper from the rucksack and began writing again:

November 24, 1968

Dear Janie,
*   Well, my training is done. I*
passed Recondo School, and now
I'll be going back to the Hundred
and First. I hope some of my old
buddies are still up there. I know
you have probably written, but
so far none of your letters have
arrived. Hopefully, when I get set-
tled in with my new unit they'll
come. I like what I am doing now.
It's much better. At least there's

some sense of control. The mon-
soons have begun again, and I
don't think I've ever seen it rain
so steadily for so long. Please send
me some pictures when you can.
Love,
Buck

Buck reported to the LRRP Company HQ early that afternoon. The First Sergeant opened his personnel file and read intently while Buck stood at ease. After several minutes he closed it and looked up.

"Some pretty high praise here from one of the MAC-V instructors. He thinks you're ready for a team leader slot. What do you think?"

"I'd rather work with an experienced team for a while, learn your SOPs and get to know some of the men."

The First Sergeant nodded slowly. "Don't worry. I'm not giving you one of my teams till you and I both know you're ready. Go back down the road to the second hooch on the right. That's Second Platoon. If Sergeant Robertson is there, tell him I need to see him."

Buck sloshed his way back down the road, through the steady onslaught of the monsoon rain. Walking through the sandbagged entrance into the huge tent, he found a dim interior lit by a couple lanterns. Several men in boxers or fatigue pants lounged around on the cots. Buck tossed his rucksack on an empty one.

"Who the hell are you?" a soldier asked.

"Buck Marino. I just reported in."

Another soldier in the shadows at the back of the tent beyond a low sandbagged wall jumped to his feet and came his way.

The first soldier pointed to Buck's rucksack. "Well, *Buck*, FNGs are expected to have some manners and ask where they can bunk. Take your shit to the back and find an empty cot."

The soldier's voice was laced with sarcasm, and it was obvious Buck was once again going to have to prove himself with another new unit.

"Buck?"

It was the man approaching from the shadows at the back of the tent. Buck turned and squinted in the darkness.

"TJ?"

"What the fuck are you doing here, mon?"

"What are *you* doing here?" Buck responded.

TJ grabbed him, wrapping his arm around his neck and turning toward the first soldier. "This ain't no FNG, Sarge. This is the guy I told you about, the one from my old unit who's up for the Medal of Honor."

Buck shook his head. "Sorry to disappoint you, buddy, but it was reduced to a DSC."

"What do you mean, mon. How can they do that?"

"I got into some trouble back in the States. I'll explain later."

The first soldier extended his hand. "Ron Robertson." He glanced at Buck's rucksack still on the adjacent cot. "Sorry. You can leave your gear there."

Buck shook his hand. "The First Sergeant said he needs to see you."

"Well, shit," Robertson said. "My fatigues were damned near dry."

Pulling the dripping poncho over his head, the team leader tossed it on the floor and called his men together. The monsoon rain still pounded the top of the big tent.

"The good news," Robertson said, "is that Marino's joining our team as the assistant team leader. The bad news is our new mission is in the hills on the western side of the A Shau."

The team leader unrolled a topo map.

"An as-yet-unidentified NVA regiment crossed over into the valley a week ago. The One-Oh-One has two battalions looking for them, but they've had no luck. Three of our teams are up there as well. If the weather breaks, we'll replace one of them. Mad Dog, you will be point man. Zorro, you're walking slack. I'll follow with the first radio, and Marino will be behind me with the second. Marshal, you'll be tail-gunner."

He spread the map on the cot.

"There'll be no fly-over recon. We're inserting on an LZ right here," he pointed to a tight circle of contour lines. "There's a line company already there. We'll depart from there and move to higher ground to give them some extra eyes in the area."

The briefing continued for another half-hour. Buck was told to draw a variety of new equipment that included a CAR-15, magazines, ammo, two Claymores, a couple blocks of C-4, a variety of fuses, smoke, frags, starbursts, carabiners, rope, blood expander, tiger-striped fatigues, compass, PRC-25 with a spare battery, a long range antenna, and a five-day supply of LRRP rations. He also requested a bayonet, which he began sharpening to a razor edge on both sides the way Crowfoot had taught him—a violation of Army SOP, but an invaluable tool for hand-to-hand combat. The rain slackened, and after a quick trip to the firing range to check out the CAR-15, he was ready.

Dawn the next morning S-2 reported only a fine mist of fog was hanging in the A Shau Valley. The mission was a "go." The team waited to board a slick on the acid pad, and Buck was reading the first letter he had gotten from Janie in weeks.

November 10, 1968

Dear Patrick,
I love you. Please write when you can. I am on my way home now,

and looking forward to seeing my father and Montana again. I talked with my dad on the phone the other day and told him about you. He seemed pleased. I also told him how you got your nickname from your mother's old car and he laughed so hard he could hardly talk. I haven't heard him laugh like that in years. He also said they have already had several snows. I never thought I'd be happy about seeing snow again, but I'm actually looking forward to it. Maybe when you come home we can go skiing together. Right now, I've been on this plane for so long I can hardly hold my eyes open. I'm going to sleep awhile and will write to you again when I get home. Please be careful. I love you. Write soon.
Janie

He handed the letter back to TJ who had come to see them off.

"Leave it on my cot. Will you?"

"No problem, ma friend. Is that from the nurse you met down at Phu Bai?"

"Yeah. She's on her way home."

"That's cool. You gonna hook up with her when you get back to the world?"

"I hope so."

TJ grinned. "I reckon we gotta better chance gettin' home by doing this recon shit than when we were in the line company. You know?"

"Goin' hot," the chopper pilot said.

The turbines began a low groan and the main rotor started a slow rotation.

"Load up," Robertson said.

TJ stuffed the letter in his pocket and trotted to the edge of the pad. After a few minutes the turbines were at a high-pitched whine, and the rotors were spinning rapidly. The ground lurched away as the chopper rose and tilted to the west. Buck gave a fist in the air salute to TJ as his figure grew smaller far below. Once again, it was show-time.

The LZ was atop a hill on the western edge of the valley, and their arrival was uneventful as they disembarked and walked past several hollow-eyed grunts lying about in sandbagged holes. When the chopper was gone, a captain in muddy fatigues approached. Robertson shook his hand, and the team took a knee while they talked.

"We know there's an NVA regiment close around here somewhere," the captain said. "They hit us every night with probes and mortars, and the goddamned trails look like pig paths, but we haven't been able to find their main force. If we don't find them first, sooner or later we're going to stumble into those little bastards and they're going to chop us up bad."

"What's the plan from here, sir?" Robertson asked.

"That's why we asked for you guys to help out. We're on the left flank of the battalion. We're supposed to move off this hill and up the side of that valley over there. I just need for you guys to get up there somewhere on that ridge to the northwest and stay out ahead of us. Watch our flank and let us know if you see any movement coming our way. Right now, we're waiting on resupply choppers that were supposed to have already been here. As soon as they arrive and we get organized, we'll begin moving. I'd say no more than two or three hours."

"Give us as much time as you can," Robertson said. "We have to cross down into the valley and climb that ridge over there."

21

DANCING WITH THE ENEMY

November 1968

After trading frequencies and call signs with the captain of the line company, Robertson motioned for Mad Dog to take the point. One of the grunts on the perimeter pointed out the trip flares and Claymores as the five lurps passed. Buck made eye-contact with him. The tired soldier looked up and both nodded in recognition of the other. This tired grunt was the reason Buck had returned. Maybe, just maybe, he was the one that his coming back here would save. Within a few seconds the LRRP team was again under a thick jungle canopy and moving downhill into the valley. Despite maintaining total silence, they were moving faster than they should, but it was necessary to get up the ridge before the line company began moving.

One at a time, they quickly crossed a stream at the bottom of the mountain valley, and began the climb up the next ridge. After nearly an hour, Mad Dog brought them to a halt and motioned Robertson to the front. Buck followed. They'd come upon a well-worn trail. It came down the ridge and crossed the deep mountain valley, leading up the next ridge to where the line company would be moving in the next few hours. The team crossed the trail and Marshal cleaned up their tracks behind them.

After a while Mad Dog began moving slower, and for good reason. Buck sensed it, as did the others. There were no birds calling, no monkeys chattering, nothing but silence. The team slowed to a cautious crawl, two, three steps then a pause to listen. Something had the jungle in silence mode, and it was likely the enemy. Buck sensed the growing tension in his team members as they double-checked weapons and scanned the surrounding jungle, their eyes digging deeper back into the shadows, searching, looking for that tiny telltale sign that might save them all.

Buck sucked in the dank jungle air through his nostrils. Sometimes you could smell them before you saw them—an odor of wood-smoke, defecation, or even the rotted fish sauce they called Nuoc Mam. For now, there was nothing but the odor of the rotting vegetation on the jungle floor.

A few days prior to this mission, TJ had told him how some of the teams were pretty slack with discipline. This group, though, seemed sharp, and every man remained focused. Robertson appeared competent and professional. He directed the team with quiet confidence. Zorro—real name Garcia—a happy-go-lucky Tex-Mex back on base, had transformed into a hardened hunter, his dark brown eyes seeming to miss no detail. Marshal—real name Dillon—was a laconic West Virginian who moved with a natural ease in the mountainous jungle. Mad Dog was the only one whose persona Buck had difficulty figuring. He was quiet, hardly speaking except when necessary. He seemed more like a Buddhist monk than a lurp. The team turned, taking a harder angle up the ridge.

There came the sudden sounds of jostling of equipment and men running. Everyone froze. Coming from the left further up the ridge, the sounds grew closer, and before the team did little more than raise their weapons, NVA soldiers were running past, only a few feet away. All five lurps had their weapons trained on the jungle at point-blank range while a line of enemy soldiers continued passing. No one fired as the enemy ran single-file down a trail passing no more than ten feet in front of Mad Dog.

Frozen like a statue, with his weapon trained on the passing column, Buck began counting. Catching only fleeting glimpses of the enemy passing through the thick vegetation, he counted at least thirty-four NVA regulars before the sounds dissipated and they disappeared down the ridge. Their path would take them directly across that of the line company coming up the far ridge. It was obvious the NVA were getting in position for an ambush. Buck didn't wait for Robertson to give the order as he pulled the handset from his pocket and radioed the line company's CO.

The team had taken a knee, and waited while Buck whispered the coordinates into the radio. When he was done, Robertson gave him a silent nod of approval and stood. There came another muffled rustling from up the ridge. Robertson went back to his knee and the entire team raised their weapons as another group of enemy soldiers streamed past on the same trail. Mad Dog was close enough to spit on them as they crossed rapidly to his front. Buck was all but unnerved and soaked with sweat as he lightly caressed the trigger on his CAR-15.

The second column also passed without incident, but down the ridge, probably no more than two hundred meters, Buck heard them leaving the trail and spreading in a line just above the stream. They were forming a classic "L" shaped ambush to catch the line company passing on the opposite slope. Buck again contacted the line company while Robertson motioned to Mad Dog and Zorro to move back away from the trail.

"That's at least sixty of those little bastards down there," Robertson said. "Buck, tell the captain to hold up and get small. We're gonna call in an airstrike, but first I want to move further back up the ridge so we aren't too close ourselves."

The team moved out, straight up the ridge, parallel to the enemy trail. When they had moved several hundred meters Robertson called them to a halt.

"We'll call in the strike from here," he said.

"Sarge?" Buck said.

Robertson raised his chin and looked his way.

"The ones that are left will probably come back through here. Why don't we put a couple of Claymores on the trail and be ready for them?"

"Damned good idea," he whispered. "Zorro, Mad Dog, put your Claymores out down there and keep an eye on the trail."

Robertson eyed Buck for a moment before giving him a nod. It felt good getting this experienced team leader's approval.

"We might be dancing with these bastards in a few minutes," Buck said, "but I don't want to kiss any of them. I'd send Marshal back up the trail behind us to put out his Claymore and watch our backdoor."

"You heard him, Marshal, go."

When the team was deployed, Robertson knelt beside Buck and talked with the X-ray team on the radio as he gave the coordinates for the airstrike. They were told it would be at least fifteen minutes before the assets were on station.

"Well, at least they were already airborne," Buck said.

"What do you mean?" Robertson asked.

"I don't think they could have scrambled from the ground and gotten back this far that fast."

Robertson smiled and nodded. The two men knelt and listened, straining to hear, but there was nothing. There wasn't a hint of a breeze, and there wasn't a sound anywhere, not even the call of a bird. Buck wiped the sweat from his face. The ringing in his ears was the only sound, something that had been continuous since his squad was overrun near the village on 547. One too many grenades, he figured. Of course it didn't help when Mo opened up on the attacking NVA with his muzzle beside Buck's ear.

The radio broke squelch. "Romeo Tango One, this is Bird Dog Foxtrot Charlie, over."

It was the airborne FAC. The forward air controller was going to fire some rockets to mark the target and direct the jets on their bombing run.

"What do you think?" Robertson said. "The way I see it they're gonna have to come southeast to northwest up the valley over the line company."

Buck nodded. "Yeah. Let's make sure they know where the line company is and where we are."

Robertson whispered into the radio and for several minutes the only sound was the buzz of the forward air controller's aircraft off in the distance. Robertson held the radio handset to his ear.

He looked over at Buck. "Bird Dog says he's coming down to mark the target with rockets. We can correct from here if we need to."

Robertson whispered into the radio, and a few moments later the FAC aircraft came up the valley, firing a volley of rockets. They struck just to the north of the NVA positions. Robertson called in the correction, and the men waited. Buck listened, and for a moment he thought he heard the distant roar of a jet engine, but then there was nothing—more silence. The men watched and waited.

When he first saw it, a streaking green blur above the trees, there was only silence, but an instant later an extended shriek followed the blur of a green and tan camouflaged F-4 Phantom. The roar of its afterburners thundered overhead as the treetops in the valley below became inundated in a mushrooming cloud of orange napalm.

It was only seconds before a scattered line of panicked NVA soldiers came up the ridge. Most were on the trail. Some weren't. Mad Dog and Zorro detonated their Claymores. Screams and sporadic gunfire came from the surrounding jungle, some of it mere feet away. A panicked NVA soldier burst through the brush, plowing over Robertson. Buck was on him in an instant, smashing his head with a grenade. Mad Dog and Zorro opened up with their rifles. Two more enemy soldiers plowed through the undergrowth stumbling over Buck and Robertson. Buck shot one, his barrel inches from the enemy soldier's torso. Robertson was bowled over by the second soldier's momentum. There was a momentary struggle, but it was over in an instant when the team leader pushed his forty-five against the man's body and pulled the trigger.

An intense cloud of smoke, heat, and ashes rolled up the hillside. Buck's eyes watered and he could hardly breathe as he contacted the line company on the radio.

"Let's get out of here," Robertson said. "Go get Marshal. I'll get Mad Dog and Zorro. We'll rally back down the ridge near that first trail we crossed."

Buck pushed through the undergrowth and sprinted up the trail where he found Marshal crouched and bug-eyed.

"We got movement up there," he said, pointing up the trail.

"Put a time-delay fuse on the Claymore and let's go. We're moving out."

The sounds on the ridge above increased as Marshal armed his Claymore with a short fuse.

"Hurry up!" Buck hissed.

"I'm coming, dammit!"

A moment later Marshal ran past him, but as Buck was about to follow, an NVA soldier appeared on the trail up the ridge. Aiming carefully with his CAR-15 he fired three rounds sending the enemy soldier reeling. He turned and followed Marshal.

"Over here," Mad Dog called out. There was no more whispering.

Buck and Marshal pushed through a wall of vines toward the voice, finding the other team members huddled together. Robertson talked on the radio.

"Wassup?" Buck asked.

"Too much shit up this way," Zorro said. "He's telling the grunts we're pulling back to the LZ. The captain is arguing with him, but I think it's his Six who doesn't want us to pull back."

"Fucking colonel better sober up quick," Buck said. "We can't go toe-to-toe with them in here. Too much cover and we don't know how many we're dealing with. I think it's that missing NVA regiment."

Robertson cut his eyes up at him, but said nothing as he listened to the RTO on the other end.

"I roger, Aiming Eagle Six, but we're still moving to your rear for now. Too much activity up this way. Out.

"Let's go," Robertson said.

The team moved out, back the way they had come earlier. From the valley below came the sporadic pop and chatter of small arms fire. A while later the team came to the first trail they had crossed. After studying the approaches for a minute or so, Robertson motioned the men to cross one at a time. Buck came up for his turn to cross and stopped.

"Come on!" Robertson whispered. "It's clear."

Buck pointed at the clutter of tracks on the trail. "Look," he said.

"What?"

Buck glanced up at his team leader. Robertson had not noticed the difference.

"The tracks were all moving *up* the ridge this morning. These are all going down that way." He pointed down the ridge toward the valley where the path led up the far slope to the rear of the line company.

Marshal stepped up behind them. "What's the problem?"

"A bunch of those bastards are flanking the line company back this way," Robertson said.

"We better get them on the radio quick," Buck said.

They contacted the line company, and the captain's voice said it all. The LRRP team had again given him and his men a reprieve. The problem now was which way to go. Robertson and Buck talked it over. There was no good answer. Beyond the ridge behind them was probably the entire NVA regiment. To their front was a portion of them who were flanking the line company. Going back west would put them in the jaws of a trap. Going east was to disengage entirely.

"How many Claymores do we have left?" Buck asked.

The team took toll. There were four left.

"I say we set up right here on the trail, put out three Claymores to our front and one to the rear."

"You got big balls," Robertson said.

Buck shrugged. "We can E&E to the east if you want."

Robertson looked around at the other team members. Their black and green face paint was streaked with sweat and cuts from the undergrowth they'd been fighting all day. It had been a hairy eight hours, and everyone was exhausted.

"I say we stay and try to do what we were sent here for," Zorro said.

Robertson looked around at the others. Marshal shrugged. "I agree with Zorro, but I say we move down the ridge closer to the company. It'll get us further away from the bastards behind us."

Robertson glanced at Buck. "We can move a little closer," the team leader said, "but we don't want to get too close. We'll get greased by our own people."

"Agreed," Buck said. "Why don't we move down to the blue line and set out the Claymores. At least we'll be able to see a little more from there."

Just before dark the team again spoke with the captain. No rookie himself, he had sent a reinforced squad to his rear to set up with two M-60s and wait in ambush for the NVA force coming his way.

A deep red sun broke through the clouds just before falling behind the mountains in the west. Total darkness followed in minutes. Up the slope on the opposite ridge, parachute flares began blossoming, leaving an eerie orange afterglow on the undersides of the low-hanging clouds. This was where the line company had formed their perimeter, nine hundred meters away.

Other than the pop and the subsequent glow of the drifting flares, there was little else to hear or see. Forty meters to the team's front, the mountain stream gurgled as it tumbled through the rocks. Buck hoped his influence on the team hadn't put them in an untenable situation. The lurps were spread in a line, no more than an arm's reach from one another, waiting for the firefight that was sure to come.

They didn't have long to wait. The ridge six hundred meters away silently lit up in a shower of red and green tracers, punctuated with bright white flashes, followed a moment later by the sounds—stuttering pops and cracks of automatic rifles, along with the echoing roar of detonating Claymores. The captain's men had sprung their ambush, and a full-fledged firefight had ensued. Like so many of these small battles, it was over in less than a minute as the din of weapons-fire quickly diminished to a couple shots, one more, then silence.

Up on the ridge more parachute flares descended through the clouds, casting a collage of shadows and spooky amber light over the jungle. In the valley from where the LRRP team watched, it remained black as the inside of a cave. The team had set out their Claymores in a line across the trail, knowing the enemy would likely use the same route to retreat after the ambush. Buck held the clacker for one of the Claymores, but with the night so totally devoid of light, he depended on his ears to tell him when the enemy was approaching. They would come. There was no doubt in his mind. He only hoped he heard them before they got past the Claymores.

The first sounds out of the ordinary were splashes in the stream below, followed seconds later by that of men breathing heavily as they came up the trail. Buck slammed his thumb down on the clacker and a brilliant white flash lit the jungle below. At least a dozen enemy soldiers were silhouetted coming up the trail from the stream. It was a black and white freeze frame of men caught in midstride the last moment of their life. To his right, Buck felt Mad Dog shift his weight backward. His teammate was about to throw a frag down the trail.

From below came the groans of wounded enemy soldiers. To avoid giving away their position, no one on the team had yet fired a rifle. Mad Dog threw his grenade and dropped back to the ground. Buck wrapped his arms over his head and burrowed lower as the grenade spoon pinged and the fuse popped. A few seconds later another flash and roar lit the jungle followed by the spattering of shrapnel all about.

Two AK-47s opened up from down near the stream. Their tracer rounds scattered randomly across the ridge. Buck punched Mad Dog and handed him another frag. Mad Dog was lying closest to the trail and able to throw the grenades down the hill without striking the trees. Buck felt his partner in the darkness as he jerked the pin from the grenade, came to his knees and threw it down the hill. Again there was another flash and roar, and the two AKs went silent. More shrapnel spattered all around.

No one moved. The radio handset in Buck's pocket broke squelch. It was barely audible, and he wasn't sure how the radio had gotten switched on, but it was more noise than he wanted at the moment. Cupping his palm over the ear piece, he muffled it. Other than the parachute flares floating above the line company's perimeter nearly a thousand meters to the northeast, there was nothing—nothing moving and no sound, except for the gurgling mountain stream below.

22

FLASHLIGHTS AND NAPALM

The A Shau Valley, December 1968

Utterly exhausted, Buck ignored the streams of green tracers streaking past the chopper as it climbed from the jungle LZ. He had nothing left. Lying on the deck of the chopper, he closed his eyes as the steady chug of the door gunner's M-60 lulled him to sleep.

The worst had come that first day, but the team had remained in the field and coordinated with the line company for another week. Out of water, out of rations and with no more than a couple hours' sleep a night, the team was only a couple hundred meters ahead of NVA trackers when they called for extraction that morning.

The normal debrief with S-2 was postponed as Buck and his teammates stood under hot showers drinking beer and whiskey, while their adrenaline high ebbed and the coiled spring of tension inside each man slowly unwound. It was noon when they plodded through the mud back to the hooch, wearing boxers and jungle boots with towels around their necks. Buck lay back on his cot and passed out. When he awakened he could see the light of day still shining through the nearby doorway, but he felt strangely rested and very hungry.

He glanced around. Robertson's cot was empty as were Marshal's and Zorro's. Mad Dog was sitting on his cot reading a letter by the light of a lantern. He noticed Buck sitting up and folded the letter.

"Wassup?" Mad Dog asked.

Buck motioned toward the empty bunks. "I reckon they went to get some hot chow for supper?"

Mad Dog laughed. "Breakfast, maybe, but not supper."

Confused, Buck wrinkled his brows and tried to make sense of what his teammate had said.

"You've been asleep since yesterday afternoon," Mad Dog said.

"Damned." At least that explained why he felt so rested and so hungry. He'd slept almost sixteen hours. Mad Dog switched on a cassette tape player and turned up the volume. It was a Righteous Brother's tune, "Unchained Melody." Buck listened while he dressed.

Lonely rivers sigh
"Wait for me, wait for me
I'll be coming home, wait for me."

Everything Mad Dog did belied his name.

Later that afternoon the team was cleaning weapons and reloading magazines when Robertson showed up. He'd been gone since breakfast.

"Buck, Top needs to see you ASAP," the team leader said.

After lacing up his boots, Buck buttoned his fatigue shirt and trotted up the road to the company HQ. He stepped inside to find the First Sergeant sitting behind a table stacked with papers.

"Sergeant Robertson said you wanted to see me, Top."

The First Sergeant looked up. "Relax, Marino. I'd tell you to take a seat, but I don't have an extra chair. Look here. I know we said you were going to run a few missions with an experienced team, but Robertson says you are more than ready for a team of your own. We're giving you an E-5 stripe and a team, now."

"But, Top, I don't—"

"Hold up." The First Sergeant raised his hand. "Robertson has agreed to give up the best man on his team, Mad Dog Morgan. He'll hold your hand and help you over the rough spots, but from what Robertson tells me, you can handle most anything yourself. And if Robertson says that about a man, I believe him, because he's one of our best team leaders.

"Along with Mad Dog, I'm giving you three steady performers, Arcenaux, Sloan, and Burch. They were on a team that lost two men last month. One of them was their team leader. I'm giving you two days to get them squared away, run some reaction drills and figure out who can do what the best. I can already tell you that Sloan is a fucking artist with a thump gun. They say he can put five rounds in the air before the first one hits the ground, and all *will* be spot on target. Besides Mad Dog, Burch is your most experienced man. He's steady and can do most anything you ask. Arcenaux is the little guy they call Cajun. He's your most inexperienced, but he seems to have a lot of spunk. You shouldn't have much trouble bringing him up to speed.

"Your first mission will be in three days. We'll keep it simple by inserting you near a good observation point to watch the main valley. If all goes well, you'll be extracted in four or five days. Questions?"

"Why are we running only five men to a team?"

"Not enough people right now. We're supposed to get some men in a week or two."

Buck nodded.

"Do we have an area close around here where we can pull some mock patrols? I want to see these guys in action."

"Not a problem."

The First Sergeant went to a map on the wall and pointed out Camp Eagle and the area where the teams ran practice patrols.

"Let me know if you need anything else."

Buck nodded, and turned to the door.

"Oh, and one more thing," the First Sergeant said.

Buck stopped and looked back.

"It seems someone back at Bragg removed some things from your personnel file. Is it true you whipped the hell out of several National Guardsmen and made them polish their boots and cut their hair before they performed funeral escort for your platoon sergeant?"

"Like most stories, Top, that one's been stretched a bit. I only roughed one up a little because he came at me."

The doubt on the First Sergeant's face was plain.

"Maybe we can have a drink sometime and you can tell me about it. Go get your team squared away."

After meeting with his new team, Buck sat down and wrote a quick letter to Janie.

December 9, 1968

Dear Janie,

This new duty is nothing like what I was doing before. It seems that as long as we don't do something stupid we are in better control of our destiny. I can't write much about it, but suffice it to say so far so good. I have my own team now and we're going to train for a couple days before going back into the field. It's like two days of R&R considering all the rain we're having. At least we'll be able to change into dry clothes each night.

Please write every chance you get. Your letters are like gold and sometimes the only connection I have with sanity. I am looking forward to coming home when I can. I hope you have a good Christmas.

Love,
Buck

Three days later the team lay dog in a rock pile near the top of a mountain above the A Shau. The valley below spread before them in a broad panorama. While gazing down through the haze hanging above the valley floor, Buck found himself again thinking of Janie. He figured she understood why he had to come back here. She was intuitive that way. Understanding it himself was difficult, but he wasn't leaving Nam without finding a way to say good-bye to Rolley, Crowfoot, Dixie, and all the men whose blood now soaked this ground. He didn't know what else he hoped to accomplish, but quitting and walking away meant their deaths were futile sacrifices.

The shadow of dusk fell over the valley below, while back to the west the last orange remnants of sunlight faded. A slight mountain breeze stirred, bringing a chill with it. Buck wrapped his poncho liner across his shoulders and began studying something far up the valley near the northern horizon. He would have thought it was the first sparkle of an evening star becoming visible, except it was below the horizon.

"TJ," he whispered. He motioned for the little Cajun. "Come look at this."

They watched for nearly thirty minutes before the single light became a cluster of lights that soon took on a linear formation as they streamed southward down the center of the valley.

"Jesus, Mary, and Joseph," TJ muttered. "There's gotta be a thousand of them flashlights down there."

"Yeah, and they say only every third man carries one. Let's raise the relay and see if we can tell the TOC what we have. We'll try to see where they're going and maybe put some nape on them after daylight."

The men took turns watching and marking the progress of the column snaking its way down the valley. As the sky began graying up at dawn the flashlights began disappearing, first one or two at a time, and within minutes they all had flickered out. From somewhere out over the valley came the buzz of a Bird Dog aircraft. The Forward Air Controller was the spotter for the jet attack aircraft that Buck knew weren't far behind. He brought him up on the command net and called in the coordinates for the last location he'd seen the lights.

"Roger, Bird Dog Foxtrot Charlie, I can hear you, but I can't see you," Buck whispered.

"Shadow Walker One Zero, I roger. Watch carefully. I'm gonna hit my nav lights for just a second. Let me know if you can get a fix on me. I've got a covey of fast-movers inbound and want you to help me mark the front and rear of the column you spotted. Do you roger?"

"Bird Dog Foxtrot Charlie, Shadow Walker One Zero. I roger."

"On my mark, Shadow Walker One Zero. Now."

"There he is," Mad Dog whispered. "He's still a ways down the valley."

"We have you, Bird Dog, but you're still too far out for a visual without the lights. Keep coming."

The buzzing drone of the little aircraft grew louder as the men strained to see it.

"There! There!" TJ said.

"Where?" Mad Dog asked.

TJ pointed down into the valley.

"I've got him, too," Sloan said.

Finally, Buck spotted him as well.

"Bird Dog Foxtrot Charlie, this is Shadow Walker One Zero, we have a visual. On my mark, you will be passing over the last point where we saw the front of the column. Three, two, mark."

A line of white smoke followed what was obviously a smoke canister dropped by the pilot. The valley below erupted with streams of green tracers shooting skyward at the little aircraft.

"Ah, Shadow Walker One Zero, this is Bird Dog Foxtrot Charlie." The pilot's voice was incredibly calm. "We may be onto something. Give me another mark when I reach the rear of the column. Shit!"

There were now showers of tracers climbing all around the little aircraft.

"That dude has big balls," Mad Dog said.

"You okay, Bird Dog?" Buck asked.

"Yeah, just got a couple new holes in the wings."

"Okay, stand by for the next mark. Three, two, one, mark."

Another stream of white smoke plummeted earthward as the aircraft's engine climbed to a high pitch whine. A moment later from somewhere to the south came the low roar of jet aircraft.

"Okay, Shadow Walker One Zero, the fast movers are inbound. Let me know what corrections you need."

By now the entire valley was lit up like a Fourth of July fireworks display as heavier enemy anti-aircraft weapons began firing from the surrounding hills. Buck spotted the first jet streaking up the valley. A moment later roiling clouds of orange flames billowed skyward. A second jet followed the first, extending the line of napalm up the valley.

"Bird Dog, this is Shadow Walker One Zero. Your guys are right on target."

The jets followed one after the other.

"What do you think?" Buck whispered to Mad Dog.

"I think we just put a big hurt on those little fuckers, but there are a lot more of them in these hills around us, and they're going to be pissed. I think we need to call the TOC and relocate. If the gooks have any triangulation gear up here, they probably know where we are by now."

Mad Dog was right. No sense taking chances. Buck dialed up the relay frequency and told the X-ray Team he was relocating. Moving off the mountain, Mad Dog walked point and led the team across an adjacent slope toward a secondary extraction point. All day, they moved thirty or forty meters at a time, one slow deliberate step after another, stopping and listening for several minutes before moving again.

Sweat trickled into Buck's eyes. This was his team, and he was responsible for their lives. Slowly and carefully he pulled a sleeve across his face. The slope above was a visually impenetrable wall of jungle growth. He glanced back at the other team members. The men stood motionless, blending into the jungle. He motioned Mad Dog ahead, but there came a sound only a few meters away—the murmuring of voices. The team froze as an NVA patrol passed within a stone's throw.

The enemy had been gone for ten minutes when Buck nodded for Mad Dog to move out. In an abundance of caution, he directed Burch to dust their back trail with powdered CS. Twice more in the next hour the team's stealth paid off as they came within a few meters of enemy patrols without being detected. All of the patrols were moving toward the mountain where the team had been. Mad Dog was right. It now seemed almost certain the enemy had triangulation gear and had homed in on the team's radio transmissions.

23

THE DEAR JOHN LETTER

Camp Eagle, December 1968

Mad Dog ripped the letter in two and wadded the pieces together. After stuffing it in his rucksack, he shoved the pack beneath his cot, and glanced around. Buck quickly dropped his head and pursed his lips. He had seen it happen before, and it was deeply personal. Mail call was always an intense affair with everyone hoping for a letter from home. It was a link to another world where they imagined sanity ruled, or was at least accepted as the norm.

Yet, there were often those who received nothing, and they simply shrugged and walked away in a futile attempt to hide their disappointment. But then there were those like Mad Dog Morgan who had just ripped open an envelope only to be crushed by the "Dear John" letter inside. Buck was pretty certain that was what had just happened. He wanted to say or do something encouraging, but it was better to simply be here for him.

"Hey, man," Buck said.

Mad Dog turned up the volume on his tape player.

Oh, my love, my darling
I've hungered for your touch
A long, lonely time

It was the Righteous Brothers' "Unchained Melody." Mad Dog glanced up at Buck with a half-assed smile of feigned nonchalance.

"Wassup?"

"You are probably the most easy-going guy in the entire platoon. So, what's up with the 'Mad Dog' tag?"

This time Mad Dog's smile was a little more genuine. "It's something that dumbass brother Greg Jefferson came up with. He started calling me Morgan David after Mogen David wine. Then he shortened it to Mad Dog 20/20, something he always drank. Now, they just call me Mad Dog."

"And let me guess: you don't even drink wine, right?"

"I prefer beer," Mad Dog said.

"He also hung the Marshal tag on Dillon."

"I've got to meet this guy," Buck said. "What team is he on?"

"He's not. He got killed last month trying to save his team leader. They were on the team we have, now."

The echoing boom of outgoing artillery sounded somewhere in the distance. Mad Dog dropped his chin on his chest. "I should have seen it coming," he said.

"Seen what?"

He motioned toward the rucksack beneath his cot. "That damned letter."

"Your girlfriend?" Buck asked.

"Fiancée. She wrote a while back telling me how her college professor was such a wonderful guy and so intelligent. Her next letter said he was telling her and the rest of the class that we were all murderers and killing innocent people over here. I wrote back and told her the guy was full of shit. She didn't write for a month after that. When she did, it was more crap about how she adored his brilliant mind."

Are you still mine?
I need your love
I need your love
God speed your love to me

Mad Dog's eyes had reddened to the point of tears.

Buck looked away as he spoke. "A friend of mine told me that most of those professors don't have a clue about what's *really* happening over here. They're just college students who never got a real job."

"Your friend is pretty smart."

"*Was*," Buck said. "He got killed a couple months ago up northwest of Hue."

"Was he one of the guys you were trying to save when you got wounded?"

"How did you know about that?"

"The Cajun told me. Little fucker thinks you're the baddest SOB this side of the Philippines."

"TJ embellishes. Rolley and Crowfoot were my friends, and I was only doing what they would have done for me."

"I'm proud to be on your team," Mad Dog said.

Buck nodded. "Thanks. You want to go get a beer?"

"Sure. Why not? We better celebrate while we can. Robertson said they're sending several teams back into the A Shau in a couple days."

Late that evening Buck and Sloan supported a very drunk Mad Dog as they escorted him back to the hooch. After pulling off his boots and throwing a poncho liner over him, Buck sat down and began writing another letter to Janie.

> Dear Janie,
>   It stopped raining for a little while this evening and there was one of those beautiful Vietnam sunsets out there in the mountains. I don't think I will ever be able to do anything over here that will make up for the friends

we lost. I'll be ready when it's my turn to come home. One of the guys on my team got a Dear John letter today, and he played that Righteous Brothers song, Unchained Melody, on his cassette tape player again. I took him out and got him drunk. It may sound kind of sappy, but the lyrics of that song remind me of you, and it has become a long lonely time over here. I'm not sure what I will do to make a living in Montana, but, God-willing, I will be coming home to you.
I love you,
Buck

Buck's team had just returned from another mission. Although exhausting, it had been a relatively uneventful five days poking around in what turned out to be a dry hole. They had finished their showers that afternoon when the company clerk came running up.

"Hey Buck. Top wants you to report ASAP. He said to tell your guys to gear-up, now."

"Must be another team in trouble," TJ said.

"Sounds that way. Tell the guys to go light on the rations and load up with extra frags and ammo."

Within minutes Buck had met with the First Sergeant and was trotting back up the road to the hooch. The team was inside, lacing up boots, taping their equipment and applying face-paint. They all looked up at once when he walked in.

"There's a Bird Dog down on the west side of the A Shau. They got a signal from him. He's still alive and hiding from the NVA somewhere up there. We'll finish with our gear in a minute. Let's take a look at the map and talk about the mission first."

TJ, Mad Dog, Sloan, and Burch listened while Buck gave the briefing. "A FAC aircraft was hit across the fence in Laos, but he made it back over the mountains to the western A Shau Valley before going down in this area." Buck pointed at a spot on the topo map. "Last word from the pilot was he was escaping and evading downhill toward the valley floor. His name is Captain Rider. Problem is he has a broken ankle."

"Any enemy contact reported?" Mad Dog asked.

"None, as yet."

"We can't get trigger happy either, because there'll be an SF team in the area along with another one of our teams."

"How come they didn't just pick him up with a chopper?" TJ asked.

"His radio quit, and the mountains up there are socked in with clouds."

"So how are we going to get in?" Sloan asked.

"If we get there in time, we're going to insert just below the cloud line on the mountain and climb up to where he is."

"Lovely," Burch said.

"Okay, let's go over the frequencies and call signs, and we'll get going."

The chopper had been airborne for thirty minutes, and Buck's eyes watered as he looked out the open door toward the valley up ahead. The tops of the mountains were shrouded in a layer of low-hanging clouds. This mission probably carried more risk than any yet, and it would be blind running luck if they found the pilot, but they had to try. Fifteen minutes later the chopper skirted the mountainside just below the cloud line.

Because of the steep terrain and the high jungle canopy, the team planned to rappel from the chopper. Everyone was prepared as the helicopter hovered into position just above the trees. Buck had rappelled several times down at Nha Trang, but this was his first in an actual combat situation. Mad Dog and TJ were already out on the skids facing the door. Buck checked their gear and gave them the nod. They dropped down through the trees. Within a couple minutes the entire team was on the ground, and the sound of the chopper was quickly fading away down the valley.

Moving silently, they climbed up the mountain a couple hundred meters before stopping. The clouds left the jungle dripping wet, and a dusky twilight made it seem later than midafternoon. After ten or fifteen minutes of waiting and listening, Buck motioned the team together.

"Okay," he whispered. "We'll move straight up the mountain from here. The crash site is supposed to be up that way, maybe another half click."

Slowly, Mad Dog led the team another two hundred meters up the mountain before Buck called them to a halt.

"TJ, you and I are going to move across that way to the south. Mad Dog, you, Burch, and Sloan move northwest, over that way. Let's see if we can locate a trail. We'll meet back here in forty minutes."

"What if we don't find a trail?" TJ asked.

"We'll execute plan 'B'."

"What's that?"

Buck grinned. "Don't know. Haven't thought of it yet."

"This is like searching for a needle in a haystack," Burch whispered.

"Move out," Buck said.

Buck and TJ had moved only fifty meters when TJ's radio broke squelch. He motioned to Buck. "Mad Dog said they found a trail."

"Okay. Tell him to sit tight, and we'll head back his way."

"Roger that."

The team rendezvoused beside the trail.

"We'll wait here a while and see what comes along. It's a long shot, but maybe our boy will find the trail, too."

"What if an enemy patrol comes along?" Sloan asked.

"If the pilot's not with them, we let them pass."

"What if he is?" TJ asked.

"Put a single Claymore against that tree over there so that it fires straight across the trail. I'll hold the detonator. We'll have to rush them quick or they'll kill him."

It was a risky plan, similar to a prisoner snatch, but one with a zero-margin for error.

"Don't shoot unless you know exactly what you're shooting at," Buck said, "and no auto-fire. Pick your shots."

The men nodded in silence. Buck glanced at his watch. There were barely two hours of daylight remaining, and a light drizzle had begun falling. Crawling beneath the ferns, the team lay within ten meters of the trail. It was crazy close, but with the gathering shadows they'd be hidden, yet close enough to recognize the pilot. Within minutes there came a slight sound from down the trail toward the valley.

Buck brought his CAR-15 to ready. A moment later an enemy soldier appeared, walking steadily up the trail, his eyes darting nervously about. A fine sheen of perspiration coated his copper face, but his body language said it all. The enemy knew the team was in the area.

No one moved. Within a couple minutes fourteen NVA regulars had passed.

After several minutes one of the lurps on his right moved. "Anyone piss in their pants yet?" Burch said.

"I could smell those bastards," TJ whispered.

"Ssshhh," Buck hissed. He had heard another sound coming from up the trail in the direction the enemy patrol had gone. There came a scuffing sound and a grunt. Buck was on the far left of the line and cut his eyes up the mountain trail. A lone figure was hopping on one leg, dropping to his knees, crawling, then rising to hop on one leg again. Buck rose to his feet and stepped up to a tree beside the trail. It was the pilot, and he stopped less than a foot away, unaware of Buck's presence. He gazed back up the trail while gasping for breath.

"Captain Rider," Buck whispered.

The pilot froze and stopped breathing. He didn't look left or right.

"You best come with us, Captain Rider."

The pilot slowly turned his head until he was looking directly into Buck's eyes.

"Holy shit! Where in hell did you come from?" the pilot asked.

"Put your arm over my shoulder and let's get off this trail," Buck said.

When the team had moved back a hundred meters off the trail, they gathered around the pilot.

"Damned. For a minute I thought I was asleep and this was all just a dream," he said. "This is the second miracle I've experienced today."

"What was the first?" Buck asked.

"When I woke up after the crash, I was still strapped in my seat and hanging upside down twenty feet off the ground. Are you guys Special Forces?"

"75th Rangers, attached to the 101st at Camp Eagle."

"Shit, y'all are some spooky lookin' fuckers."

"Burch, you and Sloan give us your Claymores. Keep your weapons and ammo. I want you guys to swap off carrying the captain. TJ, raise the X-ray team and tell them we made the recovery. We're moving to the extraction point. Hurry up. We need to get down below the clouds. It's getting dark fast."

Buck nodded to Mad Dog, who began pushing his way through the undergrowth. Something hit the ground with a thud at his feet, and Buck, thinking he had dropped something, reached down and picked up a Chi-Com grenade. It was more reflex than thought as he quickly gave the grenade a sideways toss.

"Grenade!" he hissed.

The explosion scattered shrapnel everywhere. Buck began pulling pins on grenades and bracketing the area. Burch and TJ were doing the same. After a moment Buck realized there was a struggle in the brush only a few feet to his front. Coming to his feet, he jumped forward to find Mad Dog fighting with three enemy soldiers trying to drag him down the mountain. With the element of surprise, Buck quickly shot two of them. Mad Dog dispatched the third with his knife, just as a fourth enemy soldier burst out of the undergrowth. The soldier had his AK-47 trained on the two LRRPs.

A ripping clatter of CAR-15 fire sent him flying backward the way he had come. Buck glanced back. It was TJ. He slid down the hill beside him. Muted voices of more enemy soldiers came from the ravine below.

"Sloan said he heard voices behind us, too," TJ said. "They've got us surrounded, mon."

"Go get Burch and Sloan," Buck said. "We'll wait here for you."

After retrieving his CAR-15, Mad Dog began going through the pockets of the dead and dying enemy soldiers, searching for maps and other documents. Buck pulled his last two frags from the pouch. A moment later the other three LRRPs slid down the hill behind them, carrying the pilot. No one said a word as they all stared expectantly at Buck.

"We're screwed if we stay here," he said. "Put a Claymore behind us with a short fuse aiming back up the mountain. I'll set out some toe poppers then we'll toss a few frags down the hill and run that way. We might get lucky and bust through. At the least we'll take a few with us."

"You fuckers are crazy," the pilot said.

"You got a better idea?" Buck asked.

"We can split up and try to slip past them."

"Captain, sir, you're not slipping past anybody with that broken ankle. We'll all make it out of here together or we won't. If anyone gets hit bad enough you can't run, sound off. We're not leaving anybody on this mountain."

Burch set the Claymore, while Buck spread the toe poppers along the team's back trail. When they were ready, Buck, TJ, and Mad Dog pulled pins on their frags and threw them down the mountain. The grenades exploded and the team came to their feet. Running forward, they tumbled, regained their feet and made their way down the steep slope sixty meters before bursting through a wall of vegetation into the midst of a half-dozen NVA soldiers.

The fight was close, furious and confusing, but over in seconds. The enemy had never suspected the team would charge at them. Buck glanced around. All his men, including Captain Rider, were still standing.

"Anyone hurt?"

"One of 'em stuck me with a bayonet," TJ said.

Buck glanced at the little Cajun. "Where?"

He pointed at his hip. "Right here, mon, but I don't think it's gonna be bad. It ain't bleeding much."

"Can you make it?"

TJ nodded.

"Okay, we can't stop. Let's keep moving."

The continuing drizzle deadened the sound of their movement as the team crept quickly down the mountain. After another couple hundred meters, Mad Dog came to a stop. The jungle was quickly fading into darkness. Buck moved up beside his point man.

"What's up?" he whispered.

"I heard more voices." He pointed down the slope.

"Dammit! Okay, let's turn and move across toward that ridge over there."

"Good move," Mad Dog said.

Buck knew the enemy would expect the team to follow the path of least resistance. Climbing the steep parallel ridge was probably the last thing they expected them to do.

"Move out, but slow down," Buck said.

After moving another three or four hundred meters, he again brought them to a halt. They knelt and listened. After five minutes, Buck was about to motion Mad Dog ahead, when there came the distinct bark of a dog from back up the mountain.

"Shit."

He reached forward in the darkness, and ran his hands over Mad Dog's rucksack. After a couple seconds, he found what he was after, a canister of CS powder. The same stuff used to make teargas, it was an effective deterrent for the enemy tracker dogs. The team clustered together in the darkness.

"Stay close. Follow me," Buck whispered.

He climbed the steep ridge for seventy or eighty meters before stopping. The dog barked again, this time closer, but still well up the mountain. Walking past his men, Buck scattered the CS powder on the trail and their boots.

"Okay, we're turning east from here and heading down toward the valley. Stay butt-cheek close. We can't afford to get separated, and we still need to get below the clouds by morning for extraction."

It was well after midnight when Buck called the team to a halt. Soaked from the mist-covered vegetation, they had covered several hundred meters without further contact. Sloan and Burch were exhausted from carrying Captain Rider, and TJ's wounded hip was causing him to struggle to keep up. The only good option was to give the team a rest. The jungle was enveloped in total darkness as the team huddled together and waited for daylight.

Buck had dozed when he heard the tiniest scratch come from TJ's radio as it broke squelch. He opened his eyes. The fog-shrouded jungle had begun reappearing in the first gray light of dawn. He held the radio handset to his ear and answered. It was the X-Ray team. Two Hueys were inbound along with a pink team. One slick was a backup for the other that would actually extract the LRRPs. The pink team, a C&C chopper and a couple of Cobra gunships, would provide air cover. First, the LRRPs had to move further down the mountain to an open area where the choppers could land.

He shook the others awake, and within a minute or two they were moving silently through the wet jungle, stopping, listening, forty, fifty meters at a time. They were headed toward an area of scrub palm, ferns, and bomb craters created by an Arc Light Strike. Out beyond the main valley came the distant thump of rotors. It was the extraction choppers approaching. For the first time since the evening before, Buck was beginning to feel he and his team might make it out alive.

He silently motioned for them to take a break and keyed the mic on the PRC-25, "Charlie Echo Niner, this is Shadow Walker One Zero. Do you read me? Over."

"Ahh, roger, Shadow Walker, gotcha Lima Charlie. Hotel Mike? Over."

"Likewise, Charlie Echo Niner. We've had a lot of activity until the last several hours. Moving cold for now to Echo Papa One."

"Roger, Shadow Walker. We've got a couple snakes and a spotter on hand if we need them. Over."

"Roger, Charlie Echo Niner. As soon as we reach Echo Papa one, we're going for a low profile with a couple panels. Over."

"Roger, Shadow Walker. We'll give it a try, but there's a lot of fog and haze out here. Over."

Buck glanced down the ridge, spotting the clearing that extended along the hills at the base of the mountain. The marker panels would be safer than using smoke or flares, which would probably draw the enemy's attention. His biggest concern was getting there. Everyone was exhausted, and it would take the team at least fifteen more minutes to reach the extraction point.

"Roger, Charlie Echo Niner. We still have about four hundred mikes to go. I will re-contact you in One-five. Do you roger?"

"Roger, Shadow Waker. We'll be standing by. Out."

Buck motioned for Mad Dog to move out. Reaching down, he pulled TJ back on his feet and pulled his arm across his shoulders. He glanced back at the others. Burch and Sloan helped Captain Rider to his feet. So far, so good. Other than the distant thumping of the inbound choppers, it was quiet.

The team reached the edge of the LZ. Huge, water-filled craters pockmarked the terrain for as far as Buck could see. He signaled for the men to spread out, pulled out a bright yellow marker panel and eased out into the open. Crouching low, he crept out as far as he dared and spread the panel. When he returned to the edge of the jungle, Mad Dog was already on the other radio notifying the choppers.

"He's going to do a high fly-over and try to spot the panel." he said.

A moment later the chopper came from the southeast. The team watched until it was directly overhead.

"Bingo," Mad Dog whispered into the mic. After a few seconds, he looked over at Buck. "He never saw the panel, but he said to get ready. He's got a pretty good fix on us and is coming down. He wants us to pop smoke."

Buck pulled a smoke canister from TJ's rucksack, yanked the pin and threw it out into the open. A few moments later the chopper correctly identified the purple smoke as "goofy-grape" and came in low from the main valley.

"TJ, Mad Dog, you guys move out there and give us some flank security. Burch, Sloan, you guys leave the captain here with me, and cross over to that first crater. You can provide cover fire from there if we need it. I'm going to wait here with him till the chopper is about to land. Move out."

The team sprinted across the clearing just as the chopper flared over the LZ, but a shower of green tracers burst in a crisscross pattern and two B-40s exploded nearby. Too late, the pilot tried to pull up as yet another explosion wrecked the tail rotor. The chopper set down hard beside the crater as the enemy fire continued unabated.

Buck and the captain waited and watched from the jungle's edge as the team along with the helicopter's crew scrambled toward the bomb crater. The helicopter was already enveloped in flames.

Buck keyed the mic on his radio. "Mad Dog, anyone hurt?" he asked. There was no answer. Buck pressed the radio mic to his ear, turned up the volume and listened.

"Charlie Echo Niner, this is Shadow Walker One-One, over." It was Mad Dog on the other radio.

"Standby, Shadow Walker. The snakes are inbound to your position. We'll give you three-sixty cover fire and bring in the second chopper. Can you give me a sit-rep on my crew down there?"

"Charlie Echo Niner, your crew is okay," Mad Dog said. "Negative on the three-sixty. We still have two men about seventy-five mikes to our Sierra Whiskey."

Buck grabbed his compass, shot a quick azimuth toward the crater and keyed the radio handset. "We're at two-hundred and ten degrees from the downed chopper. Do you roger?"

"This is Charlie Echo Sierra One. I roger."

"Charlie Echo Sierra Two. Roger."

The two Cobra Pilots were on the same frequency and the C&C chopper began giving them specific targets. Within minutes they had all but silenced the enemy ambush as the second Huey approached from the east.

"Shadow Walker One Zero, this is Charlie Echo Niner. The most we can lift out of here with is seven. We have another chopper coming, but he's still about thirty mikes out."

Within seconds the second extraction chopper set down beside the flaming wreckage of the first. The four lurps and three crewmen from the wrecked chopper leapt from the crater and ran to the helicopter. A moment later the door gunner gave the pilot a thumbs-up and the chopper labored into the air.

Buck glanced over at the captain. He was still crouching beside him.

"They didn't have enough lift for all of us, did they?" the captain said.

Buck nodded. "I hope that second chopper hurries. I'm down to two magazines of ammo."

The captain smiled and began pulling magazines of ammo from his pockets. "That little Cajun guy gave me these before he ran out to that crater. And here's a couple frags he gave me, too."

He set two fragmentation grenades on the ground in front of Buck.

"You already knew we weren't all going to ride out on that first chopper, didn't you?"

The captain grinned. "I wasn't sure, but I do have my moments. Besides, *someone* has to take care of you dumb grunts."

There came the sound of voices nearby. Buck peeked over the top of the grass. A hundred meters away, several NVA soldiers were standing, gazing at the smoking remains of the first chopper.

"They must think we were all on that second chopper," he whispered. Rider nodded while Buck whispered into the radio mic. "Charlie Echo Niner, this is Shadow Walker One Zero, over."

"Go ahead, Shadow Walker."

"We've got company out here. You guys still around?"

24

FINDING A NEIGHBOR

A Shau Valley, December, 1968

Buck watched intently. One of the enemy soldiers pointed back toward the jungle where he and the pilot, Captain Rider, were still hiding.

"Negative, Shadow Walker One Zero. Assets are returning for fuel."

He whispered into the handset, "What about that other extraction chopper?"

"Shadow Walker, he's inbound about fifteen mikes out. Call sign Angel Fire Three. Over."

The enemy soldiers in the clearing were joined by others as they began fanning out toward the jungle.

"What are we going to do now?" the captain whispered.

"Disappear," Buck said. "Stay with me as best you can."

With that he began crawling through the grass until they were well within the cover of the jungle. He stopped and looked back. The captain was struggling to catch up.

"Where are we going?" Rider asked. He was red-faced and in obvious pain.

"We're going over there to that pile of dead trees and burrow under it." Buck pointed to one of the many mounds of brush and trees blown into heaps by the Arc Light Strike. "First we're going to sprinkle ourselves with some more CS powder in case that damned dog is still around."

More murmuring came from a few meters away as Buck quickly shook the powder on their clothes.

"Let's go," he whispered.

Within minutes both men had crawled, scratched, and made their way well into the darkened confines of the log pile. The sing-song voices of the enemy soldiers were now coming from all around them. Buck glanced at Captain Rider. The whites of his eyes reflected in the shadows. The voices suddenly ceased, and from somewhere outside came the steady thump of rotors. The extraction chopper was approaching.

Buck whispered into the handset of the radio. "Angel Fire Three, this is Shadow Walker One Zero. We've got dinks all around us."

"I roger, Shadow Walker. Pop smoke, and we'll light up the rest of the area. Over."

"Negative, Angel Fire, no can do. They're too close."

"Okay, Shadow Walker. It's your call. What's the plan?"

The only plan Buck had was not to end up as a prisoner. He grabbed his compass and shot another reading on the approximate position of the downed chopper.

"Angel Fire Three, are you packing any ordnance? Over."

"Packing heavy, Shadow Walker. We're normally an attack chopper."

"Roger, Angel Fire. We're about two hundred and twenty-five degrees from the downed chopper. Light up everything else."

"Roger, Shadow Walker. Get small and standby."

The ticking buzz of a Vulcan machine gun came from somewhere above, followed quickly by the voices of a panicked enemy.

"Let's ease out where we can see," Buck said.

Peeking over a tree trunk from beneath the brush pile, Buck spotted several NVA soldiers still hunkered down only a few steps away. The helicopter fired rockets and sprayed the surrounding jungle with their machine guns. Buck backed up, colliding with Rider behind him.

"Back up," he hissed.

"What?"

"We're not going anywhere. Those bastards are still out there."

The two men crawled deep beneath the log pile.

"What are we going to do?" Rider asked.

"Just sit tight and wait. We don't have much choice. Besides, I don't think they know we're here."

Buck keyed the mic on the radio. "Angel Fire Three, I want you to put some ordnance on the downed chopper. Over."

"Shadow Walker One Zero, that chopper is pretty much…..no nee…." The transmission was garbled.

"Just do it!" Buck whispered into the radio.

"Roger, Shadow Walker. Stand by."

A few moments later there came a series of explosions from out on the LZ.

"Okay, Shadow Walker. The wreckage is scattered to hell and back. What now? Over."

"Angel Fire Three, we're still surrounded but laying low. It's a no-go on the extraction. We're going to wait till our company departs and try to relo when we can. Roger?"

"Ah, roger, Rome…go…eh….er."

"Awww, shit," Buck muttered.

"What now?" the captain asked.

"The radio battery is going dead."

"You have a spare?"

"The spare was in TJ's rucksack."

Rider's eyes locked with Buck's.

Buck shrugged. "Just hang with me, Captain. We're gonna get out of this mess."

The men had remained hidden beneath the log pile for several hours. The only sounds were those of an occasional helicopter somewhere far overhead.

"How old are you?" Rider asked.

"Nineteen. Why?"

"How old do you think *I* am?" the captain asked.

"Hell, I don't know."

"I'm twenty-five years old."

"Reckon I'll have to start calling you Pops."

"Buddy works for me. That's what my family calls me." Buck pulled a small can from his rucksack.

"What's that?" Buddy asked.

"Camo face-paint. Rub some on your face and neck." He gave the can to the captain.

"How did you become a pilot?"

"My father is a crop-duster pilot down in the Mississippi Delta."

The Mississippi Delta stretched for several hundred miles, but this was the closest Buck had come to a person he could call a "home boy."

"No shit? Where?"

"A little wide spot in the road on Forty-Nine West, in Sunflower County, Mississippi."

"You're fucking kidding me?"

"Why?" the captain asked.

"I'm from Tallahatchie County, right next to the Sunflower County line."

"Where?"

"You ever hear of a place called Bois de Arc?"

Rider almost laughed aloud, and Buck clamped his palm over the captain's mouth. The two men stared wide-eyed at one another in the shadows of the log pile.

"Sorry," Buck said. "You were gettin' a little loud."

"My father sprayed crops for several farmers over that way."

Buck paused. Here he was nine thousand miles from Bois de Arc talking to a neighbor. He was having one of those eerie out-of-body experiences that caused him to question the reality of the moment. "Well, if we're gonna get back to Mississippi, we've got to relocate from here. You up to it?"

Rider wagged his head. "My fucking ankle is broken, dude. Look at it. It's flopping around like a rope. I can't go anywhere on my own."

"We'll make it, Cap...Buddy. Just don't give up. You hear me?"

Rider stared back at him for several seconds before responding. "You're one hard-core bastard for a nineteen-year-old."

"It's not all that difficult being hard-core when half the people you've ever known are dead."

"You got family back home?"

"No. Parents died in a car wreck, but there is this one girl I'm crazy about. She lives in Montana."

"Maybe she'll be there for you when you get home."

"We'll see. For now, we've got to plan on how we're gonna get there."

"How did you meet a girl from Montana?"

"She was a nurse over here—met her at the 22nd Surgical in Phu Bai. We gotta get movin'."

The sun had set, and Buck crawled out to where he could see. A fog was settling across the valley. It was quiet. The gray shapes of the mountains loomed in the evening mist. He felt suddenly very small and insignificant, except for one thing. That was the realization of what he meant to Janie. It was all that mattered. And if he could return her love, if he could bring her the happiness she had brought him, nothing else much mattered.

"Are we gonna make a break for it?" Buddy asked.

It jarred Buck from his thoughts.

"Not yet. Sit tight while I take a look around."

He slipped from the log pile and crawled to the edge of the jungle. The open area was quiet and without movement, except for the smoldering remains of the helicopter, where wisps of smoke still rose vertically into the still mountain air. He turned and crawled back to the log pile.

"Okay, crawl out here in the open, and get on my back. We're gonna move."

With Buddy draped across his shoulders, Buck began a slow and careful walk along the inside edge of the clearing.

"I don't want to cross that open area to get down to the valley. We're going northwest and cross up that way, then head down."

"Damned!" Buddy whispered. "That's gotta be a mile or better."

"Just shut up and enjoy the ride," Buck said.

It had been hours, and even though his body screamed with pain, Buck refused to stop. His calves, his buttocks, every muscle burned. He had reached the end of the bombed-out area and was pushing his way down toward the main valley. Buddy hadn't spoken for the last hour, and Buck thought he heard him snoring at one point. Except for moving downhill, he had lost all orientation in the darkness, and only when he noticed a change in the light on the horizon did he begin to have hope. It had to be the edge of the valley.

"Does this trip have any stop-overs?" Buddy whispered.

Buck stopped. Almost immediately his legs began cramping.

"Why?" he asked.

"I gotta piss."

Buck released him, and the pilot hit the ground with a thump.

"Shit!"

Buck fell beside him.

"Sorry."

"I'm revoking your chauffeur's license."

"That's okay. The fucking chauffeur is give-out. Let's sleep a while."

Buck jerked awake. It was a new day, and the sun was shining overhead. Buddy was still curled in a fetal lump with his head buried against his knees. It felt somehow empowering to be on a first name basis with an officer he respected, and who in turn respected him. They were now simply two men fighting to survive. Birds were chirping in the trees above, and a soft breeze wafted through the palms. This was a good sign. Buck pulled two packets from inside his fatigue shirt. One of Buddy's eyes cracked open.

"What are those?" he muttered.

"Shhh! Whisper! They're LRRP rations."

Buddy uncurled and sat up. He began rubbing his swollen ankle.

"Which one do you want?" Buck asked.

"What are the choices?"

Buck held up the two envelopes. "Chicken and rice, and chicken and rice."

"In that case, I believe I'll have the chicken and rice."

Buck tossed one of the envelopes into Buddy's lap.

"Here," Buddy said, handing it back. "You need to keep up your strength. Eat them both."

Buck tossed it back again. "The Air Force will be pissed if I let you starve to death. Eat it."

From somewhere far down the valley there came a steadily growing drone of a small aircraft.

"Sounds like your buddies are coming to look for you."

Buddy scooped the rice from the packet with his fingers.

"What are we going to do?"

"Finish that first. We'll move out into that elephant grass down there and try to signal them with the mirror. I'm not firing a starburst till I hear some choppers around."

Buck's legs felt like jelly as he pushed through the undergrowth with Buddy across his back. When they reached the elephant grass the two men landed in a heap, and Buck pulled the signal mirror from his pocket. The small O-1 Bird Dog had begun circling high above the original extraction point. Steadily working the mirror against the morning sun, Buck tried to get the pilot's attention.

"There's a mile of water-filled bomb craters between him and us," Buddy said. "With all that shining in his eyes, I seriously doubt he'll see us."

Buck continued working the mirror. "You're probably right."

After nearly two minutes of signaling, he noticed the Bird Dog had stopped circling. Shading his eyes with his hand, he squinted into the morning sun. The little aircraft was coming their way. A few moments later, it began circling, still very high, but directly overhead. Buddy worked the mirror against the sun, still trying to signal the plane.

"Damned! I think he's spotted us," Buddy said.

The little Cessna was steadily dropping closer. Several green tracers shot up from the jungle further up the mountain. The aircraft straightened and flew back out over the valley, waggling his wings as he departed.

"I just hope a chopper gets here before those little bastards up the mountain do," Buck said.

"You think they'll come down this way to check things out?"

"No doubt in my mind," Buck said. "Climb on, and let's move back into cover till a chopper arrives."

The men didn't have long to wait, as the steady thump-thump-thump of multiple choppers reverberated up the valley. Buddy gripped a starburst flare and waited.

"Once I fire this thing, the enemy is going to know exactly where we are. I'm going to wait as long as I can."

More green tracers began passing overhead as the enemy fired out across the valley at the approaching helicopters. Buck snatched the ring on the flare sending it streaking skyward, where it burst into a shower of sparks. Several cracks and zips sounded around them. The enemy soldiers up the mountain were now shooting directly at him and Buddy. He flicked the selector switch on his CAR-15 to "Auto" and emptied the magazine into the jungle above.

Buck was inserting a fresh magazine when he caught movement from the corner of his eye. He turned just as a Cobra gunship rose above the trees, its guns blazing in a continuous *BURRRRRPPPP*. It flared away as a Huey came in behind it and hovered down into the elephant grass.

"Let's go," Buck shouted. With Buddy draped across his back, he struggled toward the chopper.

The door gunner swung about and began firing up the mountain as more green tracers zipped past. Buck's legs wobbled beneath him as he continued running. The chopper was now less than sixty meters away. Something stung his left buttock, throwing him off balance. His legs gave way, and he pitched forward sending Buddy sprawling.

Buck groped with his hand, feeling for the wound to his hip. Buddy crawled his way.

"Come on," Rider shouted.

He stood on his one good leg and pulled Buck up. The rotor wash buffeted them, knocking them both from their feet. Buck looked down. His leg was bent at a sickening angle.

"I'm not going anywhere," he shouted.

A helmeted figure leapt from the chopper and ran toward them. More tracer rounds zipped past. It was the door gunner.

"Take the captain first," Buck shouted.

The chopper crewman grasped Buddy beneath the arms, and began dragging him. Buck tried to follow, crawling through the grass, but his body had reached its limit.

A rocket-propelled grenade flew over the chopper and exploded in the jungle below. The helicopter rose slightly from the ground. An easy target for another RPG, it couldn't remain stationary much longer. Buck shielded his eyes from the flying debris. His only hope was that Captain Rider was safely aboard. The chopper was taking too much fire to remain on the LZ.

He buried his head in the grass. This was it, but at least he had done his job. He had gotten Captain Rider out safely. He reached down and pulled out one of his last two frags. The enemy was not going to take him alive. A moment later he felt the arms of the helicopter crewman lifting him off the ground. "Let's go, Sarge. We've got to get the hell out of here."

25

January 1969

Buck's right leg was in a cast up to his hip. An enemy round had grazed his butt, throwing him off balance, but the worst wound came when his knee collapsed, tearing the ligaments. They had been reattached during surgery, but his tour was ended. He was going home. Mail Call came and he got another letter from Janie.

> Dear Patrick,
> I love you. Please come home, and I promise you will never get one of those "dear john" letters from me. We can make a great life here in Montana, and I will do my best to make it worthwhile

for you. Just come home and be with me. All I want is to have your babies, be your wife and make you happy.

By the way, the hospital is paying my tuition to return to school. I am going to become a Registered Nurse. I'll be burning the midnight oil for a couple years, but it'll be worth it in the long run.

My dad said we can have some land and build a house on his place if you want when you get home. He has a ranch and guide service on several hundred acres south of Missoula. I already know the place I want to put the house, with your approval of course. It's beautiful. It's near the Bitterroot River north of Stevensville. I promise you will love it. Stay careful, Stay true and come home soon.
I love you.
Janie

"Soon" was coming a lot sooner than she could ever imagine, and Buck planned to surprise her.

Of all the terrible experiences he had endured during this war, what troubled Buck most was his friends dying for the thankless protesters back home. It seemed the sacrifices the soldiers had made were pointless. The very people for whom they had died held posters and signs and sneered at him as he made his way on crutches through the Oakland Airport. Buck wanted to respond. He wanted to stop and tell them about Rolley, about Romeo, Crowfoot, and Dixie. Instead his thoughts got lost somewhere back in Nam, and his eyes stared in the distance, beyond the protestors and their righteous ignorance, to a place from which there seemed no escape.

He steeled himself for more of the same when he arrived in Missoula, but Montana was different. The people at the Missoula Airport treated him like royalty. Strangers smiled and patted his back while airport staff put him in a wheelchair and carried his duffle bag. It became a mini-homecoming parade as pilots, baggage handlers, stewardesses, and passengers escorted him through the terminal to a waiting taxi.

He had already called ahead to Saint Patrick Hospital. The operator there said Janie was on duty. She was putting him through to her, when he quickly hung up. While riding in the cab up Broadway, Buck scrawled a note. When he finished, he carefully folded the paper and put it in his pocket as the cab stopped out front.

Buck asked to leave his duffle bag with the hospital receptionist, and after discovering his purpose, she called an aide to escort him to Janie's work station. With crutches, he walked beside the young woman up the hallway until he spotted Janie bent over, writing. Even under the hospital's fluorescent lights her face shone with radiance. A lump swelled in his throat. He stepped back out of sight.

"Take this note, and give it to that nurse sitting there behind the counter. Don't say anything. Just hand it to her. If she asks you anything, just don't answer. I'll take care of the rest."

The young nurse's aide smiled. "Got it."

Buck peeked around the corner, watching as Janie wrinkled her brow and took the note from the aide. After she unfolded it and began reading, he quickly made his way toward the nurse's station.

> *Dear Janie,*
> *When you see me again, I will have a cast on my right leg and be walking with crutches. Don't freak out. I busted the ligaments in my knee and the doctors said I'll be walking just fine again when they heal. The good news is the war is over for me.*
> *See you REAL soon.*
> *Love,*
> *Buck*

He heard her voice as she looked up at the aide.

"Where did you get this?"

The aide turned and looked toward him, and Janie turned as well. She threw her hand over her mouth and let out a muffled scream as she leapt to her feet. Scrambling madly, she ran to Buck, who dropped his crutches with a clatter to the floor. Doctors and nurses came running from all directions as Janie sobbed uncontrollably in his arms. Buck fought back his own tears as he tried to maintain his balance. It had been a long trip since his parents had died and the year in Vietnam, but he had found life again. He had found the person with whom he could make that place called "home."

The last two months should have been the happiest of Buck's existence. One day he was a filthy, mosquito-bitten grunt running through the jungle, shooting at the shadowy figures of enemy soldiers, knowing he would likely die before sunset, and within days he was home—home where beds had sheets, music played and people had no clue about the misery soldiers were suffering on the other side of the world. But there were the long-haired freaks at the airports, most of whom had never had a job, never studied enough history to really know much about wars, yet they were experts on this one. He tried to ignore it. It didn't matter. It was as he had written in his note to Janie: His war was over. And now that he was home, he no longer cared who was right. Or at least he tried to tell himself as much.

Today was Sunday, a rare day when Janie didn't have to work or go to school. He sat beside her, feeling the warmth of her body—the woman with whom he hoped to spend the rest of his life. Huddled on the couch beneath a quilt, they sipped hot coffee and gazed out at the magnificent Bitterroot Range of the Rocky Mountains. Still laden with snow in late March, the mountains glowed in the amber light of an early morning sunrise.

"How are you feeling? Janie asked.

"I'm good."

He couldn't lie. She knew he had a hangover, but he was determined to give her a good day.

"Do you ever get accustomed to looking up at those mountains?"

And this was the wonderful thing about Janie. She knew he was struggling, and she gave him space encroached only by gentle persuasion.

"Sometimes life distracts you, and you take them for granted, but then there are mornings like this."

Buck gently pulled her by the chin and pressed his lips against hers. When they parted, she raised her brows and smiled. "I can only imagine what my coffee-quenched dry-mouth tastes like this early in the morning."

"Sweetheart, your mouth tastes like the inside of a honey jar."

"And Patrick Marino, you are *so* full of crap."

He ran his hand under her pajama shirt and began tickling her.

"Stop! You're making me spill my coffee."

A moment like this should have led to making love, but ligaments heal slowly. The cast remained on his leg, making sex awkward at best. He settled for snuggling.

"Buck…"

"I know."

For two and a half months not a day passed without him enjoying the warm benefits of several shots of bourbon.

"I'm here for you, but I also need you. You've got to let it go."

No longer able to look into her eyes, he turned and stared out at the mountains. She was right. The only relief he found was half way down into a fifth of Evan Williams. There was nothing good behind him, but he couldn't stop looking back and wondering why—why his mother and father had died just when the rewards of all their labors were finally coming to fruition, why his mother, instead of living as the wife of some wealthy landowner, had married truck farmer Joe Marino and worked beside him, purchasing parcels of land and building the farm that Buck now owned.

He also wondered why men like Rolley, Crowfoot, Dixie, Romeo, and so many others had to die in a war no one cared about. And why had Rolley become so careless that he chose to walk out across open ground that day?

Was it because of the fiancée he had lost to a similar senseless accident?

Buck understood little, except the thing which he feared most—that he too might someday decide to take that careless walk into eternity. Janie was right when she said the war had him. It did. It had stolen forever any remaining sense of peace he had with life. The fear that it might happen again haunted him—that like his parents, Rolley, and Crowfoot, he might lose Janie. The thought of her dying left him cold inside. It made him want to run, to leave her safely behind so she too wouldn't die like everyone else. It made no sense, but fear un-tempered by reason never did.

Buck and Janie had another argument. It had occurred the previous afternoon before she left for her shift at the hospital. He was drinking too much, and it was their usual. He had no defense. She was right, but quitting anytime soon was impossible. Whiskey was his lifeline, his only link to sanity, and with more time, he could work through it. If only she could be patient. It was as if she thought his memories of Vietnam had a switch he could throw to make them instantly disappear, but he couldn't. He was still ducking and flinching at every loud noise.

The argument had grown ugly, and Buck said things he never imagined would come out of his mouth. Janie left for her twelve-hour shift in tears. Another apology was useless. It had grown into a litany of "I'm sorrys." There was little he could say, but he wanted her to understand that he cared. She had no idea how much.

Driving Janie's old pickup along the Clark Fork River, he headed into downtown Missoula. The crystalline waters of the river tumbled over rocky shoals, and the hills above town were still wrapped in an early morning mist. Janie had come home that morning and gone straight to bed without speaking. He drove across the river and down several streets before stopping to ask about a local jewelry store. "It's called the Jem Shoppe," the woman said, and she gave him directions.

The rings were expensive, but easily affordable with his savings from the military. He walked out of the jewelry store that day with a huge diamond solitaire and a matching wedding band. He popped open the white box with his thumb as he drove back to the apartment late that morning. Gazing at the rings nestled in white satin, he smiled. This would prove to her just how much he truly cared.

Buck stopped the pickup in front of the apartment. Janie's car was gone. She had only slept five hours after her twelve-hour shift. As soon as he let himself inside Buck spotted the note on the kitchen table. Janie said she was going to stay with a nurse friend for a couple days. That was all it said. He dropped the ring box into his pants pocket and went to the window. Should he leave? After all, it was *her* apartment.

Two days later she returned. Buck had been drinking heavily the entire time. They spoke to one another, but things were different. Perhaps he had pushed her away once too often. He put the rings away without showing them to her. Turning inside himself, he tried to avoid confrontation, but the result was the same. He was pushing Janie away, but she refused to give up.

Sometimes angry, sometimes patient, she looked deep into his soul, denying him the comfort of blaming anyone but himself. And although she could have, Janie never pointed to herself as an example of compartmentalizing the past. She too suffered at times, but she was a hell of a lot stronger woman than he was a man. He tried again and again to quit drinking, not for his sake, but for hers. It was no use. He could see their lives floating apart as they tried to navigate the ocean of tragic memories both had experienced in Vietnam. It ruled his past and his every thought, and he was destroying Janie's life along with his.

Nine months slipped by while Buck continued drinking away the memories. Outside of the occasional "good days" he and Janie shared, drinking was his only solace, but he still functioned. He had driven Janie's pickup into the mountains. Sitting with the doors open and the radio tuned to a rock music station, he sat on the tailgate, half-stoned and gazing out at the magnificence of the snow-covered peaks. It was winter, but he felt no pain, as he sipped the bourbon straight from the bottle. It was an escape of sorts, and he was enjoying the crisp mountain air when he heard the announcer say, "Jefferson Airplane, with their 1967 hit, 'White Rabbit.'"

He recognized the voice of Grace Slick, but he had never listened closely to this one. Sitting up, he suddenly found himself remembering the discussion he had with Rolley two days before the ambush that killed PJ Goodson. The music, like the lyrics, was spooky and surreal, and he was certain it was Rolley speaking to him from beyond the grave.

And if you go chasing rabbits, and you know you're going to fall
Tell 'em a hookah-smoking caterpillar has given you the call
And call Alice, when she was just small

The DJ called it psychedelic rock, but it was scarily real. It was Rolley's spirit speaking to him, except Buck didn't know what he was trying to say. What could Rolley possibly want to tell him? None of it made sense. The crisp mountain air turned cold, and only then did he understand that forgetting was hopeless. He could never forget Vietnam. It was woven into the fabric of his life, but it was Janie who was bearing the brunt of his insanity. She begged for a simple life of peace and harmony, but the ugly specter of the war still owned him.

He loved her. He wanted her. He needed her, but he had to free her from the hell he brought into her life almost every day. There was but one thing he could do. He had to set her free. By the end of the year he had made up his mind to leave, to return to Mississippi and fight his demons alone. Perhaps she would have him back someday, but for now, it was the only way out.

New Year's Eve came, bringing with it the haunting refrain of Auld Lang Syne, and he saw them again, smiling and walking beside him as if nothing had changed. Rolley, Crowfoot, Romeo, Dixie, they were all there. The music tortured him as he raised cup after cup of "kindness" until they disappeared in a jungle mist, and he no longer felt the pain. And there was Janie faithfully close beside him with a stoic patience he didn't deserve. She too had been there, and he was putting her through it again. Buck awoke with another hangover on New Year's Day 1970 and finally made the decision to go.

At first she fought him with tears and anger. She offered to give up everything and go with him, but he refused. She needed a friend, a man who would be there for her when life became a trial, but he was not the person. Janie had seen the travesty of war as well, and she needed him, but he was too weak. And when he again forced himself to say cruel things, she saw through it. He had met his match. She was a woman who not only had heart and cared, but she was actually smarter than he was. And when she realized he was set on leaving, she had the wisdom to give in.

"Go if you must, Buck," she said. "I'll always be here waiting for you."

He said nothing in reply that day when he walked out. It was for the best. Janie was grief-stricken, but she could pick up the pieces when he was gone, perhaps meet a well-to-do surgeon, or someone who could at least remain sober for more than a day or two. He wanted to tell her this, but he was too pissed off at the world and at himself.

26

THE BOTTOM OF THE BOTTLE

Bois de Arc, Mississippi, June 1970

Buck had been in Mississippi for months, and he hadn't missed more than a night or two at Reilly's Grill. Old Man Reilly's place was more bar than grill, and a watering hole for local farmers, construction workers, hunters, and fishermen. It had been there since he was a kid. Joe Marino had stopped here on occasion for a shot of his favorite bourbon. Now, Buck stayed every night till closing time, and he was pretty certain his dad's old pickup truck had developed its own homing beacon, because most nights he never remembered leaving. If Janie knew, she would have quit work, school, and everything else to come down and look after him.

She had tried calling at first, but when he didn't return her calls, she wrote him regularly, saying the snow was melting in the high country, and the Bitterroot River was running at the top of its banks. Later, she wrote about the mountain flowers and told him she was still waiting, but he didn't write back. Life after Nam was a pointless activity. He was at Reilly's again and well into another long-necked bottle of Evan Williams. Outside, the summer moths fluttered beneath a buzzing sodium vapor light, while inside, the music played from an old juke box.

Several locals were sitting with their beers at the bar and at tables when he heard the song again. Someone had put some rock music on Old Man Reilly's jukebox. It was Grace Slick singing "White Rabbit." He looked around. There were construction workers sitting at the bar. Buck wanted to unplug the jukebox, stop the music, and find peace, anything but hear those painful lyrics again, but it wasn't his nature. He killed his drink.

When the men on the chessboard get up and tell you where to go
And you've just had some kind of mushroom, and your mind is moving low
Go ask Alice, I think she'll know
When logic and proportion have fallen sloppy dead
And the white knight is talking backwards
And the red queen's off with her head
Remember what the dormouse said
Feed your head, feed your head

Buck elected to feed his head, and he felt the warmth of the bourbon as if he were resting his head against Janie's breasts. He wasn't blind to what he was doing, but the bourbon let him forget those terrible times. It let him sleep for a little while without the nightmares. For a few hours each night he wasn't dragging Rolley or Crowfoot across the canal, or Blondie through an inundating hail of bullets and shrapnel. He didn't see TJ at the bottom of the trench, his crimson blood soaking into the mud, or Mo with a bloody hole in his face. The bourbon gave him a very real sense of relief, and tonight he sipped it, as always, straight over ice.

That night turned into more weeks and the weeks into more months. The cotton bolls were full, and the soybean leaves had yellowed. Old man Reilly often came to his table when he had the time, sitting and talking with him. Buck told the old man about the hell he had been through, and Reilly always coaxed him with kind words, asking him to slow down on the drinking. Buck would thank him and continue drinking. It was the only way he could find peace, even if it was only for a few hours' sleep each night—a sleep void of nightmares, void of memories, void even of his own existence.

Buck had never failed to find the door and drive home, but this night his mind was a jumble of confused paranoia as he drank, thought about the war, and wondered how people like Wade McKinney had never gone to fight. Wade had come in with a group of friends. It was the first time Buck had seen him in years, and his cousin pointed him out to his friends. Despite his anger, Buck could do little more than hold his head up off the table.

Wade called him a drunken fool with a hero complex, but when Buck tried to explain that the heroes were all dead, Wade laughed and said, "Except for you, right? Yeah, I saw you profiling with all those medals in that newspaper picture. People 'round here think you're some kinda badass paratrooper hero or something, but you ain't nothing but a piss-ant drunk."

Buck no longer cared. He uncapped the bottle of bourbon and poured his glass full. Wade and his friends continued laughing—making a fool of him in front of everyone in the bar. It didn't matter. He killed the glass of bourbon, and laid his head down on the table.

The cold air jarred him back to consciousness as he realized someone was carrying him outside to a vehicle in the parking lot. It was dark, and he didn't know if he would wake up tied to a concrete block in the bayou or face-down on the concrete floor of the county jail. At this point the difference was irrelevant. He was too drunk to care and there was nothing he could do about it.

He cracked open his eyes as the man dumped him into the seat of a pickup and shut the door. A moment later the door on the driver's side opened and he rolled his head around to see who it was. He instantly recognized the man's face, which made him realize he was simply having another nightmare. He squeezed his eyes shut tight. When he opened them, the man's face was still there, glowing blue in the dim light of Reilly's neon sign. Buck again squeezed his eyes shut.

"Hey," the man said. "You awake?"

It was dark, and with the surrounding shadows there was no way of knowing who might be out there. Buck felt for his CAR-15 in the darkness as he clumsily pressed his finger against his lips. "Sshhh. The enemy will hear you."

"Old Man Reilly is right. You are absolutely demolished."

Carefully opening one eye Buck found the morning sun shining brilliantly through the window—a window he didn't recognize. The nauseating smell of sausage and eggs frying drifted into the room. Despite his "delicate" state, he sat up and put his feet on the floor. It was cold, and his head swam in the morass of another hangover. He was still fully clothed except for his shoes and jacket, but he had no idea where he was.

The door creaked, and he looked up. It was that face again—the same one he had seen last night. He squeezed his eyes shut and held them closed. Separating himself from a dream and waking up had never been as difficult as it was now. He hoped he wasn't slipping into a psychotic state.

"I should be puttin' down defoliant for some folks today, but instead…well."

Buck's eyes flew open. It *was* him—Buddy Rider.

"What the f...?" Buck rubbed his temples, and squeezed his eyes shut again.

"Old Man Reilly and my father go way back. He called me last night, said you'd mentioned my name and were in need of a friend. I had planned on looking you up, anyway, but I thought you were living with your girlfriend up in Montana."

Buck was certain the morning sunlight could be no less painful than splinters of broken glass in his eyes.

"You got any aspirin?"

"Sure, and how about some sausage, eggs and biscuits?"

"Oh, no, no, *hell* no!"

Buddy might have laughed, but he didn't. He simply nodded.

"Okay, sit tight."

A couple minutes later he returned with a glass of milk and four aspirin. Buck took the glass, but sniffed it when he detected the odor of something besides milk.

"It's got some of the dog that bit you in it," Buddy said. "The milk will help coat your stomach, and the bourbon will reduce some of the pain, while you sleep it off."

Buck finished the milk, and gave a small belch as he fought to keep it down.

"I've got to ride over to the strip and prep a plane. I'll be back around dark, and we'll see if you're ready to eat then."

It was dark outside when Buck heard a truck door shut. Buddy was returning. He walked in and tossed his cap on a chair.

"You feeling any better?" he asked.

Buck nodded, but his psyche was wrecked by the thought of how he had made a fool of himself in front of his cousin.

"Do you want to try to eat? I can bake some chicken in the oven. That shouldn't be too rough on your stomach."

"I reckon so. Did you meet my cousin, Wade McKinney, last night?"

"No. Him and his friends were gone when I got there, but Old Man Reilly told me about them running their mouths."

Buddy took a package of raw chicken from the refrigerator and began cutting it in pieces with a butcher knife.

"When did you leave your girlfriend in Montana?"

"Hell, I don't know—almost a year ago, I think."

"She must have turned into a real bitch."

Buck looked up at Rider. He didn't sound like the captain he had carried out of the jungle.

"No. As a matter of fact, she was…" He paused. After a moment or two he continued. "She was the closest thing to perfect I could ever imagine."

Rider finished cutting the chicken, placed it in a pan, sprinkled it with salt and pepper, and shoved it in the oven. He turned back to Buck.

"Did you know your cousin was fixin' to piss on you last night when Old Man Reilly ran him off?"

"Piss on me? What do you mean?"

"What I mean is he was literally getting ready to piss in your ear while you were passed out on the table. At least that's what he told everybody in the bar. He had unzipped his pants and was pulling out his pecker when Old Man Reilly ran his ass out."

Buck shrugged. He probably deserved it for getting so drunk. Rider grew red-faced.

"Shrug if you want, but you've let yourself sink to the bottom. You know, I worked with the best of the best—SOG Spike teams out of FOB 1 in Phu Bai—Green Berets. I flew Covey riders across the fence. Before I went out the first time, I went with a team on the ground, so I could better understand what they were doing. Do you know why I'm telling you this?"

By now, Rider's voice was growing louder. Buck shook his head. "No."

"I'm telling you this because several of those men became my friends, and some got killed—a couple because I didn't get the airstrikes exactly where they needed them. I'm telling you this because I've seen you in action, and I know you were as good as the best of them."

Buck shrugged, and the red-faced Rider threw the heavy butcher knife across the kitchen, burying it to the handle in the sheetrock on the far wall. He reached into a cabinet and retrieved a bottle of bourbon. Quickly turning, he smashed it against the edge of the table, spraying glass shards and bourbon across the kitchen.

"Good stuff, whiskey." His voice suddenly receded to a whisper. "It helps on occasion, but when you let it control you, you degrade not only yourself, but the memory of the people who served with us. Do you know if it hadn't been for you, I would never have made it out of the jungle that day?"

"Look. It wasn't—"

"No, Buck! Let me finish. While you were passed out on that table last night, Mr. Reilly told me a lot of what you've been telling him the last ten months. He told me about your friend Rolley. He told me about your nightmares."

Rider paused for several long seconds. Buck could no longer look him directly in the eyes. Rider was right. He was at rock-bottom.

"I had nightmares, too," Rider said. "And I can tell you with certainty that whiskey isn't a cure. The only way you get past them is to look outside yourself, start looking ahead and stop looking back. You can't change what happened in the past, only what happens in the future."

Buck stood. "You gotta mop and a broom around here?"

"Leave it. I'll clean it up. What you need to do right now is make up your mind. I'm here for you, but I can't fix you. Only you can do that."

Buck realized that for two years he had done nothing but look back. Finding a future still seemed a daunting task, but it was that or risk never finding his way back.

"You're right, Buddy. I promise. I'm going to try."

"Bullshit with trying! I know you, Buck. You can do any damned thing you set your mind to. Don't try. Just do it. Turn it loose. Move on. And anytime you need help, I'll be here for you."

Buck walked over to the wall and jerked the butcher knife free from the sheetrock.

"Where did you learn to throw a knife like that?"

"I didn't. It was a blind-luck throw."

"Well, just the same, remind me never to challenge you to a knife fight."

27

TO SAY GOOD-BYE

Bois de Arc, Mississippi, November 1970

Buck opened his eyes. His chest was pounding and his breath was coming in gulps. He reached out to touch something—or perhaps it was someone, but nothing was there. Shaking, he tried to clear the cobwebs from his head. It was just another nightmare disturbing his late afternoon nap—or was it? A stark yellow beam of fall sunlight angled through the window. Much like a dirty spotlight in a topless bar, it illuminated the framed ribbons and medals from his tours of duty in Vietnam.

Sitting on a shelf in the mahogany bookcase, they reminded him not of the war, but of something else. The dream had taken him someplace strange, and he had seen something deep within himself. It was a path, and he was being beckoned to follow it. He had but one thing to determine: whether it led to a new beginning or to the end.

Pushing himself from the chair, he walked across the hardwood floor. Most of the two years since he left Nam had been filled with nightmares, but this one was different. It wasn't about the combat or the war, but it had shaken him to his very core. His shadow blocked the sunlight as he looked down at the ribbons and medals pinned to the green velvet background. It seemed like only yesterday that he returned home.

Janie had mounted the medals in the frame and given it to him. Running the tip of his finger over the glass, he pushed a diagonal streak through the dust. The red, green, and yellow Vietnam Service Medal stood out most, but it was the Purple Heart hanging askew that drew his attention. It had been that way for some time. A sudden compulsion overcame him, and he began prying the back from the frame.

Feverishly, he bent the nails with his bare fingers, until he pricked his thumb. A drop of blood, dull red in the shadow, became bright crimson as he turned toward the sunlight and continued bending the nails one by one until he could remove the medals from the frame. He set the glass aside, and a large drop of blood fell, spidering outward as it penetrated the green velvet.

Walking back to the chair, he carried the pieces of the frame, the glass, and the medals, laying them in his lap. He stared at the telephone. The silence in the house seemed as eternal as the void in his heart, not a sound anywhere—not the hum of the heater, nothing except the stark echoes from the past. Buck wondered where Janie might be now. Probably married with a different last name. He picked up the phone and dialed the long-distance directory for area code 406.

"Missoula," he said. "Jorgensen, Jane Jorgensen." The operator gave him the number. Janie still had the same last name, but he wondered if she might have found someone else. Life after Nam could be extremely lonely, and he couldn't blame her.

Grabbing his pen, he scribbled the number, smearing more blood across the notepad. He hung up and stared back at the dusty beam of sunlight, now illuminating the empty spot on the bookcase. It had been a bad time that day when he walked away, and he told himself that he had done it more for her than he had for himself. The real truth was he was running—running to escape the past.

After an hour the sunlight faded into the gray twilight of dusk. Buck dozed, and standing before him were Rolley and the rest of the squad—TJ, Crowfoot, Mo, Romeo, Lizard, Blanch, and Blondie. He was there with them again in Vietnam. Rolley's steel pot sat crooked on his head and his sixteen was slung over his shoulder. TJ, who was hollow-eyed and grinning, had his arm resting on Lizard's shoulder. And there was Blondie, the one who probably best represented them all. Crowfoot and Romeo seemed to stare through him at something in the distance. Buck grinned and called out to them, but one by one each man turned and walked away, disappearing into the mountain mist.

When he awakened the house was dark, but there was a distinct sound coming from the bookcase. It was the ticking of the clock; second by second he had let the last two years disappear. Fumbling for the switch on the reading lamp, he turned it on and looked down at the frame and medals in his lap. The notepad was still there, but the blood from his thumb had blotted out part of Janie's phone number. He tried to scratch away the blood, but the paper tore. Pausing, he stared at it. He had been two weeks without a drink, but he was still lost. After a while he crumpled the paper and tossed it into the wastebasket.

By early December, more lost days had become more lost weeks, and Buck stared out the window at nothing in particular. The memories were unavoidable, but the nightmares had become fewer, and he was no longer compelled to drink himself into a daily drunken stupor. Problem was he was stuck. Buddy had made him see the futility in the drinking, but the rest was up to him. He recalled a lesson Rolley had taught him long ago. Perhaps it was the answer. Many times they had talked into the night about their experiences, and Buck had asked him how he could remain so calm—really almost nonchalant—when the bullets were flying.

Rolley said, "You have to embrace your fear and the things that cause it. Own them, lest they own you. Look the beast in the eye and flip him off." Rolley laughed that day and added that you also had to kill him after you flipped him off. Buck now smiled at the thought.

Rolley was still speaking to him across the years. He had been talking about owning one's self, one's problems, and one's weaknesses. And that lesson had come full circle. Only now had Buck come to realize the only way to escape the past was to own it, to own his weaknesses and to take control. It had been almost a year since he last saw Janie. His heart ached for her, but there came a new fear—one that was far worse than any he had faced in Nam. He feared that he may have ruined his only chance for a decent life. He picked up the phone and again dialed the number for long distance information.

After scribbling her number on a pad, he quickly dialed it. There was an eternal pause before it began ringing. The ring seemed as distant as the months and the nearly two thousand miles that separated them. It rang again and again, and the Bitterroot Valley of Montana seemed the most remote place on the planet. But when it seemed no one would answer there came a click on the other end.

"Hello?"

It was her. He would recognize that soft western drawl a thousand years from now.

"Hello?"

Buck froze. He put his hand over the receiver. He didn't know what he wanted to say. He wanted to tell her he was no longer drinking every day, but that simply wasn't enough. Carefully, he hung up the phone.

His head was clearer than it had been in the last two years. Even knowing all the while that he and Janie were meant to be together, it had taken him a long time to find equilibrium. Only recently had he been able to say good-bye to his mother, his father, Rolley, Crowfoot, Romeo, and the others—to let them go. He would never forget them, but saying good-bye had freed him. He was beginning to see a future where he and Janie could live out their lives in the peace they and their friends had paid for so dearly—if only she would still have him. The fear of what he had done to their relationship was very real, but he had to face it. He would call again, when the time was right. Until then he had to think about what to say when she answered.

The screen door slapped shut behind him as he stepped out on the front porch and stretched. The December air was crisp and cool. The sun had nearly set, but high overhead its amber light shone as a reflection against V-formations of snow geese that stretched all the way to the horizon. He walked back inside and called Buddy.

"You been duck hunting today?"

"No, not today. What's up?"

"Not much. How 'bout let's go up to Reilly's place and grab a bite?"

"Sure, but I gotta wash some of this crud off first. I've been working on the Ag-Cat all afternoon. How about I come by and pick you up in about an hour?"

"That'll work," Buck said.

It was after six when they arrived at Reilly's Grill. It had become a regular meeting place for them. Old Man Reilly always kept a pot of oil hot and was known for his catfish sandwiches and french fries. The two men sat at a table after ordering their food.

"Something wrong with one of your planes?" Buck asked.

"Nah. Just doing some PM on the motors while things are slow."

"Look, just so you know, I'm going to call Janie, and if she will still have me, I'm probably going to head up that way."

Rider pressed his lips together and gave a knowing nod. "It's been a long time, you know?"

Buck heard the skepticism in his voice.

"Yeah, I know."

"Is she still working at that Saint Patrick Hospital?"

"As far as I know."

"Well, I hope it works out."

Buck raised his brows. "Yeah, me too."

"What are you gonna do with your place?"

"That's what I want to talk about. I was kind of hoping you'd act as caretaker for me. You know? Son Freeman and his folks are still running the vegetable operations, but with his church, he can't do everything.

I need someone to take care of the crop lease and other administrative details, maybe find a renter for the house, and look after those old folks living in the sharecropper shacks. You can keep whatever's left after maintenance and taxes."

Rider shook his head. "I'll be the caretaker for the place, but I'm not taking your money. Letting me duck hunt over there is all the pay I need. Best duck hole in the Delta. I reckon what I'm worried about is this plan of yours."

"You mean going back to Janie?"

"Yeah. What if she's found someone else? You're not gonna go back to drinkin', are you?"

Buck glanced over at the bar. He had wondered the same thing.

"No. I mean—well, I reckon I'll tell her I'm sorry and move on."

Buck knew it would crush him, and going back to the bottle would be an easy escape, but he was going to take life one day at a time. There came the roar and rumble of engines as tires crunched to a stop in the gravel parking lot outside. Buck looked over his shoulder. Men were spilling out of two big pickups, laughing and talking. A moment later the front door slammed open and a cold night air rushed in as they entered the bar. Buck did a double-take.

"Aw shit. It's that loudmouth Wade and his buddies."

"You want to head out?" Rider asked.

"Yeah, reckon so."

Buck reached for his jacket, but it was too late. Wade swaggered up to the bar. He was still wearing his camouflaged hunting coat, and turned to look their way. One glance and Buck knew his cousin was already under the influence. He had probably sat in the duck-blind all afternoon with his buddies, swilling beer and shooting more ducks than the game laws allowed.

"Well, I *WILL* be damned, if it ain't my little dago cousin—the war hero."

Rider, who had his ball cap pulled down low, pushed his chair back and started to stand. He spoke without facing Wade. "Why don't you give it a rest, partner?"

"Who the hell are you?"

The other men, who had been talking loudly while dragging chairs up to a table, grew suddenly silent. Wade had always been bigger than most of the boys and continued putting on weight even into his late twenties. Buck figured him at maybe six-three and around two hundred and eighty pounds.

"Let me introduce you," Buck said. "This is a friend of mine. His name is Buddy Rider."

Buck wasn't sure whether it was from walking in out of the cold air or being drunk, but Wade's nose was running. The big man pulled his coat sleeve across his face.

"Hell, I know who you are. You're the crop duster pilot. You sprayed a lot of our fields this summer."

Rider extended his hand, but Wade didn't seem to notice.

"What can I get for you fellas?" old man Reilly asked.

"Bring everybody a Budweiser," Wade said. "It's on me, and bring a couple beers for these boys, too—whatever kind they want."

"We're going to pass," Buck said. "We were just headin' out."

"What, you too good to drink a beer with me and my buddies?" Wade turned and looked back at the men standing around the table behind him. Reaching into the large cargo pocket of his hunting coat, he pulled out a long-necked bottle of Jim Beam. It was three-quarters empty.

"You always drink the good stuff, anyway, don't you?"

He twisted off the cap and took a swig.

"Here," he said, extending the bottle toward Buck.

Buck stood and took the bottle. Smiling, he set it on the table. "Look, Wade. You're drunk. So, why don't you just take it easy? We're gonna go ahead and leave."

Wade stepped in front of him, blocking his path to the door. "You're a fine one to talk about somebody being drunk. You ain't going nowhere till we discuss you letting me hunt my duck hole on that land you cheated us out of."

The land was eight hundred acres where the cypress-lined Bayou Bois de Arc flowed. It was also adjacent to both the McKinney land and Buck's father's land. Hoping to someday buy it, Buck's father had told him how he planned to sell the timber from two hundred acres of prime hardwoods on his place in order to get the money. That was before he died in the automobile accident.

The first thing Buck did when he returned home was sell the timber and make an offer on the eight hundred acres. The absentee owners accepted immediately, but unknown to Buck, the McKinneys had a long-standing low-ball offer they had also made on the parcel.

"No one cheated you out of anything, Wade. I didn't even know y'all had made that offer. Besides, your offer was for only half of what the land was worth."

"Yeah, and those niggers were fixin' to sell it to us if your dumb ass hadn't come along and bought it out from under us."

"Wade, those people were our neighbors before they moved away. If anyone was about to get cheated, it was them. Besides, they said you were planning to evict all their poor relatives still living in those shacks along the bayou. I told them they could stay."

"I didn't expect much more out of you, Marino. Your dago daddy and those niggers have been going around buying up our land for years."

Buck smiled. Rider glanced at him. Buck had his eyes fixed on Wade.

"No, Buck," Rider said.

Buck continued smiling.

"Let's just go," Rider said. "Come on." He stepped around Wade.

Buck bowed his head, shaking it slowly side to side. Wade poked Rider's chest with his finger. "Why don't you mind your own business, partner. I'm talking to Marino." Wade turned back to Buck. "What are you grinning about?"

Buck raised his head. "You don't seem to realize that this man here, who you just poked in the chest, is a friend of mine, and he was awarded the Air Force Cross in Vietnam." He was still smiling as his eyes met Rider's.

"Oh, shit!"

Buck focused every ounce of his energy, all his concentration and every muscle in his body into his right fist and a point a few inches behind Wade's jutting chin. He was still smiling when the blow struck, a lightning bolt that drove Wade's chin back with an audible crack. The big man hit the floor with a thud and didn't move. Buck and Rider found themselves facing the other five men standing at the table. One of them stepped forward and looked down at the comatose Wade then back up at Buck.

"Nick?" Buck said. "Damn, I almost didn't recognize you."

"Been a long time," Nick said, again glancing down at his older brother.

The other men stood nervously shifting their weight from leg to leg.

"Well?" Buck said. His eyes were now fixed hard on Nick's.

Nick glanced again down at Wade. "I reckon he had it coming."

"What the…?" one of the other men said. "Are you gonna let him sucker punch your brother that way?"

Nick shrugged. The second man stepped up beside him. "I say we take 'em."

"Nick," Rider said, "I expect you better stand back 'cause your cousin Buck is fixin' to mop the floor with these boys' asses."

Nick held his arm across the other man's chest. "No. Wade started it by running his mouth. Let 'em go." Several seconds passed, before Nick spoke again. "Y'all go ahead, Buck. We're done here."

Rider walked out the door, and Buck followed, leaving Nick and his friends tending to Wade.

Rider was driving Buck back to his place, and they were several miles down the road before he spoke.

"You know you broke that big ape's jaw, don't you?"

"Yeah, I know."

"You've become a mean bastard since you cut back on your drinking."

"Yeah, I know."

"I was just kidding. Stop worrying about it. Like that Nick fella said, he had it coming."

"Reckon so."

The now barren cotton rows fluttered past in the headlights in a geometric progression of monotony as the pickup sped down the highway. Buck watched as if they were his entire life passing in a continuous pattern—a never-ending series of conflicts, losses, and pain. He was desperate for a reprieve, for a life of peace where no one was dying needlessly, one where no one was getting hurt—simply a life where things seemed normal—whatever that might be.

"Reach under your seat," Rider said. "There's a bottle of Evan there. I'll pour us a short one to knock the edge off when we get to your place. How's your hand?"

Buck held up his right hand and flexed his fingers. "It's okay. How did you know I was fixin' to deck him?"

"What do you mean?"

"You hollered 'oh, shit' just before I hit him," Buck said.

Rider didn't answer. And several minutes later he turned into the drive leading to the house. A herd of deer scampered across the field and into the darkness beyond the headlights.

"It was pretty obvious," Rider said. "You were smiling with everything except your eyes, and when they turned stone cold, I knew the shit was fixin' to hit the fan. That's the way they looked that evening when you found me up in the A Shau Valley. Scared the shit out of me then, too."

Pulling his pickup to a stop in front of the house, Rider switched off the headlights. Friends welded to one another in the heat of battle were friends for life. Buddy Rider was one of those people. Buck reached under the seat and found the bourbon.

"I'll try not to telegraph myself so much next time."

Rider laughed. "Hell, that stupid bastard never saw it coming. He probably *still* doesn't know what hit him."

Buck uncapped the bottle and tipped it up.

"Whoa, boy. Just a swallow. You don't need to get back into the habit."

"No worry. It just got a little crazy tonight, and I really need this one."

Rider grinned. "Yeah, you're right. You did get a little crazy back there, but then most of you LRRPs have a loose screw or two, anyway."

Buck looked over at him with a flat smile. "Thanks, Buddy, but I never landed a plane upside down in the jungle."

28

Bois de Arc, Mississippi, December 1970

Another week slipped by while Buck tried to come up with a plan. Calling Janie on the phone simply wasn't going to work, but showing up in Missoula unannounced didn't seem like a good idea either. He talked with Buddy, and he suggested writing her a letter. Buck agreed, but several days later he was still laboring over it. Buddy said he was over-thinking it. It was only two days before Christmas, and he had written a dozen letters, ripping up every one and restarting again and again. He could tell her he was sorry. He could say he loved her. He could say a lot of things, but he wanted to say them to her face. He wanted to hold her in his arms again, and never let her go.

The headlights of a vehicle flashed across the windows on the front of the house. It was raining hard that night, and he walked to the front window to look out. It was after midnight. Buck was tired and not ready to entertain anyone. It was probably Buddy, but with the pouring rain and the darkness he didn't recognize the vehicle. He went to the front door and cracked it open. Someone in a hooded rain jacket got out of the pickup and ran toward the porch.

He stepped outside and walked across the porch. It looked like a woman. An instant lump stuck in his throat as he remembered the girl who ran the same way up a road toward him years ago back at Phu Bai. She stopped at the bottom of the steps, still out in the rain, and stared up at him. Buck felt his legs collapse beneath him as he dropped down on the wooden porch, where he sat staring back at her.

Janie walked up the steps out of the rain. Pulling back the hood of her rain jacket, she sat down beside him, and they both stared out into the nighttime storm. Buck wasn't sure how long they sat. He wanted so much to say the right thing, but his mind was overpowered by a jumble of sorrow, relief and joy. As always it seemed Janie was the one who knew what to do. She turned toward him.

"Buddy Rider called me. I've been driving since he called early yesterday morning."

He reached and took her hand. Her moist brown eyes and her golden-blond hair glowed beneath the dim porch light. Buck tried to fight back the tears, but it was useless. They held one another for a long while, there on the porch without speaking. He felt the thump of her heart behind her breast as well as the deep sense of redemption settling in his own heart. A low and distant thunder rumbled from somewhere beyond the night-time horizon, and the rain ran in sheets from the roof above the porch.

"Buddy Rider said you saved his life."

"He's probably saved mine, too."

Janie looked up at him. "We can live here if you want. It doesn't matter, as long as I am with you."

Buck stood, pulled her to her feet and opened the screen door.

"I think I'd rather live in Montana."

"Really?"

"Yeah. The mountains remind me that I'm not the center of the universe, and that's pretty damned liberating if you think about it."

They walked down the hallway, stopping at the door to the study as Janie gazed about.

"So, this was your parent's house." She motioned toward the mahogany bookcase in the study. "Were all those books your dad's?"

"No. Most of them are mine. I've been doing a lot of reading this last year."

Janie let go of his hand and walked to the bookcase. Buck's military decorations were there, scattered about beside the disassembled frame.

"What happened to our medals?"

"Our medals?" he said.

"Yes, *our* medals, Patrick. Don't think for a minute that I didn't live every moment with you, thinking about you, worrying and trying to keep up with what was happening while you were in the boonies."

She held up the empty frame. "I mounted these medals in this damned frame for both of us. I am you. I am so much a part of you…"

She stopped as the tears streamed from her eyes. Buck stepped up and put his hands on her shoulders.

"You're right. I woke up one day and realized the Purple Heart was hanging crooked, so I took the frame apart. That's when I realized the medal really wasn't mine, at least not mine alone."

Janie said nothing as she bit her lower lip and bowed her head.

"It's Rolley's. It's Crowfoot's, and Romeo's, and Dixie's. It belongs to a lot of people who helped me make it. But more than anyone, it is especially yours."

She looked up at him. There was no smile, but her face said what a smile and words couldn't express. Buck picked up the Purple Heart. Pushing open Janie's jacket, he carefully pinned it to her blouse.

"You earned it."

Janie thumbed the medal and looked up at him. "This has been the most difficult two years of my life, Patrick—worse even than the time I spent in Vietnam, but giving me this medal means more than—"

"Be careful what you say."

Janie cocked her head sideways.

"What do you mean?"

"There's one more thing I want to give you. Stay here. I've got to run back to my bedroom. I'll be right back."

Buck hurried to his room where he pulled open the drawer of the bedside table. He remembered putting the engagement and wedding rings there, but he hadn't seen them in nearly a year. He rapidly stirred the paperclips, flashlight, ink pens, scissors and other items in the drawer. He pulled it open wider. His eyes searched frantically. No sign of the rings. He jerked the drawer all the way out and dumped the contents on the bed. Still nothing. He slammed his fist on the mattress, bouncing the clutter upward. Some of it landed on the floor.

Whirling about, Buck glanced desperately around the room. He must have moved the rings, but where? Outside came the deep rumble of more thunder as the bedroom windows vibrated in response. And slowly it came to him. He remembered one of those nights long ago when he had returned from Reilly's. He had taken the rings from the drawer, walked into the study and sat in the big chair. He had opened the box and put the engagement ring on the end of his pinky finger. Too much time and drink blurred the memory, and he couldn't remember what he'd done with them after that.

He hurried back to the study.

"What is it?" Janie asked. "What's wrong?"

Buck glanced into her eyes then up at the shelves of the bookcase.

"Give me just a minute."

Something had caught his eye, an ivory inlaid wooden box on a high shelf. It was where his mother had kept her rings and other jewelry when she was working on the farm. He didn't remember putting his rings there, but it was worth a look. He took the box down and opened it. His mother's rings were there along with the ring box from the Jem Shoppe in Missoula. He opened the white box. They were there.

"What's that?" Janie asked.

Buck exhaled and turned to her with a self-conscious smile. He took the engagement ring from the box and held it up.

"When did you buy that?" she asked.

"I bought it last year in Missoula. I was going to ask you then, but...well...if you'll still have me."

Janie wrapped her arms around his neck.

"Let me have your hand," Buck said.

The tears flowed anew as he slid the engagement ring on her finger. "What do you say we go on R&R the rest of our lives? You can work at the hospital, I'll work for your dad, and we'll make him a bunch of grandkids."

Janie laid her head on his chest. Drawing a quivering breath, she made a fist and stared at the ring.

"I'm ready," she said.

"You drove straight through all the way from Missoula?"

"Yeah. I pulled over twice and slept for an hour or two, but that was it. I could hardly hold my head up the last few hours." Janie's voice was growing weaker by the moment.

"Well, I'm taking you to bed before you pass out."

Buck scooped her up in his arms and carried her down the hall, through the great room and back to the bedroom. He set her on the bed, cleared away the spilled contents of the drawer, and pulled off her jacket. Unbuttoning her blouse, he slipped it from her shoulders. After removing her jeans, he unsnapped her bra and couldn't help himself as he gazed down at her naked breasts.

"I have a gown and some clothes out in the truck."

"Don't worry. I have you covered."

Walking over to his dresser drawer, he found an extra-large T-shirt and pulled it over her head. He then lifted her legs onto the bed and she lay back on the pillow. Buck covered her with a blanket. Janie gazed up at him with tired eyes as he bent over and kissed her forehead.

"You're obviously too tired for any extracurricular activities, tonight. We can begin planning our future in the morning."

She had already closed her eyes, but gave him a faint smile.

Stripping to his boxers, Buck crawled beneath the blanket and curled up behind her. The rain outside continued as a subdued roar. After a moment he heard her breathing heavily. Janie had already fallen asleep. He pulled her close, buried his face in her hair and cradled her abdomen as he too faded into a peaceful sleep.

EPILOG

Second Squad and First Platoon were among the most decorated small units in the Vietnam War.

———

William (Billy) "The Lizard" Reilly—was Wounded In Action and returned to his unit. He finished his tour of duty in November 1968. Billy received the Combat Infantryman's Badge (CIB), the Bronze Star Medal with an Oak Leaf Cluster, and a "V" for Valor, the Purple Heart Medal, and the Republic of Vietnam Gallantry Cross. He returned to his home near Greensboro, North Carolina, where he owns an auto parts store.

Pete "Blondie" Sevrenson—was twice Wounded In Action. He received the Purple Heart Medal with one Gold Star, the Combat Infantryman's Badge, the Silver Star Medal, and the Bronze Star with Oak Leaf Cluster and "V" for Valor. Blondie eventually became a college professor in Minnesota.

Maurice Boggs—was reported to have been Killed In Action by hostile enemy fire. He received a Combat Infantryman's Badge and the Purple Heart Medal. Boggs's family was indigent and requested he be buried in the National Cemetery in Memphis, Tennessee.

James Lee "Dixie" Greenbaugh—was Killed In Action in 1968. He received the Congressional Medal of Honor (awarded posthumously) and the Republic of Vietnam Gallantry Cross, as well as the Purple Heart Medal with one Gold Star (awarded posthumously). He also was awarded the Combat Infantryman's Badge, the Bronze Star Medal with an Oak Leaf Cluster and "V" for Valor, and the Good Conduct Medal. Dixie is buried at Arlington National Cemetery in Virginia.

John Merrit "Doc" Gilbert—was awarded the Combat Infantryman's Badge, the Bronze Star Medal with an Oak Leaf Cluster and "V" for Valor and the Silver Star Medal. Doc Gilbert was one of the few medics in Vietnam who were never wounded in combat. He returned to Texas where he became a Registered Nurse and went to work for a VA Hospital.

George Albert Gruenstein—completed his tour of duty in early 1969. He received the Combat Infantryman's Badge and Bronze Star Medal, and worked several jobs after returning from Vietnam. He is presently unemployed, and has been in and out of a VA facility in New York several times over the years suffering from what was finally diagnosed in 1981 as post-traumatic stress syndrome.

Johnny Crowfoot—was Killed In Action in 1968. He received the Purple Heart Medal with a Gold Star (awarded posthumously), the Combat Infantryman's Badge, the Silver Star Medal, and the Bronze Star Medal with an Oak Leaf Cluster and "V" for Valor. Crowfoot is buried on the Standing Rock Reservation in North Dakota. His medals and commendations hang with his photo in the Sioux Nations Museum.

Robert Earl "Mo" Joyner—was Wounded In Action and did not return to combat duty. He was awarded the Combat Infantryman's Badge, the Purple Heart Medal, and the Bronze Star Medal with an Oak Leaf Cluster. After leaving Vietnam he went to work at a General Motors Plant in Michigan. For therapy purposes to aid in the recovery of the wound to his tongue and jaw, doctors recommended Mo begin playing a harmonica. He later became one of the most sought-after musicians at Mo-Town Records.

Roland "Rolley" Zwyrkowski—was Killed In Action in 1968. He received the Combat Infantryman's Badge, the Silver Star Medal, the Bronze Star Medal with an Oak Leaf Cluster and "V" for Valor, the Republic of Vietnam Gallantry Cross, and the Purple Heart Medal. His parents eventually moved back to northern Wisconsin, and have Rolley's military decorations and commendations framed and displayed in their home.

Victor "Romeo" Lopez—was Killed In Action in 1968. He received the Combat Infantryman's Badge, the

Purple Heart Medal, and the Bronze Star Medal with "V" for Valor. His medals and ribbons are in a frame beside his mother's bed in East LA.

Doyle Henderson—was Killed In Action. He received the Purple Heart Medal and the Combat Infantryman's Badge. He is buried in Ohio.

Thomas "Blanch" Blanchard—completed his tour of duty in 1968. Blanch received the Combat Infantryman's Badge and a Bronze Star Medal with an Oak Leaf cluster.

Thomas Joseph "TJ" Arcenaux—was twice Wounded In Action and received the Purple Heart Medal with a Gold Star, the Combat Infantryman's Badge, and a Bronze Star Medal with an Oak Leaf Cluster and a "V" for Valor. He volunteered for LRRP training and joined the 75th Rangers attached to the 101st Airmobile Division before leaving Vietnam in 1969. TJ returned to southern Louisiana where he became a foreman on an off-shore drilling platform in the Gulf of Mexico.

75th Rangers attached to the 101st Airmobile

Ronald Allen Robertson—served two tours of duty in Vietnam. He was Wounded In Action in July, 1970 while on patrol near Firebase Ripcord. Robertson was awarded the Purple Heart Medal, the Bronze Star Medal with an Oak Leaf Cluster, and the Combat Infantryman's Badge. He remains in the army as a non-commissioned officer.

Thomas "Marshal" Dillon—was killed in action May, 1969 while on patrol in the A Shau Valley. He was awarded the Purple Heart Medal (posthumously), the Bronze Star Medal with an Oak Leaf Cluster, and the Combat Infantryman's Badge. He is buried near his home in the mountains of West Virginia.

Javier "Zorro" Garcia—served two tours of duty in Vietnam. He was awarded the Silver Star Medal for heroism while on patrol near Firebase Ripcord in July, 1970. He was also awarded the Bronze Star Medal with an Oak Leaf Cluster, the Republic of Vietnam Gallantry Cross, and the Combat Infantryman's Badge. Garcia remains in the army as a Command Sergeant Major.

David Michael "Mad Dog" Morgan—was Wounded In Action in May, 1969 while on patrol near Dong Ap Bia, later known as Hamburger Hill. He was awarded the Purple Heart Medal, the Silver Star Medal, the Bronze Star Medal with an Oak Leaf Cluster, and the Combat Infantryman's Badge. Morgan was later elected to the United States Congress, House of Representatives from the state of Oregon.

Patrick "Buck" Marino—was Wounded In Action three times. He was nominated for the Congressional Medal of Honor, received the Distinguished Service Cross, the Silver Star Medal, the Bronze Star Medal with an Oak Leaf cluster and "V" for Valor, and the Purple Heart Medal with two Gold Stars. He volunteered for Long Range Reconnaissance Patrol duty and joined the 75th Rangers attached to the 101st Airmobile Division before leaving Vietnam in 1969. He now lives in Montana with his wife Janie and their two sons and one daughter. Buck is a respected hunting and fishing guide in the Montana Bitterroot Valley.

The End

If you enjoyed this story, please go now, while it is fresh in your mind, and write a review of it on Amazon.com and Goodreads. com or the vendor site of your choice. You can learn more about other novels in the Vietnam War Series at www.rickdestefanis. com. Regardless of your decision, please accept my sincerest thanks and appreciation for the time you invested with my book.

Rick DeStefanis

GLOSSARY OF TERMS

AAR: After Action Report, normally submitted by officers after combat

ARVN: Army of the Republic of Vietnam, the South Vietnamese Army

AIT: Advanced Infantry Training

AK-47: Russian assault rifle used by the Viet Cong and North Vietnamese

AO: Area of Operation

Bingo: Radio acknowledgement of a direct fly-over

Bird Dog: Forward air controller who flew a small aircraft and directed air strikes.

Braniff International: An airline company that also provided charters for transporting troops to Vietnam (known for crews wearing color-coordinated uniforms matching the exterior of its jets—often unconventional colors such as pink, purple and red.

Blue Line: Jargon for rivers and streams marked on topo maps as blue lines

C-130: Four engine turbo-prop air transport

CAR-15: A cut-down version of the M-16 with a shorter barrel and stock.

C&C: Command and Control

C-Rations: Canned rations provided for troops in Vietnam, also called "C's."

Cherry: a soldier newly arrived in country

Chinook: A large transport helicopter with two main rotors.

Chopper: slang for helicopter

CID: The Criminal Investigation Department of the army.

Claymore: an American anti-personnel mine carried by troops in Vietnam

CO: Commanding Officer

Cobra: A helicopter gunship with heavy armament and firepower, sometimes referred to as a "Snake."

Covey Rider: : An experienced Special Forces member who rides in the back seat of a birddog aircraft to assist teams on the ground

CP: Command Post, a unit's headquarters position in the field

Danger Close: Generally a range within 600 meters of a friendly position whereby artillery or air strikes might endanger soldiers or civilians.

DEROS: Date of Estimated Return from Overseas Service

Di di mau: Vietnamese command to hurry. Pidgin use by American soldiers "di di" meaning "to hurry."

Dustoff: A helicopter used for a medevac mission

E&E: Escape and Evasion

FAC: Forward Air Controller identified and marked targets for attack aircraft.

F-4 Phantom: American jet fighter/attack aircraft first used in Vietnam

FNG: Slang for a soldier newly arrived in country, F------- New Guy

Frag: Slang term for a Fragmentation Hand Grenade, also the act of attacking with a fragmentation grenade.

FO: Forward Observer (usually calls for and directs air strikes)

FSB: Fire Support Base, primary purpose is to provide a secure location for artillery units

HE: High Explosive

Hooch: term referring to any form of shelter—tent, hut or bunker.

Green Tracers: Enemy tracer rounds were green. American tracers were red.

HQ: Head Quarters

Huey: Nickname for the Bell UH-1 Helicopter, used primarily to transport troops and for Medevac missions

I Corps: Pronounced "Eye Core"--the northern most military tactical operations area in the Republic of Vietnam

KIA: Killed in Action

Kit Carson: A Vietnamese scout used to assist American patrols, often a turn-coat enemy soldier.

Click: One kilometer

LAWS: The M-72 Light Anti-Tank Weapons System—hand held rocket launcher that replace the bazooka.

Lay Dog: A term meaning to rest and hide in a position for an extended period.

LP: Listening Post, often place out beyond secured lines to detect enemy movement.

LRRP: Long Range Reconnaissance Patrol, members were also often referred to as Lurps.

LT: Lieutenant

LZ: Landing Zone, often cleared in the jungle for helicopters to land

MACV: Military Assistance Command Vietnam

M-16: American made assault rifle first introduced during the Vietnam War. Also referred to as a "sixteen," it fired a 5.56mm round.

M-60: American made light machine gun, air cooled, belt fed, 7.62mm ammo, also called the "pig." It weighed 26 pounds.

M-79: American grenade launcher, often called a thump gun, fires single 40MM rounds

Medevac: Medical Evacuation, often references a helicopter used for that purpose.

MIA: Missing in Action

Napalm: A Jellied Petroleum Compound used in bombs that burned with extreme heat.

NCO: Non-Commissioned Officer—a sergeant

NCOIC: Non-Commissioned Officer In Charge

NDP: Night Defensive Position (usually a foxhole dug in a perimeter)

NVA: North Vietnamese Army

OD: Olive Drab (standard Army color)

PFC: Private First Class—second lowest enlisted man's rank

Pink Team: A helicopter extraction team usually consisting of one or two Hueys, two Cobras and a C&C helicopter

Prick-25: Slang for the PRC-25 Radio, normally carried by troops in the field

Purple Heart: Medal awarded to American soldiers killed or wounded in action

RIF: Reconnaissance in Force: a large unit patrol in search of the enemy

RPD: Soviet made light machine gun

RPG: Rocket Propelled Grenade

R&R: Rest & Recuperation-a brief respite given after six months combat duty

RTO: Radio-Telephone Operator, the man who carried the radio

Sapper: Vietcong or NVA Commando that usually carries explosives

SERTS: Screaming Eagle Replacement Training School—training the 101st Airborne provided for new men just arriving in Vietnam

Sit-Rep: Situation Report

Slack: The man who walks directly behind the point man of a patrol

Slick: A chopper (usually a Huey) used to transport troops

SOP: Standard Operating Procedure

Spec-Four: The Rank of Specialist Fourth Class

Strings: Jargon for the ropes LRRPS used to rappel into the jungle

Swiss Seat: A rope configured with leg holes LRRPS used to be lifted out of the jungle

TAC: Tactical Air Cover-often referred to as "TAC Air" whereby aircraft provided support for ground troops

TOC: Tactical Operations Center, home base where the higher ups communicated with their LRRP teams in the field.

T&T: Through and Through Wound, One that enters and exits body

VC: Vietcong, members of the National Liberation Front

WIA: Wounded in Action

Willy Peter: Military slang for White Phosphorous, a white hot burning chemical used in grenades and rockets.

X-Ray Team: Radio operators positioned somewhere between the area of operation and the tactical operations center to relay radio communications to teams in the field

A preview of Book #3 in the "Vietnam War Series."

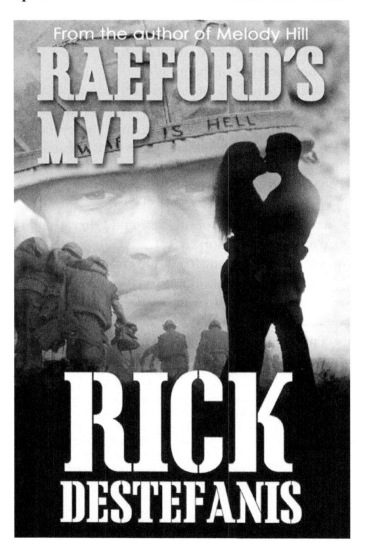

1

PUT A CANDLE IN THE WINDOW

Central Highlands, Republic of Vietnam, 1970

Billy Coker sat on a sandbag, smoking a cigarette and staring out at the fog-shrouded mountains of Vietnam. It was another dripping wet afternoon—quiet, except for the muffled voices of his men, playing cards in the bunker below. The rain had passed, and somewhere on the firebase behind him a radio played Credence Clearwater Revival. John Fogerty's plaintive voice came from the outside world, "Put a candle in the window." It was Billy's invitation to become human again, because in less than thirty days the freedom bird was taking him home. He'd have a real bath, sleep in a real bed and no longer worry about dying or watching others die. He was happy to be leaving Vietnam alive and unscathed, but without a clue as to why. It was as if somewhere along the way his life had ended, and he didn't even know when it happened.

He dropped the cigarette into a puddle, and fished another from the pack in his pocket. Other than escaping his current predicament, a total lack of anticipation had him teetering on the finest edge between happiness and despair. Those years in high school when he thought he was on top of the world now came back to haunt him with guilt and regret. And the strangest part of it all—he wasn't even thinking about the last eleven months in Nam. His thoughts weren't about the futility of the war or any of the recent events that should have culminated as the defining experiences of his life. He wasn't thinking about the man he'd become, or the men he'd seen die in the mud and rain—men like Butch and Danny, men closer to him than his own brother.

He absentmindedly rubbed his thumb over the Saint Sebastian medal hanging around his neck. He rubbed it as he had a thousand times in the last eleven months. He had clung to the silly medal like a raft in a storm. It was a gift from Bonnie Jo Parker. He smiled at the thought.

Were she given the chance, Bonnie Jo probably could have charmed the pants off of most men, but she wasn't that kind of girl. She was one of the fat girls at Raeford High who wore glasses and laughed too much. She laughed, not because she was silly, but because she was happy. Billy had spent time talking to her when he could—just to be nice—but Bonnie Jo wasn't his type. Perhaps, this was why he thought about her so much.

Seems the fat girls never got a break, and he sure as hell never gave Bonnie Jo one.

Of course, they hadn't been *close* friends—only buddies of a sort—but he'd seen her almost every day. He ran cross-country track, and he was good at it. Back then he was skinny as a rail, and he liked the running. It was a way to clear his mind, not that there was much to clear. But cross-country track was the only thing he did well, besides chasing girls. Billy lit another cigarette as he thought about his after school runs. Crossing the pasture behind the school, he took the same course every day, down the hill to the creek and up through the woods. Skirting the back of town, he went behind the drive-in and around the old gravel pits, making a six-mile circuit. And Bonnie Jo was almost always there sitting at the tables behind the Dairy Queen with a couple other girls. When he passed on the trail in the woods, they waved, but he seldom did more than raise a finger in acknowledgment.

They had been in school together since their freshman year. He'd passed her in the halls almost every day, but the first time they spoke more than two words was at the beginning of their senior year. It was a Saturday in September when she walked out of the dollar store in Raeford. Billy was staring at the sale sign in the window, "Women's Summer Clothes 50% Off", thinking of—what else?—a girl with half her clothes off.

"Hey, Billy."

Bonnie Jo stopped and smiled, but he was daydreaming his way into Sissy Conroy's pants, and several seconds passed before he realized she had spoken. She started to turn away, but he snapped out of his trance.

"Oh, hey, Bonnie Jo."

She turned back. "What's up?"

He cast another glance back at the sale sign and lingered a moment before giving up on his daydream.

"Oh, nothing. Just trying to figure out how I'm gonna pass natural science this year. I failed the first test."

Billy began walking toward his truck. It was parked down by the Laundromat. Bonnie Jo tagged along.

"The way the football players talk, I thought you helped them with their studies."

"I only help those assholes with English," he said. "Grammar and comp are easy, but I'm not worth a crap with math and science. I missed all the test questions on population statistics."

"Why do you call them assholes?"

" 'Cause they are—and so are most of the cheerleaders and the rest of their cliquey friends."

"Hmmm," she said. "I thought you were part of their group."

"Not really. I just run cross-country and try to survive in their world. All I want to do is graduate and get the hell out of here."

"I can probably help you if you want."

"You think?"

"Sure."

Climbing in, he cranked the truck and rolled down the window.

"Need a ride?"

"You don't mind?"

He glanced over his shoulder to see if anyone was around. Giving a fat girl a ride in Raeford, Mississippi got you permanently stigmatized by the Lizards. The name was his personal invention—one he was proud of. They all wore shirts with little Alligators on them—but he figured they were more like lizards.

"Get in," he said.

"My house is out that way, off the highway." She pointed up the street then glanced down at the schoolbooks on the seat. "So, let's start with what you know."

She picked up the science book and opened it.

"That won't be hard. I don't know shit about natural science."

Bonnie Jo giggled but stared straight ahead down the road.

"What's so funny?" he asked.

"Nothing," she said, "except that's not what I've heard."

"Huh?"

"Never mind. I was just kidding."

It finally dawned on him what she was implying.

"You can't believe the crap you hear," he said.

It was better to lie than to be like the jocks who bragged about their sexual conquests, most of which Billy was pretty sure were with their hands and not with the girls they claimed. He continued driving past the traffic light, and headed east out the highway. The roadway narrowed just outside of town passing a pasture ripe with the odor of cattle manure. White cattle egrets roosted on the backs of Black Angus that grazed in scattered groups all the way to a distant tree line.

"Oh, well, I'm glad it's not true," she said.

The tone of her voice was patronizing, but he let it pass as she thumbed through the first chapter.

"So, tell me," she said. "What do you consider the best relationship for humans to have with their environment?"

"What the hell does that have to do with anything?" he asked.

"It's the first chapter, dummy—Humans and Their Relationship with the Environment."

"You mean like what's my idea of a perfect world?"

"Okay, what's your idea of a perfect world?"

"Are you sure you want to know?"

"Sure," she said. "Tell me about your Utopia."

It was time to give goody-two-shoes a dose of reality—show her what really matters.

"Okay," he said. "In a perfect world there's a high school called Beaver Valley High, and all the girls have perfect bodies and wear cheerleader outfits year round. And on weekends they're barrel riders in the local rodeo, crouching low on their quarter-horses with their perfect little butts bouncing high in the air as they whip around the barrels with auburn, blond and chestnut hair flowing from beneath their lady Stetsons."

She laughed. "Like I said, I've heard this about you, Coker."

"Heard what?"

"That you have a one-track mind."

She seemed so self-assured. It was time to turn up the heat.

"Hell," he replied, "You just don't know what *really* makes the world go 'round. Do you have a clue about the power women have over men?"

"Power?" she said.

"Yeah. If women could find a way to make men mainline that stuff, they could rule the world with a syringe. I mean they practically own it anyway, but they can't disengage their hearts long enough to really take charge."

She rolled her eyes. "You're confusing 'means' with 'motivation'."

"Means and motivation?"

"Yeah, most girls just don't think that way."

He turned and looked at her. "You think I'm crazy, don't you?"

Bonnie Jo pointed to a blacktop road up ahead. "Turn up there on that road," she said. "No, you're not crazy. Your hormonal overload isn't any worse than most guys your age. That house down there on the right."

"So you think it's only the guys that are crazy, huh?"

He slowed his old truck and turned into her drive. A long gentle curve of pavement took them through mature oak trees and up to the house. One of the nicer places around Raeford, the house had large gables and a big front porch.

"You want to come in?" she asked.

He shook his head. "I can't. I gotta get home to check on Mom."

"Is she sick?"

"No, not really—I mean, I don't know. It's just—she hasn't been doing so well since dad got killed last winter. Too much nerve medicine, I reckon."

Bonnie Jo looked off to the side and squinted. "I read about it in the paper," she said. "I mean, when your dad died."

"What's done is done," Billy said. "So, when do we have our first tutoring session?"

She gave him a sad smile and shrugged. "What's a good time for you?"

"How about Monday after I run?"

"Where?"

This was something he hadn't considered. The tables behind the Dairy Queen came to mind, but if he was seen hanging around town with her, the Lizards would harass the hell out of him, and it would definitely cost him some popularity points. He noticed a wooden swing hanging from a huge oak in her front yard.

"How about over there?" he said.

She shrugged.

"Weather permitting, it works for me."

"Sergeant Coker!"

Jarred back to reality—such as it was in Nam—Billy realized someone was calling him from somewhere in the warren of sandbagged bunkers encircling the firebase. Firebase Echo had been home as of late for his airborne infantry battalion. They'd been holed-up there for a month overlooking a road crossing near the A Shau Valley—'interdiction and pacification' they called it. George Custer tried the same thing with the Sioux. Billy almost laughed at the thought.

The surrounding mountains were crawling with North Vietnamese regulars, and the battalion had been whittled down to the equivalent of three lean companies of men. This was bad-guy territory, and the enemy called most of the shots. They even had anti-aircraft guns somewhere in the surrounding hills, which made resupply choppers few and far between.

Again, someone call his name. Martin, one of Billy's men, stuck his head out of the bunker below. "It's one of the cherries," he said. "You want me to go get him, Sarge?"

"Yeah, if you don't mind. Go get him before a sniper takes his dumb-ass head off. And stay down."

They'd made him squad leader, probably by default, because had there been any competition, Billy was pretty sure he'd still be a buck private. Instead he'd spent the last three months trying to keep his men all in one piece. He figured that was the most important thing, because nothing else about this war made sense. He remembered how Bonnie Jo always said he was too cynical—especially when he called the Lizards egotistical jerks. If only she could see him now. He'd perfected cynicism in Nam. It was his forte, and he'd raised it to its highest form.

Martin crouched as he trotted back down to the bunker with the cherry. "Cherry here says Bugsy wants you up at the CP. Says it's real important."

Billy turned to the cherry. Dumb-ass nodded earnestly as if his role as messenger gave him some kind of authority. "If you don't stop wandering around in the wide-ass open, you ain't gonna live long enough to really enjoy this war."

"But, Sarge."

"No 'but' to it, dumb-ass. If you want to stay alive, start thinking like a soldier. These goddamn hills are crawling with NVA snipers, and they *will* put a round through that thick head of yours if you don't start using it for something besides a helmet holder."

Lieutenant Busby—or 'Bugsy' as the men called him—was the platoon leader. Billy decided to finish his cigarette. Sitting back down on the sandbag, he looked out across the mountains, wondering who he had become and where he was going when he left this godforsaken place. Other than eight weeks of Basic, nine weeks of Advanced Infantry Training and Airborne school, his resume before getting to Nam would say he'd read a few books and did a focused study on female anatomy. It was a damned shame. Here he was just nineteen years old and CMFIC of a combat infantry squad.

The CMFIC—that's who they ask for when they want to talk to the person in charge. People often thought it was an official military acronym, an understandable assumption, but an incorrect one. Billy exhaled a cloud of smoke into the stagnant afternoon air. CMFIC was an *unofficial* military acronym, that stood for Chief Mother Fucker In Charge. The real kicker was that his men actually thought he knew what he was doing. He was their squad leader, and they watched his every move, hoping he could show them something that would keep them alive just one more day. It would have been laughable had it not been so serious.

It was simply a matter of the one who'd been here longest leading the ones who'd just shown up. If it wasn't for the war, most of them, himself included, would have been down at a McDonalds by nightfall, trying to pick up chicks, drinking Old Milwaukee talls and listening to Hendrix or Steppenwolf. Instead, they were here on this godforsaken firebase, and Billy only hoped he could make a difference whenever the shit hit the fan.

Order *Raeford's MVP* now at: http://amzn.to/2rMkQpX

More Exciting Books by Rick DeStefanis, available in Paperback and Kindle editions from Amazon.com

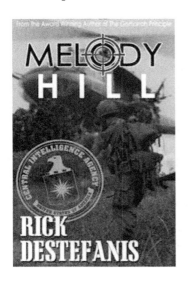 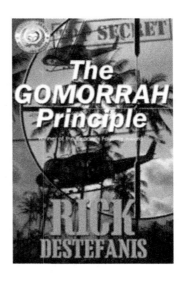

Read more about these books and award winning author Rick DeStefanis
at
www.rickdestefanis.com

Printed in Great Britain
by Amazon